# PAWN'S GAMBIT

# PAWN'S GAMBIT

## THE PAWN STRATAGEM BOOK I

### DARIN KENNEDY

*Dearest Kiersten —*

*The first move is yours!*

*Darin Kennedy*

*To Dad, who taught me a lot more than just chess.*

*The chess board is the world, the pieces are the phenomena of the universe,*
*the rules of the game are what we call the laws of Nature.*
*The player on the other side is hidden from us. We know that his play*
*is always fair, just, and patient. But we also know, to our cost,*
*that he never overlooks a mistake,*
*or makes the smallest allowance for ignorance.*
Thomas Henry Huxley

*The Pawn is the soul of Chess.*
François-André Danican Philidor

*Tenuous king, slanting bishop, fierce queen,*
*straightforward tower and cunning pawn*
*Over the checkered black and white terrain,*
*they seek out and enjoin their armed campaign.*
*They do not know that the scarred hand*
*of the player governs their destiny,*
*They do not know that an adamantine fate*
*controls their will and their journey.*
Jorge Luis Borges

# 1

## CORNERS

Steven Bauer sat with his back to the bar, his gaze wandering across the crowd of humanity occupying the checkered dance floor. The last sip of his whiskey sour did little to banish the headache pulsing behind his right eye in time with the thumping house music. He turned back to the bar to order another as the man to his right nearly fell off his barstool.

"One too many?" Steven shouted over the music.

"No such thing." The man, at least twenty years Steven's senior, steadied himself and shot him an inebriated grin. "What're you drinking?" His breath smelled like a distillery.

Backlit by the enormous aquarium looming behind her, a cute bartender with blue eyes and a blonde bob leaned across the bar and retrieved the man's empty glass. "Before you start offering to buy rounds, you might want to settle up first."

The man pulled out his wallet and dropped a ten on the bar. "That's all she wrote today," he said, doing his best to stay atop his barstool. "Now, how about a shot for me and my new friend here?"

Steven rested a hand on the man's back. "Thanks, pal, but I think we'd better call you a cab." He slipped the bartender a pair of twenties. "That cover his tab?"

"Right at it."

"Good. Get this guy home." Behind a forced smile, Steven gritted his teeth. "He's in no shape to drive."

A quizzical look flashed across the bartender's face. "You even know this guy?"

Steven tilted his head to one side. "Just sowing some good karma."

Seconds later, a bouncer Steven didn't recognize escorted the man out, leaving him alone at the bar. He downed another whiskey sour as quiet words from the past echoed in his mind.

*"Character is what you do when no one is looking."*

Even after eighteen months, Katherine's voice was as clear as if she'd just left his side.

And if keeping a drunk driver off the road was the worst thing he did tonight...

The headache flared again and Steven held the drink to his brow. His eyes slid shut as he offered a silent prayer an angel would come and take the pain.

"A kind heart," came an unfamiliar voice, low and sultry. "Not too common these days."

Steven's downturned eyes opened on a pair of graceful ankles in black stiletto heels. His gaze trailed up the woman's form. Her black dress slit to mid thigh, its plunging neckline threatened to hold his stare. Lustrous dark hair spilled past her shoulders, framing a face that belonged on a magazine cover. Her green eyes burned through him like an emerald flame.

"Care for some company?" The woman placed her black sequined clutch on the bar, her mouth turning up in a questioning smile. "Unless, of course, you're waiting for someone."

Steven glanced at his phone. "No text. No call. Doesn't look like she's going to show."

The woman took the recently vacated stool and leaned in close. "Her loss." Unlike the stool's previous occupant, her breath smelled of raspberries.

"Thanks." Steven took a sip of his drink. "I'm guessing you're meeting someone."

She raised an eyebrow. "I thought I was meeting you."

"Oh." His pulse raced as he took her offered hand. "I'm Steven. And yours?"

Smiling, she ignored the question and motioned to his glass. "What's your poison?"

Steven's brow crinkled. "Whiskey sour."

"Delightful." She signaled the bartender. "I'll have what he's having." Her accent hard to place, a hint of Irish lilt colored her words. "So, what's a good-looking guy like you doing on this end of a broken date?"

"No idea." Steven let out a chuckle. "No offense, but if you're looking for me to explain the inner workings of the female mind, I'm afraid I'm fresh out of insight."

The woman laughed, her wide smile sending Steven's heart racing. "Fair enough."

"My first time out to Corners during business hours," Steven said. "Not bad for an old mill, eh? Amazing what you can do with a few million dollars."

"It's certainly different than I remember."

"Oh. You saw it before the big renovation. You live in the area?"

"Not for a few years. I'm in town on business. Flew in this evening." Her wistful look suggested an untold story. "It's been far too long since I've visited the Windy City."

More than a few stares came in their direction, surprisingly more from women than men. Though Steven guessed it wasn't him they were watching, his simple button-down shirt and slacks suddenly seemed inadequate. He brushed a lock of brown hair from his eyes and offered the woman his best smile. "So, what business brings you to Chicago?"

"Acquisitions. My employer sent me to pick up a little something he needs for a project he's working on." The bartender rested a glass before her and the woman downed the drink in a single gulp. "He'd rather I keep it all official, but I figured there'd be no problem having a little fun while I'm in town."

"And how long is that going to be?"

"Tonight." Her gaze meandered around the room. "I'm heading east in the morning for another job."

"You staying nearby?"

Her tongue ran across her mouthful of even teeth. "Why do you ask?"

Heat rose in Steven's cheeks. "Just making conversation."

The woman smiled. "I like your accent. I'm guessing... southeast?"

"I grew up in Virginia. Moved here from the D.C. area about a year and a half ago."

"Change of scenery?"

"You could say that." Steven had left Georgetown less than a month after Katherine's funeral. He had no desire to go back.

"Sorry. Seems I hit a nerve." She brushed his wrist with her fingertips. "So, what do you do around here for fun?"

"When I'm not working, I'm usually out pounding the pavement. I'm training for the Chicago Marathon this October." Steven leaned in, intoxicated by the woman's dancing eyes. "Do you run?"

"Only if someone's chasing me." She twirled a lock of dark hair around a well-manicured finger. "A marathon, huh? You must have some serious endurance."

"It's my first one, but I'm getting there. Trying my best not to overtrain."

"And what is it you do?"

"I'm a consultant at an employment agency. You might have seen our ads: 'Winds of Change. Where finding a job is a breeze.'"

"How... clever." Her forced laugh left Steven wishing the words back into his mouth.

"I've been with the company a little over a year. Even helped a few of the staff here land their jobs. Otherwise, I doubt I'd have gotten past the rope tonight."

"Well, we're both here now." Her gaze flicked out to the mob of gyrating forms to their rear. "Are we going to sit at the bar all night?"

"Oh." Steven's heart leaped up into his throat. "Want to hit the dance floor?"

"I thought you'd never ask."

Steven slid from his barstool and took the woman's hand. "Fair warning. It's Retro Night. Most of what they've been playing is a bit before our time."

Her lips curled into a wicked smile. "Speak for yourself."

She pulled Steven into the crowd and led him to a dark corner where even the flashing lights above their heads seemed afraid to shine. Their bodies moved in concert to the techno beat roaring from the speakers. Seconds later, the music downshifted into a slow R&B groove and the woman drew even closer. The rhythm took possession of her, her supple hips shifting with every passing beat. The scent of her, like sweet lavender, filled his senses, and for a moment, Steven forgot about his headache, the eighteen months of hell, even Katherine.

The woman wrapped her lithe arms about his neck and pulled him in tight to her well-toned body. The warm moisture of her breath a promise, she whispered, "If you're interested, my hotel room is only two blocks away." He half-believed he'd imagined the words, but the lust in her eyes left little doubt.

"But I don't even know your name."

"Does it matter?" She took his hand and pulled him toward the exit, only to be blocked halfway across the dance floor by a dark mountain of a man in a purple suit and black turtleneck.

"Hey, Jonas." Steven didn't like the look on the bouncer's face. "What's up?"

"Sorry to interrupt, but some taxi driver out front says he needs to talk to you. A friend of yours just puked all over the inside of his cab."

"Friend?" Steven asked.

Another of Katherine's favorite sayings echoed through Steven's mind: *No good deed goes unpunished.*

"Well?" Jonas said. "You coming?"

"If it's that guy from the bar, I don't even know him." Steven raised his hands in mock surrender. "I was just trying to help him out before he made a mess of himself."

Jonas let out a quiet chuckle. "Oh, he's made a mess, all right."

"And that's my responsibility?" Steven's voice rose a decibel or two.

Jonas shook his head. "Look, he's already complained to the manager. I stood up for you, and now the boss is pissed at me. Cabbie's refusing to leave till somebody pays up."

"I'm guessing that means me." Steven's brow furrowed. "What does this guy look like?"

"Late forties, maybe. Weird accent."

Steven laughed. "You just described half the taxi drivers in Chicago."

"Wait a minute." The woman, silent to that point, took Steven's hand. Her fingers felt hot, almost feverish. "The Good Samaritan thing was cute before, but you're not seriously going to cough up your hard-earned cash because a complete stranger can't hold his liquor, are you?" She squeezed his fingers. "Stay here with me and let your friend do his job." Her gaze dropped to the bouncer's nametag. "Unless this is the best you can do for patrons who actually pay for their drinks, Mr. Turo."

Jonas bristled. "Now, hold on a minute. I'm—"

Steven raised a hand. "Don't worry, Jonas. I've got this. In for a penny and all that." He pulled close enough to whisper in the woman's ear. "Five minutes?"

"Sure." Cold frustration flashed across the woman's features. "I needed to make a call anyway." Without another word, she stalked in the direction of the ladies lounge and disappeared around a corner.

"What the hell is her problem?" Jonas rested a firm hand on Steven's shoulder. "Nobody talks to me like that."

"I have no idea." Steven scanned the room for the mysterious woman. "I've known her for all of ten minutes."

"I'd watch yourself, man. She's got a mean streak, that one." Jonas chuckled. "I'd hate for you to wake up tomorrow in a bathtub of ice missing a kidney or something."

Steven shot him a withering stare. "Thanks a lot."

"No sweat." Jonas turned toward the front of the club. "Come on. I'll get you out of the front door quick so you can get back to business."

Steven followed Jonas, the crowd parting like the Red Sea as the bouncer strode toward the door. A few seconds later, they stepped out into the warm night air. He clasped Jonas' shoulder. "Hey. Thanks again for getting me in tonight."

"No sweat." Jonas motioned for the other bouncer to go inside and took his position at the rope. "Just to let you know, I hope I'm wrong about your lady friend."

"That makes two of us." Steven peered out at the busy street. "So, where is this guy?"

"He was parked across the street a minute ago." Jonas raised the rope, allowing passage to a pair of women in dresses that left little to the imagination. "It's funny. I haven't seen a ride like that in years."

"Keep an eye out." Steven stepped toward the street. "If I'm not back in five, call 911."

"Give him hell." Jonas' gold-toothed smile faded into purposeful indifference as he turned back to face the mob of hopefuls stranded at the velvet rope.

At first, Steven didn't see it. The street was littered with the usual hodgepodge of motorcycles, cars and SUV's. A stretch Hummer filled with college students in tuxes and formal dresses sat parked at the curb. As the eight of them disembarked and their land yacht pulled away, the object of Steven's search came into view.

A holdover from a different age, the red-and-white-checkered taxi was a product of late-seventies Detroit and had clearly seen better days. Its battered bumper hung slightly lower on the driver's side, the grille was fractured, and only three of its four headlights worked. Steven remembered reading an article in the late nineties about the retirement of the last checker cab in New York City and couldn't recall ever seeing such a vehicle on the streets of Chicago. He waited for an ebb in traffic and jogged across the street. Strangely nervous, he knocked on the driver's side window. A few seconds passed before the window opened a crack.

"Pardon, sir, but I'm off duty." The driver's accent was strange on Steven's ear, blending the crispness of the Queen's English with the smooth diction of French or Italian.

"I don't need a cab." Steven peered through the driver's side window, but could only make out the man's fedora and a hint of facial hair through the tinted glass. Otherwise, as best he could tell, the cab was empty. "I'm here to settle up for the guy who puked in your back seat."

"Ah, it's you." The driver chuckled, as if waking from a pleasant dream. "My sincerest apologies, but that fabrication was a necessary evil. I needed to speak with you away from the noise of the discotheque."

"Discotheque?" Steven murmured under his breath. "Look, pal. I'm not sure what kind of shit you're trying to pull here, but—"

"Quiet. We can argue semantics later if you like, but for the moment, there is simply no time." A quiet anger colored the man's words. "Now, get in the cab."

"Are you kidding me?" Steven's hands flew in the air. "I'm not going anywhere, especially not in this wreck." He pointed back at the door to the club. "Things were just getting interesting in there when you yanked Jonas' chain and tricked me into coming out here."

"Interesting, eh?" The driver let out a sarcastic chuckle. "You have no idea. Know one thing, young man. The woman who waits for you inside? She is not who she seems."

The words sent a chill through Steven's midsection. "Who the hell are you?"

"A friend." The driver turned his gaze to meet Steven's. The lights of a passing car illuminated his pair of slate-grey eyes, just visible above the cracked window.

"What the hell are you talking about?" Steven whispered. "Are you stalking her?"

"Though I know many things about the woman in black, understand I am not here for her." The back door of the cab opened as if by remote control. "I am here for you."

"Screw this." Steven turned and headed for the club. "I'm not ending up on the ten o'clock news tonight."

"Do not walk away from me, Steven Bauer." The driver opened his door and set one foot on the pavement. "You are not safe here."

Steven sprinted for the club and found Jonas replaced by a man resembling an Armani-clad linebacker.

"Whatever you do, don't let that freak inside," Steven shouted as he dove under the rope and through the door.

"Hey. You can't—" The bouncer's voice was cut off as the door slid shut. Michael Jackson's *Thriller* faded into a remix of Depeche Mode's *Master and Servant*. The thumping bass did little to help Steven's throbbing head as he worked his way back through the crowd. Back at the bar, he found Jonas hunched over the spot where he and the woman in the black dress had been sitting minutes before.

"Hey, Jonas." He rested a hand on the bouncer's shoulder. "You all right?"

"I don't... feel so good." Jonas lifted his head from the bar and squinted at Steven through bleary eyes. "Think I need to take a break."

"I know what you mean. I'm having the weirdest night. That head case in the taxi was talking some crazy shit. I'm not sure what he—"

Jonas rose from the stool. "Need to take a break." He lumbered past Steven and into the crowd as if he were sleepwalking. Steven's incredulous stare followed his friend until Jonas' massive form disappeared into the mob.

"Has everybody gone nuts?" Steven took Jonas' stool, his eyes growing wide at the circle of cardboard resting on the bar before him.

During his half hour wait at the bar, Steven had ample time to study every detail of this, the newest club in downtown Chicago, right down to the design of the coasters. Each displayed the black and gold Corners logo on one side and a famous quotation on the reverse. Steven's had featured Nietzsche's often-maligned line, "That which does not kill us makes us stronger."

The coaster resting at his elbow was not one of those.

Checkered red and white like an old-fashioned diner tablecloth, the cardboard disc was an endorsement for the Red Checker Cab Company, complete with phone number and the logo "Our promise – To get you home safe and sound." As old and battered as the cab waiting outside the doors of the club, it too appeared to have come from a different time. More interesting, though, was the message penned across the bottom.

*She is not who she seems.*

Steven scanned the crowd, his every instinct screaming he was being watched, but neither the woman with emerald eyes nor the mysterious cab driver were anywhere in sight. His heart racing in time with the music blaring from the speakers, he stole a furtive glance around, pocketed the coaster, and rose from the bar. Before he could take a step, a soft voice from across his shoulder sent the hairs on his neck snapping to attention.

"Why, Steven," came the already familiar Irish lilt. "Did you think I left without saying goodbye?"

## 2

## BAPTISM

Steven spun around to find the woman in black staring at him, her mouth twisted into a quizzical yet amused smirk.

"Everything go okay with the cab driver?" she asked with more than a hint of derision.

"Yeah." Steven cast a quick glance back at the front of the club. "All taken care of."

"You're all flushed." She put a hand to his damp cheek. "So, where were we?"

"You know, all of a sudden, I'm not feeling so hot." He rose from the barstool. "Give me another minute?"

Steven headed for the men's room, an unsolicited image of the woman in black training a gun at the back of his head hastening his steps.

*She is not who she seems.*

Locking the door behind him, he went straight to the sink and barely recognized the harried gaze looking back from the mirror. He splashed some water on his face, hoping he would wake from whatever nightmare had taken over his life. In a fit of desperation, he tried the window, only to find it nailed shut.

"Great," Steven whispered. "Heaven help this place if there's a fire."

Massaging the knot forming at the base of his neck, he cracked the restroom door and peered out at the crowd. The mysterious woman in the black dress was nowhere to be seen. Relief washed over him, at least until he realized her absence meant she could be anywhere.

As Steven stepped through the door, a firm grip from the shadows descended on his right shoulder. He whirled about, fists up and ready to fight.

"Steven." Jonas' deep base cut through the cacophony of the club. "Come with me."

"God, Jonas. You scared the crap out of me. What are you—" Steven stopped, not understanding what he was seeing. Jonas' eyes were different, their usual dark brown now the grey of a January sky. "Okay, what the hell is—"

"Quiet." Jonas' voice was dead. "This is far from over."

"What are you talking about?" Steven's eyes narrowed as understanding overtook him. "Where is she?"

Jonas scanned the crowd through squinted eyes and pointed a trembling finger. "There."

Steven followed Jonas' gaze. The mysterious woman in black stood atop the bar at the far end of the room, her head cocked to one side as if listening to something. Or someone.

Somehow unnoticed by the surrounding mob, she fixed a cold stare on Steven like a jungle cat surveying its prey. She shook her head in mock sadness and her frown turned up into a gleaming grin. Steven sprinted for the door, his heart pounding. Halfway across the crowded room, he chanced one last glance across his shoulder and immediately wished he hadn't.

At the woman's casual wave, eight jets of black flame shot out from around her feet, swept down the bar, and onto the floor. The twenty or so people closest to her screamed in unison as the dark fireball set their clothes and hair aflame. Their agonized wails went silent as the middle third of the bar exploded in an erupting volcano of ebon fire. Chunks of wood and concrete flew in all directions, the largest impacting the face of the mammoth aquarium behind the bar. The glass held for the briefest of moments before shattering outward like an enormous aquatic bomb, the shards of glass and coral cutting down at least a dozen more.

"My God," Steven whispered.

The room continued its descent into chaos as several thousand gallons of rushing salt water filled with flopping, gasping fish flooded the space. Forced toward the door, hundreds of bodies scrambled over each other like panicked cockroaches. Steven watched helpless as a young woman an arm's length away was crushed beneath the crowd's trampling feet. He lost sight of Jonas in the mad rush, and before he could form another coherent thought, Steven found himself outside. The scene just inside the club's open door sent ice through his veins.

The woman in black swept across the checkered floor as if carried by a gale force wind, the dark flames playing about her feet like excited bloodhounds.

*The cab driver. He tried to warn me.*

Steven spun around and scanned the opposite side of the street. Where the red-and-white-checkered vehicle had been parked rested a silver Honda decorated with a "Gore/Lieberman 2000" sticker from the most recent election.

"Shit." Steven's pulse pounded in his head as he sprinted up the street. Alternating north and east for several blocks, he took refuge in the shallow doorway of a corner coffee shop marked "Open Soon." A quick inspection confirmed he was alone and the block deserted.

Across the street, an empty construction site shone in the filtered moonlight like the ribcage of a giant's skeleton. He hunched over for several seconds, working to catch his breath, and felt in his pocket. Pulling out the red-and-white-checkered coaster, he rubbed the bridge of his nose and reread the scrawled writing at the cardboard's edge.

*She is not who she seems.*

"There's a news flash." Steven flipped the coaster over, eyed the number printed there, and reached for his phone only to find it had been lost in the shuffle.

"Dammit. Now what?"

Across the street at the edge of the construction site, a section of not-yet-destroyed wall sported an old payphone just visible in the dim light. One more look up and down the street and Steven sprinted across the four lanes of downtown boulevard. His hands trembling, he pulled a couple of coins from his pocket, dropped them into the phone, and dialed the number from the worn coaster. The phone rang several times before a strained voice answered.

"Hello?"

"I need a cab right away." Steven squinted in the dim light at the road signs at the corner. "I'm at the intersection of—"

"Look." The voice on the other end went from strained to irritated. "This stopped being funny years ago."

"What do you mean?"

"Red Checker went under in 1988, dumbass. Look it up."

"But—"

"I told her we should change this damn number." The man's voice grew quieter with each angry word.

"Wait. I need your—"

*Click.* Then nothing but dial tone.

Steven slammed down the receiver and pulled it back to his ear to dial 911. A flicker of movement on the periphery of his vision caught his attention. A block away along a sidewalk that had been empty seconds before, the woman in black bore down on him. Like a dark swan on a placid lake, she glided effortlessly down the sidewalk faster than Steven would have thought possible for a woman in heels. Closer and closer she drew and Steven did his best to ignore the impossible fact his senses screamed was true.

Her feet weren't touching the ground.

She lit on the opposite corner and inclined her head to one side as she had done in the club. Their gazes again met and her eyes narrowed with cruel design. Gone was the Hollywood smile, replaced by a mask of utter disdain. The face of a killer.

A snap of her fingers and obsidian flames flared to life at Steven's feet. He leaped backward half a second before the concrete beneath him erupted in dark fire. He turned to flee and found his way blocked by the fence surrounding the construction site. After failing two attempts at scaling the twelve feet of chain link and barbed wire, he chanced upon a torn section and scuttled under. Steven sprinted across the concrete slab, too terrified to look back. Though his ears registered no footsteps but his own, he took little comfort in the surrounding stillness.

Halfway across the maze of steel and concrete, a hurried look back in the direction he'd come confirmed he was again alone. He stopped for a moment to catch his breath and took cover behind a pile of bricks. Perking his ears for any hint of his pursuer, Steven heard nothing but his own raspy breathing. He rose from his hiding place only to find the woman in black waiting in the moonlight.

"Steven, Steven, Steven. Are you really going to make me chase you all night?" Her smile had returned, though in the darkness it more resembled the bared teeth of a predator closing in for the kill. "And here I thought you and I had real potential."

Steven took a step back. "What do you want with me?"

"Merely to continue our date, hopefully in more luxurious surroundings." Her stiletto heels clicked on the concrete. "I promise a night you'll never forget."

"Back off, lady." He picked up a piece of rebar from the concrete. "I'm not afraid to use this."

Her smile faded, replaced with a cold look of regret. "Very well. This could have been so easy and, no doubt, quite pleasant, but if you insist, I suppose we can do this the hard way."

In a blink, a halo of black iridescent light surrounded the woman's lithe form, the effect reminding Steven of a photographic negative. Her eyes filled with detached contempt, she raised her right arm. A sphere of shimmering darkness enveloped her hand. The ball of crackling energy expanded for several seconds before dissipating like a snuffed candle. Where the dark electricity had been, the woman now held a cylindrical object in her clenched fist.

Between the low light of the construction site and the waves of darkness emanating off her body, Steven could just make out the object's shape. No longer than the woman's arm with a serpentine relief fashioned into the dark metal, the rod culminated in a fist-sized orb of dark crystal. An unbidden image of the Queen of Spades flashed across his mind's eye, the Bed Post Queen from his college poker days. He caught his breath as the scepter crackled with the same obsidian force that surrounded his pursuer's form.

"Nobody move!"

Steven spun in the direction of the unheralded shout and found a uniformed guard standing next to a concrete column. Though his sidearm was leveled at Steven, the guard's attention remained focused on the woman.

"This is private property," the guard said. "State your business."

He approached them, retrieving a radio from his belt with one hand while keeping the gun aimed at Steven with the other. Respecting the firearm aimed at his chest, Steven let the rebar fall to the ground and put his hands in the air though he too kept his eyes on the real threat, the woman clothed in darkness.

"Not even a Pawn in the struggle." The woman directed her attention to the guard and sighed, a contemptuous smirk spreading across her face. "I almost pity you."

Black fire erupted from below her feet and raced in the guard's direction, the fiery trail stopping just short of his protuberant belly. Without warning, a tongue of flame shot up and licked his fingers. His hand's reflexive jerk sent his sidearm flying. Disarmed, the guard gaped as the woman snapped her fingers and disappeared from her end of the river of black flame. A moment later, she reappeared before him, the serpentine scepter held high above her head. Still nursing his blistered hand, the guard's knees hit the unforgiving concrete, his previously boisterous voice reduced to submissive whimpering.

"Little man, you have seen what must not be seen." Her gaze shot to Steven. "And you. You just had to run, didn't you? It's a shame, really. No one else had to die tonight."

Steven charged the woman who in turn leveled her scepter at the terrified man, her face no more affected than if she were about to swat a fly. The countless gems and stones decorating the engraved serpent's coils shone with a dark inner fire, the cold glimmer of the jewels mirrored in her icy stare. The guard hands before his face did little to protect him from the jet of black flame that flew from the scepter's tip and engulfed his entire body.

The horror of the moment stopped Steven in his tracks. His stomach threatened to rebel at the crackling sound of burning flesh mixed with the stench of singed human hair. The man's eyes bulged from his head and his skin fissured while his tormentor looked on, impassive. One last burst of flame and the guard's soul-wrenching screams ceased. As his immolated corpse fell at the woman's feet, she again turned her attention on Steven, her cold green eyes alight with a dark fire all their own.

Steven sprinted for the fence, fighting off another wave of nausea, all the while trying to banish the man's dying screams from his mind. Only fifty yards of concrete jungle remained between him and the next street, but it might as well have been a mile.

As what remained of the guard's body disintegrated into grey ash, black fire again erupted from the ground at the woman's feet and followed Steven as if he trailed gunpowder. The flickering trail of obsidian flame shot past him and with an audible snap of the woman's fingers, she again appeared squarely in his path.

"You can stop running any time now." Her tone wavered between sarcasm and boredom. "You're only making this harder on yourself."

"You killed that man. All those people." Steven trembled with anger. "Why?"

"Our Game isn't a spectator sport." The woman took a step in his direction and raised the scepter above her head. The trail of flames ending at her feet grew low, the fiery orchestra hushing as their dark maestro prepared to start the final movement.

*This is it.* Too terrified to even pray, Steven's eyes slid shut in preparation for the firestorm that was sure to come. Katherine's smile flashed across his mind's eye, followed by an unbidden image of his father's face. *He'll never know what happened.*

The flash of high beams and the piercing screech of squalling tires jerked Steven back to the present. He opened his eyes to find the red-and-white-checkered cab hurtling at his enemy. Striking the fence like a runaway train engine, the car penetrated the chain link barrier as if it weren't there. A mix of anger and surprise flashed across the woman's features, and then, in the blink of an eye, she was gone.

The cab screeched to a halt inches from where Steven stood. His knees threatening to buckle, he gasped when the back driver's side door again opened of its own accord.

"Get in," the driver grunted.

This time, Steven followed the command without question. The door slammed shut behind him like the jaw of a rabid dog. "Get me out of here," he said between panting breaths. "God, get me out of here."

"As you wish, Steven." The mysterious man behind the wheel let out a quiet chuckle. "Buckle up."

# 3

## JAUNT

The cab hurtled along Chicago's darkened streets, the roar of the engine a guttural counterpoint to Steven's pounding heart. One block at a time, the driver zigzagged across the city, his gaze shifting constantly from road to mirror. Too frightened to speak, Steven clutched the dark leather seat to keep from being flung from side to side. At every turn, he expected the vehicle to explode into black flames and more than once considered leaping from the cab to take his chances with the rushing pavement.

"Where are you taking me?" Steven could barely keep the tremor from his voice.

"Away from her, for a start." The driver's tone was flat with a hint of fatigue.

Steven's entire body tensed. "Take me home. Please. Whoever you are. I can pay cash, check, whatever you want. My address—"

"I know where you live, Steven Bauer. Going to your home, however, would be far from prudent. As the opposition has determined who you are, it is fair to assume they also know where you live, work, even where you take your breakfast on Saturday mornings. They could be at your home this very moment, awaiting your return."

The driver took a screeching right turn. "And you are in no way ready to face them a second time."

"A second time?" A crawling sensation played along Steven's scalp at the mere thought of another encounter with the woman in the black dress.

"Your opponent is playing quite aggressively this time," the stranger continued, "and seems to be ignoring the rules at his whim. This steps up our timetable considerably."

"Timetable? What are you—"

The driver accelerated through a left turn, sending Steven careening into the door. "I can guess many of the questions running through your mind, though the most important ones are those you have yet to consider."

The cab's engine whined as the driver sped beneath a yellow light and narrowly avoided an oncoming garbage truck. The truck's headlamps filled the cab with light and something that had nagged at Steven sprung to the forefront of his mind. Despite multiple turns and the lights of dozens of vehicles, he couldn't recall seeing so much as a glimpse of the driver's face. He craned his neck in an effort to catch the man's profile or perhaps a reflection in the rear view mirror, but regardless of the lighting or angle, the driver's features remained hidden in shadow.

*Except his eyes. Those piercing grey eyes.*

"Who are you?" Steven asked.

The driver met Steven's gaze in the rear view mirror. "Names as a convention are funny things, but for now, you may call me Grey. More importantly, I am someone in need of your particular services."

"My services?" Steven let out a solitary chuckle. "I work for an employment agency. You want me to find you a job?"

Grey laughed. "No, Steven. This job is yours, the first of many. I have several open positions to fill and I am seeking individuals who meet my very exacting requirements."

"Right." Steven rolled the man's words over in his mind. "And that crazy bitch who tried to flash-fry me. Who was she?"

"A representative of your opponent, and not someone to trifle with."

"What the hell does she want with me, anyway? I've never even seen her before."

"You are not being pursued for anything you have done, Steven, but for the road you are about to walk."

"And you're not listening to a word I'm saying. I haven't agreed to any part of this." Steven peered out the window as the car slowed in an unfamiliar neighborhood. "I don't even know what *this* is."

"Trust that all your questions will be answered in due time, but first we must get you to safety." The cab pulled to the curb along a dimly lit side street. "If memory serves me, your dinner plans this evening were interrupted. You must be famished." Grey exited the cab and proceeded up a narrow alley.

His warring instincts telling him simultaneously to make a run for it and to trust the enigmatic stranger, Steven followed Grey into the murky alley. A solitary streetlamp flickered to their rear, its intermittent illumination barely able to penetrate the hazy mist playing about his rescuer's feet. Cloaked in a full-length duster, the man known as Grey remained a mystery. An inch or two taller than Steven, his shifting form melded with the shadows like an out of focus image on a movie screen. As they reached the other end of the alley, Grey stopped before a dilapidated green door and brushed the dust from an old wooden sign marked "Stage Exit."

"We're going to a theater?"

"This door leads to a safe location, albeit in a roundabout sort of way." Grey rummaged in the pocket of his well-worn gabardine coat and produced an old-fashioned skeleton key along with a bundle Steven couldn't identify in the dim haze. He brushed the door twice with the bundle, leaving an "X" in the dust and cobwebs, and placed the two-pronged key into the lock. Shooting a quick glance back at the mouth of the alley, he turned the key. The aged tumblers resisted briefly, but in the end, relented.

The door swung open, but instead of a darkened room or musty stairwell or even the inside of a building at all, the doorway opened onto a cobblestone street. Damp air with a hint of chill poured through the open door. Grey stepped through without hesitation and waited on the other side. Steven followed, feeling like Alice at the rabbit hole, all the while doubting his own senses. An abrupt drop in temperature coupled with the pungent smell of salt water made it clear they were no longer in Chicago. Outside the doorway waited not the murky alleyway they had just left, but the inside of a coffee shop after hours, lights off with chairs upside down on the tables. Grey closed the ornate glass and wood door behind them and again turned the key.

"What are you doing now?"

"Locking up." Grey's matter of fact tone held a touch of levity. "It is common courtesy, is it not?" He pocketed the key and proceeded down the sidewalk at a brisk pace. Steven followed in silence, jogging to keep up. The odd pair passed block after block of shops along the cobblestone street, the storefronts a strange mixture of contemporary and vintage. Occasionally, between some of the buildings, Steven glimpsed a large body of water he had a sneaking suspicion wasn't Lake Michigan.

"Where are we?" Steven asked.

"This is Old Port. Nice town. Quite pleasant this time of year."

"Old Port?"

"The oldest section of Portland. Have you never visited Maine before?"

"We're in Maine? Are you kidding me?"

"You tell me, Steven. When was the last time you took an ocean-side stroll in Chicago?"

Steven stopped at the next intersection and peered out at the water. "Point taken. You've got to admit, though, this is all a little..."

"Insane? Do not fear. All will be made clear soon enough."

Grey headed inland, leaving the main street of shops and restaurants behind, and again, Steven followed. Strangely, though the streets held a smattering of joggers, dog walkers and couples out for an evening stroll, no one acknowledged their presence. Some would politely step out of the way or head to the opposite side of the street, but not one made eye contact with either of them.

"It's strange, Grey. It's like these people can't..." Steven's breath caught in his throat at the sight of shadows shimmering off Grey's coat like raindrops. He looked to the side and his mysterious rescuer all but vanished, only to reappear when Steven refocused on the man's form.

"How the hell are you doing that?"

"Hold that thought, Steven. We have arrived."

They stood before a white two-story house with black shutters, a quaint front porch with several hanging ferns, and the obligatory pair of rocking chairs.

"At last." Grey's boots, loud upon the cobblestone walkway, echoed on the warped wood of the porch steps as he approached the front door. Even there, beneath the porch's lone incandescent bulb, his face remained hidden.

Despite the late hour, lights shone from several rooms of the house. The unmistakable wail of a Louis Armstrong solo emanated from an open window. The dulcet jazz tones sent Steven back half a decade to a much happier time.

*The senior dance at Georgetown. The jazz band from New Orleans. The feel of Katherine's velvet dress beneath his fingers, the two of them shifting in time to the music.*

Grey knocked three times on the wooden door, jolting Steven back to the present. The music stopped, leaving only the distant whistle of a train to break the stillness. "It has been far too long," Grey whispered.

Footsteps approached from within, followed by a gruff voice from behind the door. "Who in the blue blazes is knocking at this hour?"

Grey chuckled. "You might say, 'a long-expected party.'"

"Holy saints," proclaimed the voice from beyond the door. "Could it be?" The door cracked an inch, and a pair of eyes scrutinized Grey from below a brass chain.

"Hello, Arthur."

The door clicked shut for a moment and then flew open to reveal a man in his eighties grinning broadly. His build slight, he wore his thick, white hair combed neatly to one side. Dressed in old jeans and a flannel shirt, his well-used apron proclaimed in faded red letters "Kiss the Cook." He regarded Grey with glad recognition and seemed oblivious to Steven's existence.

"Unbelievable. Rex Caesius standing on my doorstep." Tears formed at the corners of Arthur's eyes. "It's been quite a while."

"It has indeed," Grey said. "You look well."

"You too, Rex, though I see your preferred appellation is finally starting to catch up with you." Arthur laughed. "About damn time." He glanced back into the house. "I hope you're hungry. We didn't get a proper dinner tonight, and Ruth is just finishing up our evening snack."

"I am well, thank you, though my companion could probably use some refreshment."

Arthur squinted past Grey and caught Steven's eye. "Wait. Is that—"

"This is a new associate of mine," Grey interrupted. "His name is Steven Bauer. We met earlier this evening to discuss a business proposition, but our rendezvous was interrupted. We needed a place away from certain prying individuals to discuss the specifics. I apologize for the lateness of our call, but yours was the first place that came to mind and, as I remember, you usually have some scraps lying around for hungry passersby."

"Scraps?" Arthur pushed past Grey and shook Steven's hand. "Good evening, young man. I'm Arthur Pedone. Welcome to our home."

"Thank you, sir." Steven was sure they'd never met, though a glint of recognition and a hint of gratitude shone in the man's old eyes.

"Well, come on inside. Don't be shy. Scraps. The very thought." He put his hand to his mouth and called down the hall. "Ruth?"

A plump woman of Arthur's vintage stepped into the hall from an adjoining room. A simple apron and the mouthwatering smell of cooking meat suggested she had been busy in the kitchen. Her face screwed up when she saw the three of them, her eyes squinting over the pair of rectangular glasses perched precariously on her nose. "Well, love? Are you going to leave them standing on the porch or invite them in?"

"But I—" Arthur stammered.

"Please excuse my husband's poor manners." Ruth shot them all a wink. "Come inside, all of you. It's damp out tonight, and we don't want anyone catching colds." Grey beckoned for Steven to enter before disappearing with Arthur into the next room. Steven moved to join them but stopped at the old woman's raised hand.

"Don't mind those two," she said with a knowing grin. "They have some catching up to do. Please make yourself at home." Her dark eyes sparkled. "I'm Ruth."

"Steven." His gaze wandered around the room. "Nice to meet you."

"Do you know why you're here?" Ruth fiddled with her necklace, a simple silver chain, her fingers absently stroking the dragonfly-shaped pendant that rested above her heart.

Steven swallowed. "Do you?"

Ruth took Steven's hands, her long-suffering smile implying she understood his life had become anything but ordinary. "I'd best not say. You'll get your answers soon enough, most of which I suspect you'll wish you could give back."

Her hands were calloused but warm. As the two of them stood there, another bit of déjà vu filtered through Steven's thoughts, as if he had stood with her before just like this, but in another place, another time.

"I'm sorry, Ruth." Steven locked gazes with the old woman. "Have we met?"

Arthur stepped back into the hall. "The teapot is whistling, love, and I suspect the corned beef is almost ready."

Ruth dropped Steven's hands and turned to face her husband. "Is everything all right?"

"Everything is fine." Arthur's expression suggested otherwise. "I just have a few things to take care of outside." He embraced his wife and gently kissed her wrinkled forehead.

"I'll go finish up, then." Ruth shot Steven an anxious look and headed down the hall for the kitchen. Arthur cracked the front door and peered out into the darkness before stepping out onto the porch.

"Wait," Steven said. "Where are you going?"

Arthur turned and met Steven's nervous gaze. "You can go ahead into the next room. He's ready for you." The old man forced his lips into a tight smile and pulled the door closed behind him. The deadbolt lock turned from outside.

"Looks like I'm not going anywhere." Steven's eyes passed from the locked door to the opposite doorway that apparently led to all the answers his mind craved. "Ready for me, huh?" A sarcastic chuckle escaped his lips. "The real question is whether I'm ready for him."

# 4

## GREY

Steven stepped through the arched doorway into a den furnished with three mismatched chairs and a well-worn leather sofa. A pair of bookshelves sagged under the weight of hundreds of volumes. A small Panasonic television complete with rabbit ears sat abandoned in the corner, the screen so covered with dust, he suspected it hadn't been turned on since Clinton sat in the Oval Office. He turned to call for Ruth and found a grey duster draped across the back of the old sofa. Just a few feet away, his mysterious rescuer stared intently at a framed black-and-white photograph hanging on the wall.

He hadn't been there a second before. Steven rubbed at his eyes. How could he have missed the man?

No longer cloaked in canvas and shadow, Grey sported a charcoal and white-checkered tunic that hung midway down his thighs, cinched at the waist with a woven leather belt. His jet-black, shoulder-length locks accentuated the few strands of white at his temples. Made of grey leather, his well-worn boots shone with a high luster.

"Shark skin." Grey's eyes didn't budge from the photograph.

Steven took a step closer. "Excuse me?"

"The boots. They are fashioned from shark skin."

"That's… interesting. What's up with the picture?"

Grey turned and sat in a battered claw-footed chair where a pair of lace doilies decorated the armrests. "My apologies. I was reminiscing on happier times."

Captivated by Grey's steely gaze, Steven took a seat on the sofa opposite his strange rescuer. The weathered lines of the man's face spoke volumes, while his aquiline nose and square chin suggested nobility.

"I was thinking. I never really thanked you for—"

"No thanks are required, Steven." Grey spoke with authority though an undercurrent of weariness colored every word. "Your importance in the coming days necessitated every risk I have taken this evening."

"I don't get it." Steven buried his face in his hands. "Floating women, black fire, exploding security guards, not to mention our little interstate jaunt an hour ago. Please tell me I'm lying in a gutter somewhere dreaming all this."

"If only this were a dream. As difficult as it may be for you to believe, all you have seen tonight is real." A rueful grimace spread across his face. "Far too real."

"There has to be some sort of explanation, then. Something that makes sense." Steven shoved his hands into his pockets to keep them from trembling. "Why is all this happening? What do you want from me?"

"As I said in the cab, I have need of your services."

Steven's stomach knotted. "And if I don't accept?"

"It is not your choice." Grey stroked his sparse beard. "This position chooses you, not the other way around."

"I'm guessing the woman in black doesn't want me to take the job."

Grey studied the floor, his brow furrowed. "I am still unclear as to how she found you. By every convention, you should have been untouchable, at least until the others were gathered. My best thought is that despite all my precautions, the enemy became aware of your identity through me. I am truly sorry your life was endangered before you were ready."

"Like I was ever going to be ready for a supermodel assassin sporting a flamethrower? Not to mention I've never laid eyes on you before tonight."

"Oh, we have indeed met, Steven Bauer, though I sincerely doubt you would remember. I have approached you in friendly guise on multiple occasions, much as I did earlier this evening through your friend Jonas. I hoped to avoid alarming you until I had confirmed you were in fact the man for the job. Tonight's events unfortunately demonstrate that my efforts to maintain your anonymity have failed."

"You think?" Steven's eyes grew wide. "Consider me officially alarmed. That woman—whatever she was—knew exactly who I was. She killed all those people trying to get to me." He pondered for a moment. "Is this a CIA thing or something like that?"

Grey shook his head. "You saw what your pursuer could do this evening. Try as you might, you will find no explanation that makes sense to you in the world you know. Your paradigm must shift. If you wish to understand tonight's events and your role in the coming struggle, you will have to open your mind to possibilities you have never considered."

A sniff from the hall caught their attention. Perched at the edge of the arched doorway stood Ruth, her face half-hidden in shadow.

"Food's ready, boys." A quiet insistence filled her words. "You can wash up in the back."

As Ruth vanished back down the hall, Grey rose. "Shall we continue our discussion over dinner? Ruth is quite the cook."

Though Steven bristled at the interruption, he found it difficult to argue with the rumbling of his stomach as the aroma of corned beef wafted into the room. He followed Grey down a hallway filled with fifty years of framed photographs to the Pedone dining room.

Clearly the showplace of the home, white columns on either side of the doorway opened on walls of deep magenta and a cherry hardwood floor. A simple wrought-iron light fixture hung over a small oval table with four place settings. Four glasses of iced tea and an impressive assortment of rolls and croissants occupied the center of the table.

"Have a seat," Ruth said. "Arthur should be back any moment."

As Steven and Grey took their places around the table, a jangle of keys at the front door brought a relieved smile to Ruth's face. A moment later, Arthur joined them.

"Well, that's done." Arthur grabbed one of the hot crescent rolls and gestured across the table. "Can someone pass the preserves?"

"Come now, love," Ruth said. "We haven't blessed the food."

"Yes, yes." Arthur took Ruth's hand and then Grey's. After an uncomfortable silence and a not too subtle nod from Ruth, Steven followed suit. Grey's firm grasp was a sharp contrast to the nervous tremor in Ruth's fingers. Steven bit his lip as the other three closed their eyes and bowed their heads, something he hadn't done since he was a child.

The truth was, he didn't recall the last time he asked for God's blessing on anything. Katherine had dragged him to her church in Georgetown on occasion, though any desire to set foot in a place of worship died the day of her funeral.

Grey cleared his throat, and Steven realized he was crushing the man's hand. He relaxed his grip and tilted his head in apology. Ruth began to pray.

"Father, we come before You today with thanksgiving in our hearts for the bounty You have put before us, for health, for security, for old friendships that never fade, and for new faces to brighten our day. For all the blessings of each and every day, we give You thanks. Amen."

Waiting until Arthur and Grey had echoed the final word of the prayer, Steven opened his eyes to find Ruth already up, humming a pleasant tune and assembling a plate. He reached for a sandwich and felt Grey's hand on his arm.

"Don't you lift a finger, Steven." Ruth shot him a wink. "My house, my rules."

Though the fare was humble, the aged woman served the simple sandwiches as if their meal were the finest of feasts. She moved with a facile grace that belied her age, the veil of years lifting occasionally, allowing glimpses of a young woman from half a century before to peek through. As she worked on Steven's plate, her face flashed with something like recognition.

"Hold on." She stepped into the kitchen and returned with a white bowl covered in cellophane. "I'm betting you'd rather have a bit of cole slaw on yours."

"Thanks," Steven said. "Never was a big fan of sauerkraut."

"My pleasure." A hint of color playing in her cheeks, Ruth spooned a bit of the sweet smelling cabbage onto Steven's plate.

"Bit of that for me as well, please." Grey set the salt back on the table, deftly exchanging it with the pepper as Ruth served him. "Ever the consummate hostess, Mrs. Pedone."

"My Ruthie's one of a kind," Arthur said. "Don't know what I'd do without her."

"You silly boys," Ruth said. "It's just cole slaw."

"Best cole slaw you've ever had." Arthur grinned. "Sixty years of nothing but the best."

"Stop it, love." Shooting Steven a furtive glance, Ruth sat back at the table and did her best to avoid his gaze. "You're embarrassing me."

An awkward silence fell over the table.

"Thank you for your kind hospitality, Ruth," Grey said, steepling his fingers below his hawkish nose. "As always."

She nodded, taking a sip of her drink.

Steven turned to Arthur. "I'm curious. How do all of you know each other?"

Arthur's eyes shot to Grey and the two men shared a knowing look.

"We go back quite a way," Grey said. "Longer, I imagine, than either Ruth or Arthur care to remember."

"And they know why I'm here?" Steven's eyes flashed with something like hope. "Have they been through this?"

"Thank heavens, no," Arthur said. "I've never even seen the shoes you're wearing, much less walked a mile in them."

"But you do know why I'm here. I can see it in your eyes. Ruth all but spilled it in the hall before. Why won't anyone tell me what's going on?"

"Do not worry," Grey said, eyeing Ruth. "These two have only your best interests at heart. They are privy to knowledge few on this planet know or understand. Their reticence to share with you is at my request alone."

"As for how Rex and I know each other," Arthur rested his glass on the table. "It was the Big One, Steven. June of '44. The shores of Normandy." He slapped Grey's shoulder. "Wouldn't have made it off Omaha Beach if it weren't for this old coot."

Steven slid back from the table. "I don't think I'm following you, Arthur. You're talking D-Day. You I can buy, but 'Rex' here isn't even as old as my dad." Steven scrutinized Grey's features for a second time that evening. "Unless I'm missing something."

Arthur's gaze shot to Grey. "He doesn't know?"

Something akin to frustration washed across Grey's visage. "We had not quite come to that part." He rose from the table and stepped into the hall. Steven moved to follow him, but at Arthur's raised hand, sat back down.

"Still has a flare for the dramatic, that one." Arthur poured Steven another glass of tea. "Don't worry. I have a feeling I know what he wants to show you."

Grey returned a few seconds later with the framed picture from the other room and handed it to Steven. Closer inspection revealed it wasn't a mere photograph, but a newspaper clipping, a vintage Steven had only seen in museums. The aged newsprint had yellowed, but the picture, a group of soldiers disembarking from a US Navy frigate, remained clear. The caption beneath the photo read, "Corporal Arthur Pedone and Sergeant Rex Caesius of the 29th Infantry Division disembark at New York Harbor." In the upper right corner, nearly covered by the frame, the paper's date read, "January 4, 1946."

In the lead were two familiar figures.

The first, an unbelievably young Arthur, walked proudly down the dock with a stuffed duffel bag held across his shoulder. He looked nineteen or twenty, his smile that of a man with his entire life before him.

The second bore an uncanny resemblance to Grey, as if no more than a day had passed since the photo was taken. Other than the hair, which was cut in the military style of the time, his mysterious rescuer stood unchanged from the photo taken three generations prior.

Steven laid the frame on the table. "How is this possible?"

"I have lived long enough to say goodbye to more friends than I care to recall." Grey rested a hand on Arthur's shoulder. "I remember walking off that boat with Arthur like it was yesterday. That year represented one of the great watershed moments in human history, and I have been present for far more than my share. Every other person in that photograph is long gone, but I still remember every name."

"Stop," Steven said. "What you're talking about is impossible."

"Impossible is a state of mind," Grey whispered. "Were you not standing in downtown Chicago less than two hours ago and now find yourself breaking bread in Maine?"

"All right, though you still haven't explained what any of this has to do with me."

"Very well." Grey sat and stroked his beard. "Tell me. What do you know about chess?"

# 5

## PAWN

"Chess?"

Grey raised an eyebrow. "You have played the game, I assume."

"Enough to go a few rounds with you." Steven grinned. "It's been a few years, though. What's that got to do with anything?"

"Everything. What lies ahead of you is a game of chess, the most important of your life. But be warned. This contest is no mere meeting of the minds."

"That woman," Steven said. "She mentioned something about a Game."

"I have no doubt she did. You and others like you comprise one side of a coming conflict, the woman you met last night and her associates the other. The gathered White are soon to face their dark opposition across a checkered battlefield and fight until only one side remains."

"This chess game. It's not metaphorical, is it?" Steven put down his sandwich and placed his hands in his lap to hide his trembling fingers. "You're crazy if you think I'm signing up for more of this shit. That woman killed those people at the club without a second thought.

Burned that security guard alive right in front of me. Hell, if you'd arrived a few seconds later..."

Grey rubbed at the bridge of his nose. "I know your role in this must seem without hope after your encounter with the woman in black this evening, but let me assure you when you next face the enemy, you will be far from helpless and, if all goes well, no longer alone."

Steven massaged the knot forming in his neck. "So, assuming neither of us is in serious need of medication, you're saying I'm part of this Game of yours whether I like it or not." His gaze fell. "And powerless to do anything about it."

"Not powerless." Arthur's voice quivered with excitement. "Tell him, Rex."

Grey eyed Arthur, his patient gaze clouding for a moment. "For a time, you and others you have yet to meet will embody the various pieces of the chessboard. Once conscripted into the Game, each of you will possess abilities commensurate with your position therein."

"Abilities?" Steven asked. "And these others you keep talking about? Do they know about all this?"

"No more than you did," Grey said. "Five more await the call, each of them as oblivious to their destiny as you were earlier this evening."

Steven shook his head. "Shouldn't someone let all the soldiers know they've been drafted before they're dumped in a war zone?"

Grey sighed. "You have hit upon the crux of the matter. Tonight's skirmish was the opening salvo in the latest iteration of a struggle that has gone on for more than a thousand years. In the fifteen centuries since the inception of the Game, it has come to this only a handful of times. Each time, both sides stood assembled and primed before contact with the opposition was feasible, much less allowed. Your opponent has not only ignored this convention, but as evidenced this evening, has been quite proactive in his recruiting. Your future compatriots are in grave danger, Steven, and I fear we can do little but continue with the gathering."

"I don't know much about chess," Ruth said, "but removing pieces from the board before the game begins sounds like cheating to me."

"Indeed." Grey shook his head, his dark eyes cast downward. "If the Black are successful in this endeavor, they will possess an insurmountable advantage before the Game proper can even begin."

"How do they even know who they're looking for?" Arthur asked.

"That remains a mystery." Grey rested a hand at a bulge at his hip hidden beneath the edge of his tunic. "Without this—"

"Stop it, all of you." Steven shot out of his seat, sending his chair crashing to the floor, and went to the window. "Listen to yourselves for God's sake."

Arthur joined him by the fogged glass. "I know all of this sounds crazy, but over the years I've learned to accept a few things on faith. I believe God looks down on me every day, hopefully with a smile on his face. I believe I managed to land one of the few perfect women ever born into this world." He glanced back across his shoulder at Grey who remained seated at the table. "And if there's one thing I haven't a shred of doubt about, it's that the world according to Rex Caesius, as strange as it may sound, is the truth."

Steven righted his chair and sat back down, the familiar dull pain flaring again behind his left eye. "It's still a lot to take, Grey. One night of weirdness and I'm supposed to accept that my life has been transformed into some magical game of chess?"

"I appreciate how difficult all of this must be for you," Grey said. "You do not and cannot understand your place in the world as you are now, but you soon will." He reached beneath the edge of his tunic and retrieved a small leather bag. Steven recognized the bundle Grey had brushed across the stage door in Chicago. Handing the bag to Steven, he said, "Until this time of conflict is over, this will be your guide and your burden."

Steven eyed the white leather bag. "What's so special about your little knapsack?"

"Knapsack." Grey ran his tongue across his teeth, his impassive features clouding over with frustration. "The *Hvitr Kyll* is a tool, a guide, a resource. Old beyond measure when even I was young, this pouch and its dark sister contain the dual essence of the Game itself."

Steven studied the pouch, its heft unnaturally warm in his hands. Fashioned from faded white leather, it was cinched at the top with a length of silver cord. Strange letters stamped into the thick band surrounding the mouth were of no language he'd ever seen. A low drone emanated from the mouth of the pouch, its volume growing and the warm leather pulsating in his hand like a human heart.

"Open it," Grey said. "The answers you seek are inside."

Steven looked to Grey and Arthur, though it was Ruth's silent nod that prompted him to untie the cord. He peered inside, the throbbing drone crescendoing with every passing second. A white glow shone from within, growing brighter with every beat as it pulsed in time with the pounding sound.

"This is incredible. Can you guys see—"

Steven looked up from the pouch only to find himself somewhere else. Far from the Pedone dining room in Portland, Maine, he stood atop a ragged cliff overlooking the ocean. The sun descending into the expanse of water to the west left the cloudless sky a burnt orange. A gentle breeze brought the scent of the churning surf to his nostrils. He turned from the edge and nearly collided with an aged man in colorful striped robes walking with a teenage boy dressed in white. Though their language was foreign, Steven understood every word.

*"Ten thousand dead in two days," the old man said. "Twelve hundred years under the arrangement of our ancestors and still men die in droves at the whim of an unforgiving universe. Over a millennium, and we have accomplished nothing."*

*"But Grandfather," the boy said. "Has not the arrangement kept the great catastrophes at bay for the same twelve centuries? You have always taught me to trust the wisdom of our forbears."*

*"And what wisdom is that?"*

*"To always serve the greatest good."* Though harsh on Steven's ear, the voice of the boy was strangely familiar. *"Did you not instruct me the needs of the many must always come before the needs or wants of the few?"*

*"Ten thousand dead, young one. Ten thousand. I believe even Aristotle would agree in this case, the sacrificial few have become the many."*

*The boy picked up a smooth stone from the ground and rubbed it between his fingers. "I and a friend have spent hours deliberating over this. We may have come upon a solution."*

*"What would this grand solution of yours be, my grandson?" The old man stopped and faced the boy. "And who is this friend of whom you speak?"*

*The boy studied the ground at his feet. "Zed returned from the Orient yesterday." He flung the stone sidearm off the edge of the cliff. "He brought with him an idea. A game."*

*"Zed is a wandering fool, and I know far too well the kind of games he plays." The old man turned away from the boy and headed inland. "You would do well to avoid him."*

*"Won't you hear me out, Grandfather?" The boy's eyes grew wide with emotion.*

*The old man stopped in mid stride, though he didn't turn to face his grandson. "Speak. Tell me of this game."*

"Ah, to be that young again."

Steven spun to find Grey standing at the cliff's edge, a hint of moisture forming at the corners of his cloud-grey eyes.

"He's... you." Steven stared at the boy in white.

Grey turned to face the setting sun. "I truly thought I had the answer. The centuries have proven it was I, not Zed, who was the fool."

"Slow down, Grey. What are you talking about?"

"Forgive me. There is so much for you to understand." Grey's eyes darkened with emotion. "What you are witnessing is, in many ways, the Game's beginning, though the seeds of its creation were planted long before this day, this conversation."

"They... you were discussing an arrangement of some kind?"

"The history and legends of every culture on the planet are filled with references to great catastrophes that occurred in the all but forgotten past. A great flood that nearly destroyed all life on earth. A once great city sent to a watery grave. Pestilence. Famine. Even the fossil record your scientists worship proves the worldwide extinction of one dominant species after another. Practitioners of the ancient arts sought a way to end these great cataclysms that had plagued man for all of history."

"They tried to stop... nature?"

Grey offered Steven an apologetic smile and picked up a stick from the ground. Holding the fragile twig delicately between his fingers, he maneuvered it like the balancing pole of a tightrope walker. "In a way. The forces responsible for these great cataclysms are ever present, much like the tides or the shifting phases of the moon. They lie in eternal opposition, usually in some semblance of balance, with most changes to their equilibrium occurring over millennia or longer. This perpetual state of flux, however, is punctuated at times with rapid corrections, when reality snaps back into place with speed and violence." With a crack, Grey broke the stick across his knuckles and allowed the two pieces to fall to the ground. "Like an earthquake occurring after centuries of subtle tectonic shifts, these corrections have the potential for destruction beyond imagining."

"I still don't see what this has to do with me," Steven said, "or chess for that matter."

Grey raised a hand. "My ancestors set in place a solution that stopped the great disasters from occurring, at least at their previous magnitude. The arrangement involved channeling the forces in question into the constantly warring tribes of the world. By allowing the opposing energies to come into direct and violent opposition through the endless conflicts of man, they achieved a new and more fluid equilibrium. The great disasters ceased and a multitude of innocent lives were saved. The cost, however, was greater than they could have imagined."

"Dad always said no one could see the future." Katherine's smile flashed across Steven's memory. "All you can do is make the best decisions possible with the information you have."

"Your father is a wise man, though the outcome of this particular solution was almost worse than the problem it solved." Grey lowered his head. "The forces previously responsible for the great cataclysms became simply another aspect of the face of war, a new and terrible aspect no one had prepared for. The immense power pouring into and through the warring armies would often escalate hostilities, protracting for years strife that should have lasted mere days. The death toll of these conflicts grew to staggering heights, outmatching even that possible with modern technology, often eradicating entire tribes or races from the planet. Still, the cataclysms stopped, as if some dark god had been appeased with the blood sacrifice of countless men."

"Like how dropping the bomb on Hiroshima ended World War II," Steven said. "Still, you haven't explained what any of this has to do with me or this Game you keep talking about."

Grey's eyes slid shut. "Fourteen centuries ago, Zed and I proposed a solution to the rampant slaughter necessitated by our ancestor's arrangement. A simple contest to replace the great wars while maintaining an equilibrium set in place long before my time."

"Ah." Steven's eyes flashed with recognition. "The Game."

Without warning, reality twisted around him, a swirling kaleidoscope of light and colors that pulsed in time with the drone from the pouch. Faces, images, locales all flashed by in a rapid torrent of experience. Then, as abruptly as before, Steven was somewhere else and again alone. Far brighter than the previous location, he squinted to take in his new surroundings. A mountain of sand beneath his feet, pyramids peeked above the next ridge, while in the valley below, a scene both game and battlefield played out.

Atop sixty-four squares of alternating marble and obsidian, two opposing forces waited, one garbed in white and gold, the other in jet and silver. Each side sixteen strong, foot soldiers from both front lines had already begun their advance. Their forms indistinct due to the distance, Steven gasped at the unmistakable silhouette of four of the combatants.

*Are those... elephants?*

Steven sprinted down the hill to get a closer look at the battle unfolding before him. With each square at least twenty feet across, the enormous chessboard was better than half a football field in size. Behind the front line of foot soldiers, the four corners of the board held bronze chariots manned with armored warriors and drawn by massive steeds. Next in, mounted soldiers armed with either mace or flail awaited the command to go into battle. Flanking the middle squares of both black and white, a quartet of elephants waited. Armored head to toe, a pair of archers sat atop each of the elephants, as if the creatures' bronze covered tusks weren't sufficiently intimidating. Finally, the two center squares of each rear file held a pair of men, one clothed in the ornate dress of royalty and the other dressed in simple robes and sandals.

"That's odd," Steven said. "Where are the queens?"

"A good question." Stepping out of nothingness, Grey appeared by Steven's side. "In Chaturanga, and later in Shatranj, the pieces in question were known as viziers. The ministers to their respective kings, they were only marginally more capable than a pawn. The piece you know as queen did not come along for another six hundred years."

"Six hundred years?" Steven asked. "When is this? What are we seeing?"

"The first iteration of the Game, over fourteen hundred years ago."

Steven continued his sandy trudge toward the board. "They can't see me, can they?"

"There is no one to see, Steven. You are not actually in this place. As real as all this may appear, you are nothing but an observer to events that occurred long before your time."

Steven swept his arm outward in a grand motion, indicating the gathered forces of light and darkness. "Who are they?"

"Mere men, much like you," Grey said. "Empowered by the Game, however, this day they faced each other with the power of gods."

"Men like me…" Steven watched as one of the elephants thundered along a diagonal line of white squares to the far end of the board. "What happened to them?"

Reality warped around Steven again, the hot sand replaced by yellow grass and the bright blue of the Egyptian sky with dreary grey. At the center of a rugged plain, another enormous chessboard stretched out before him, the far end littered with the mangled remains of better than a dozen forms, their white garb stained deep crimson. Vultures circled above while a murder of crows availed themselves of the bloody spread.

Steven stepped onto the board and moved in the direction of the carnage. Bile rose in his throat, the stench of death growing stronger with every step. Within seconds, he stood over the first body. Covered in armor of silver plate, the young man lay crushed beneath the flank of his ivory steed, his breastplate caved in as if struck with a battering ram. His face, barely visible beneath a medieval helm, was frozen in a rictus of fear.

"This is a slaughter." Steven looked to the sky. "Why am I being shown this?"

Grey appeared from a shimmer in the air. "You must see what has gone before if you are to understand what is happening in the present."

"This is what you created?" Steven asked. "What's waiting for me?"

Grey stared at the maimed bodies at his feet. "The first iteration of the Game ended without bloodshed, exactly as I imagined it. The lives of countless innocents had been saved and the correction contained, its energies returned to the ether from whence they came. I was so proud, and so naive. Here in this place and on this day, however, any sense of pride or naiveté was extinguished along with the lives of those you see before you. You see, the conclusion of the first iteration revealed a truth no one save my opposite had considered."

"Zed?"

"Zed." Grey spat the name. "Stripped of their dramatic conclusions, these corrections leave an abundance of raw, undifferentiated energy in their wake. For a brief period, the checks and balances that govern reality are distorted, and a person adept at the Art can manipulate the energies in question to accomplish anything they desire. Zed tasted that power at the conclusion of the first iteration, and greedily awaited the second to claim it for his own."

Steven knelt at the body, running his fingers along the man's crushed helmet. "Looks like he made damn sure he won this time."

"The winning side is responsible for the final disposition of the forces remaining at the end of play, an aspect of the Game Zed insisted on and to which I unfortunately agreed." Grey walked among the butchered bodies, his face a mask of regret. "These were good people, Steven. I trained them myself, ensured they were ready, but not for the onslaught they faced this day." His grey eyes caught Steven's gaze. "They barely lasted two minutes."

"The woman who came for me tonight." Steven shivered. "She's the current Black Queen, isn't she?"

"Indeed," Grey said. "Though she is new to me, the role she plays in this Game I helped create is not."

"But why send her?" Steven's downward gaze met the young foot soldier's dead eyes. "Why not come for me himself?"

"Truth be told, I have no idea. He certainly sent a most beguiling emissary. I suppose it is within the realm of possibility that he wished merely to capture you."

"You saw her. What she did to all those people. I got the distinct impression I wasn't part of any sort of catch and release program."

Grey offered a solemn nod. "As I said before, regardless of how well I know Zed, his motivations in seeking you out before the Game proper can begin are unclear." His eyes darkened. "Outside the obvious, of course."

Steven's entire body tensed. "You faced Zed once in Egypt and a second time... wherever this is. How many times has this happened?"

"Only once more. Antarctica. 1537." Grey looked away, a new tremor in his hands. "The third iteration ended in... a stalemate."

"Antarctica." Steven bit his lip. "Did they all freeze to death?"

"It doesn't matter. The balance was maintained." Grey gazed into the distance. The coolness in his eyes sent a shiver through Steven's core. "Suffice to say Antarctica is a place I hope to never see again."

Steven stared into the opaque eyes of the dead man at his feet. "How is it this Game of yours has been going on for centuries, yet no one has ever heard of it?"

"Clandestine by its very nature, the Game has ever been a part of history, though no history you ever learned in school." Grey stepped into an adjoining square. "Countless misconceptions and outright falsehoods have been passed down from generation to generation for centuries. Much of what you and the rest of society accept as fact is simply a more palatable fiction. This history of lies is for the best, though. The truth is more than most could take."

Steven's eyes narrowed. "I don't understand, though. You didn't stop war. Millions died in the two World Wars. Then Korea, Vietnam, Afghanistan, Iraq. What's the point?"

"Man has killed man from the beginning," Grey whispered. "Technology has only made it easier with every passing century. Still, the death that would come if the Game did not take place would make any war in your history books pale in comparison."

Steven rose from the dead man's battered form. "So, lesson's over?"

"Not quite yet," Grey said. "There is still one last game for you to see."

As Grey's form faded into the air, Steven turned to go back the way he'd come and discovered where the pouch had brought him. More breathtaking than all the pictures he'd seen, the ring of colossal stones to the west seemed fitting, as if gravestones for the fallen had been placed generations before in preparation for this day. He stepped off the board and rested his hand on the jutting stone that pointed to the heart of Stonehenge.

"Africa. England. Antarctica." Steven took a deep breath. "And now, America."

Steven's surroundings again spiraled into a kaleidoscope of colors, though this time the experience was different. Scenes from his own life flashed by in rapid order: dinner with Ruth and Arthur, his bold rescue by the man he now knew as Grey, a conflagration of black flames with their dark mistress resting at their heart, his lonely months in Chicago, the accident, Katherine dancing in her red cocktail dress, grad school, college graduation, high school prom, his mother cooking breakfast, and finally, his dad arriving home from work where a much younger Steven waited to play their favorite game.

Everything slowed to a crawl, and a strange compulsion drew Steven's attention to his family's old coffee table. There, frozen in time, he and his father sat perfectly still, hunched over an old wooden chessboard.

Steven remembered this game well. Thirteen years old at the time, the watershed moment marked the first time he ever defeated his dad at anything. In this particular match, Steven played white and his father black. In the end, it came down to his king, bishop, knight and remaining pawn against his father's king, queen, knight and the remnants of his front row. Though his father's remaining pieces gave him the numerical advantage, Steven managed to keep the opposing king in check for several turns and eventually forced him into a corner.

He remembered the look of defeat in his father's furrowed brow several moves before the end. One of many small steps in the inevitable progression of boy to man, the recognition had thrilled him at the time. Only in later years did he look back on that moment with a soberer understanding of the day.

His younger self reached for the pawn, advanced the piece to the seventh rank and placed the black king in checkmate. Time stopped for a moment before resuming its normal cadence. Then, his father shook his boy's hand like he would a man before mussing his hair as they walked into the next room, leaving adult Steven alone with the old chessboard.

Every scratch in the wood, every dent of the checkered surface, every blemish on the old chess set roared back as if only minutes had passed since this game rather than years.

Above all, the lesson he learned that day echoed in his mind: Even the weakest piece on the board, when employed correctly, can bring down the king.

In an instant, Steven's perspective changed. Shrunk to the size of a chess piece, he stood in the seventh rank of his father's old board, the black king to his forward right. The white king to his rear protected him from capture while the white bishop and knight, each in their respective squares, blocked the black king's every escape.

"It is time."

Grey's voice echoed in the space, and in a blink, Steven found himself back at the Pedone dinner table. Ruth and Arthur looked on in wonder as the groan of the pouch grew louder, pulsing in time with Steven's heartbeat. A stirring of the air caused the candles at the table's center to flicker. Grey rested a hand on Steven's shoulder. "Reach into the pouch and show me what you find there."

Steven rose from the table, held the pouch before him, and stared down once more into the silver glow. His father's chessboard filled his vision, though only one piece remained on the sixty-four squares of alternating pine and walnut. Steven reached into the bag, the low drone now amplified to deafening volume. His fingers grasped something cold and hard. His clenched fist emerged from the pouch, knuckles white.

"Open your hand," Grey whispered.

Steven loosened his grip on the object. Lying in his palm was a marble chess piece, a sphere positioned atop a tapering column with a wide, rippled base. He looked up at Grey, the shock in his eyes fading into simple resignation. "I'm the Pawn."

"So it would seem."

"What do I do now?"

"That is for you to decide, Steven. The first move is yours."

A streak of shimmering darkness shattered the room's lone window and flew between Steven and Grey, ripping the pouch from Steven's hand. An inch in diameter and scintillating with ebon energy, the black arrow imbedded itself in the dining room wall with a resounding thunk, impaling the pouch on the blood-red surface.

Grey's brow curled into a frustrated scowl. "At least in theory."

## 6

## STONE

The pawn icon shimmered in Steven's hand, the silvery glow a brilliant counterpoint to the waves of darkness emanating off the ebony shaft and fletching protruding from the wall. A moment later, a searing pain ripped through his core, sending him to his knees. Steven clutched his side in agony as a second arrow flew past his head.

"Steven!" Ruth crawled to his side, a distinct edge to her voice. "Are you okay?"

"Other than feeling like I'm about to puke up my shoes, I'm doing all right."

Flipping the heavy oak table onto its side, Grey pulled Arthur to the floor and motioned for Steven and Ruth to take cover. Fighting off alternating waves of pain and nausea, Steven scrambled to the makeshift bunker with Ruth close behind.

Arthur pulled his wife to him and held her close, eyeing the man he called Rex with a potent mix of fear and concern and a hint of anger. Steven dropped to one side as a barrage of arrows tore into the oak tabletop, their scintillating razor tips piercing the thick wood like paper.

"What's happening to me?" Steven fought off a wave of nausea. "I feel like I've just drunk a gallon of antifreeze."

"Have you not guessed?" Grey peered above the edge of the over-turned table. "Your icon is alerting you to the enemy's presence."

Steven coughed out a laugh. "A bit late for that, don't you think?" He held his clenched fist up to his face, the icon within shining like a miniature sun. "Message received, you lousy piece of shit."

"Actually, your icon is performing precisely as designed," Grey said. "What you feel is a call to action. As long as you remain vulnerable, the pain will continue."

"You've got to be kidding me." Steven clutched his side in agony. "Thing feels like it's ripping me in half."

"Stop complaining, then," Grey grunted, "and defend yourself."

"Defend myself?" The stabbing in Steven's midsection continued to pulse in time with the icon's oscillating glow. "How?"

"In your mind's eye. Summon an image of a shield. Will it onto your arm."

Steven closed his eyes, his mind running through image after image of shields, anything from movies to art to his high school visit to the Tower of London.

"You are wasting time," Grey said. "They will be upon us any moment."

"Fine." Steven took a deep breath and focused. The icon disappeared from his grip, scorching his hand with a flash of silver fire. When his eyes cleared, he found a circular shield better than two feet across strapped to his left arm. The convex disc fashioned from a lightweight metal resembling brushed platinum, its mottled streaks reminded Steven of the pawn icon's marble surface. A subtle white iridescence shimmered from its burnished surface. Like a switch had been flipped, the pain in Steven's belly faded to a dull ache.

"That's better." Steven rose into a low crouch. "The pouch?"

"The target of their initial strike was no accident." Grey's gaze shot to the wall where the pouch hung limp below the darkly shimmering shaft. "Without the pouch's capabilities, none of us will leave this place alive."

"At least there's no pressure." Steven peered across the table.

"What's going to keep William Tell out there from shooting me in the back?"

"I can shield you from the enemy's eyes, at least for the moment. I suspect their archer, unfortunately, may be the least of our concerns." Grey's eyes slid closed, a low hum escaping his lips and his body swaying to an unheard rhythm. The lights dimmed and the air in the room filled with electricity. Grey stretched out his arm and every shadow in the room obeyed his silent command, leaping to the window and forming a swirling mass of obscuration.

"How did you do that?" Steven asked.

"Time is short." Grey's eyes flicked to his rear as another group of arrows flew through the window. "Hear me, Steven. As Pawn, your shield will protect you from any attack from the front, but you must ever watch your back."

"Thanks for the tip." Steven clambered to the wall on all fours and stared up at the shimmering shaft of darkness. Keeping as much of his body behind the shield as possible, he snaked a hand up and used the hanging pouch to protect his hand as he gripped the arrow. Despite his best efforts, the dark shaft didn't budge.

"Dammit. The arrow's stuck in a stud."

"Maybe a bit of brute force is the answer." Arthur pushed Steven out of the way. "This should do the trick." The old man raised a battered old sledgehammer above his head and brought the head down upon the arrow's barbed tip. The resultant explosion threw Arthur and Steven to the ground.

"Arthur," Ruth screamed.

"I'm fine," Arthur said. "I've survived worse. Didn't help though."

"Crap." Steven made his way to his feet. The blow had shattered the shaft, but left the pouch pinned to the wall by the arrow's dark barbed tip.

"Hurry, you two." Grey's voice grated with strain. "I can only maintain the Feast of Shadows for a few more seconds."

Yet another arrow hit the wall, this one so close, the fletching tickled Steven's ear as it flew past.

Arthur rose from the floor and handed the sledgehammer to Steven. "Maybe your younger hands will have better luck."

"The wall." Grey made a motion like a hammer strike. "Aim for the wall."

"Got it." Steven brought the ten-pound mallet above his head and a tingling sensation ran up his arm like an electric current. In a flash of silver, the sledgehammer vanished, replaced in an instant with its medieval cousin. The worn wooden handle now shining steel, the face of the hammer formed a serrated rectangle, its claw a tapering tip like the tooth of some metal monster.

"Everybody. Heads down." Steven brought the hammer down upon the drywall, the blow sending a shudder through the entire house and shattering the underlying wooden beam. The barbed arrowhead clattered to the floor and the pouch fell from the splintered timber and landed at Steven's feet.

"All right. Let's get out of…" The hair on the back of Steven's neck stood on end. Dropping the hammer, he spun around and raised the shield just before a trio of arrows crashed through the remnants of window glass and impacted the metallic disc, the resulting sound a triple beat of thunderous crashes.

"Excellent," Grey said. "Now bring the pouch and let us be away from here."

"It's not over." Ruth clutched the chain at her neck, her knuckles white around the small dragonfly pendant. "Something is happening."

"What is it?" Arthur asked.

"Amaryllis," Grey said. "I had almost forgotten."

"I ignored her first warning," Ruth said. "The second was more emphatic."

"What are you two talking about?" Steven asked.

A rumbling like a passing train roared outside.

"Steven." Grey said, his eyes wide with fear. "Get them away from here. Now."

"What about you?"

"I will follow if I can." Grey's eyes flicked toward the rear wall of the house, the rumbling sound outside hitting a fever pitch. "The theater door in Chicago. Do you remember?"

"I remember."

"The front foyer should serve your purpose well." Grey helped Ruth and Arthur to their feet. "Find the others. Keep them safe."

"But—"

The back wall of the dining room erupted inward, a battering ram of black stone protruding through at the center of the explosion.

*No, a fist. An enormous stone fist.*

Ruth screamed, blood trickling down her face where a stray piece of flying stone had grazed her scalp. Catching her as she fell to one side, Arthur stared up at Steven, his eyes filled with desperation. Another pair of arrows sailed into the room, flying like thunderbolts from the cloud of whirling shadows by the window.

"Go." Grey turned to face the dark conglomeration of stone. "I will find you."

"Come on." Steven grabbed Ruth's hand and dragged her and Arthur toward the front of the house.

"What about Rex?" Arthur asked.

"He's coming," Steven said. "Right behind us."

"He's pulled that one before, back in '44," Arthur said. "I won't leave him again."

Another crash echoed from the back of the house. Steven pulled Ruth and Arthur into the foyer. "We're out of time. We've got to go now." Gripping the mouth of the pouch in his hand, he touched the bag's warm leather to the door.

"Take us far from here," he whispered, turning the knob.

Outside the Pedone front door awaited a sight both familiar and foreign. The porch and cobblestone walk remained, though at the edge of the yard, a fifteen-foot wall of black stone blocked all view of the street. Catching a flash of dark energy from atop the wall, Steven slammed the door shut just before another pair of black arrows buried their barbed tips in the door's thick wood.

"I must not have done it right. How did Grey—"

An echo of the low rumbling from the back of the house sounded from beyond the door and grew in volume with each passing second.

"Move!" Steven pushed Ruth and Arthur into the adjoining room a split second before the front door splintered inward, the foyer demolished in a horizontal avalanche of black stone.

"Front door's gone. Any other way out?" Before Ruth or Arthur could answer, Steven spun around and headed for the back of the house. "Scratch that. Follow me."

Steven led the old couple through the formal living room and into the hall, keeping his shield high as arrow after arrow flew crashing through the front window. He shouted for Grey as they passed the remnants of the once beautiful dining room. Answered only with silence, he paused at the room's elegant entrance. The rear wall now merely a gaping hole, his mysterious rescuer was nowhere to be seen.

"Guess that means it's up to me," Steven groaned.

The rumbling from the front of the house began anew. A moment later, the mass of black stone rounded the corner and rocketed in their direction.

"Shit." Steven sprinted down the hall, and caught up with Ruth and Arthur at the door to their bedroom.

"What now?" Arthur asked. "That thing's coming for us fast."

"Don't you think I know that?" Steven wiped the sweat from his brow. "Let me think."

With a granite roar, a tendril of black stone charged down the hall after them like an angry tongue.

"It can't end here." Ruth gripped Arthur's hand. "It can't."

"Wait." Steven grasped Ruth's shoulder. "I remember."

He brushed the four corners of the door in a large X and whispered, "Anywhere but here." A silver glow shimmered around the door's edges. "Come on."

He jerked the door open onto a smoke-filled room, the air reverberating with a loud techno beat. Shoving Ruth and Arthur through the doorway, he took one look back at the rushing wall of stone and leaped through himself, slamming the door shut behind them.

"Made it." Steven's vision blurred as his knees gave way beneath him.

"Steven!" Ruth's shout was the last thing he heard before everything went dark.

# 7

# DESTINY

Steven awoke to a splitting headache, the pain flaring in time with the booming bass of AC/DC's "Highway to Hell." His addled mind placed him back at the club in Chicago, still waiting on the reportedly cute librarian his buddy's wife had fixed him up with.

"Look, dear," came a man's voice. "He's coming around."

"Thank God." The woman's voice, filled with concern, sounded vaguely familiar.

Steven raised his head from a table and gazed blearily into the eager eyes of the elderly couple seated across the booth.

"Arthur?" he asked. "Ruth?"

"Glad you still remember our names," Ruth said. "We were getting worried you weren't going to wake up."

Steven massaged his neck. "How long have I been out?"

"About half an hour," Arthur said. "We were letting you rest."

"Are you two okay?"

"We're all right." Arthur locked gazes with his wife. "Considering."

"Wait." Steven's heart skipped a beat. "Where's Grey?"

"Rex?" Arthur shook his head. "We haven't seen him since the attack."

Steven cursed under his breath. "At least I got the three of us out of there. Where did we end up anyway?"

"Well..." Ruth peered around the darkened room, her eyes alight with amusement.

"Coming to the stage." A boisterous male voice came across the loudspeaker above Steven's head. "Everyone put your hands together for... Destiny!"

A woman in a brown Stetson and a leather coat that fell just past the top of her toned thighs strode past their table heading for the stage at the far end of the room. The five-inch heels on her knee-high boots echoed as she crossed to the brass pole at the center of the platform. An upbeat country-western tune blared from the speakers.

"Wow," Steven said. "When I told the pouch to take us away, this wasn't exactly what I had in mind."

"It's all right, Steven. We're safe here, at least for the moment." Ruth swirled the ice cubes in her glass. "Not to mention, this place has a senior discount."

"You can't be serious." A flood of memories filled Steven's head. The swarm of arrows. The fist of stone. The dark granite ram tearing apart the Pedone home from the inside out. "Those... whatever they were. They destroyed your house."

"We'll get by." Ruth stroked her husband's shoulder. "We always do."

"Don't worry about us, Steven." Arthur kissed his wife's hand. "Ruthie and I have been around the block a few times."

Ruth wiped away the tear coursing down her cheek. "As for the house, it's just four walls and a roof." She patted her chest above her heart. "Everything important is here."

"And right here next to me. I love you, sweetheart." Arthur pulled her close and kissed her wrinkled forehead. "Always have and always will."

The scent of Katherine's hair wafted through Steven's mind. He did his best to bury the strange envy that welled up in his heart.

"I'm sorry. You guys are very kind, but it's still my fault. These people are hunting me. If Grey had known what was coming, I'm sure he would've handled things differently."

"Oh, he knew," Arthur said. "He hoped it wouldn't come to this, but he warned us to be prepared for anything."

"He knew?" Steven's face grew hot. "And he still brought me to your home?"

Ruth brushed Steven's hand. "It's all right. We knew the risks when you showed up on our doorstep. Remember, we've known Grey a long time."

"Still, he could have taken us anywhere. Why would he possibly bring the enemy down on you two?"

Ruth shrugged, an unexpected half-smile sneaking onto her face. "Sometimes things work out the way they're supposed to. We're just glad you're safe. We owe you so much."

Arthur shot a sharp look in Ruth's direction. "What Ruth is trying to say is we know how important it is to keep you hale and hearty. You've got a long road ahead of you."

"Speaking of long roads, Grey could've at least told me how much the door to door pouch travel was going to take out of me. I feel like someone let the air out of my tires."

Ruth smiled. "Rex took us to Paris a few years ago. Our fiftieth anniversary. Said we didn't need to bother with any 'silly aeroplanes.'"

Arthur laughed. "Instead, he made us get all dressed up in our Sunday best and marched us down to the local bait and tackle shop. We both thought he was joking, that is till he opened the door and we stepped through into a French bistro."

"As he explained it," Ruth said, "you've got to go where the power is if you want to travel. Otherwise, traveling takes it out of you instead."

"Sort of like jet lag on steroids. I guess that explains why we landed in that café when we first hit Maine." Steven let out a chuckle. "Grey didn't happen to leave a trail guide to magical doorways laying around, did he?"

"So, Steven," Arthur said as another dancer took the stage. "What now?"

"I suppose we find a room for the night," Steven said. "Any idea where we are?"

"This is Club Sapphire, honey. Hottest girls in town and the coldest drinks." The server held her full tray at shoulder height. The sleeve of her violet T-shirt faded into a tattooed snake coiled around her arm. She winked at Steven and flashed an amused grin. "Glad to see you back among the living, handsome."

"Thanks," Steven said. "I'm starting to feel better."

The server scooted into the booth next to him. "Little too much to drink this evening?"

Steven massaged his neck. "Let's just say it's been a rough night."

"So…" She eyed him quizzically. "You usually bring your grandparents along when you hit the strip club?"

Ruth bristled. "I'll have you know in my day, I could have danced the pants off any of these girls." Her gaze drifted to the stage. "Not that our current entertainer seems to need any help in that respect."

The server's eyes narrowed, though her face broke into a smile. "You know what? I like you. You've got spunk." She rested a drink before each of them. "That'll be twenty even."

Steven handed her a wad of cash. "Keep the change."

"You got it, gorgeous."

As their server headed back to the bar, Steven turned up his glass and swallowed the contents in a single gulp. "Whiskey," he said with a shudder. "It's like you read my mind."

Ruth grinned. "Thought you might need something with a little kick."

Steven rested his glass on the table. "So, you used to dance?"

"Back at the beginning of time." A wistful look crossed Ruth's features. "I was taking ballet when Arthur and I met. Pursued it for another couple of years, but after we got married and started our family, my priorities shifted. I never looked back."

"My Ruthie was a sight to behold." Arthur beamed. "Still is."

Ruth shot Steven a wink. "I even did burlesque for a few months not long after I met Arthur."

"You did burlesque?"

She batted her eyelashes. "I wasn't always eighty-two, Steven."

He laughed. "No, I guess you weren't."

Arthur cleared his throat. "It's got to be closing in on midnight,

Steven. If you've got your legs back under you, I think we should head on."

Steven, Ruth, and Arthur stepped out of the club and onto a sidewalk covered in broken glass. The neon sign outside proclaimed "Club Sapphire, The Hottest Babes in Baltimore." The competing stenches of cigarette smoke and urine nearly made Steven retch.

"At least we ended up on the good side of town."

"There's got to be a motel or something around here." Arthur peered down the street and Steven followed his gaze. The only lodging in this part of town most likely charged by the hour. "Maybe we should—"

"Arthur." Ruth grabbed her husband's arm, her gaze trained down the alleyway between the club and the dilapidated cigarette store next door. "We should go back inside."

"What's is it, Ruth?" A phlegmy cough from behind them sent a chill up Steven's back.

"Hand over your wallets," came a voice from the darkness. "And whatever else you've got on you." A form emerged from the shadows by the dumpster. Dressed in oversized jeans and a baggy football jersey, the man face remained hidden within his yellow hoodie.

"You've got to be kidding me," Steven stepped in front of Ruth and Arthur. "Look, man. This isn't—"

"I don't have all fucking night," the man grunted. "Now give it."

"Listen, young man," Arthur said. "All we have with us are the clothes on our backs."

"Don't try and bullshit me, Grandpa. Club Sapphire has a ten-dollar cover." The man from the shadows cocked his head to the side. "You got enough money to watch those bitches shake their asses, you got something for me. Don't make me take it from you."

"All right," Steven said. "Give me a second. Just don't hurt anybody." He reached for his wallet, shifting the pawn icon in his pants pocket to hide it from view.

"Hey," the mugger grunted. "What you got there?"

"Nothing. Just let me get my wallet and you can go on your way."

The mugger drew closer. "Let me see what's in your pocket."

Steven's eyes narrowed. "You really don't want to do this."

Arthur stepped forward. "Now, see here, young man—"

The man grabbed Steven's shirt and jammed the business end of his pistol up under his jaw, sending Steven's heart into overdrive. Arthur raised both hands and backed away, stepping between the mugger and his wife. Ruth gasped, but wisely kept her silence.

"Do I look like I want to talk?" The mugger pulled back the hammer on his pistol. "Now, show me what's in your pocket, or I swear I'll get it myself and trust me—you don't want that."

"All right." Steven reached into his pocket and wrapped his fingers around the pawn icon. A subtle vibration in the cool marble he hadn't noticed before sent a tingle through his fingers. "I'm getting it for you, okay?"

"Slow, man. Slow." The man backed away as Steven brought the icon out, its white marble shimmering subtly in the darkness. "Now, give me it."

The pale light of the icon revealed the figure from the shadows was just a kid, no more than nineteen. Regardless, the gun trained on Steven's midsection remained steady.

This definitely wasn't the kid's first rodeo.

"Here. Take it." Steven handed the pawn to the robber who took it greedily, never taking his eyes or gun off Steven.

"What the hell is this supposed to be?" The man examined the marble icon. "Looks like some kind of chess piece."

"That's exactly what it is."

Unbidden, an image formed in Steven's mind. A point, an edge, a curved blade, all at the end of a wooden pole. The icon's silver shimmer tripled in intensity and light poured between the mugger's fingers.

"Turn it off." The man pointed his gun at Steven's head. "Turn the damn thing off."

"Very well." Steven raised his hands before him in mock surrender. "Pike."

The single word fell from Steven's lips and a flash of heat and brilliance filled the space. The pawn icon vanished from the robber's hand, replaced with an eight-foot pole arm.

"Arrh!" The man shrieked and flung the pike at Steven. "Fucking thing burns!"

Steven snatched the pike from the air and spun to the side, sweeping the thug's feet from beneath him with the blunt end of the pole. His assailant landed in a heap on the concrete. Steven brought the shining tip down upon the man's pistol and cleaved the barrel in two.

"Holy shit," the man screamed. "What are you?"

"What I am is very angry." The voice was Steven's, but deeper, older, wiser. He leveled the pike's razor tip at the man's throat. "Leave us and forget you saw any of this, or I swear we will meet again. Do you understand?"

Without a word, the robber stumbled to his feet and ran. He didn't look back.

Steven studied the weapon resting in his hand. Strong and resilient, the pike felt light in his grasp. A low hum rose as he passed the weapon before him, the eight feet of smooth poplar culminating in a bright, silver tip that combined the best features of axe and spear. Though he questioned the utility of carrying around an eight-foot pole with a pointy tip in the age of tactical nukes, his heart raced at the feel of the wood in his hand.

Images flashed in his head, scenes from countless movies he'd seen over the years. *Excalibur, Braveheart, Gladiator*. Line after line of soldiers at the battle's front, long spears dug into the ground, tips raised high awaiting the inevitable onrushing horde.

"Steven." Ruth rested a hand on Steven's shoulder. "Are you all right?"

He smiled. "Never better."

## 8

---

# DRAGONFLY

Steven and Katherine, their faces lit by the flicker of a lone candle, intertwined their fingers as they waited for the decadent mountain of chocolate that was their favorite dessert. The same bistro as their first date, they sat at their usual table, the one by the bay window. Steven made the reservation better than a month before, and despite the torrential rain pounding the roof, he had every intention of carrying through with his plan.

Katherine ran her fingers through her dark, gentle curls. The crash of shattering plates from the kitchen drew her attention. Steven slipped his hand into his coat pocket. His trembling fingers closed around the velvet box and the world narrowed and stilled. The boisterous couple at the next table faded into the background. The rushing wait staff became invisible. The pounding rain on the roof seemed quiet compared with the hammering in his chest. In that pregnant moment, he saw only Katherine and the endless possibilities dancing in her hazel eyes.

Eyes that a moment later grew wide in terror. No longer in the restaurant, Katherine screamed from the passenger seat of Steven's car. The squall of screeching tires rent the air. Rushing high beams filled their car with light.

The events played out as they had a thousand times before.

Except for one detail.

Behind the wheel of the dark SUV, the woman in black bore down on them, her cruel smile the last thing Steven saw before he jerked awake.

Rubbing at his eyes, Steven peered around the darkened motel room. In the dim light, he could just make out the rise and fall of Arthur's chest in the next bed. Steven rolled over and sat up, the popping of his back like the crackle of arthritic knuckles, and found Ruth seated in the large recliner in the corner staring at him.

"Trouble sleeping?" he asked.

"I'm surprised you were able to sleep at all." Ruth took a sip from one of the hotel mugs. The aroma of coffee filled the room.

Steven yawned. "What time is it?"

"A little before six."

He motioned to Arthur's sleeping form. "At least one of us can leave it at work."

"Arthur could sleep through a bomb." Ruth chuckled. "And actually, he has."

"What about you? Couldn't sleep?"

"I lay there as long as I could." She looked away. "I've got a lot on my mind."

"The house?"

"That's part of it." Ruth glanced over at her husband's sleeping form. "When someone like Rex is a part of your life, you learn to prepare for the worst. Arthur and I have suspected for years it might come to something like this. Still, you can only prepare so much." She rose from the chair, sat on the corner of Steven's bed and patted his foot through the covers. "You were having a nightmare. Tossing and turning like the Devil himself was chasing you. You okay?"

Steven closed his eyes and a toothy grin that always used to raise his pulse flashed across his mind's eye. "It was nothing." His voice cracked. "Just a stupid dream."

"Don't ever play cards, dear," Ruth said with a sympathetic smile. "Your poker face needs some work."

"What are you and Arthur going to do now?"

Ruth sighed. "I suppose we'll take the train back up to Maine and see what's left. Find out if Nationwide covers magical terrorist attacks."

"I'm so sorry, Ruth." Steven shook his head. "I don't know what else to say."

"Stop," she said. "I told you it's okay. In fact, I want you to have something." She unclasped the dragonfly pendant from her necklace. "I don't claim to understand all you're going through, but from what little I do know, I'm guessing you have a long road ahead of you. I have carried this dragonfly over my heart for many a year, and she has always brought me good fortune."

She placed the dragonfly in Steven's palm. "Amaryllis here was a wedding gift from an old friend."

Steven examined the gift in silence. The body of the dragonfly was two inches long with a similar wingspan. The most intricately detailed piece of jewelry Steven had ever seen, its entire length shimmered with green iridescence. The four wings formed a tight X and despite their fragile appearance were quite sturdy.

"Amaryllis?"

Ruth nodded. "You might find she comes in handy if you get in a pinch."

"I can't possibly accept this." Steven attempted to return the gift. "You've given up too much already."

"You can and you will." She took the dragonfly from his hand and placed it over his heart. "I don't think I'm going to need her anymore."

"But I don't even have anything to hang it—" Before Steven could complete the thought, the insectile clasp gripped his shirt as if the dragonfly were alive. Ruth ran her aged fingers along the metallic wings, her downcast eyes glimmering with a hint of regret.

"Don't you go and lose her, Steven." She stroked the wings once more and rested her hands in her lap. "Keep my Amaryllis by your heart and she'll keep you fine."

The bejeweled dragonfly weighed heavy on Steven's chest, and for a moment he imagined he saw the quartet of metallic wings flutter. He took the elderly woman's hand, her graceful fingers cool in his grasp. "Thank you, Ruth."

"My pleasure." Her gaze dropped to her lap. "Steven, listen. There's something else I need to—"

"Can't leave you two alone for a minute," came a half-asleep voice.

Ruth and Steven turned to find Arthur sitting up in bed.

"You silly man." Ruth sighed, the moment passed. She climbed onto the bed next to her husband and gave him a quick peck on the cheek. "We were just talking."

"Most people at least wait for the sun to come up." Arthur's eyes fixated on Steven. "You get enough shuteye last night to save the world?"

"I suppose we'll all see soon enough." Yawning, Steven shot Ruth a grin in the room's dim light. "Any chance you made more than one cup of coffee?"

"Sir, we've got people waiting." The cashier scrutinized Steven through horn-rimmed bifocals. "Cash, debit, or credit?"

With images of his various near-death experiences from the preceding twenty-four hours flashing across his memory, Steven grinned and handed her his credit card. "Charge it."

She crinkled her nose. "And what do you want me to do with this mess you came in wearing?"

Steven glanced down his body at his new T-shirt, jeans, and boots, and slid the charred remnants of the previous night's clothing into the trash can by the counter.

"Rough night." Steven took back his credit card and slipped his wallet into his pocket. "Don't ask."

"I always tell my boys," she said. "You need to watch yourself when you're working with fire. It just takes a second."

"You have no idea." Steven turned to go when a familiar warmth radiated from his hip. As a low-pitched drone filled the air, he jerked the pouch from his belt and cast his gaze around the department store, vigilant for any sign of attack. The heat and sound lasted for another few seconds. Then, as quickly as it started, the white leather bag grew cool and silent. He scanned the crowd for a reaction, but no one seemed to have noticed anything other than a crazed man holding an old pouch before him like it was a stick of dynamite with the fuse burning.

"You all right, honey?" The cashier put on a practiced smile.

"Did you hear something?" Steven asked. "Anything?"

"Nope." She shook her head. "So, what's in the bag?"

He considered for a second. "A couple sandwiches."

"You know, that thing looks like it was made a couple hundred years ago. We have lunch bags in the baggage department on the third floor."

Steven shot her a sideways grin. "This one serves its purpose just fine."

He headed into the mall corridor, his stomach rumbling. Hours wandering the streets of Baltimore since leaving Ruth and Arthur at the bus station had left him famished. Following his nose to the food court, he grabbed a slice of pizza and found a table. A quick scan of a discarded newspaper continued a disturbing trend he'd noticed over the preceding weeks. Out of season torrential rains and flooding in the southwest, strange seismic activity in Kansas, an unprecedented heat wave in…

*Heat.* The pouch grew warm at his side and the drone returned. He untied the silver cord and again slid the pouch from his belt.

"What is it? What do you want?" Steven received more than one odd look as he sat addressing the white leather sack, though it seemed no one but him could hear the pouch's drone. He moved to an exit door near the room's periphery and pulled the pawn icon from his pocket. Not even a glimmer of the previous night's radiance remained.

"No glow. No pain. Can't be the bad guys." Steven moved to return to his table, the drone growing subtly louder with each step. "Another Piece." He returned the pawn icon to his pocket. "That has to be it."

Holding the pouch before him like a mystical Geiger counter, Steven headed for the center of the busy food court. The rising and falling drone reminded him of a game he played with his mother when he was a child.

*Warmer. Warmer. Colder. Now warmer.*

As he walked between the tables like a dowser searching for water, the locals all gave him a wide berth. A pair of security guards across the way rose from their table and moved to converge on him at the room's center.

"Crap," Steven muttered. "How are you supposed to use this thing without looking like some kind of terrorist?"

As if in answer to his unspoken request, an opaque white mist rose from the marble floor. The white fog encircled his body, transforming into a hooded cloak of white that hung to his ankles. Steven pulled the hood back and Ruth's dragonfly climbed up his chest and clasped the cloak at his neck.

The two guards returned to their table, suddenly oblivious to Steven's presence, while the worried glances he'd been receiving from the other patrons ceased, much like everyone ignored him and Grey as they walked the streets in Old Port.

Not to mention the Black Queen who stood unnoticed atop the bar before her attack.

*The rest of the world can't see us.* Steven admired the pawn icon. *Shield. Pike. Cloak. This thing's loaded for bear.*

"Hey, you. Move it." Steven spun around to find a man in his fifties trying to edge past him to get to the trash can. "I don't have all day."

"Sorry." Steven stepped to his left and allowed the man to pass.

*Inconspicuous? Yes.* He pulled the cloak about him. *Invisible? Apparently not.*

Steven continued his search, the drone of the pouch rising and falling with every step.

*Warmer. Warmer.*

*Now, colder. Colder.*

*And now, warmer. Warmer. Warmer...*

*Hot.*

Steven jerked his hand away from the pouch's sudden searing heat. As he bent to retrieve it, he was nearly bowled over by two pairs of denim-clad legs moving in the opposite direction. Clutching the still warm pouch, he spun around to find a young couple hand-in-hand stepping onto the down escalator. He clambered to his feet and followed, racing down the moving staircase after them. The pouch grew warmer with each step, its drone building as Steven closed the gap between him and the young lovers. He followed the pair through the mall for several minutes, keeping his distance despite the concealment afforded by the cloak.

Steven's best estimate put the pair in their late teens. The boy was about five eleven, well muscled, and wore a tight green T-shirt and jeans hung low on his hips. His dark-brown curls fell into his eyes. He walked with a confident swagger, not quite a man but well on his way. Despite his tough exterior, a different truth became apparent when the young man looked at the girl.

Slightly shorter than the boy despite her two-inch platform sandals, the girl's denim capri pants and tight, yellow blouse revealed a well-toned athlete's body with an olive complexion. She wore her hair long, her lustrous brown locks kissing the small of her back. Her brown eyes revealed more spark and discernment than he would expect in someone so young.

The pair stepped into a shoe store and headed for their respective sections to check out the selection. Steven saw his opportunity to determine which of the two the pouch was keying in on. Before he could take a step, however, the boy's cell phone went off. One look at the flipped up display and his expression went cold.

"Lena." The boy's shouted voice was filled with pain. "It's Carlos."

Lena's gaze shot across the store, the color draining from her face. She rushed to her boyfriend's side, tears welling at the corners of her eyes as she read the text. Shaking, she pulled the boy to her and held him tight. Steven looked away, guilty for intruding on such a private moment. He was distracted no more than a second, and when he again looked in their direction, they were gone.

Steven ran out into the main corridor and scanned the crowd, spotting the pair heading for the escalator. The boy jogged up the moving staircase while Lena trailed a few steps behind. Steven launched into a dead sprint, knowing full well he would never find them again if he lost them in the crowd. He hit the escalator a second before Lena stepped off at the next floor. Thwarted by a throng of pre-teens, he reached the next floor in time to glimpse Lena's dark tresses vanish behind a door leading outside.

Steven weaved through the shoppers like a professional quarterback and made his way out into a deserted parking deck. He closed his eyes and listened, for what he wasn't sure. As he headed up the stairs to the next level, the distinctive sound of a motorcycle rumbling to life echoed through the space. Seconds later, Lena and the boy zoomed past on an arrest-me-red Honda, the roar of the engine still quieter than the deafening whine of the pouch.

Steven sprinted for the stairs, puffing as he took the steps five and six at a time in a desperate effort to outrace two teens on a rocket with wheels. He exploded out of the ground-level doorway and headed for the street, dodging between rows of parked cars only to arrive at the main thoroughfare in time to see the two teens ignore the light and speed out of sight.

"Brilliant." Steven plopped down on the sidewalk, panting. The pouch quiet and again cool to the touch, he sat there for a minute until his breathing slowed to normal and the pang in his side resolved.

"I'll never find them now." Steven's fingers rested on the pouch's cool leather. "Unless…"

Steven turned back for the door he'd come through. Pulling the pouch from his belt, he rose from the sidewalk. The white leather sack hummed as he passed it across the door twice in a large X and a familiar silver shimmer appeared at the door's edges.

"All right, pouch." Steven's eyes narrowed. "Take me to the boy."

## 9

### EMILIO

The pouch flashed white-hot as Steven opened the door. Rather than the sprawling parking deck, the door opened onto a hospital ward. A metal sign with the word EMERGENCY emblazoned in backlit scarlet letters hung from the ceiling.

*This is going to hurt.*

Steven stepped through the door and into the fluorescent light of the hallway. Fatigue assaulted his limbs as though he'd run a marathon. Kicking the door closed behind him, he leaned against a wall and slid to the floor. Grateful he didn't pass out again, he barely had time to catch his breath before another door at the far end of the hall burst open.

With whatever strength he had left in his legs, Steven curled into the wall, narrowly avoiding the wheels of the oncoming stretcher hurtling past him through the double door leading into the emergency room. His cloak still wrapped around him, the trio of blood-covered paramedics barely acknowledged his presence as they passed.

One navigated the unwieldy gurney down the wide hallway while the other two pounded away on the patient's crimson-soaked chest and squeezed bag after bag of air into the man's lungs. The tube projecting from the bloody pulp that had been the man's face was stained red inside and out, the rusty fluid from his lungs advancing and retreating with every forced breath. The paramedics pumped at his chest, his ribs crunching like broken twigs.

Steven rose from the floor and followed the paramedics into Emergency as fast as his wasted limbs would move. No sooner were they through the door than half a dozen staff descended on the wounded man. His skin appeared the same hue as the white hospital linen that lay beneath his tattooed arm.

"That leg looks bad," said a man in black scrubs who appeared to be in charge. "All right, people. Chest, abdomen, pelvis and right femur films and call the lab. Four units, O negative."

"Blood's already on the way, Dr. Ott. Antibiotics going in now." One nurse pierced the hub of the man's intravenous line and injected the medicine while another drew blood from his opposite arm. The man moaned as she inserted the needle but didn't pull away. Such an effort was no doubt beyond him.

"What are his vitals?" Ott asked.

"Pulse 160 and thready. Respirations 28 and labored. BP 60 over palp."

"He's bleeding out." Ott passed a penlight back and forth across the young man's eyes. "Right pupil looks blown. Keep bagging him, get me trauma surgery on the phone, and get that blood up here, stat." The doctor's grim expression grew more alarmed as he pressed his stethoscope to the man's chest.

"God, this kid can't catch a break." He pulled a syringe from a nearby drawer and Steven winced as Ott slid what looked like two inches of needle into the man's chest a finger width below his collarbone. The doctor sighed at the hiss of escaping air, smiling at the nurse standing across the body. "Most beautiful sound in the world." A moment later, the chest resumed its rhythmic rise and fall with each forced breath.

"Surgery's on the line," shouted a nurse from the central desk. "It's Dr. Paard. You want him on speaker?" At Ott's nod, she pressed the button.

"This is Paard. What've you got?"

"Mid-twenties Hispanic male, unresponsive, through and through gunshot to the right chest, entrance wound in the right upper quadrant, two gunshot wounds to the right leg, collapsed lung on the right—"

"Just send him," Paard said. "OR-3 is open. Neuro is finishing a case, so they're available. I'm sending my resident down to bring your guy up."

"We'll get him ready for transport." Ott checked the man's pulse and glanced up at Steven, raising an eyebrow before turning to the nurse at his side.

"Prep this kid for surgery and call x-ray. Tell them to catch up to him in OR-3 to shoot that right leg and his chest to check tube placement." The nursing staff continued their work and Ott stepped out of the bay, confronting Steven in the hallway.

"Can I help you?" Ott asked.

Steven's jaw dropped. "Uh… sorry. I was looking for someone."

"Are you a patient or family member of someone in Emergency?"

"Not exactly." Steven's hand went to his neck. "I was supposed to meet someone here."

"We're very busy right now." Ott escorted him out of the treatment area and dropped him off in the waiting room. "You can wait for your friend out here."

Steven caught the man's shoulder. "You can see me?"

"Yes, young man. I can see you." Ott rubbed at his neck and returned to the ER muttering, "Guess I'll be calling psych down later."

Steven wandered among the rows of chairs, his father's old saying about how you can't fool all the people all the time echoing through his mind. He settled for a seat next to a hacking toddler, the mother's half-closed eyes adorned with the dark circles of too many sleepless nights.

No sooner did he sit than his hip erupted with heat as if set aflame. The pouch droned so loudly he clutched it to his side until he recalled that no one but him could hear it. A moment later, Lena and her boyfriend appeared at the main entrance and headed for the reception desk.

"I'm looking for Carlos Cruz," the boy said between panting breaths. "The police said the ambulance brought him here."

The receptionist punched away at her keyboard for several seconds before looking up, nonplussed by neither the boy's insistent tone nor the girl on his arm fighting back tears. "You two family?"

"I'm his brother, Emilio." His voice trembled with anger and adrenaline. "Is that family enough for you?"

"All right, Mr. Cruz. Stay calm. Your brother was brought in a few minutes ago. I'll go check on him and—" Before she could complete her thought, the intercom barked to life.

"*Attention, please. Surgery to Emergency, stat. Repeat, Surgery to Emergency, stat.*"

The receptionist's eyes fell.

"What does that mean?" The tremor in Emilio's voice grew stronger, the rage replaced by simple, unabashed fear. "Is that Carlos?"

"Let me go check." The woman excused herself and walked through a door to her rear. Emilio paced the floor while Lena stared off into space, her trembling fingers absently twisting her long, brown hair into tight coils.

Steven absently caressed the dragonfly clasped at his neck and drew the cloak close around his body. The pouch grew white-hot on his hip as Steven fell into line behind Lena and Emilio, the drone reaching a fever pitch when he brushed the boy's shoulder. A moment later, the receptionist returned with one of the nurses Steven had seen working in the back. Their shared expression spoke volumes.

"Mr. Cruz?" the nurse said.

"That's me," Emilio said. "What's going on with my brother? Cops said he was shot up pretty bad. Did he pull through? Is he—" Lena put her arm around Emilio's waist as his words faded into choked whispers. The nurse pulled them into a side room. Steven followed and stood at the door, straining to hear her hushed words.

"Your brother's up in surgery, but it doesn't look good. He was in pretty bad shape when he got here. He was shot multiple times and he'd lost a lot of blood. One of his lungs that collapsed in the field has been reinflated and he has a tube in his throat to help him breathe. The doctors in the OR are working to stabilize him as best they can." She looked away. "I'm sorry to say, they're not optimistic."

Lena sobbed and buried her face in Emilio's chest. Emilio, on the other hand, took the information in stride. A look of bold defiance spread across his face. "Take me to him."

The nurse led Emilio and Lena down the hall toward a bank of elevators. Steven waited a few seconds before heading out into the main hospital hallway. He perused the floor legend posted by the stairs and then, ignoring the fatigue in his limbs, sprinted up three flights to the surgical floor.

As Steven exited the stairwell, the nurse led Emilio and Lena past him and down the hall to a small waiting room. An older man in scrubs and surgical cap soon joined them, and Steven followed. Inside, Lena's cheeks were wet and even Emilio's stony visage had cracked, a single tear working its way down his cheek. From his position outside the door, Steven only caught snippets, but the meaning of the doctor's words came through all too clear.

"... large caliber handgun... heart and lungs... nothing we could do... your parents..."

"... just us... only family... want to see him..."

"... cleaning him up... when he's ready..."

The surgeon and nurse withdrew from the room, leaving Emilio and Lena alone. He passed Steven in the hallway, giving him no more than a cursory look as he pulled his surgical mask across his nose and headed back to the operating room. No sooner was he gone than Emilio broke down into tears, while Lena, who had cried nonstop since their arrival to the emergency room grew quiet. She held Emilio's head to her chest and stroked his curly brown hair.

"I'm sorry, *papi*," she whispered.

Steven moved down the hall to give the young couple a bit of privacy, pacing the blue and ivory checkered tiles of the hallway for the better part of half an hour as they all waited for the doctor to return. At first, he did his best to appear inconspicuous, but found regardless of what he did or where he stood, everyone who passed ignored him. Only one small child noticed anything out of the ordinary. Wide-eyed, he peered out at Steven from an open elevator. Steven held his finger to his lips and smiled until the doors closed.

*Kids. Not so easily fooled.*

After an interminable wait, the surgeon returned and ushered

Emilio and Lena down the hallway toward the operating rooms. Steven followed them into one of the recovery rooms. The surgeon led the young couple to a corner sequestered by a curtain. Hearing Lena gasp, Steven drew close and peered behind the curtain.

The body of Carlos Cruz lay beneath the starched hospital sheet with only his head uncovered. Steven was grateful his mutilated face was all they could see. He knew all too well what horror rested beneath those thin sheets of cotton.

Lena sat at the foot of the bed sobbing while Emilio stood and stared at the wall, his body shaking with grief and rage. After a while, Lena gathered herself, rose from the bed, and wrapped her arms around Emilio from behind. The room remained quiet save for the boy's occasional bursts of angry muttering in both English and Spanish and the girl's soothing words.

Steven marveled at the power of young love, a distant pain echoing in his heart.

Emilio eventually disengaged from Lena's embrace and headed for the door. As he drew near the pouch again grew hot and the crescendoing drone reminded Steven why he was there.

"Emilio Cruz?" He stepped into the boy's path. "May I speak with you?"

"Who are you?" Emilio stopped and wiped the tears from his eyes. "What do you want?"

"My name is Steven Bauer." A surge of guilt rushed through him. He avoided Emilio's indignant glare. "I'm sorry to hear about your brother. I know the doctors here did everything they could—"

Emilio put a hand in Steven's face. "To this hospital, my brother was just another banger. I'm sure the doctors did their best, but the last thing I need right now is to hear how sorry everybody is."

"Believe it or not," Steven said, "I know what you're going through. I know what it's like to lose someone. Trust me, the last thing I want to do is make this day any worse for you, but there's something you need to know." Steven cleared his throat. "Listen—"

"No, you listen, *pendejo*." Emilio said. "You think you understand me? For the first time in months, everything was finally getting better, and now my brother is dead with Salvatrucha bullets in his chest."

Emilio crossed the room to the sink and splashed his face. The water washed away the salty trail of tears running down his cheek. "I know what I gotta do now." Emilio's voice trailed off. "I know what I gotta do…"

"I told you I'm not listening to that crap, Emilio." Lena came out of her chair and joined her boyfriend by the door. "You're not going anywhere near those bastards. Do you want to end up like your brother? Chest full of lead and your blood spilled on the ground?" Her voice trembled with a potent mix of panic and fury.

"My only brother is dead." Emilio said. "You don't understand."

"I understand if you go down there and start mouthing off to the wrong people, I'll be attending two funerals instead of one."

"What do you want me to do, Lena? Let it go? Forget everything Carlos did for me?"

"I've been telling you for weeks to call the police, *papi*. It's too late for Carlos, but not for you. Let them handle this."

"The police won't do shit. Another banger dies in the *barrio*, and they couldn't care less." Emilio's eyes grew distant. "What I gotta do is go down there, find who did this, and…"

Lena pulled away and headed for the door. "And throw away everything Carlos ever wanted for you. If that's what you've got to do, you can do it without me." She stormed past Steven and out of the room.

"Lena." Emilio took off after her. "Wait."

"Great," Steven muttered under his breath. "Here we go again."

## 10

## BARREL

T he hospital's main entrance opened onto an urban
nightmare, the road so congested not even a pair of ambu-
lances, lights on and sirens blaring, could move an inch. The
cacophony of blaring horns only punctuated the chaos. Sprinting
between the cars, Emilio and Lena led Steven by fifty yards, ignorant
they were being pursued or that their lives had changed irrevocably
the moment he entered their lives. *Ignorance won't save them if Black
finds them unprepared.*

The pouch barely warm at his side, Steven stopped at the sidewalk
and pulled the cloak tightly about him. Emilio caught up to Lena at
the corner and the girl spun around to let him have it. Though he
couldn't hear her words, her expression and body language were
more than clear. The passionate exasperation reminded Steven of—

*No time for that now.*

As Lena and Emilio's one-sided chat continued, Steven's patience
wore thin. No matter what else had happened, he still had a job to do,
not to mention the Black was still on the hunt. He had taken no more
than a couple of steps in their direction, however, when the fight
ended. Lena pulled Emilio close, gently stroking the curly locks at the
nape of his neck, and Steven's voyeur's guilt returned in spades.

After a moment of making up as only young lovers can, Emilio led Lena over to the red Honda motorcycle and started the engine. She held tight to the boy's chest as he maneuvered the bike through the parking lot and out into the throng of immobile cars clogging the street.

As the motorcycle disappeared around the corner, Steven headed for the nearest door and unfastened the pouch from his belt. The polished glass of the hospital's front entrance reflected a face filled with confidence and purpose, a face Steven hadn't seen in some time. Then, with no more thought than if he were boarding an elevator, he crossed the door and stepped across the metal threshold.

Fifteen minutes later, Emilio brought his bike to a halt at the entrance of a run-down apartment complex. Graffiti covered the brick and faded trash littered the ground. Lena climbed off the back of the bike, took Emilio's hand, and led him to a first-floor apartment marked 1217. Emilio produced a large ring of keys, unlocked the three deadbolts, and followed Lena inside.

From the window of the laundromat across the street, Steven looked on with no small measure of relief. His latest jaunt had left him exhausted, though the quarter hour spent waiting for Emilio and Lena to catch up to him had returned some of the strength to his weary limbs.

Steven had no idea how to approach all of this with Emilio. The pouch would no doubt do its thing when the time was right, though getting an angry and grieving teenager to listen to anyone about anything was likely a tall order. Not to mention, the problem of what to do with the girl, Lena.

"And this kid's only the first." Steven's hand brushed the pouch, the smooth leather again warm to the touch and humming like a hive of bees. He stepped out of the laundromat and turned toward the apartment when a sticking pain at the base of this throat made him jump.

"What the hell?" Steven stopped in his tracks and jerked the dragonfly from his chest. "You pinched me." As he decided which made him crazier, chatting with a leather sack or yelling at a piece of jewelry, a new set of players entered the scene.

A cluster of Latino males in their teens to early twenties converged on apartment 1217. Eleven in number, all were dressed in some variation of white ribbed tank tops, baggy black jeans and flashes of blue. A third of them didn't appear old enough to need a razor.

"Amaryllis." Steven stroked the dragonfly and returned it to his chest. "Thanks, Ruth."

Steven pegged a tall *hombre* with greasy locks swept back under a blue bandana to be the leader of the group, his gait marked by the swagger of a man accustomed to respect. He pounded twice on the heavy wooden door. After a few seconds, the door opened to reveal Lena's angry glare. Her small frame filling the doorway, her face flushed crimson as she spewed a rapid-fire barrage of curses in alternating English and Spanish. Though Steven's two semesters of foreign language at Georgetown were a distant memory, the girl's message was clear.

Steven edged closer in case things went south, stopping beneath a nearby covered bus stop. Without warning, a cramp took his breath. Clutching his side, he watched the drama across the street unfold, hoping the twinge in his side was merely an aftereffect of his latest jaunt. In his heart, however, he knew all too well what the pain meant.

The gang stood impassive in the face of Lena's anger. Blue Bandana maintained a distinct air of disinterest while a few at the back snickered at her outburst. This did nothing but escalate her fury. Spitting on the sidewalk at their feet, she slammed the door on the whole lot.

Blue bandana raised a hand. "Just wait, boys."

Less than a minute passed before the door opened again. Despite Lena's fervent shouts, Emilio stepped out and locked the door behind him. The group encircled Emilio and Steven wondered if they were going to jump the boy. The pain in his side faded to a dull ache and Steven craned his neck to listen as Blue Bandana slapped a firm grip on Emilio's shoulder.

"Hey, *esé*. Sorry 'bout your brother."

"Don't feed me that bullshit, Vago." Emilio brushed off the tattooed hand.

Blue Bandana's face betrayed no emotion. "Traviezo was playing with fire, and he got burned, bad."

"Don't call him that. My brother's name was Carlos. Last time I saw him, he said he was leaving all this shit behind."

"Is that what he told you, *manito*?" Vago shook his head in mock sadness. "Carlos always said he'd make sure you made it to college, but trust me. He was going nowhere."

"Screw you, man. My brother had more brains than all of you." Emilio's volume continued to escalate. "He was even thinking about college himself."

"El Traviezo in college." Vago laughed. "He always did talk a big game."

"Look. You and your homeboys get the hell out of here and don't come back." Emilio turned to rejoin Lena inside, but stopped cold at Vago's next words.

"We know who the shooter is." A smug expression broke across Vago's face.

Emilio turned from the door and faced him. "What?"

Vago nodded. "And we know where to find him."

Emilio went nose to nose with Vago, his already flushed face darkening to a deeper shade of crimson. "Tell me his name."

"Alvarado. New guy with the Salvatruchas. Maybe a year younger than you." Vago spat on the sidewalk. "Whacking your brother was his ticket."

Veins bulged along Emilio's neck.

"One of our boys heard this Alvarado kid talking about it downtown, bragging about how your brother went down after one shot to the chest. Said he unloaded three more rounds into him just for target practice."

Emilio balled up his fist and swung at the wall, fracturing the shutter by the window. Blood poured from his knuckles as he pulled his injured hand from the splintered wood.

Vago laughed. "Carlos never let you come around, but I always guessed you had the same fire."

Lena cracked the door and peered out. Her eyes grew wide when she spotted Emilio's bleeding knuckles and the broken shutter. "*Dios mío*," she said. "What happened?"

"It's nothing." Emilio's lips turned up in a pained smile.

"Like hell it is. Come inside, Emilio."

"No, *manito*. Come with us. We'll take you to Alvarado and… take care of business."

"I'm sorry, *mami*." Emilio avoided Lena's gaze. "Somewhere I gotta be."

Vago's smile was that of a cat closing on a wounded bird.

Lena grabbed Emilio's arm and forced him to look her in the eyes. "We've already discussed this. You're not going anywhere with these… people."

Vago put his hand on Emilio's shoulder again. "You gonna take orders from this little *chola* or are you gonna be a man like your brother?"

Emilio caught the unwelcome hand and with a fluid movement, brought Vago's muscular arm up into the small of his back, doubling the bigger man over. A grimace of surprise and more than a little pain replaced his smug grin.

"Don't talk about her." Emilio brought his mouth close to the side of Vago's head. "Don't even look at her. *Comprende?*"

Two of the others grabbed Emilio, but Vago held up his free hand and signaled them to back off. Steven gripped the Pawn, his knuckles white, but held his ground.

"It's all good, boys," Vago grunted. "*Manito* here is just all worked up, right?"

"Stop calling me that." Emilio forced Vago to his knees before releasing his arm. "I'm not your brother, and I'm definitely not your friend."

Vago took a few seconds coming to his feet, his self-satisfied smirk tarnished. "So, *vato*, looks like you did learn a few things playing wrestler last year. Carlos always said you were unstoppable on the mat." Vago stroked his chin. "I'm impressed."

"The last thing Emilio needs is approval from a criminal," Lena said. "Now you and your gang leave before I call the police."

Vago laughed. "You sure know the talk, *cholita*, but come on. When was the last time you saw a cop around here? Pigs don't care about what happens in our little *barrio*. El Traviezo bled half an hour before they showed." He shot a sidelong glance at Emilio. "Why don't you go back inside, *chica*, and let the men talk?"

"Emilio." Lena's voice was half command, half pleading. "Come inside."

Emilio stared at the ground, refusing to meet her gaze. "They know where the bastard is who killed Carlos."

"I know this is all about your brother, *papi*, but think. Is this what he would want? He spent his entire life keeping you from all of this so you could have it better than he did. You've got a full ride to Maryland, and you're about to flush it down the toilet because this *pendejo* is pushing your buttons."

Emilio turned away from Vago, his eyes welling with tears, and pulled Lena close.

"I've got to do this. For Carlos." Emilio's gaze dropped. "He'd do it for me."

Tears streamed from Lena's swollen eyes. "Carlos is dead, Emilio, but if he was standing here right now, he'd tell you to walk away."

"Listen, Cruz." Vago's smile was gone, replaced with a look of cold resolve. "The Alvarado kid said he enjoyed watching Carlos bleed. In or out, we're going to go take care of this. Last chance to join."

Emilio met Lena's gaze, his pleading expression bringing fire to her eyes.

"No." Lena pushed him away. "Go with these guys, you end up as dead as your brother."

"Don't worry, *chica*. We've got his back." Vago signaled to one of his gang. A kid, no more than fifteen with the worst case of acne Steven had ever seen, pulled an automatic pistol from the waistband of his jeans and handed it to Vago.

"So, *manito*, you ever handle one of these?" He placed the weapon in Emilio's uninjured hand. "Beretta, 9mm, one round in the chamber, fourteen in the magazine. The safety's on so you don't shoot yourself in the foot."

Emilio stared down at the gun. Smiling, Vago positioned the boy's arm, pointing the automatic pistol out into the street. Lena looked away in disgust.

"You drop the safety here," Vago said, revealing the red dot on the side of the weapon, "and when you're ready, pull the trigger."

The hate that filled Emilio's eyes lasted but a second. Dropping the gun to his side, he shook his head as if waking from a bad dream. Steven followed Emilio's gaze and discovered the reason for the sudden shift. Across the street, a small window framed a child's terrified gape, a child Steven guessed had seen more than his share of violence.

Emilio rubbed his brow and placed the weapon back in Vago's hand. "When I'm through with this kid, he's gonna wish he'd never been born, but if you want him dead, you're talking to the wrong man."

"We'll see, little brother, we'll see." Vago returned the gun to its owner. "Now, say goodbye to your girlfriend and we'll go have a chat with the Salvatruchas." He stepped off the stoop and sauntered away, the rest of his gang falling in behind their leader like a line of infantrymen heading off to battle.

Emilio nuzzled Lena's chin and brought her gaze back to his. A single tear betrayed his brave facade. "You stay here and don't leave the apartment until I get back. Understand?"

Without a word, Lena shook her head in disgust and stepped back into the apartment. The deadbolt clacked into place with a gavel's finality.

Emilio paused on the doorstep before rushing to catch up to Vago and the others. The entire procession walked within five feet of where Steven stood, his appreciation of the power inherent in his cloak growing with each breathless moment. The pouch pulsed at his side, its volume rising as Emilio grew close and quieting as the boy disappeared from view.

As the last of Vago's gang rounded the corner, Steven broke from his hiding place and headed up the street after them. Before he had gone ten feet, the roar of multiple engines and the squall of tires on gravel let him know the gang, and most likely Emilio as well, had left the area. He looked around for a convenient door with which to jaunt ahead and noticed Apartment 1217 standing wide open. A moment later, Lena poked her head out and did a quick sweep of the street before emerging with a battered old aluminum baseball bat in her hand. Her eyes barely lit on Steven as she stole up the sidewalk in the direction Emilio and the others had gone.

"Excuse me," Steven shouted as he sprinted to catch up to her.

Lena spun around, the bat raised above her head as if she were waiting for a fastball. "Who are you?"

Steven took one hesitant step forward. "I need to speak with you for a—" He clutched his side, the gnawing below his ribs flaring like a miniature supernova.

"Are you all right?" Lena didn't lower the bat an inch.

"I'll... be okay... in a minute." Steven could barely string three words together without retching. "Been through this before."

"All right," Lena said. "I get it. You're sick and need help, but I've got to... Wait. You're the guy from the hospital."

"My name is Steven Bauer." The nausea began to pass and the pain in his side returned to its previous low smolder. "I've been looking for you."

Lena stepped back, her knuckles pale around the bat. "You look different."

*The cloak.* "I'm sorry, Lena. I don't mean to spook you, but—"

"How do you know my name?" she said. "What do you want?"

"It's about Emilio. It's important I talk to him, and soon."

"Well, Mr. Bauer, you're out of luck. You just missed the big idiot." Her voice cracked. "He's off trying to get himself killed." Lena took off down the sidewalk.

Steven rushed to catch up to her. "Maybe I can help."

"How? Have you got a SWAT team with you?" She picked up her pace.

"I could ask you the same." Steven gestured to the aluminum club the girl held across her chest. "You planning on bailing him out or knocking some sense into him?"

"Somebody's got to look after that macho dumb-ass." The tremor in her voice betrayed her stoic expression.

"I can help, if you'll let me," Steven said. "Take me to him."

Lena's expression remained decidedly unimpressed. "And what exactly are you going to do? You a cop or something?"

"I'm no cop, but I can help. I swear."

Lena stopped at the corner and studied Steven with apprehensive eyes. "What is it you want from us? I've never seen you before in my life."

"You're right, Lena. You don't know me from Adam, and I do come with an agenda. Right now, though, I don't see anybody else knocking down the door to give you a hand." Steven's cheeks burned with guilt. Regardless of Emilio's current predicament, what he had to offer was at least as dangerous. In fact, a part of him suspected Emilio would be better off if the two of them never met again.

*But if the Black could find me...*

"I have a proposition for Emilio." Steven attempted a smile. "A job opportunity."

"Look, I don't know what it is you're selling, but every second we spend here talking puts my man in deeper trouble. Help me drag his butt out of this bullshit, and you can talk his fool head off for all I care." Lena resumed her jog down the fractured sidewalk. "I just hope you know how to handle yourself in a fight."

Steven took a deep breath. *That makes two of us.*

He kept up with Lena for the first couple of blocks until the stabbing in his side flared again, nearly sending him to the broken concrete. Paralyzed by the pain, he watched as Lena rounded the corner ahead. Stumbling through the agony and nausea, Steven did his best to follow, the streets dirtier and more littered with each passing block. The few stores in the area still in business had bars on the windows and every building he passed sported more than its share of graffiti.

Even more unnerving, despite the cloak's facade, Steven couldn't escape the notion he was being watched. He scanned the area, but other than an emaciated dog and a couple of cars, the street was deserted. The cramping in his side eventually let up enough to allow Steven to run again, and he applied every bit of speed and endurance at his command to catch up to Lena.

He rounded the corner of what must have been the twentieth city block and spotted her. Leaning with her back against a rusty El Camino, Lena's chest heaved as she worked to catch her breath. The pouch, cool and silent at his hip, grew warm, its familiar drone returning.

Two blocks past Lena, dozens of men and boys filled the street, their colors alternating between blue and black. Vago and his boys had found the Salvatruchas.

Lena popped her head above the El Camino's hood to survey the situation and moved down the street toward the growing mob. Steven sprinted to her vacated hiding place and then followed her to the next block and concealed himself behind a pile of old tires.

Peering from his spot, Steven had no trouble making out Vago. A few inches taller than the rest of the throng, he argued with a man Steven didn't recognize. He guessed a certain high school wrestler with an underlying death wish was also there, right in the thick of it.

As Lena closed on the growing throng, another wave of nausea sent Steven to his knees, the pain in his side returned with a vengeance. He retrieved the pawn from his pocket and found its marble surface glowing with a white shimmer that pulsed in time with the throbbing in his abdomen. The radiance grew more brilliant and the stabbing sensation in Steven's side flared into sheer agony. He shifted his gaze skyward to avoid the icon's blinding brilliance.

There, above the gathering crowd and atop a two-story office building, stood a man of medium height and dark complexion. His attire was black as midnight, a twisted depiction of a Native American warrior's garb. He wore headgear fashioned in the likeness of a bird of prey, the curved beak coming to a point above the bridge of his nose. A traditional Native American breastplate covered his neck and torso, an intricate lattice of bone hairpipe, buffalo horn and leather. A horizontal line of white accentuated the skin around his eyes, eyes that sparked with a familiar dark scintillation. His well-muscled arms held a longbow the color of night nocked with a cruelly barbed arrow, its shaft easily half an inch in diameter.

The pain in Steven's side flashed white-hot as he looked past the arrow's dark fletching and caught the man's steady gaze. The archer studied him for several long seconds, his grimace slowly evolving into an almost congenial smile as if to say, "this is not for you." Once he had Steven's full attention, he shifted his attention to the increasingly belligerent crowd below him and altered his aim to target the heart of the rabble. Steven took off at a dead sprint for the center of the crowd, splitting his attention between the danger before him and the threat above.

Before he crossed even a quarter of the distance, the archer drew the bowstring with a slow, deliberate pull and let the bolt fly.

# 11

## EN PASSANT

The black arrow left the assassin's bow with a crackle of obsidian energy and sped toward its mark. *Too little.* A split-second estimate placed sixty additional yards between Steven's position and the heart of the mob. *Too late.* With a brand of hope familiar only to the desperate, Steven gripped his icon and dove forward.

Time slowed to a crawl mid step as Steven's five senses simultaneously expanded and focused. The sensation was foreign, yet familiar, as if he had lived that exact moment before, but in another time, another life. The fleeting stillness coupled with his heightened senses brought the surrounding world into crystal clarity.

The angry mob stood before him immobile and silent, unaware of the temporarily postponed death sentence approaching from above. The ebon missile hung in the air, its inexorable progress halted for the moment. The archer's static gaze remained fixed on the crowd below, a gleeful smirk frozen on his thin lips. Before Steven's mind could grasp what was happening, the hand gripping the pawn icon made a swift but subtle forward movement, as if moving the game piece over an invisible chessboard.

An instant later, Steven's entire perspective shifted.

No longer a spectator, Steven found himself amid the unmoving mob and standing back-to-back with Emilio. The short jaunt landed him in the archer's direct field of fire. The barbed missile, its tip pointed at Steven's heart like a compass to magnetic north, hung frozen in the air less than twenty feet away. Another breath, and time began to resume its relentless march. The bolt gradually accelerated toward the center of Steven's chest, and that's when instinct took over. His mouth had no more than formed the word "shield" than the shimmering icon in his hand vanished, replaced by a body-length rectangular shield strapped to his left arm, a subtle white iridescence emanating from its polished surface.

A split-second later, the lethal projectile struck Steven's hastily created defense with a force more like a wrecking ball than an arrow. The impact sent both him and Emilio sprawling, and though the shield held, he half-expected one or both of them to be skewered by the archer's follow up shot.

The mob scattered like roaches in the light. Clearly, many had seen the attack, but with the cloaks of the Game in play, Steven couldn't begin to guess exactly what it was they saw. The fleeing gang members fired off a few rounds, the gunshots all aimed skyward at their dark assailant. In seconds, he and Emilio stood alone in the kill zone.

Steven scrambled to his feet, shield held high in anticipation of a second arrow that never came. He helped the winded Emilio up from the pavement, all the while scanning the rooftops for any sign of movement. He found nothing but empty sky. The only evidence remaining of the mysterious archer's existence was the shattered bolt lying on the pavement, the dark glimmer of its barbed tip diminishing with each passing second.

Steven grabbed Emilio's arm and led him to cover behind a purple SUV decked out with custom chrome rims. A part of him wanted to start tracking their assailant, but the sheer terror etched on Lena's face as she sprinted across the open street prompted him to stay put.

As she reached their bit of cover, Lena threw herself down between Emilio and Steven and wrapped her arms around Emilio's broad chest. "*Papi*, are you all right?"

"I'm good, thanks to this guy." Emilio looked back and forth from Lena to Steven, his expression a picture of confused recognition. "Who are you, anyway?"

"This is Steven," Lena said. "He was at the hospital, remember? He's here to help." She eyed Steven with a mixture of gratitude and apprehension. "You look like you're feeling better."

"I am." *Defend yourself*, Grey had said at Ruth and Arthur's. The pain and nausea faded into a tingling at the back of his head that oscillated in time with the shield's fading brilliance.

Emilio's gaze swept the rooftops. "Who the hell was that? Why was he shooting at us?"

"You stopped that bullet," Lena said. "Are you wearing a vest or something?"

*Bullet?* "Look, you two. I promise to explain everything as soon as I can, but right now I've got to get you out of here."

Lena nodded, but Emilio remained unconvinced. "Wait," he said. "I remember you now. You were in Carlos' room." He shot Lena a glance. "How do you know his name?"

"Just listen to him," Lena said. "He... knows things."

"In that case, mystery man, why don't you tell us all what's going on?" Vago, along with several of his boys, approached from their flank. Steven had been so intent on the threat from above, he had all but forgotten he was standing in the middle of an impending gang war.

"Two questions. Who the hell are you, and who was that on the roof?" Vago swayed back and forth, like a cobra in a snake charmer's basket, a menacing grin plastered across his face. "Tell us what you know and maybe you walk." As Vago's boys moved to surround the three of them, Steven noted the sound of more footsteps approaching from the opposite direction.

"I'd like to hear what this *hombre* has to say as well." A well-muscled twenty-something Steven took to be the leader of the Salvatruchas sauntered over, flanked by at least twenty-five men and boys dressed in black and denim. Between the two gangs, Steven estimated they were surrounded by at least sixty, every last one primed for violence after the attack from above.

The Salvatrucha chief dropped his half-burned cigarette on the ground at his feet and blew smoke in Vago's direction. "Hell, Vago, I figured you brought the shooter. That kind of chicken shit is right up your alley."

"It'll be a cold day in hell when I need second-story backup to take care of your punk ass, Cortez." Vago took a step into Cortez's space, any hint of smile now banished from his face. "Anyway, it wasn't *you* the bastard was aiming at."

"What're you trying to say?" Cortez stepped forward as well, his nose an inch from Vago's. A thin trail of smoke escaped his pursed lips.

Vago raised one shoulder, taunting the Salvatrucha leader with a noncommittal shrug. "After the thing with the kid's brother this morning, nothing would surprise me."

"I don't know what you're talking about." Cortez stood his ground defiant, but flashed another Salvatrucha a questioning look.

Emilio clenched his fists in silent rage. Lena stroked his arm.

Vago's devilish grin made a return appearance. "Besides, how would I get one of my guys up there anyway? This was Salvatrucha turf last time I checked."

Cortez's eyes narrowed, but he kept his silence.

"Sounds like the only person who knows what's going on is this guy." Vago's eyes fastened on Steven. "So, mystery man, spill. What do you want with my *manito* here?"

"I'm not your—"

Lena hushed Emilio as Steven stepped between the two rival gang leaders and leveled a no-nonsense gaze at Vago. "That's none of your business."

Vago bristled at Steven's tone. "You don't tell me what my business—"

"I'm taking these two away from here." Steven's eyes narrowed. "I recommend none of you get in our way."

"Dammit, I am not a child." Emilio shrugged off Lena's hand. "I don't need you to protect me, Lena, and I sure as hell don't need some stranger coming down here and getting in my business."

He turned to face the gathered Salvatruchas. "My name is Emilio

Cruz, brother of Carlos. Whoever the bastard is who killed my brother, let him step out and face me if he thinks he's man enough."

For a moment, surprised amusement colored both Cortez's and Vago's features. Steven's concern was echoed on Lena's face, but he somehow kept his silence as the girl stepped forward to take a spot to Emilio's right, her aluminum bat at the ready.

"Now, now, *chica*, that won't be necessary." Cortez scrutinized Emilio. "All right, Little Traviezo, what's all this about your brother?"

"Look, Cortez. I didn't come down here to listen to you talk out of both sides of your mouth. Bring out the bastard who killed my brother so we can get this over with."

Any pretense of cordiality left Cortez's face. "Boy, you really don't want to piss me off." The two Salvatruchas flanking Cortez drew pistols. Steven and Emilio found themselves on the business end of two nickel-plated Colt .45's. Cortez drew a snub-nosed Ruger from his jeans and trained its sights on Vago's chest. "As Vago here pointed out, this is Salvatrucha turf."

A twinge of pride hit Steven as Emilio stepped in front of Lena, though the irrelevance of this action wasn't lost on him. With Salvatruchas and Blues on all sides, if the bullets started to fly, none of them would survive.

"Look." Emilio's voice cracked. "I didn't—"

"Tread careful, kid," Cortez said, "and show some respect."

Emilio's fists clenched, but he managed to keep a passably civil tone. "I got no problem with you, Cortez. All I want is Alvarado. I thought you of all people would understand." Emilio's voice was confident and strong, but the beads of sweat running down his face told another story. Cortez clasped Emilio's shoulder with his free hand in an almost fatherly gesture.

"I feel you, Cruz. Somebody offed my brother, you bet I'd be standing right here mouthing off to whoever'd listen. If I knew who capped El Traviezo, I'd be more than happy to introduce you, believe me, but if you're looking for Alvarado, we've got a problem."

"And what's that?" Emilio spoke in as even a tone as he could muster.

"Alvarado's dead. Drive by, last week. In the ground three days." Cortez offered an unaffected shrug. "He's not your man."

"But..." Emilio stammered, "I thought..."

Vago took advantage of the moment to change the rules. Before anyone could react, a pistol appeared in his hand, its barrel positioned three inches from Cortez's left eye.

"A Desert Eagle can shoot through a foot of solid brick. I can't wait to see what it does to your skull." Vago rested the tip of his handheld Howitzer on Cortez's brow. "Now, you and your boys put your shit away."

A sense of dread blossomed at Steven's core. The two modern-day gunslingers stood transfixed in the momentary standoff, each vigilant for the slightest sign of weakness in their opponent. After several tense seconds, Cortez inclined his head and his two lieutenants leveled their weapons at Vago's chest. The surrounding Salvatruchas drew weapons on various members of Vago's gang, and within seconds, both sides were fully armed and ready for war. The invincibility of youth coupled with the haze of fear was a recipe for disaster. The only reason gunfire hadn't erupted, Steven guessed, was that no one wanted to be the first to fire. The concept of mutual assured destruction, the fodder for countless Cold War era movies, drifted across his thoughts. The deadlock stretched on for seconds that seemed like hours, and tensions on both side boiled.

Cortez's impassive stare betrayed no emotion while Vago's ashen features spoke volumes. Emilio somehow managed to keep his cool, and more remarkably, his tongue. Only Lena's trembling hands betrayed her mask of bold defiance. With the four principles caught at an impasse, the figure that prompted Steven to action was actually a bit player in their little drama.

In the periphery of his vision, Steven glimpsed a black bandana-topped fourteen-year-old kid on the verge of hyperventilation, his quivering pistol trained on Vago's right ear. The boy squinted and turned his head to the side like a toddler about to pop a balloon. Steven brought the shield before him, and with no idea how he was going to survive the next thirty seconds, commenced upon the only course of action left to him.

"Pike."

The eight-foot weapon appeared in his right hand, the smooth poplar warm to the touch, its tip gleaming in the sunlight. Steven took a deep breath, unsure if it would be his last.

"Uncloak."

At his command, the cloak dissipated, leaving his pike and shield revealed to a crowd of astonished faces. Within seconds, every eye and weapon was trained on him, the standoff between the rival gangs momentarily forgotten. Steven smiled ruefully, remembering the old joke about bringing a knife to a gunfight. Then, for the second time in as many days, a whispered word he barely knew left his lips.

"Phalanx."

## 12

# PHALANX

Steven disappeared in a flash of blinding white light. The crack of gunfire filled the air, followed by a mix of disoriented shouts and mumbled curses. As the collective vision of the crowd cleared, they found Emilio and Lena encircled by eight armored warriors, their interlocking full-length shields and upraised pikes resembling an armadillo's scales armed with porcupine quills. Their garb was uniform: white tunics trimmed with silver under a vest of fine chain mail, tan pantaloons, an intricate helm of silver metal, sturdy leather boots of russet color and gauntlets of leather and steel. Their most interesting commonality, though, was that they all bore the same face.

Reality blurred as Steven coped with seeing the world through eight pairs of eyes. Like trying to watch an entire bank of televisions at once, the eightfold divergence overwhelmed his senses. His very consciousness unraveling, an image of Katherine's face flashed across his mind's eye—so real he could smell the lingering scent of her perfume, those eyes full of love suddenly backlit by the twin head-lamps of the speeding Chevy Suburban.

"No." A switch went off in Steven's head and the disparate thoughts of his eight minds congealed back into a single awareness.

What had been discordant noise now played through his collective mind like a well-rehearsed orchestra as the small army surrounding them opened fire.

Every banger with a clear shot unloaded their weapons at the eight anachronistic newcomers. The circle of Pawns, in turn, closed ranks and brought their shields up to defend against the barrage of bullets. This violent display of firepower lasted for over a minute, eventually dwindling to a sound reminiscent of the last kernels in a bag of microwave popcorn.

Other than a couple of gang members who were hit as their rounds ricocheted off the circle of impenetrable shields, not a single bullet found its mark. The silence that followed was as striking as the preceding pandemonium. The sixty or so men and boys stood agape, staring mystified at what was most likely the strangest sight any of them would ever see. For the moment, any division between the Salvatruchas and Vago's boys was swept away by the recognition they were facing something beyond their ken.

The brief stalemate ended in a symphony of martial expression. The four Pawns at the cardinal points of the circle closed tight around Lena and Emilio while the remaining four moved to engage the two gangs. The first vaulted into the air, spinning the eight-foot pole arm about his head like the blades of a helicopter. He landed amidst a group of Salvatruchas and disarmed nine before any could get off a shot. The second, alternating between shield and pike, bludgeoned a path through the mass of bodies, avoiding the bullets of the few who retained the mental capacity to fire their weapons. The third ran interference for the inner circle, incapacitating anyone brave or stupid enough to come within range of his pike's gleaming tip. The fourth rushed Vago and Cortez, the spear-axe tip of his weapon a flashing silver arc. Their weapons clattered on the pavement and the two men howled in unison, clutching their hands in pain.

"What the hell is this?" Vago bellowed, the confidence in his voice a distant memory.

In answer, the Pawn engaging the two gang leaders brought the point of his pike to rest at Vago's midsection and spoke in a voice both Steven's and not Steven's at all. "You were warned not to interfere in things that do not concern you and are fortunate to still have both your hands. Now, I am leaving with Emilio and Lena. Stay clear of our path and hold your tongue, Miguel Fausto Vasquez, or I may be forced to teach you more about actions and their consequences."

Shaken by the use of his proper name, Vago didn't say a word. All that moved were his eyes, their rapid beat reminiscent of a fox trying to find a way out of the hen house. Cortez followed Steven's admonition as well and kept his silence, his cold stare almost as unnerving as Vago's shifting gaze.

One of the Pawns defending Lena and Emilio turned inward to check on the two teenagers. His voice resuming its normal tone, Steven asked, "Are you two okay?"

Lena looked up from her crouched position on the ground and nodded. Emilio looked himself over and signaled he was all right as well. Steven took a moment to survey the situation through his eight-fold perspective before helping Lena to her feet.

"We're going to get the two of you out of here." The Pawn took Lena by the hand and led her and Emilio through the crowd. The seven remaining Pawns configured themselves into a moving wall surrounding their brother and the two teens. The mob parted as they went, most of them too befuddled to do anything other than watch in silence as the tightly defended circle passed through their ranks. The Pawn holding Lena's hand smiled, though the moment of self-satisfaction lasted but a second.

"Stop." Within the circle of Pawns, Emilio stopped in his tracks, effectively halting the entire procession. "Doesn't anybody understand?"

He turned to one of the Pawns. "I get it. Something big is going down, and somehow I'm tangled up in it. That's why you're here. I appreciate you pulling my can out of the fire, but I'm not going anywhere. Not yet."

"Emilio." Steven tried to calm the fuming teenager. "Listen—"

"No, you listen," Emilio said. "My brother was murdered today, and you expect me to walk away. Pretend like it never happened? I didn't come all the way down here to run like some whipped dog. The bastard who killed my brother is here somewhere, and I'm not leaving till he has the balls to come out and face me."

Emilio moved from Pawn to Pawn within the circle, attempting to free himself from his cell of flesh, bone, and steel, but each time was denied by Steven's apologetic but unyielding stare. Emilio, however, was having none of it. His efforts to leave escalated till it became clear he was willing to fight his way out if it came to that.

With a heavy heart, Steven willed one of the Pawns to step out of Emilio's way and watched with eightfold dread as the defenseless boy left the safety of the circle.

Emilio made a beeline through the crowd, ignoring Blues and Salvatruchas alike, and headed straight for Cortez. An unbidden image of the boy grabbing a rattlesnake by the tail and holding it up to his face flashed across Steven's mind's eye.

Neither Cortez nor Vago had moved from the spot where Steven disarmed them minutes before. Either of them walking away would have been seen as a sign of weakness. More than that, however, Steven suspected that they, like everyone else present, were merely waiting to see what would happen next.

"So, Cortez," Emilio said, "if this Alvarado kid didn't kill Carlos, who did?"

Dumbfounded by the boy's sheer audacity, Steven half-expected Cortez to gut him on the spot, and was surprised when the Salvatrucha leader's face broke into a wide smile.

"I got to admit, boy," Cortez said, "you got some brass ones. I see a lot of your brother in you." His smile faded. "Look. My boys know better than to even breathe without checking in first. They sure as hell wouldn't cap somebody, especially somebody I respected as much as your brother, unless the order came directly from me."

"You're lying," Emilio said. "Vago told me he heard one of your boys bragging about it today. He said Carlos was Alvarado's initiation. He said..." Emilio paused and looked back and forth from Cortez to Vago. Cortez glared back, indignant but calm, while Vago avoided Emilio's gaze completely. "Vago?"

Vago peered up from beneath his blue bandana, his head cocked to one side as if he were about to speak, but remained silent. All confusion left Emilio's face as his eyes narrowed and his lips parted to reveal a feral snarl. He charged the man his brother had called friend.

Vago's gaze swept the surrounding blacktop. Spotting his Desert Eagle lying a few feet away, he dove for the weapon, but came up short as Emilio caught him mid-leap, plowing his shoulder into Vago's exposed flank.

"You bastard." The two of them went to ground, a tangle of arms and legs. Emilio soon gained the upper hand, swinging his winded opponent's arm behind his back in a hold similar to the one he'd used before. Planting his knee in the small of Vago's back, Emilio ground his face into the asphalt. Cortez motioned for his Salvatruchas to stay out of the fight while the Blues watched impotent as their leader's face was pummeled into the ground again and again. A pair of them moved to pull Emilio off their leader, but retreated when they found their way blocked by a pair of crossed pikes. Vago fought back for as long as he was able, bucking and kicking in an attempt to break the young wrestler's grip, but the winner of the fight was never in doubt.

Emilio came to his feet and stood over Vago's limp form, his chest heaving with rage and adrenaline. He slid his foot under the man's ribcage and flipped him onto his back.

"Wake up, *pendejo*."

After a few seconds, Vago came around. He glared up at Emilio through the bloody pulp that minutes before had been his right eyebrow, but said nothing.

"Why?" Emilio hissed through clenched teeth.

Still dazed, Vago sputtered through broken teeth. "Man... I swear... I didn't..."

"Don't lie to me." Emilio dropkicked Vago's already bruised flank.

Vago spat a thick stream of blood onto the asphalt as Emilio knelt to retrieve the Blue leader's weapon. The Desert Eagle swallowed his hand as he leveled the handheld cannon at Vago's head. "You and I both know what this gun can do. I got no problem ending you right here, right now, so listen up 'cause I'm only gonna ask you this once. Did you kill Carlos?"

Vago stared listless at Emilio for several seconds before turning his head to look up at the gathered Blues and Salvatruchas. Faces from both sides bore the same questioning expression. Vago spat out another mouthful of blood, but kept his silence. Despite the battering his face had taken, Steven could see the man's mental wheels turning in earnest.

In an instant, Steven was twelve again, crouched on his parent's driveway and staring at a trail of something that looked a lot like spattered red paint. He followed the string of wine-colored circles into their family's garage and around his mom's silver Buick. In the corner, whimpering, he found their neighbor's dog bleeding from her mouth and side. He guessed the old sheltie had been hit by a passing car and managed to make it to the shade of their garage before collapsing.

He stood to go for help, and the dog let out a whine. Steven reached out to stroke the dying dog's fur and his world disappeared in a sea of red. His father heard the screams and ran to Steven's side, but by the time he arrived the dog had released Steven's hand and fallen unconscious. Steven still bore the scars of that day, and his father's words still echoed in his mind over a decade later.

*Never trust a wounded animal, especially if it's cornered.*

"All right, *manito*," Vago sputtered. "You want the truth? Your brother was a traitor."

Emilio's grip on the gun tightened. "Careful."

Vago's lips turned up in a snarl. "Last few weeks, he treats me and mine like we're stinking garbage, and today he spouts all this stuff about getting out and moving on. I told him he wasn't going anywhere." He spat out a bloody tooth. "He said he'd go to the cops if he had to, and that didn't go over so well."

Emilio's eyes went cold. "So you did kill him."

"You disrespect me, you break loyalty, you pay." Vago's battered face turned up into a distorted likeness of his trademark smug grin. "So, what you gonna do about it? You gonna cap me, *esé*?" Vago kept up his pretense of cool, but the tremor in his voice told another story. "Get your revenge, Little Traviezo?"

"Maybe," Emilio said. "I don't get it, though. Why did you lie about all of this? Why bring me down here?"

"Tactics, kid." Cortez shot Vago a sarcastic grin. "He gets you pissed off, you come down here, mouth off to the wrong people and get yourself killed, he doesn't have to worry about kid brother coming after him somewhere down the road. Pretty much what I'd expect from this piece of chickenshit."

"Shut up, Cortez," Vago said.

"No, you shut up." Emilio brought the gun down and placed the barrel against Vago's temple. "You killed my brother, you bastard. I'm not even gonna feel bad about this."

Lena, who had remained silent through the entire fight, left the relative safety of the circle of Pawns and stood by Emilio. Steven let her go in hopes she could talk Emilio down in a way he couldn't, and instantly cursed himself for a fool as an image of Lena's bloodied form flashed across his mind's eye. Steven knew more about survivor's guilt than he liked to admit, even to himself, and could only imagine how much worse it would be for Emilio if anything happened to the woman he loved.

"Are you going to kill him, Emilio?" Lena's voice cracked as tears trailed down her high cheekbones. "Are you really capable of that?"

"What do you want me to do, Lena?" Emilio bared his teeth in fury. "You want me to let him walk? Carlos was all the family I had left."

"I'm your family now, *papi*. Please don't do this."

Emilio's hand trembled. The barrel trailed along Vago's furrowed brow and up into the man's greasy hairline as Lena pled her case.

"He's already confessed to killing Carlos. The police will sort all this out, but if you pull that trigger, he'll be dead, and they'll be taking you away instead." Emilio didn't budge, but the tremor in his hand became more pronounced, the tip of the automatic pistol now dancing by Vago's head like a drunken bumblebee.

"This is not what Carlos would want for you, *papi*. He spent his whole life keeping you away from this crap so you could get out of here and make something of yourself. Don't waste the opportunity he bled and died for."

Not a word was spoken as the war in Emilio's mind played out on his young face. Steven tensed as the dance of the Desert Eagle stopped and the barrel came to rest once more on Vago's drenched cheekbone. Vago closed his eyes and busied his lips mouthing a prayer to whatever God would listen to his murderer's confession. Steven's heart grew cold as Emilio's finger tightened on the trigger.

"Do it," Cortez whispered. "You know he deserves it." Cortez's smug patter brought fire to Lena's eyes.

"You're as bad as he is," Lena fumed. "All of you. I wish every last one of you would—"

"No." Emilio lowered the gun to the ground.

"*Papi?*" Hope flickered in Lena's features.

"We're done here." Emilio placed the pistol at the feet of the closest Pawn and wrapped his arm around Lena's shoulders. "Let's get out of here." Emilio and Lena turned to leave.

"You think you're going somewhere?" Cortez's derisive tone stopped Emilio in his tracks. "I don't get how you think you can come around here, get in our business and then walk away clean."

Steven's entire body tensed.

Cortez ran a hand through his greasy locks. "The way I see it—hell, the way Vago sees it—this is all pretty cut and dried. Capping him is justice, eye for an eye. It makes you one of us, and we look after our own. But you don't walk away from this. That makes you nothing but a witness." As if on cue, every Salvatrucha within earshot leveled weapons at Lena and Emilio. Cortez turned his attention to the nearest Pawn, his smug smile firmly in place.

"You freaks may think you're pretty tough in all that King Arthur getup, but not one of you is fast enough to save these kids if I give my boys the order to open up." Cortez went nose to nose with the Pawn. "You and the others drop all your pointy sticks and get the hell out of here or I swear I'll make them both bleed."

Steven surveyed the situation with eight sets of eyes, and lost count of the number of guns aimed at Lena and Emilio at around thirty. The element of surprise now a distant memory, Steven found himself out of options and desperate for a diversion.

Any diversion.

As if in answer, a familiar gnawing mounted in his collective side. The dragonfly at his neck shifted nervously as the shields all regained their previous luster. The spear-axe tips of the eight pikes gleamed even brighter than before. Even the tip of the shattered black arrow regained its dark shimmer.

*Oh no.* Steven cast about for any hint of their true enemy. *Not now.*

A flash of black along the roofline declared the arrival of a Black Piece. Another flash followed, and then another. The eight White Pawns all shifted their attention skyward, and even Cortez had the good sense to shut up and pay attention.

Steven and his seven Pawn brethren formed a tight circle around Lena, Emilio, Vago and the few Salvatruchas close enough to protect. Cortez took refuge behind one of the Pawn's shields and aimed his weapon at the roofline, his dispute with Emilio for the moment moved to the back burner. Salvatruchas and Blues alike followed suit, and Steven allowed himself a moment of hope they might still survive the day.

From his perch, the Blackfoot archer stepped to the rooftop's edge and hailed Steven with a brisk salute. A second later, from a building across the street, the assassin's mirror image stepped forward and offered a similar greeting. The humble Baltimore street corner soon became a kill zone as the remaining six Black Pawns revealed themselves to the crowd gathered below.

The dark archers controlled the high ground, arrows nocked and bows drawn. Steven and his seven Pawn brethren raised their shields and steeled themselves for the hail of arrows sure to follow. From within the circle of Pawns, Cortez cursed under his breath, and though the Spanish was beyond Steven's understanding, he echoed the sentiment.

*What are they waiting for?* Steven didn't have much time to mull over the question.

Another flash of black appeared along the skyline accompanied by a brief but intense flare of pain through Steven's belly. Though he had no doubt as to the identity of the new arrival, his heart still skipped a beat as she stepped forward and looked down on him from the dilapidated rooftop, her emerald eyes cold and flickering with dark energy. Her movie star smile tarnished only by the malice in her gaze, the Black Queen broke the silence.

"Hello, Steven," she breathed, her voice carrying on the wind. "You must know, I was quite disappointed our date last night was cut short, but that's yesterday's news." She tilted her head to one side, darkness crackling in her gaze. "If nothing else, you'll find I'm all about second chances."

She raised her scepter above her head, a black bolt of energy from the darkening sky pouring into its serpentine form, and leveled her weapon at the circle of Pawns. The Black Queen's smile disappeared, replaced by a contemptuous sneer, as she issued a whispered command that echoed down from above like rolling thunder.

"Fire."

# 13

## CRUCIBLE

The octet of archers let fly their first cruel volley. While the majority of the bolts shattered on contact with the glowing platinum of the encircled Pawns' shields, a single errant arrow found its way into the thigh of one of Vago's boys.

"*Diablos,*" the wounded kid screamed.

*Devils.* "Close enough, kid." The nearest Pawn broke formation, grabbed the injured boy by the scruff of his neck, and dragged him into the relative safety of the circle. The boy's eyes were wide as rhythmic spurts of crimson jetted from his thigh where the dark shaft protruded, a shaft Steven wasn't certain the boy could even see. "Try to stop the bleeding," he said to Lena as he reconfigured his eightfold perimeter to block the second volley of arrows. "I'll do my best to keep us covered."

Lena dove at the boy and clamped her hands over his pumping wound while another of the Blues, no more than thirteen himself, whipped out a bandana and fashioned a crude tourniquet at the top of the screaming boy's thigh. It took only seconds for the surrounding mob to disperse, leaving the circle of Pawns defending ten: Lena and the two Blues, Emilio, Cortez, Vago, and four others, their gang allegiance for the moment inconsequential.

While Lena and her resourceful assistant continued to work on the wounded boy's leg, Cortez and the remaining Blues and Salvatruchas raised their weapons and returned fire. The archers retreated, taking cover from the barrage of small arms. The Queen, conversely, moved even closer to the edge, her green eyes crackling with obsidian fire as she leered down at the circled Pawns below.

Steven's suspicion the Queen had nothing to fear from bullets was soon confirmed. The few that came anywhere near her flared and evaporated like meteors passing through the stratosphere. Still, a window had opened. Steven barked commands like a seasoned soldier.

"As long as they've got the high ground, we're sitting ducks." Steven gestured to Lena and the Blue helping her with the wounded kid. "You two. Grab him and head for that alley."

"What about me?" Emilio asked.

"Grab Vago and try to catch up with Lena."

"No way," Emilio said. "I'm not touching that piece of—"

"Do it." An arrow whistled past one of Steven's doppelgangers and ricocheted off the ground at Emilio's feet. "Now."

The octet of Pawns formed a screen to their rear and herded the group en masse toward the narrow alley. Lena grabbed the wounded boy's hands and dragged him along while the other kid kept tension on the tourniquet tied high on the boy's right thigh.

As Emilio stooped to help Vago to his feet, Cortez shook his head in disbelief. "He wouldn't do that for you, *manito*."

Emilio grunted a coarse reply, draped Vago's arm across his shoulders, and followed Lena's lead.

As the third and fourth volley of arrows came in, Steven struggled with his next move. To go any faster would compromise the already minimal cover the eight shields provided, but every second in the kill zone was a fatality waiting to happen.

That's when the Queen made her move.

Steven had kept at least one set of eyes on her throughout their scramble for the alley. As a stream of black flame shot from her feet and rushed down the store facade toward the street below, the eight Pawns cursed as one.

"She's coming," Steven grunted. "Hurry."

Though no one but Steven could truly see the threat he referred to, they moved nonetheless. A pair of Salvatruchas took the kid with the injured leg off Lena's hands and fireman-carried him the rest of the way with Lena close behind. A pair of razor-sharp arrows narrowly missed her as she rounded the corner into the alley. With a roll of his eyes, Cortez took Vago's other arm and he and Emilio dragged the Blue leader away with the phalanx of Pawns bringing up the rear. As the last of his doppelgangers passed into the alley and out of the archers' field of fire, Steven looked frantically for a door.

No sooner had Steven discovered a decrepit service entrance at the far end of the alley than a tongue of ebon flame snaked halfway down the alleyway and pooled there, a lagoon of black fire. A blink, and the Queen appeared within the circle of dark flame. She snapped her fingers and the eight archers materialized before her, aligned as if the blacktop below their feet hid a life-size chessboard.

Steven sent seven of his doppelgangers to defend their end of the alley, their shields and pikes at the ready, while he focused on getting everyone else through the open door to safety. Most of the Salvatruchas went through first, carrying the wounded Blue away from the battle, leaving only Emilio, Vago, Cortez and Lena to guard.

From behind her own line of Pawns, the Black Queen scowled, raising her scepter at Steven's hastily formed wall of flesh and steel. Her eight emissaries moved forward in a careful advance, launching another barrage of barbed missiles. *Make certain none of them leave this alley alive*, her whisper echoed through the space.

The line of seven Pawns held their position as the archers pressed forward. Volley after volley of black bolts impacted the line of gleaming platinum shields, the echoed clangs making it nearly impossible to think. Behind his hard-pressed defensive line, Steven worked to convince a balking Cortez to step through the open doorway at the alley's far end. A weathered sign above the door read "Patrick's Hardware," but what lay beyond was anything but a hardware store.

"Where'd you say this goes?" Cortez peered through the doorway at a long, sterile hallway lit with fluorescent light that had no business being behind that particular door.

"Not sure," Steven said. "Should be a hospital." He watched through the portal as the mixed gang of Salvatruchas and Blues disappeared around the far corner of the hospital hallway with the wounded kid in tow, a trail of crimson marking their path. "All I know is that it's somewhere far from here. Now go."

"You first," Cortez said.

"There's no time to argue. Go now, or I'll leave you here with them." Steven jerked his thumb at the advancing line of archers. Cortez weighed his options for all of two seconds and dove through the door. Steven closed the door behind him and recrossed the frame, muttering under his breath, "Take us away from here." The pouch groaned as Steven opened the door onto a midday beach scene. A gull rested beyond the threshold, snacking on sand fleas as a wave broke upon the deserted shore.

"Lena," Steven said. "Go."

The girl shot a hesitant look in Emilio's direction. "But, Steven—"

"Trust me, Lena. I'll make sure nothing happens to Emilio, but you have to go now."

Lena ran to the open doorway. Staring for a moment in disbelief at the impossible scene on the other side, she stepped from cool Baltimore asphalt onto the hot afternoon sand of someplace else. With Lena out of the picture, Steven returned his attention to the enemy assault. Frustrated by their failure at range, the eight dark archers dropped their bows and drew short axes fashioned of wood and steel. In spite of everything Steven had already seen, their bloodcurdling cries as they charged his line shook him to his collective core.

"Emilio." Steven's voice took on a renewed urgency as the wave of oncoming Blackfoot warriors broke on his wall of White Pawns. "Your turn."

"Got it. Just one question. What do we do with *this*?" Vago, still half-conscious and draped across Emilio's shoulders, appeared to be in no shape to even stand, much less fight.

"I guess we'll have to bring him along." Steven said. "Head for the door and we'll sort it out on the other side."

"Better idea," Vago said as he slid from Emilio's grasp. "Why don't we sort it out now?" Far less injured than he had led them to believe, he maneuvered his muscular arm around the boy's neck and squeezed. "Shoe's on the other foot now, ain't it, Little Traviezo?" Vago positioned Emilio between himself and Steven, the boy's struggling form an effective human shield. "And don't get any ideas, Steven, or whatever it is you freaks call yourselves." Vago slipped a five-inch blade from his boot and held it to Emilio's throat.

"Way I see it, these guys want the kid dead, and I got no problem with that. So either back off and tell your bag of tricks there to get me the hell out of here, or I'll hand him over." He pulled the blade in tight to Emilio's neck and drew a thin trail of blood below his left jawbone.

"All right," Steven said. "Don't hurt him. We can talk about this…" Steven's voice trailed off as a troubling realization hit him like a battering ram. Though her octet of Pawns continued their efforts to penetrate Steven's line, the Black Queen had somehow faded into the background and was nowhere in sight. His father's words echoed in his head.

*The pawns are there to defend and distract, Steven. Don't forget the little guys. They can kill you like the rest, but always keep an eye on your opponent's heavy artillery. That's where the money is.*

As the melee raged on, the black on white a schizophrenic pianist's nightmare, Steven scanned the asphalt battlefield.

"Steven," Emilio whispered as the blade inched closer to his Adam's apple. "What is it?"

"Not what," Steven said. "Who." A pinch over his collarbone prompted him to spin around. A tongue of black flame slithered up the alley from the opposite direction of the battle, the trail of dark fire coming to an abrupt halt behind Vago and Emilio.

"I think he's looking for me, boys." The Black Queen stepped out of what appeared to be the polar opposite of a camera flash and grasped Emilio's collar. "Release the boy," she ordered. "He is mine."

Vago stepped away from Emilio, shoving him to the ground at the Queen's feet. "Sure thing, *mamacita*. He's all yours."

"Sorry to disappoint you, Steven." The Queen lowered her scepter at Emilio's head. "I'm afraid your new friend has reached the end of the Game before it even had a chance to start. Better luck with the next—"

A loud thunk brought an abrupt end to the Queen's taunt. She fell forward onto the pavement revealing Lena's panting form, the aluminum bat held low at the end of its arc.

"Stay away from my man, *puta*."

The Black Queen lay dazed at Lena's feet. A small gash above her right temple left a thin trail of red running down her cheek.

Vago's smug expression evaporated as Steven, Lena and Emilio converged on him. "Look, bro," he grunted to Emilio. "She was gonna kill you anyway and—"

"Save it." Steven raised an angry hand. "You're done." He turned to Lena and Emilio. "You two, head for the door. We're getting out of here."

"You can't leave me here," Vago said. "They'll kill me."

"Not our problem." Emilio helped Lena through the open doorway and then stepped through himself onto the hot sand beyond its shimmering threshold.

Steven waited for Emilio and Lena to make their exit before retreating to the door himself. Vago attempted to follow but found the flashing spear-axe tip of Steven's pike a compelling deterrent. Willing his seven doppelgangers to rejoin him, the line of ivory-clad warriors faded into nothingness as the lone remaining White Pawn stepped through the shimmering portal and pulled the door shut behind him.

The Black Queen stared blearily from the ground as her dark archers charged through the evaporating line of White Pawns. Their axes reduced the door to splinters in seconds, but the shattered doorframe revealed only a darkened room populated by a dilapidated vending machine and a few shelves filled with dusty stock. All save one rushed the room while the last remained to help the dazed Queen to her feet.

Seconds later, the seven Blackfoot warriors stepped single file back into the alley and encircled their wounded Queen. Her core burned with hatred as hot as the dark flame that served her every whim.

As their enemy had done moments before, the Pawn who had remained by her side subsumed his seven brethren before kneeling at his Queen's feet. She motioned for him to rise and then paced the breadth of the alley like a frustrated jungle cat.

"They're not here," the Pawn said, his voice low.

"You won't find them in there, Wahnahtah. I suspect they are far from here by now." The Queen reflected for a moment. "The White have managed to elude us twice now. The King will not be pleased."

"So, what do we do with him?" Wahnahtah flicked his eyes at Vago as the leader of the Blues edged toward the far corner of the alley. "Shall I end him?"

"Not at the moment." The Queen regarded Vago with fatigued derision. "Still, we can't very well leave any loose ends lying around."

Vago turned to run and found himself encircled in black flames. His voice cracked as he turned to face the Queen. "Please. Don't kill me."

"Don't worry, little man. I suspect you may prove useful further down the path." She held her hand before her, palm up. "Time to face the music, Wahnahtah."

The Black Pawn took the Queen's hand in his and they both looked into Vago's one good eye. The circle of fire surrounding him dwindled to nothing as the Queen beckoned him to join them. After some hesitation, he crept over to their side. With trembling fingers, he placed his hand over their interlaced digits.

The Black Queen muttered an unintelligible phrase, snapped her fingers, and the trio vanished in a cocoon of darkness, leaving only a few static pops to mark their passing.

# 14

## TIDE

A ribbon of sand stretched up and down the undeveloped section of coastline. Steven, Lena, and Emilio sat halfway between the water and the wooded area fifty feet inland. A balmy wind from across the waves cooled them even as the sun warmed their backs and the pleasant scent of the ocean permeated their senses. The undulating rhythm of the waves reminded Steven of a slow waltz.

Lena lay with her head in Emilio's lap, her olive arm draped across her eyes to block the rays of the late afternoon sun as it continued its march into the treetops to the west. Emilio's eyes remained sullen, but the boy said nothing as he stared out into what Steven hoped was the Atlantic. His mind still reeling from the events of the preceding eighteen hours, the memory of his eightfold existence slipped from his thoughts like sand between his toes.

Steven's eyes slipped closed as sleep overtook him for the briefest of moments. When they again opened, Lena and Emilio both stared past him at a point south of them along the shoreline. Leaping to his feet, he jerked the pawn icon from his pocket and readied himself to face whatever threat awaited them there.

Beneath a battered, grey fedora, their visitor walked barefoot through the surf toward the three of them. His dark pants hitched way above his knees, the man's out-of-season duster remained dry despite the lapping waves at his feet.

Steven walked down the beach and joined Grey at the water's edge. The pair stood there in silence for a moment as seagulls and sandpipers fed in the waxing and waning surf.

"You found us," Steven said.

"No small feat, as you are the one with the pouch." Grey smiled. "Luckily, I am not without resources."

Steven cocked his head to one side. "Glad to know you made it out of Maine alive."

"Likewise, though I had the utmost faith you would make it through." Grey looked up the beach and met Lena and Emilio's expectant gazes. "I see you have found your second Piece."

"We got lucky. The Queen and her eight little Indians decided to make an appearance. Just glad they left the wall of stone at home this time."

"You faced their Queen and Pawn, but not their Rook?" Grey rubbed at his temples. "What is Zed playing at?"

"Zed?" Steven's eyes blazed. "What are *you* playing at, Grey? We were almost killed back there. That happens and this Game of yours is over before it even begins."

"I am truly sorry you faced your enemy alone today, though truth be told, there is little I could have done. Even were I not indisposed by the actions of our opposition last evening, I am forbidden to intervene in affairs of White and Black until the Game proper begins."

"Forbidden." Steven shook his head. "Well, isn't that convenient?"

Grey sighed. "I know all of this must seem cruel and the task before you impossible. Nonetheless, the responsibility of assembling the White is yours and yours alone."

"You're kidding, right? I'm the Pawn. Low man on the totem pole. Compared to black fire, flying walls and magical arrows, my little army of eight doesn't stand a chance."

Grey peered up the beach at Lena and Emilio. "The evidence would suggest otherwise."

"Like I said, I got lucky, but what if I'm not good enough next time?" Steven stared across the water. "These kids aren't even out of high school yet. If it weren't for Lena's quick thinking, the Queen would've french-fried all three of us. This may be your Game, but if anything happens to them, it'll be my fault."

A whimper from behind Steven revealed he and Grey were no longer alone. He turned to find Emilio no more than a few steps away with Lena by his side. Tears rolled down the girl's cheeks and onto her boyfriend's shoulder. Emilio stared off into space, his steely facade crumbling despite his best efforts.

"Listen to me," Grey whispered into Steven's ear. "These 'kids' as you call them are a part of this and can no more walk away than can you. It is the nature of the Game. Regardless of your frustrations about the manner in which things are happening or your role in the struggle, you were first and therefore are going to have to lead."

"My apologies. I didn't mean for you two to hear that." Steven motioned for Emilio and Lena to come closer. "No use keeping you two in the dark any longer."

Emilio took a step closer. "I'm guessing this is Grey."

"I see my reputation precedes me." Grey stepped forward and offered his hand.

"Grey," Steven said, "Emilio Cruz."

Emilio took Grey's hand. "Steven said you were the man with all the answers."

"Not nearly as many as I would prefer, young man." He turned to Lena. "And you, my dear, must be the clever young lady of whom Steven spoke."

"Lena Cervantes. Nice to meet you, Mr. Grey."

"Grey will suffice." A smile shone from beneath the grey fedora. "And the pleasure, Lena, is mine."

"All right… Grey." Lena trembled from head to toe despite the late afternoon heat.

"Hey, Steven." Emilio pulled him aside. "I wanted to thank you for everything you did for Lena and me. We owe you our lives and we'll never be able to repay you, but now that it's over, we want to go home." The answer must have been written across Steven's face, for the glimmer of hope in his eyes evaporated in a blink. "It's not over, is it?"

Grey answered before Steven could so much as take a breath. "Emilio, Lena, the two of you have today borne witness to events few people have ever seen, and fewer still have lived to recount. All will be made clear soon enough, but for now understand this.

"A conflict is unfolding that will impact not only you, but the entire world on an unimaginable scale. Your lives are an intrinsic part of this coming struggle, and both of you have a significant role to play in the Game to come. Steven was the first, you are the second, and soon you will be joined by others.

"The road that lies ahead has been walked before, but as you have witnessed, the forces that stand against you are ruthless and relentless in their pursuit of victory. All your usual places of refuge are no longer safe. Until the Game is resolved, for better or worse, all our lives are bound together, yours to ours and ours to yours."

Emilio turned on Grey. "You keep talking about this Game. I know we're young, but if Lena and I are really a part of this crazy mess, I think we deserve to hear it straight."

Grey shot Steven a sidelong glance. "I believe they would prefer to hear it from you."

Steven spent the better part of an hour recounting the events of the preceding day—his narrow escape from the Black Queen, the flight to Maine and subsequent escape to Baltimore, and his novice understanding of his role in Grey's Game.

As he moved into the events that led to their current coastal sanctuary, Emilio raised a hand, an incredulous expression spreading across his face. "You really should think about moving to Hollywood, Steven. You could write one hell of a screenplay." The skeptical tone rang familiar to Steven's ear. "But what does any of this have to do with me and Lena?"

"The truth, Emilio? I believe you are one of the Pieces I'm searching for."

Emilio rose from the sand. "That's what I thought you were going to say." He walked barefoot out into the ocean and stared out into the darkening sky of early evening. After a moment, he stooped over, picked up an oyster shell covered in barnacles and flung it into the ocean. Lena joined him in the churning surf and draped an arm about his waist.

Emilio peered back across his shoulder. "How do you know it's me the Game wants?"

Steven retrieved the pouch from a shrub where it hung in silence. He drew closer and the drone resumed, increasing in volume with each step.

"Listen to it. Hear how it gets louder, more insistent when it comes near you?"

Emilio shifted his gaze back out across the rippling waves. "What if I don't want what the damn thing has to offer?"

Steven joined Lena and Emilio at the water's edge, the pouch's high-pitched drone growing with his every step. "I don't think it works that way. Believe me, no one understands what you're going through better than me. Last night, I *was* you. One second everything was normal and the next, I was being chased by a Terminator in a cocktail dress. Today, Emilio, you were the target of the attack. The enemy knows who you are. It doesn't matter how they know. They'll keep coming and coming till…"

"I get it." Emilio's gaze shifted to Grey. "So, Grey, can you at least tell us where we've ended up?"

Grey's gaze wandered out across the ocean. "We stand on the eastern shore of an island located in the Outer Banks of your Carolina coast, one of the uninhabited ones. I forget its current name." He hunkered down on the soft sand. "It is lovely here, is it not? So tranquil, as close to pristine as you will find this century." His eyes lit up as he pointed a tapering finger north along the shore. "Ah, here is a sight few people get to see."

Steven squinted off into the distance and spotted movement along the woodline. A moment later, Lena squealed with delight. Coming into view, a herd of at least thirty horses ran along the edge of the trees, sand flying from their hooves in parabolic arcs. For a moment, the years fell away and Steven sat by his father on their old couch watching Clint Eastwood shoot his way across Italy in one of Sergio Leone's spaghetti westerns.

"Here, these noble beasts run free," Grey said, "living the way they did before man domesticated their ancestors."

"They're wild?" Looking into Lena's bright eyes, Steven could scarcely believe she was the same inconsolable girl from moments before. "How did they get here?"

"Untamed horses have roamed these shores for over four centuries. This herd consists of direct descendants of Iberian horses brought over from Spain by none other than Christopher Columbus. Abandoned in the early sixteenth century by a colony ravaged by disease and poor leadership, the horses adapted to life on the island, living off the coarse marsh grass and the fresh water that lies below the sand."

"They're beautiful," Lena said. The horses passed them by and continued south, sticking to the edge of the treeline. "Why are they so small?"

"The island diet retards their growth. The locals call them 'bank ponies,' though their small stature belies the wild heart beating within each one." The four of them watched until the galloping herd disappeared into the distance.

The wind coming off the water continued to cool and Lena suggested building a fire. Within minutes, Steven and Emilio gathered enough brush to get started, though they discovered dry wood of any substantial size was scarce. Fully expecting Grey to strut his stuff and start the fire with a wave of his hand, Steven was almost disappointed when Emilio whipped out a silver lighter and ignited the kindling.

After a few false starts, the fatigued quartet huddled close around the flickering heat. Grey's duster was sufficient to keep Lena warm, but Steven, Emilio, and even Grey all noted the chill as the sun finally dipped behind the woods to the west. Grey divided provisions among the four of them though the small bag of jerky and the single wineskin of water only went so far. After consuming the simple fare, the quartet all sat and stared into the fire. After several minutes of small talk, Lena brought the conversation back to the matter at hand.

"The people who attacked us, they're all like you and Emilio? Pieces in the Game?"

"That's what Grey tells me. So far, we've met their Queen, Pawn, and Rook, unless I miss my guess."

Grey nodded once in affirmation as a question that had been nagging at the back of Steven's consciousness finally crystallized.

"Tell me, Lena," Steven asked, "what did you see when we were attacked? The people on the rooftops. What did they look like to you?"

Lena considered for a moment. "They looked like... more gang members. They had guns, maybe? It's weird, Steven. I can't really remember what they looked like at all."

"And you, Emilio? What did you see?"

"The same. It's all a big blur. That woman stood right in front of me, but all I remember about her is Lena clocking her with the bat." Emilio pulled Lena in tight and kissed her forehead.

"That sounds about right." Steven smiled. "Let me show you something." He summoned his cloak and wrapped himself within its folds. "What do you see?"

"You're... different," Lena said.

"But still you," Emilio added.

"The cloak of anonymity." Grey smiled. "Excellent. I had intended to let you know of its existence and capabilities, but our conversation in Maine was... interrupted."

"With this thing on, no one gives me a second look." Steven dismissed the cloak and his attire shifted back to his ordinary T-shirt and jeans.

"I'm guessing the bad guys have cloaks as well," Emilio said. "That explains why the whole thing seems so fuzzy."

"You let them see you with your weapons before," Lena said. "Why?"

"Only thing I could think of at the moment," Steven said. "I had to do something to get their attention on me."

"Steven's necessary diversion notwithstanding, the Game was designed to take place in utter secrecy," Grey said. "Each Piece was granted the ability to move with impunity among the rest of society. In Steven's case, the focus is a cloak, though it may be different for each Piece."

"I'm guessing you don't wear the overcoat in July because you're cold," Steven said.

Grey put his finger beside his nose and gave a subtle nod.

"I'll tell you one thing," Steven said. "I can see the enemy, and they can sure see me."

"All those indoctrinated into the struggle perceive each other according to their true natures and not the artifice meant for the rest of the world." Grey's eyes narrowed. "In fact, as I am sure you can attest, senses beyond your normal five manifest when the opposition is near."

"The whole just drank a cup of sulfuric acid thing? Yeah." Steven's gaze dropped to his chest. "But that's not the only thing, is it, Grey? The dragonfly Ruth gave me…"

Grey smiled. "Ah, Amaryllis. I was pleased to see her at your neck when I arrived, though I suppose it should be no surprise Ruth gave her to you. That is no ordinary adornment you wear. Only sixteen like her were ever crafted. The methods and materials required to create such objects are long gone. Even I am unsure how many remain."

Emilio cleared his throat. "Not to break up your fascinating discussion of insecty fashion accessories, but let's focus here. What you're saying is we faced the Black side's version of you and their Queen, almost got killed by arrows and fire only you could see, and were only able to escape because Scottie beamed us away to some island off the east coast." He crossed his arms, defiant. "This all makes sense to you?"

"It sounds ridiculous every time I say it too, but here we are." Steven looked out at the lapping surf, the ambient light fading by the minute.

"So, Steven," Emilio asked, his eyes on the ground, "what position do I play on this team of yours anyway?"

"I have no idea." Steven opened the pouch, unleashing a spine-shaking pulse of sound. "Let's find out."

A strange fervor flashed briefly in Emilio's eyes, but then he lowered his head and turned away. "I'm not so sure about this."

"Emilio, look at me."

The boy met Steven's gaze across the pouch. "What?"

"I know this all seems crazy, but as Grey explains it, this Game is happening whether we like it or not. Call it destiny, fate, or whatever makes sense to you, but this isn't something you can walk away from, no matter how much you'd rather forget you ever met me and Grey." Steven took a breath. "Now, reach into the pouch and let's see what you find."

The low drone of the pouch throbbed as Emilio rested his fingers on the lip of the leather bag's glowing mouth, the pulsating sound shifting into couplets like the beating of an immense heart. Lena covered her ears to block the deafening sound, but stared unblinking at the light, entranced by the pulsing incandescence.

Emilio cast one last look at Lena and dove his hand into the shimmering white light.

# 15

# LANCE

The pouch swallowed Emilio's arm to the shoulder, its mouth a shining pool of starlight. Steven's heart raced, the wonder of what he had seen when he reached into the same shimmering light filling his mind. Lena, on the other hand, looked on in fear and awe as her boyfriend endured what appeared an intense seizure.

Long seconds passed before Emilio snapped out of his forced reverie and withdrew his arm from the pouch, his fingers encircling a long cylinder wrapped in white cloth. An image of Julie Andrews pulling an impossibly long coat rack from her paisley carpetbag flashed across Steven's memory.

Backing away from the pouch's shimmering mouth, the metallic object continued to come into view, but not fast enough for Emilio. Impatient, he grasped it with both hands and backpedaled away from Steven, gasping as the gleaming tip of a lance no less than twice his height emerged from the mouth of the suddenly silent pouch. The lance, like the Pawn's shield, appeared crafted of solid platinum, yet the weapon seemed light in Emilio's hand. The fine white metal was embellished grip to tip with ornate interlocking sigils while the handle was covered in tightly interwoven white silk. The young man held the lance aloft at his side and stared up at his strange prize. Lena gazed upon the weapon as well, her eyes filled with wonder.

"The lance." Grey's brow furrowed, his face frozen in a quizzical stare. "The weapon of the Knight. Elegant, and powerful indeed. You must be quite a special young man to pull such a weapon from the *Hvitr Kyll.*"

"What am I supposed to do with this?" Emilio shot Steven a quizzical look.

"Hey. Remember you're talking to a guy who totes around an eight-foot pike."

"I know it's impossible, but I've held this lance before." Emilio stroked the etched platinum surface of his weapon and smiled. "Is there more?"

"You have summoned the lance," Grey said. "I can only assume the rest must follow."

Emilio took a deep breath and closed his eyes. Lena reached out to touch him.

Steven caught her hand. "He's all right. Let him finish."

She nodded and backed off.

A minute passed before Emilio opened his eyes, his deliberate gaze focused on something only he could perceive. He muttered a single word.

"Plate."

No sooner did the word leave Emilio's mouth than a breastplate of the same ornately decorated platinum materialized on his upper torso. A matching plate appeared along his back, followed by pieces of armor that covered his upper arms, thighs, and groin. His jeans shifted into a pair of white pantaloons similar to those Steven wore as the Pawn, and his battered tennis shoes extended up his leg, transforming into a pair of russet cavalier's boots.

Emilio looked down upon his new attire and grinned as he whispered another word.

"Shield."

A long triangular shield blazoned with an image of a white stallion's head in profile materialized on his left arm, his hands protected by gauntlets fashioned of fine, glistening chain mail. With shield in one hand and lance in the other, Emilio spoke one final word.

"Helm."

White mist arose from the undulating surf and swam around Emilio's head, solidifying into a gleaming helmet. Silhouetted in the dying light of day, the lance shimmering against the darkening sky, the boy stood transformed, the last conquistador to walk the earth.

"What do you think?" The smile on Emilio's face almost erased the trepidation in his eyes. "Not too bad, huh?"

"Wow." Lena ran her hand down Emilio's armored chest. "I mean, wow."

"Starting to feel pretty real, I'm guessing," Steven said. "I think you're about ready."

"Not quite," Lena said. "Something's missing. I'm no expert at all of this, but shouldn't the Knight have a steed?" Revelation dawned upon her face. "The horses..."

"Indeed." The setting sun glinted off Grey's gunmetal eyes as he turned to Emilio. "For the time being, you may wish to put your weapons away."

Emilio focused, dismissing his armor and weapons, before joining the others in a tight circle around the fire. The four of them stared at the dark woodline in silent anticipation. Lena, despite the warmth of Grey's duster, shivered as the ocean breeze began to pick up. None of them spoke until, after what seemed hours, Grey inclined his head to one side.

"Here they come," he whispered.

Through the near darkness, the eclectic rhythm of scores of hoof-beats approached from the south. The light of the rising crescent moon allowed the perception of movement along the woodline, but not much else.

Lena let out a squeal of excitement as the staccato hammering of dozens of galloping horses grew louder and louder. The sound continued to crescendo as the front line came into view, the stampeding herd charging the beach-bound intruders at a full sprint.

His heart racing, Steven bolted down the sand perpendicular to the path of oncoming horses. Well down the beach before he realized he was alone, he paused and looked back. Though Grey was nowhere to be seen, he had no trouble finding Lena and Emilio.

Directly in the path of the rushing horses, neither had moved an inch.

As the herd of horses bore down on them, Lena dove behind Emilio, a move Steven guessed was futile at best. A television special he'd seen a couple years back discussed the injuries incurred by those brave or stupid enough to run with the bulls in Pamplona, and Steven couldn't help but think at least those people got a head start.

Lena gaped at the rushing horses, her panicked expression just visible in the poor light at fifty paces, while Emilio stood tall and unconcerned, a smile upon his lips. The din of the horses drowned out Steven's frantic shouts, and before he could take another breath, the rushing herd was upon them. Steven's face drew up as he prepared to watch his young friends trampled beneath hundreds of charging hooves. What he witnessed instead was, to use a word that was quickly becoming meaningless in his lexicon, unbelievable.

As the front line of horses reached Emilio, the herd split, each half continuing its frenzied charge toward the ocean. Horse after horse charged past him, the young man a boulder amidst the rushing river of equines. Steven watched in wonder, losing count of the stampeding horses at fifty. As the last stallion passed, a pattern emerged. The horses on either side maintained their frantic trajectory until they hit the surf, at which point they peeled off to the right or left, slowed to a canter, and from what little Steven could see, circled back in the direction of the woodline. The procession ended with Lena and Emilio as the focus of an enormous ellipse of horses stretching from the water's edge to far up the beach. Each horse stood still and expectant, gazing at the two humans at their center. Steven raced up the beach to rejoin Emilio and Lena, feeling almost foolish for running.

"How did you know?" Steven knew the answer before he even finished the question.

Emilio ignored Steven and turned to Lena, his expression exultant. "Can you hear them?"

"Hear what?" Lena asked.

"The horses." Emilio trembled with excitement.

Steven stepped in. "We all heard them. They're kind of hard to—"

"No," Emilio said. "Not the galloping. The whispering. Don't you hear it?"

Lena closed her eyes and lowered her head to listen. "All I hear are the waves rolling in."

"Steven," Emilio said. "Am I going crazy? I can hear these horses talking, sometimes to each other, but mostly to me. Tell me you can hear it."

Steven listened, but like Lena, only the ebb and flow of the advancing tide and an occasional whinny from up the beach registered to his senses. "I don't hear anything, but unless I miss my guess, you're probably the only one who is supposed to hear it. What are they saying?"

"They are petitioning." Grey appeared at Emilio's side. "As Lena so astutely pointed out, the Knight must have a steed, and each of these fine creatures has come hoping they will be chosen to fill that role." Grey clasped Emilio's shoulder. "Choose wisely, my young friend."

"But we can barely see," Lena said.

Grey's mouth widened in a mischievous grin. "Then let me see if I can shed some light on the subject." He turned toward the ocean and raised his arms to the sky, time seemingly screeching to a halt as the peculiar figure stood like a statue on the sand.

"Look," Lena gasped. She pointed up the beach at the line of trees where the darkness was now broken by countless tiny floating points of light. "Are they what I think they are?"

"Nature's little lamps." Grey held his arm aloft, rotating his index finger in a tight circle, and scores of fireflies flew in his direction, coalescing above his head in a gyrating cloud of phosphorescence. More and more of the luminescent insects flew into the spinning mass until individual points of light were no longer visible. The miniature sun floated ten feet above the cooling sand, its light not the equivalent of day but more than sufficient for the task at hand.

Emilio approached the nearest horse, a white mare with brown splotches along her hindquarters. As he drew close, the noble beast lowered her head in what resembled a bow. He stroked the mare's nose and moved on to the next horse in line. Emilio continued with his inspection of the herd and each horse repeated the simple gesture of respect.

Emilio had surveyed over two thirds of the horses when he came upon a medium-sized white stallion with a single brown stocking on his front left foot. This horse did not bow, but rather stared directly into Emilio's eyes, his equine expression bordering on recognition. Emilio cocked his head to one side as if listening to a quiet voice only he could hear.

The remainder of the herd became restless, whinnying and sputtering nervously. The white stallion paid them no mind as he continued to stare into Emilio's eyes. Emilio circled the horse only to find Lena standing on the opposite side, stroking the stallion's neck.

"Lena?" he asked.

"I know this is your call to make, *papi*, but I keep coming back to this one. I can't explain it. He just *feels* right."

The proud horse touched his nose to Emilio's hand before finally bowing his head in respect. When the stallion looked up and again caught Emilio's gaze, the connection between them was palpable.

"He's the one." Emilio ran his fingers along the wild horse's mane. The horse wasn't the largest or most imposing of the herd, but Steven had no doubt Emilio had chosen well.

"The choice has been made." Grey ran his hand along the stallion's muscular flank. "This horse will serve you well." As if dismissed by some unheard voice, the remainder of the horses cantered back toward the trees. Grey meandered through the fragmented herd toward the advancing surf. Steven followed, leaving Emilio and Lena to get better acquainted with their new friend. He approached Grey from behind, the man's quiet tones as he muttered to himself just audible above the crash of waves.

"The Pawn is ready. The lance drawn. The steed chosen."

Steven joined Grey at the water's edge and for a moment, the two of them stared silently into the starry eastern sky. Breaking the peace, Grey pointed out over the incoming tide, his open sleeve shifting in the ocean breeze.

"Mars, the Warbringer."

Steven followed Grey's gaze and found the red planet high on the horizon, brighter than the other stars of the night sky, its light possessing an orange-red hue. "The time of crisis is fast approaching. A torrent of death and destruction will rain down before the Game reaches its resolution this time. Of that, I am certain."

Steven wasn't sure how to respond to what two days ago would have sounded like the ramblings of a madman.

"Tomorrow, you seek the next Piece, and unless I miss my guess, you will face your greatest challenge yet." Grey moved farther down the beach.

Steven jogged to keep up. "What makes you say that?"

"Three times before have I witnessed the gathering of the White. The Pawn is first. The Knight and his Steed second." Grey turned and locked eyes with Steven. "Tomorrow you seek your Queen, the most powerful Piece on the board. Be warned. You have thwarted our enemy three times already, and Zed is anything but forgiving. I have no doubt the Black Queen has suffered even as you have succeeded. She will not underestimate you again."

"So it's only going to get harder from here. Fantastic. They've already found me twice in as many days and were about half a second shy of killing Emilio in Baltimore." Steven's brow furrowed. "Wait a minute."

"Yes?" Grey said.

"They're just playing with us. If this is nothing but a big game of chess, then all they have to do is take out our King and it's over." Steven looked out across the dark waves of the Atlantic. "What if they get to him while we're gathering the others?"

"I suspect your King is safe, at least for the moment. In every iteration of the Game so far, the King has been the last Piece found. As you no doubt recall, you first encountered the Black Queen as I was about to bring you into the Game. The Black's attempt on Emilio occurred similarly as you were drawing close." Grey's eyes narrowed. "I do not fully comprehend the entire picture as yet, but there is clearly some sort of order to our enemy's attacks, and a clear association with each of your indoctrinations into the White."

"Another thing." Steven's fingers found the leather sack tied to his belt. "If this pouch of yours is the only way to find us, how does Black keeps beating us to the punch? How do they even know who we are or where to find us?"

Grey's gaze wandered over the moonlit ocean. "Truth be told, Steven, I have been unable to discern how the enemy knows what they know. It has never been this way before. Your pouch and its dark sister are two of only a few artifacts that remain from before the Great Purge, and to my knowledge are the only means by which either side can locate and identify its Pieces. I thought perhaps the enemy was monitoring my movements, but my absence in Baltimore clearly changed nothing."

"Why haven't they hit us here?" Steven waved his hand, indicating the deserted stretch of beach. "There's nowhere to run, that's for sure."

"Would that I could tell you." Grey flung a pebble out into the churning surf. "Only my affinity for the White, not to mentions my own means of transportation, allowed me to locate and join you today."

"What?" Steven raised an eyebrow. "You call a cab?"

"Something like that." Grey's lips curled into a rare smile. "Suffice to say that the pouch is yours now. Until this iteration is over, it shall serve as your conveyance, your guide, and your means of empowering the others. Guard it well."

"Speaking of the pouch, all my other jaunts left me with a dead battery, but here I felt fine. Ruth and Arthur mentioned something you told them once. About places and power?"

"Their fiftieth anniversary. What a delightful day. Ruth had always dreamed of seeing the Eiffel Tower." Grey crouched and drew a pair of lines in the sand, forming an X. "As for your question, understand this island rests over a crossing."

"A crossing?"

"A place of power. Crossings are holes in the sieve that is the universe, places where the fabric of reality is thinner and easier to breach. The farther from a crossing your travels take you, the more the pouch requires from its holder. Still, with the coming correction, the ambient power at virtually any point should provide enough substrate to get you where you need to be."

"More power, less resistance." Steven stared at the X in the sand. "Makes sense, I guess."

"The greatest among the various crossings are well known to the world at large: Giza, Chichen Itza, Machu Picchu, Easter Island. Ancient adepts of the Art built temples and tombs at such locations for a reason. Thousands of years ago, such wellsprings of power enabled feats that to this day are still unparalleled. The Great Pyramids. The Moai."

"Stonehenge." Steven's breath caught in his throat as the man's dead eyes flashed across his memory. "The massacre."

"Precisely. Each iteration of the Game centers on a specific crossing and the players for each side usually share a geographic propensity. As evidenced by the events of the last few days, the coming conflict will take place somewhere on the North American continent." Grey walked up the beach to where the sand was dry and sat. His duster billowed about him like a dark cloud. "On a different note, I have divined the answer to at least one mystery."

Steven stretched and joined Grey on the soft sand. "And that would be?"

"The most important question of all." Grey's eyes burned. "Why the Black are able to engage any of you at this stage of the Game."

Steven let out a bitter chuckle. "They're certainly not having any trouble doing that."

"This hunting of the White by their opposition is an abomination." Grey's voice filled with venom. "The rules governing the Game expressly forbid my interference in matters of Black and White prior to the Game proper. The fact that I've been able to find and aid you to the degree I have speaks to the deplorable manner in which the Black are conducting themselves."

"So Black is ignoring the rules," Steven said. "Not the most shocking news of the day."

"It is more than that. As Zed, myself, and the remaining seven of our order created this Game, the rules of most import were the ones that ensured play, regardless of the outcome."

"Because if the Game isn't played, badness happens, right?"

"Indeed. All of us agreed that prohibition of any contact between Black and White prior to the ordained time was out of the question—much, I suspect, to Zed's chagrin."

"Then how are they doing this?" Steven asked. "They've been all over us."

"That is the missing piece. Other than the *Hvitr Kyll*, no other way to locate you and your brethren prior to conscription exists, yet somehow Zed has become privy to your identities."

"And if we're not yet a part of the Game, all bets are off." Steven's gaze fell. "Damn."

"Our enemy's newfound prescience adds a dangerous wrinkle to an already tenuous situation. For the Game to legitimately replace the bloodshed of the previous arrangement, it had to be more than just a ritual. The war before you is real, and each of your lives along with those of countless others are on the line. Zed has been patient for centuries, but now that it is upon us, it seems he will stop at nothing to gain the power of this correction."

"So, all the others are basically walking around with targets on their chests and if I don't get to them first, they're dead." Steven rose from the sand and stared at the growing number of stars in the eastern sky.

"Steven?" Emilio ambled over, Lena and the white stallion close behind. "Not that we have much of a choice, but Lena and I have been talking. As crazy as all this sounds, we're in."

Lena stepped up and took Emilio's hand in hers. Her fingers trembled, and Steven didn't think it was merely the cool night air. "I don't think we'll ever feel safe again unless we see this through to the end. At least with you guys around, we've got a chance." She bit her lip. "We are going to get through this, aren't we, Steven?"

Steven laid a hand on Lena's shoulder. "If I've got anything to say about it."

"Don't worry, *mami*." Emilio wrapped his arms around Lena from behind and pulled her close. "You've got me watching out for you."

"So, what do we do now?" Lena searched Grey's eyes for an answer.

"Wait for morning," he answered. "Rest. Prepare." Grey looked back over his shoulder as the sphere of fireflies dissipated, returning the beach to darkness. "And pray."

## 16

## INTERLUDE

The darkened room was silent save for the occasional footsteps that echoed down the adjacent hallway. Scant illumination seeped in from the space around the door, the rectangular eclipse maintaining the room in a twilight state. A hospital bed projected into the center of the room, the gentle rise and fall of its occupant's chest the only visible movement.

A darkened television was bolted to the ceiling in the opposite corner, a silver Zenith label at the bottom of the set barely visible in the low light. A corkboard on the wall bore dozens of cards filled with well wishes and prayers. The flowers in the vase on the bedside cart were wilted, a day or two beyond their prime.

The sleeping form shifted under the covers and then sat bolt upright and eyed the door. The man's dark skin blended with the shadows of the room, though his wide eyes and silver mane betrayed his position. A quiet titter escaped his lips that evolved into a throaty laugh.

"It seems I have visitors," he mused to himself in lilting, laughing tones. The hoary fellow pulled himself upright, sat on the edge of the bed, and stared in the direction of the hallway, his head cocked to one side. After several seconds, the heavy door flung itself open. Backlit by the setting sun of some faraway desert landscape, one shadowy form and then another strode into the room. The door closed itself quietly behind them and one of the overhead fluorescent bulbs flickered to life, shedding wan light on the man's after-hours guests.

The tall, slender man in the lead adjusted the waistcoat of his finely tailored black suit while the striking woman in the full-length black gown and stiletto heels looked around at the lime-green paint of the walls and sighed.

"What is this place?" Disgust dripped from her voice.

The man in the bed chuckled. "My current living arrangements, unfortunately."

The woman flinched at the words, not having registered the man's presence.

"I do not, however, intend to be here much longer. As a matter of fact, I'm quite certain my soon-to-be associates will be along to pick me up any day now." Rising from his bed, the bent figure approached the man in the black suit.

"I see you've brought Her Highness with you this time. You hoping the old man might spill a little more information if provided with some proper eye candy?" The silver-haired man emitted a muffled cackle as he openly looked the woman up and down.

The woman in black clenched her fists but her well-dressed companion calmed her with a raised hand and subtle shake of his head.

"As you are no doubt aware," the man in the black suit said, "the White Pawn and Knight have each managed to elude us despite our best efforts. No doubt their power and experience grows with each moment they are free. Your visions so far have been more than accurate, my jovial friend, but their proximity to the events in question has made it difficult for us to capitalize on that knowledge."

"My visions? You blame the visions for your abject failure? Ha! The Pawn is indeed resourceful and the Wizard, as you know, has a wisdom born of personal experience, but that comely wench standing there should have had no trouble taking out one lone man.

"As far as your other agent goes, he couldn't manage to kill two oblivious teenagers when presented with a clear shot at their collective backsides. I think your minions concentrate a bit much on show-boating, and not enough on getting the job done. Now, the Pawn is armed, they have the boy, and he has drawn the lance. He is selecting a steed as we speak."

"Again," the man in black said, "events in the now are of little use to me."

The silver-haired man ambled over to the opposite wall, shaking his head in simultaneous laughter and mock disappointment. "As the good Dr. Bersholtz keeps telling me, I really think you should look inward for the root of your problem." He spun around, sat on a plush armchair that rested in the corner of the room, and crossed his arms. His teeth gleamed, a Cheshire smile.

The man in black seethed, but maintained a cold monotone. "I am more than aware of the shortcomings of my varied associates. They both followed their instructions to the letter, but lacked sufficient initiative when their initial efforts were thwarted. I have already expressed my displeasure with their performance."

"We will not fail you again, your Highness." Despite a hint of deep purple evident below her eye, the woman's icy stare betrayed no emotion.

"So, old man," the man in black continued, "where is the quartet now?"

"What does it matter? They are, for the moment, beyond your reach. Tomorrow, on the other hand, they seek their Queen. You will find them where she lies." The old man looked off into space at some-thing apparently only he could see.

"And where might we find the White Queen?"

"I've been unable to isolate her position as I did with the others. An aura of uncertainty surrounds her, an ambience of death. I get the impression from what little I have seen that she is quite ill and not long for this world. Her own body kills her from within. Why the Game has chosen such a person is beyond me, but in this case, the woes of the world are apparently doing your job for you. I can tell you she's somewhere in the west. I see a small range of mountains, three to be exact, but that's all I can say. Return in the morning, and I may have more to tell."

"What of their Rook?" the woman asked.

"Oh, he is a strong one."

Without warning, the sarcastic tone disappeared from the old man's voice, replaced with conviction and fire. "The Rook will not fall. Do you hear? The Rook will not fall." This other person stared at the pair in black for a moment before his face resumed its baleful sneer.

"Whoops, did I say that?" The man brought his fingers to his mouth and rolled his eyes in mock embarrassment. "I swear, sometimes it's like somebody else is trying to speak."

"And what of the good Bishop?" the man in black asked with a hint of amusement.

"You needn't concern yourself with him," spat the old man. "We're like this." He brought up his right hand, his index and middle fingers interposed to form an X. "The old fool can't even muster the will to squirt in the toilet without my say so. Continue with your plans, and I will continue to hold your ace." He turned his attention back to the woman in the black dress. "Now, if you'll have Her Majesty venture on over here. I'd like to see if this old body still has what it takes."

The woman raised a toned arm and pointed an outstretched finger at the silver-haired man's mocking smile. Before she could utter a word, the man in black grasped her elbow from behind and ushered her toward the exit. He gestured with his free hand, and the solid wood door again swung open of its own accord. The pair stepped through the open portal and vanished, the old man's cackles echoing in their ears.

A few moments later, a middle-aged woman in blue scrubs popped her head through the open doorway and scanned the room. "Everything okay, Archie? I thought I heard something." The woman smiled kindly as she helped the elderly gentleman back into his bed.

"I'm all right, Gladys." Frailty not evident moments before colored his words. "Just another bad dream." His long sigh ended in a yawn. "Would you bring me some water, please?"

"Sure thing." She grabbed Archie's cup and headed for the sink in the corner. "You know, two days from now is our open house visitation and you'll likely still be with us. Do you have anyone coming to see you?"

"Actually, Gladys, I am expecting to be quite busy with visitors that day." A glint of anticipation flashed across his eyes, a stark contrast to his feeble tone. "Perhaps you could help me tidy my room tomorrow."

"Be glad to." Gladys finished tucking the old man back into his hospital bed and took a moment to stroke his silver hair before heading back down the hall. She flipped off the light switch, exited the room, and closed the door behind her with a quiet click.

Archie lay in the dark, staring at the checkerboard squares of the drop ceiling. A rueful expression crossed his weathered face. "Quite busy, indeed."

## 17

# DOOR

Gathered around the flickering fire, Steven, Grey, Lena, and Emilio talked well into the evening. The events of the day remained the focus of discussion, though as the night passed, the quartet made the first tentative steps toward becoming more than strangers stuck in the same foxhole.

Raised by his brother after his mother died a week before his tenth birthday, Emilio Cruz had excelled in high school despite every disadvantage. Finishing in the top ten percent of his class and having made All-State in wrestling his junior and senior year, he was headed to the University of Maryland on a four-year scholarship. More impressive than his accomplishments, however, was the young man's humility. At every turn, he downplayed his own talents and accomplishments and steered the conversation back to the beautiful girl shivering next to him.

Lena Cervantes was Emilio's opposite in many ways. Born into a wealthy family in Madrid, Lena had come to America when she was sixteen to spend a year with her aunt and uncle in Baltimore. Steven marveled at her spotless command of the English language.

Her initial dismay over going to a public high school vanished as she entered her first day of US History and caught the eye of the

junior wrestler in the fourth row. She and Emilio had been insepa-
rable since, and she had even convinced her father to allow her to stay
in the States a second year so they could finish high school together.
Her story reminded Steven of another first meeting, a bittersweet
memory he quenched before it could fully infiltrate his thoughts.

Through the evening, Steven kept any revelations about his
personal life succinct and avoided the painful topic of Katherine
completely. Instead, he worked to keep the focus on the issue at hand,
gleaning every bit of knowledge possible from his cryptic mentor.

Lena sat in rapt attention as Grey recounted a brief history of the
Game. Emilio, on the other hand, spent most of the evening cracking
jokes and seemed far more interested in the rumblings of his stomach
than in the rumblings of any coming struggle.

Just after midnight, Grey's jovial tone faded as his discussion of the
Game came to the third iteration. Growing silent, he stared up at the
red planet that glared down from above.

"What is it?" Steven asked.

"It is time for you three to go. You are all hungry and tired and will
need rest and sustenance if you are to succeed tomorrow."

"Why now? What's happened? What aren't you telling us?"

Grey remained silent and continued to stare solemnly into the
night sky.

"I take it we're on our own again, then." Steven made no effort to
hide the frustration in his voice. "How long are you going to stay gone
this time?"

"I thought you understood, Steven. At this stage, I am forbidden to
interfere."

"Bullshit. You've been interfering since you pulled me out of that
club."

Grey's eyes grew dark. "An intervention made necessary by Black's
misconduct."

"So Black can flaunt the rules but we have to obey? That's crap."

"Nonetheless, it is my decision to make." Grey met Steven's gaze,
the fire in his eyes fading into sadness. "The only decision I can make."
Turning away, he clicked his cheek, and the wandering stallion
cantered back up through the surf, whinnying as the cold water

splashed up on his legs. Grey waited for the horse to join them and then turned to Lena.

"There is one last piece of business before I go. Lena, your weapon, if you please." He gestured to the aluminum bat lying half-buried in the sand.

Lena recovered the battered remnant of Emilio's days in T-ball and held it before her.

"The pouch, Steven, if you will." Grey's voice barely rose above a whisper. "Miss Cervantes' cudgel may serve her well against the street gangs of Baltimore, but in the days to come, she will need something with a bit more 'oomph,' I believe the expression goes."

Steven loosened the pouch from his belt, his irritation replaced by renewed wonder as he opened the leather bag to again find the mouth pulsing, the white iridescence growing in brightness with every beat.

"Wait," Lena said. "I can't…"

"Don't worry, Lena," Steven said. "Emilio and I have both reached into the light and made it through."

Lena trembled. "What do you want me to do?"

"Put the bat into the pouch." Steven held the pouch before her. "See what happens."

"Yes," Grey said. "Let it bathe in the White."

Lena took a deep breath and dipped the bat into the shimmering light, jumping as if she'd grabbed a live electric wire. She slid the entire length of the bat into the small opening until her right arm was imbedded up to the elbow in the warm glow of the pouch. Her entire body stiffened and her expressive brown eyes grew wide with surprise.

Emilio took Lena's hand. "What is it, *mami?*"

"It's impossible." Lena withdrew her arm from the pouch's glowing mouth, her hand clad in a gauntlet of finely wrought platinum chain-mail and the bat replaced with an enormous mace. The weapon's handle fashioned of the same bright, poplar wood as the pike, its triangular tip possessed the dull luster of the lance's platinum surface. The mace hummed quietly as Lena passed it through the air before her, her slender arms wielding the massive bludgeon with ease.

"Grey," Lena asked, "what does this mean? Am I—"

"Lena, my dear, it is clear you and Emilio are meant to walk this path together, and even more clear you would never leave his side regardless. If you are to face the coming struggle with the others, it is only proper you be given implements to defend yourself."

Lena tensed. Until that moment, she had shown little consideration for her own safety, having been far too preoccupied with worry over Emilio. Now, she studied the ground at her feet, her previous aura of confidence absent. For the first time since Steven first laid eyes on her, she appeared very much a scared, seventeen-year-old girl.

"Now, now, Lena," Grey said, "do not be afraid. I have seen your steel, and though that mace may feel foreign in your hand now, I assure you when the time is right, you will more than rise to the occasion."

Grey brought Lena and Emilio close. "You two must complement each other in the coming days if you are to survive. The reach of the lance coupled with the power of the mace is a combination few can best."

As Lena and Emilio absorbed his words, Grey turned from the fire and walked toward the ocean. Steven joined him down the beach a ways at the edge of the undulating surf. As his feet touched the ocean foam, Grey spoke again, his usual timbre hushed and reticent.

"Steven, you face the most dangerous of days. The Game proper is almost upon us, and I cannot imagine the lengths the enemy will go in the coming hours to prevent you from obtaining your Queen. The White stands not even half assembled, and while our young friends by the fire are brave and true, they are both so very young. Watch after them. Prepare them. Lead them."

Steven nodded solemnly. "I will."

"Know the three of you will never be far from my thoughts." Grey peered up again at Mars the Warbringer. "If all goes well, you should have your fourth by nightfall tomorrow. However, never forget you are navigating uncharted territory. Though our enemy seems limited in their ability to scry our comings and goings, they are not to be underestimated." Grey rested a hand on Steven's shoulder. "Take care, Steven, and let the pouch take you where it will."

The pair gazed out over the dark ocean waves for one last moment before Grey turned inland. Stopping only briefly by the fire to say his goodbyes, he marched for the forest, his vague outline fading into the dense foliage. As he disappeared from view, a silver flash revealed the silhouettes of dozens of horses interspersed among the trees.

*Have they been here all night watching us? Maybe even watching over us?*

He rubbed his eyes in disbelief and when he looked again, only the shadowy outlines of the trees remained.

Steven rejoined Lena and Emilio at the fire. "Well, here we are." He flashed them a smile as he exuded every bit of confidence he could muster.

"Where did Grey go?" A hint of panic colored Lena's tone.

"He had business to attend to." Steven shook his head, attempting to hide his frustration. "He does that, I'm afraid."

"So, what do we do now?" Emilio asked.

Steven heard an echo of himself from the morning before in Emilio's plaintive question. "That's what we've got to figure out and fast."

Emilio crossed his arms. "I say we start by heading back to the mainland like the man said. I'm starving, and Lena's been shivering since the sun went down."

Steven agreed and reached for his belt, stopping mid-step as his fingers touched the pouch's silver cord. "There's no door." He searched Lena's questioning eyes. "When traveling via the pouch, I've always used a door. I'm not sure I know how to get us back."

Standing beneath the dark sky, Steven reviewed with Lena and Emilio everything he'd learned over his various mystical jaunts. His analysis was embarrassingly short.

"So," Lena said, "if this entire island is centered on one of these crossing things, the spot where we first appeared must be the place, right?"

"I suppose so," Steven said. "That doesn't solve the door problem, though. Even if it's there, I don't know how to access it."

"We'll never find out sitting around here, now will we?" Lena stepped away from the dwindling fire. "Emilio's not the only one who's hungry enough to eat a horse."

The white stallion whinnied from beyond the flickering light.

Emilio stroked the horse's broad neck. "Don't worry, fella. She didn't mean that."

"Shall we?" Lena made her way back up the beach, retracing their steps in the dim light of the crescent moon. Emilio soon joined her, leaving Steven alone by the fire.

He let out a laugh. "And I'm supposed to be leading them."

The three of them cast about for the better part of half an hour, retracing various trails of nearly invisible footprints in the sand, many of which had been obliterated by the thousands of hoofprints that divided the beach north and south. The previously lukewarm gusts from the ocean grew colder as the night went on, turning the already dismal evening into a shade above miserable. Steven's mind had begun to flirt with hopelessness when a shout from Lena drew him and Emilio to her side.

Three distinct sets of footprints all converged on an unspoiled strip of sand not far from the edge of the trees. Steven brought out the pouch and held it over the intersecting footprints. Its low hum rose in volume almost imperceptibly.

"You're right, Lena. This is the spot." Steven smiled, relieved. "So, any ideas?"

Lena thought for a moment before answering. "These crossings have been around pretty much forever wouldn't you think?"

Steven knelt by the intersecting footprints. "I suppose so."

"Then it makes sense the doors aren't the important part. It's the place."

"Maybe it just needs a little push." Steven crossed the air above the undisturbed sand and waited. The pouch's monotone hum grew louder, but other than a brief gust of wind whistling through the nearby trees, nothing changed. He tried again and met with similar results.

"Nothing's happening. I don't feel anything." Steven threw up his hands in exasperation. "If I can't figure this out, we're stuck."

"We're not stuck," Emilio said. "You're just doing it wrong."

"I'm doing the best I can here." Steven looked up at Emilio and tried to keep the exasperation from his voice. "Have you got a better idea?"

"Coach Henley taught us something last year. He called it visualization."

"Tell me more." Steven's knuckles went white around the neck of the pouch.

Emilio knelt next to him. "He said if you want to win on the mat, you have to win in your mind first. Before he'd let us face another wrestler, he'd have us play out every hold, grab, and move in our heads. We had one hell of a season." Emilio sat on the cool sand. "Does that help?"

"Can't hurt to try." Steven focused his mind on the image of a door and unwound the pouch's knotted silver cord. In his mind's eye, he turned the knob on the imaginary portal as his fingers opened the pouch's mouth wide. This time, it responded. The muted hum escalated into the familiar pulsating drone and the open mouth shimmered with silver-white radiance. In answer, the ground at their feet shimmered with light, the eerie luminescence in the shape of an eight-pointed star.

The wind picked up, whistling louder and louder above their heads, though the air between Steven and his companions remained quiet and still. Steven's eyes blinked closed for a moment, and when they opened again, an ornate double door of dark wood and wrought iron stood in their path, its lower edge transecting the glimmering figure in the sand. At least eight feet in height and six across, it reminded Steven of the entrance to a grand cathedral.

"Can you two see it?"

"The glow?" Lena asked.

"No. The door. Big as life and standing right in front of us."

The two of them stared at him, their expressions bordering on incredulous.

"Never mind. Bring the horse. We're getting out of here."

Lena clicked her tongue twice and the horse cantered over to her side. She stroked his flank and led him over to Steven.

"Steven," Emilio asked, "are you sure about this?"

"As sure as I am about anything." Steven smiled at Emilio. "All right. You came up with the way off this rock. Where do we go next?"

Emilio ran his fingers through the white stallion's mane. "That thing can find a horse on an island in the middle of the Atlantic Ocean. You think it can find us a Motel 6 and an IHOP?"

## 18

## ROCINANTE

Oregon. *I'm standing in Oregon.*

Steven stood at a crossroads next to a large boulder with the words "Welcome to Sisters" etched in the stone. Emilio and Lena stood off the pavement next to their newly claimed white stallion. The horse stood unfazed by their recent translocation and chewed on the uncut grass of the low shoulder. Through the morning haze, Steven could just make out a distant road sign with the mileage to Portland. The city lay far north and west of their current location, opposite the rising sun peeking above the backdrop of evergreens.

"Looks like we walk." Steven motioned to Lena's sandals. "We'll see if we can't get you some better shoes."

A quaint little burg, Sisters was the sort of place Katherine would have loved to explore. The siren call of the small town had always been her weakness, a penchant Steven had learned first to accept and then to adore. A pained smile crept across his face, a memory of a night stranded at a little motel south of Gettysburg crossing his mind. How a night that started with a dead alternator could have turned out so perfect was beyond him.

The pouch remained silent as Steven and his entourage moved

farther into town. The multitude of restaurants and gift shops on either side of the main strip suggested the chief business of Sisters was tourism. Lena spotted a building less than a block off the beaten path with a sign that said "Information Center." A refurbished house with a screened-in porch and a pair of wooden rocking chairs, the center was closed, which didn't surprise Steven in the least. By his best estimation, it was around 6:30 in the morning, west coast time. Fortunately, the maps posted on the outer wall were more than sufficient for their needs. The Three Sisters, a range of volcanic mountains to the west for which the town was named, were prominently marked on a larger map of the region, along with several other local points of interest.

"Population's around two thousand," Emilio said. "This shouldn't be too bad."

"I don't know. Places like this tend to be pretty spread out, not to mention tourist towns do tend to attract tourists." One of the myriad of brochures in the wall dispenser listed the catchment area for Sisters at around ten thousand people, and Steven guessed that didn't include out-of-towners. "Get ready you two. Our Queen could be anywhere."

That morning, Steven had awakened with a start, his dreams a swirl of dark arrows and flames that burned black. A beam of sunlight filtered in between the closed curtains, transecting the darkness of the room. Lena lay crashed out on the adjoining bed while Emilio dozed in the chair by the door. Steven's first instinct was to grab the boy and shake him awake. They had agreed to sleep in shifts, with Lena taking the first, Steven the second, and Emilio the last.

*Like Emilio could've done anything if they'd found us.* Steven's resignation at their situation brought cold comfort, but did put some perspective on the situation. At eighteen, the boy had likely been through the worst twenty-four hours of his life and deserved some slack.

Steven crept to the back of the small hotel room and flipped on the bathroom light. He barely recognized the exhausted face that stared back from the mirror's scratched surface. He rubbed the sleep from his bloodshot eyes and splashed some water on his face. The digital clock between their beds read 7:10 and a peek out the window at the relatively undisturbed parking lot suggested theirs was not the only party sleeping off a long night. Steven opened the window to let in the cool Pennsylvania morning air and a moment later, the sound of stirring brought his attention back to the room. Emilio stood by the chair, wide-eyed and panicked.

"It's all right, Emilio." Steven raised a hand. "It's only me."

"Steven, man, I'm sorry. I must've dozed off. It's only been a few minutes and—"

"Don't worry about it," Steven said. "We all got some sleep and made it through to morning none the worse for wear."

Emilio's furrowed brow broke into an expression of relief.

"Now, if you'll keep an eye on Lena for a few minutes, I'm going to get cleaned up."

Steven took a quick shower, the water turned up as hot as he could stand it. The few extra moments it took to shave away the day and a half of coarse stubble from his face made him feel at least moderately human again. He slid back into his sweat-stained T-shirt and jeans and stepped out of the steamy bathroom into the dark chill of the air-conditioned motel room.

"So, who's next?"

He was greeted with silence, the room abandoned, but with no sign of a struggle. Steven fished the Pawn out of his pocket and held it up for inspection. The absence of all but the faintest glimmer from its polished surface put his mind at ease, but only a bit. He slipped on his shoes, grabbed the room key, and bolted for the door, but stopped short at the sound of the doorknob.

"Who's there?" he grunted, freezing in his tracks.

"It's us, Steven." Lena's voice was sweet relief. "Sorry. We didn't mean to scare you. We went to check on the horse." The two teens entered and closed the door behind them.

For the second time in less than an hour, an almost paternal ire rose in Steven's throat. "You've got to let me know if you're going to vanish on me, understand? A lot is riding on us keeping it together and…" Steven paused. "What is it? Did something happen?"

Emilio jabbed his thumb at the door, the dumbfounded expression on his face mirrored in Lena's eyes. "You're going to have to see this to believe it."

Lena and Emilio led Steven down the stairs to the parking lot and around to the back of the hotel where they bedded down the white stallion the night before.

"Where's the horse?" Steven asked.

"Over here." Emilio led Steven over to a fenced off area containing three green dumpsters, the closest thing to a stable they had been able to find the previous night. Steven followed them inside and the cause of their awestruck expressions became apparent.

Between the second and third dumpsters where they had left the horse now rested a motorcycle, a machine like none of them had ever seen. Longer and more massive than Emilio's red Honda, the bike's trim was pearly white. The morning sun glinted off the engine's highly shined chrome. The headlight shimmered with a piercing silver-white luminescence while the quiet purr of a well-tuned engine emanated from its gleaming twin mufflers. The handlebars swept back in a form reminiscent of a crescent moon with a V-shaped projection situated near the right handgrip. A running stallion in bright silver above nine letters of gold adorned the main body of the motorcycle.

Emilio's face broke into a wide smile. "Now that's what I'm talking about." He paced excitedly while Lena stared at the letters inscribed below the image of the horse

"What does it say?" Steven asked.

"Rocinante." Lena's face was a mask of wonder. "That wasn't there before."

"Rocinante?" Steven asked. "Does that mean something to you?"

Lena smiled. "It's from Don Quixote. His horse was Rocinante." She ran her fingers along the gilded lettering. "Papa read it to me when I was very young, and it kind of stuck. He used to claim our family was related to Cervantes, though I've never been sure it that was just a joke. My brother and I would ride around on his back and

146

knock down make-believe windmills and giants." A tear rolled down the girl's cheek. "Papa doesn't even know where I am. I'm sure my aunt and uncle have called him by now. He must be so worried."

"Lena, you know I'll do everything in my power to get us through this." Steven wiped away her tear. "We'll call your dad as soon as we can afford the time. Believe me. I want all of us to see our fathers again."

"All right," Lena said. "As soon as possible, right?"

"I promise," Steven said. "So what do you two make of the motorcycle?"

"And where did the horse go?" Lena turned to Emilio. "We left him right here."

"It may sound strange," he said, "but I think the motorcycle *is* the horse, or at least how we're seeing him right now."

"The horse…" Steven said dubiously, "is now a motorcycle."

"Come on, Steven." Emilio stroked the cycle's chrome handlebar. "You walked around my *barrio* dressed like you stepped off the set of *Braveheart* and no one even batted an eye. This isn't all that different, is it?"

"Makes as much sense as any of this." Steven slid his hands into his pockets and let out a sigh. "So, why don't you take the bike out for a spin and see what it can do?"

Needing little encouragement, Emilio mounted the bike and gunned the throttle. The motorcycle answered with a guttural roar. Lena squealed, leaped on behind Emilio, and wrapped her lithe arms around his broad chest. Before Steven could say another word, Emilio gunned the motor and peeled out of the parking lot.

"And it's not even 8 a.m.," Steven mused as he watched the pair speed away. "Can't wait to see what the rest of the day brings."

After a quick breakfast at the local Pancake King, a transcontinental jaunt through the front door of an abandoned warehouse left the foursome roadside just west of the small town of Sisters, Oregon. Upon their arrival, Emilio asked Steven if he thought the motorcycle would need fuel, only to have Rocinante resume his equine form and start munching on the unmown grass between the guardrails. Now, the noble stallion sat outside a diner on Sister's main strip resting in mechanical guise, while his three companions sat inside discussing the day's strategy.

"Any thoughts on how to proceed?" The three of them had canvassed the streets for hours with nary a sound or flash of heat from the pouch. The town bustled as noon approached, and Steven felt certain they should have at least crossed paths with the Queen at some point. "I'm open to suggestions."

"I don't know," Lena said. "How did you start when you were looking for us?"

"Like this. Walking where the crowd took me. The two of you basically found me. It wasn't easy keeping up with you, but at least I'd seen what you looked like."

"I still don't see why you don't have that bag of yours take us right to her." Emilio ran the cool bottom of his glass of soda across his sweaty brow.

"I tried that two hours ago, remember? The pouch left us in the same spot we were. As best I understand it, this is where we're supposed to be."

"At a diner in Podunk, Oregon? Awesome." Steven couldn't fault Emilio's frustration. Four hours of pounding the pavement with nothing to show for it left all of them on edge.

"You three ready to order?" The waitress' nametag read "Liz" surrounded by a red oval. "We're running a special on the patty melt combo plate today, if you're so inclined."

"A burger and fries will be fine." Emilio smiled. "Hold the onions."

"Same," Lena said.

Steven offered a tired smile. "Make that three."

"Boy, somebody took the wind out of all of your sails," Liz observed. "Are you visiting from out of town?"

Steven took a sip of soda and answered. "Actually, yes. We arrived this morning. We're supposed to meet a business associate here today."

"In Sisters?" Liz asked. "Most people from around here head up to

Portland for that kind of thing. What in the world brings you all the way down to our flyspeck of a town?" Liz eyed Lena and Emilio, and Steven could only imagine what thoughts were crossing her mind.

"I work for an employment agency based out of Chicago," he said. "Emilio and Lena here are two of our summer interns. The boss wanted me to bring them along to meet our client and get a feel for our service approach."

"Huh. So, who are you meeting?" Liz asked. "I know about everyone in town."

Before Steven could formulate an answer, Lena jumped in. "We're actually meeting them halfway. Our company is out of Portland and our client's coming from farther south."

"That makes sense. Anyway, worse places you could end up." Liz turned back to Steven. "So, any jobs out there for someone with a master's in art history? I tried one of those job.com websites a few months back, but you see what I'm doing." Her gaze wandered to the blue sky just outside the window. "I guess an advanced art degree doesn't take you very far these days."

"Depends on if you're looking in the right places." Steven made a mental note to thank Lena for the distraction. "Tell you what. I'll leave you a card. I'm kind of busy for the next few weeks, but you could give me a buzz next month and we'll see if we can't work something out." He took a quick breath, silently hoping to still be alive to take the call. "Sound good?"

"That'd be great," Liz said. "So, where are you staying?"

"We just got into town." Steven was curious how long this game of twenty questions was going to last. "We haven't exactly found a place to stay yet."

"Well, good luck finding a hotel this weekend. Summer Festival is going on down at the park, and people are in from all over. Most of the bigger places have been booked up for weeks."

At her words, and so subtly Steven almost believed he imagined it, the pouch pulsed.

"Y'know, Liz, I've changed my mind. I think I'll have the special after all." Steven shot Lena and Emilio a knowing look. "So, what's all this about a festival?"

Liz turned in their order and then deposited herself at their table for a good quarter hour, waxing nostalgic about the annual Sisters Summer Festival. The telltale heat at Steven's hip let him know they were finally on the right track. Half an hour later, they rose from the table, left a generous tip, and headed for the door.

"Well, you two, I think it's clear where we go next." Steven smiled with renewed vigor. "Looks like the whole town's going to come to us."

❦

S teven, Lena, and Emilio found their way to the park and circulated among the hundreds of people milling from stall to stall. With only the one pouch among them, they initially stayed together, but after an hour, Lena convinced Steven a three-way search could increase their chances of finding this needle in the haystack. Despite their best efforts, though, their search remained fruitless for most of the afternoon.

Around three-thirty, Steven spotted Emilio meandering through the crowd with what appeared to be a reasonable candidate. Dressed in a green formal and sparkling tiara, the reigning Miss Oregon Teen USA seemed quite taken with the young wrestler.

Despite his disappointment at the pouch's continued silence, Steven couldn't help but smile watching Emilio hang on the beautiful girl's every word. After a few minutes of patter about upcoming pageants, however, Steven was ready to move on. Surveying the crowd, he caught Lena's gaze as she rounded a nearby hot dog stand, and answered her silent question with a subtle shake of his head. Empty-handed but not defeated, she made her way over and draped her arm around Emilio's shoulders. The boy looked as if he had been awakened from a very pleasant dream.

"Any luck?" Lena asked with only the slightest bristle in her tone.

"Uhh... no, not really." Emilio motioned to the girl in green. "This is Amanda."

The young blonde offered her hand, her perky smile undaunted by

Lena's intimidating stare. "Hi. You must be Lena. Emilio's been telling me all about you."

"That would be me." Lena took the girl's hand and gave it a brisk shake. "Nice to know I was on his mind."

Amanda's gaze danced back and forth from Emilio to Lena. "Well, it was great meeting all of you," she said, stepping away, "but I've got to get back. I'm doing a ribbon cutting at four and then I've got a dinner reception at six."

"Well." Lena made no attempt to hide the scorn in her eyes. "Good luck with all that."

With a bemused furrow of her brow, the lovely young girl waved goodbye and wandered down the crowded path. Emilio raised a hand to answer but drooped under Lena's withering stare until she let him off the hook with a mischievous half-smile.

"Down, boy," she said. "You're not in trouble, but you were working on it."

"But I was just looking for—"

"It's all good, *papi*," Lena said. "She's not the one, though, and we've got to keep searching." Lena shot a sidelong glance at Steven and her smirk morphed into a mischievous grin. "Let's just let *Steven's* pouch do the thinking from here on out."

By five-thirty, the festival crowd began to dissipate. Most of the stalls and shops were closing down, and a not so distant cousin of outright panic nipped at Steven's mind.

What if their failure to find the Queen meant she'd already been found?

Though he'd been on the lookout for any sign of the Black since their arrival in Oregon, the icon had remained dark. Not even the slightest twinge of pain had interrupted the day. Still, Steven couldn't get over the distinct feeling they were being observed. An ominous whisper at the edge of his consciousness prompted Steven to remain on guard, though after such a nothing of a day, his constant warnings to Lena and Emilio to stay cloaked seemed almost silly.

Almost.

"I guess today's a bust." Emilio plopped down at a picnic table and grazed on some curly fries. Steven and Lena joined him. Fatigue showed on all of their faces.

"I'm wiped out," Lena said, "and we've got nothing. Nothing to show after a whole day of this. What are we supposed to do now?" Her despondent tone mirrored Steven's mood.

"Honestly? I have no idea. I don't know what I was expecting today, but I sure thought we'd come out the other end with at least a clue of what to do next. You're both right, though. The day is shot. Any suggestions?"

Emilio inhaled to speak, the words catching in his throat at the pouch's sudden hum.

Steven surveyed the area. This section of the festival was essentially vacated. The food vendors had closed up shop more than half an hour before, the huge midday crowd had dwindled as the afternoon played itself out, and the few people remaining appeared to be saying their farewells or heading for their cars. The only person in their immediate vicinity was an older gentleman, probably in his mid-seventies, with enough insulation around his midsection to keep him warm through the long Oregon winters.

Dressed in a green and white polo, tan pants, and a black baseball cap, the old man squinted through thick spectacles. Moving from table to table, he deliberately cleared them one by one before wiping them down. A slight limp affected his every step, but the man carried himself proudly. His meandering path eventually led to their table, the low hum from Steven's right hip growing louder with his every step.

Steven rose to meet the fastidious old man, motioning for Lena and Emilio to stay put. Each step toward the groundskeeper brought another pulse from the pouch, the volume crescendoing from a hum into a low constant moan. As he came close enough to read the man's laminated identification card, a familiar searing heat flashed at his hip. A wash of welcome relief passed through his body.

*Bingo.*

The old stranger in his pressed clothes and Coke-bottle glasses gave off a rare warmth. The badge at his collar showed a grainy photo and the name Woody, a pin on his shirt denoted this was his fourteenth year with the local park service, and the man's well-worn cap identified him as a veteran of the Korean War. Steven's mind tripped through the myriad of stories his own grandfather had told for as long as he could remember and wondered if Woody and he had ever crossed paths.

"Pardon me, sir?" Steven said.

"Yes?" Woody peered at Steven through his thick trifocal lenses. "Can I help you?"

"Actually, I was wondering if we might help you. My friends and I were getting ready to leave and noticed you had quite a few tables to go. Mind if we lend a hand?"

"Y'know," the old man chuckled, "most days I'd turn you down flat. The fresh air and exercise is good for these old legs. I'm pretty worn out today, though." He smiled the smile of a man with no regrets. "Have at it."

Steven introduced Lena and Emilio and then let Woody rest his feet while the three of them made short work of the remaining garbage. In no time at all they were done and joined Woody around the rectangular table. The old man grinned and gave them a jaunty salute.

"I sure appreciate you kids helping me out. My feet were already on fire. Without your help, I would've been out here another hour at least."

"Our pleasure." Lena smiled, the weariness of the long day banished from her features.

"No problem." Emilio stared down at his wristwatch, the fingers of his other hand drumming on the tabletop.

"Thanks to you three," Woody said, "I may get to eat dinner with my granddaughter. If she's up for it, that is. She doesn't have much of an appetite these days."

"Why?" Lena asked. "Is she okay?"

Woody's grin faded into a resigned grimace. "Actually, no." He cleared his throat, though the emotion in his voice did nothing but escalate. "She hasn't been okay for a long time."

"Sir," Steven asked, "sorry if I'm intruding, but what's wrong with her?"

Woody paused, studying Steven's face for a moment. "Leukemia," he said. "The bad kind. Well over a year now. It's down in her bone marrow and the chemo's not cutting it anymore. Last appointment, her oncologist gave her maybe a couple of months." Woody choked up. "Hell, I always figured they'd have to get hospice to come take care of this fat old man, not Audrey. She was such a beautiful girl, and that damn cancer has eaten her alive."

"The doctors can't do anything for her?" Emilio asked.

"They've done all they can. She went into remission for a while, but a few months ago, the cancer came back even worse than before. The last round of chemo made her so sick and the doctors said it wasn't working anyway, so Audrey asked if she could go home. For the last few days, she's done nothing but lie in her bed and wait to die. Have you ever had to watch someone you love wither away?"

Far from the strange sensation that hit him when the opposition was near, the pang in Steven's chest was one with which he was intimately familiar. He struggled with what to say to the grieving old man when Lena, tears coursing down her face, wrapped her arms around the old man's neck and gave him a peck on the cheek.

"Thank you, child." He smiled at Lena with grateful eyes. "Sorry I'm so broken up today. It's been a hard few weeks."

"No problem." Lena said. "I wish your granddaughter all the best."

"Thank you." Woody checked his watch. "Well, it's getting late." He rose and turned to go. "Need to go see if someone can give me a lift over to my daughter's house. Thank you all again for your help and for listening to an old man's ramblings."

Emilio put his arm around Lena's waist. "Our pleasure, sir."

Woody shook his head and let out a rueful laugh. "Enjoy life while you're young, kids. Once they take your license, it's over." With that, he shuffled back toward the road, stopping briefly to retrieve his cane from the next table. As he rounded the corner of the path and out of sight, the pouch at Steven's side fell silent.

"The pouch has spoken." Steven turned to Emilio. "Catch up to him and don't let him out of your sight."

"I'm on it." Emilio headed toward the parking lot where Rocinante lay in wait.

"Maybe we can pull this day out of the fire after all." Lena turned to follow Emilio.

"Hey, Lena?"

Lena glanced back across her shoulder. "Yeah?"

"That was beautiful," Steven said. "You really connected with him. With Woody."

Lena shrugged, an innocent smile breaking across her face. "He needed someone to care about him. I'm someone. Simple as that."

"Simple as that." Steven shook his head. "Good to hear it. Now, go on. If you hurry, you can catch Emilio before he takes off."

Lena raced up the dirt path after her boyfriend, leaving Steven alone for the first time in recent memory. His mind reeled from the events of the previous two days, like a boxer between rounds waiting for the next ring of the bell to signal the pummeling about to start anew. For the moment, however, their path seemed clear.

He hadn't mentioned it to Lena and Emilio, but the pouch had flashed white hot when Woody mentioned his granddaughter's name. Though he couldn't imagine how a girl on her deathbed could possibly have a role in Grey's great Game, his gut told him she was the one.

*What was it the old man said? What was her name?*

# 19

## AUDREY

A grand window graced the front of the two-story house, the fading blue of the Oregon evening sky reflected in its burnished glass. Proud but not pretentious, the magnificently constructed home had easily seen four generations pass its massive front door. Lena and Emilio stood silent beside him, studying the enormous conglomeration of grey stone and burgundy brick. Set back in the woods at the end of a quarter-mile cobblestone driveway, the grand edifice was surrounded by dozens of great oaks and poplars, some of which must have predated even the earliest pioneers. The highest branches of these silent sentinels swayed to and fro in the early evening breeze as if beckoning the weary travelers to come closer.

Amaryllis fluttered and scratched at his breastbone.

*Or waving us off in warning.*

An overpowering sadness emanated from every aspect of the house's architecture and landscaping, as if the venerable old home lamented a lost love.

Other than a hint of light coming from one of the many second-story windows, the entire house was dark. The lawn sat overgrown and many of the potted plants on the porch desperately needed water.

Branches cluttered the roof while leaves and twigs clogged the overflowing gutters. Closer inspection revealed three stones missing from the chimney and a broken window crudely repaired with a piece of cardboard. The only audible sound other than the wind whistling through the surrounding trees was the pulsating drone of the pouch that crescendoed as they approached the covered front porch.

"This is the place?" Steven whispered, despite the fact the three of them stood alone in the home's enormous front yard.

Emilio nodded. "Lena and I saw Woody's friend drop him off at the top of the drive."

Steven stretched out his arm, holding the pouch before him, and was answered with a high-pitched whine and a flash of heat. "Our Queen is here." He clutched his side as an all too familiar sensation gathered in the pit of his stomach. "And she's not alone."

He retrieved the pawn icon from his front shirt pocket and found its subtle glow had returned.

"I feel it too," Emilio said, not that he needed to. The pain blossoming in Steven's side was mirrored on Emilio's face. Even Lena's features exhibited some signs of strain.

"What do we do now?" She bit her lip, but maintained her composure.

"Let me try something." Steven held the pawn icon before him and willed it to transform into the shield and his normal clothing into the garb of the Pawn. As expected, the pain in his side evaporated. The gnawing sensation at the pit of his stomach, however, remained, and with it the assurance the Black were close.

"The pain is the Game's way of telling us to suit up and get ready. Give it a shot."

Lena focused for a moment and the mace appeared in her hand, its silver sheen growing with each passing second. Emilio closed his eyes, took a deep breath and held out his arms, muttering hushed words under his breath. The lance appeared in one hand, the shield on the opposite arm, followed by helm and breastplate. In the blink of an eye, the high school senior was gone, replaced by the armored form of the Knight.

"All right, guys. Keep your eyes and ears open. Be ready for anything. These bastards have beaten us to the punch again, and if we can sense them, they can sense us. We have to assume they know we're here. This girl's life is on the line, and we're all she's got. Ready?"

Lena and Emilio nodded in unison with only their eyes betraying their brave facade.

"So." Steven turned to face the darkened house and grimaced. "Any thoughts on how we play this?"

Steven approached the house alone, still dubious about their thrown-together plan of action. Stepping onto the front porch, he rapped three times on the front door. The pouch continued to drone away, a pulsating hum that escalated quickly into a grating whine that made his teeth ache. That, coupled with the knot in his gut caused by the sure proximity of the Black, left him ill. The better part of two anxious minutes passed before footsteps sounded from within. The deadbolt turned, raising the hair on Steven's neck, though the response seemed silly when he saw the face peering out from the cracked door.

"May I help you?" Beneath the chain, a disheveled woman in her late-forties eyed Steven with a weary gaze. Her voice, on the edge of hoarseness, still conveyed the refinement of someone who was no stranger to the local society page.

"My name is Steven Bauer. I'm an old friend of your daughter."

"Steven?" What he could see of the woman's brow furrowed. "Huh. I don't remember meeting you before. Do you know Audrey from Stanford?"

"Yes, ma'am." Steven hoped his eyes wouldn't betray him. "We were in a few classes together freshman year. I recently found out about, you know, what's going on with her." He smiled innocently as lie after lie passed his lips. "May I come in?"

"Of course." The woman took a deep breath and unfastened the chain. "Please, come in and have a seat."

Despite her unadorned face and tousled hair, Steven caught a glimpse of the woman's intrinsic elegance shining through, though the strain of caring for an ailing daughter had clearly taken its toll. Her gaunt cheeks and poor color indicated she wasn't eating well while the purplish bags beneath her weary eyes suggested countless sleepless nights. Still, she managed a kindly smile as she showed Steven into a front sitting room.

Even from Steven's limited vantage, it was obvious housekeeping around the old home, much like the keeping of the grounds, had been relegated to the back burner. One of the bulbs in the ceiling fixture was burned out, leaving the room in a half-dark twilight state. Stacks of half-opened mail littered the floor of the cozy sitting room. A layer of undisturbed dust covered the coffee table between them, a testament to time spent on more important things.

"I need to let you know, Steven, she's not doing well." She cleared a stack of magazines from a plush armchair and motioned for him to take a seat. "Not well at all. I'm actually surprised you dropped by. Most of her other friends stopped visiting over a month ago. Most can't bear to see her this way. I'm not sure how close you two were, but you may not recognize her the way she is now. Make sure you're ready before you go in."

Wiping away a tear, she sat on a couch opposite Steven. "Don't get me wrong. It's good you're here. You have no idea how much it lifts her spirits when she sees familiar faces."

Steven let out a quiet sigh. He couldn't be less familiar if he tried.

As Audrey's mother continued to vacillate between pleasant reverie and poignant tears, Steven barely paid her any mind, his thoughts occupied by one simple fact. Though quelled by his use of the Pawn icon, the twist in his gut that signified the Black presence was still present and growing stronger by the minute.

*What are they waiting for?*

Some framed photos on the wall caught Steven's attention. In the upper left corner was a picture of the woman who sat before him, albeit with a few less years and infinitely less worry etched into her features. Next to it hung a faded picture of a teenager in bell-bottoms hugging a man who had to be Woody in his prime. Other family shots hung from the wall as well, all surrounding a portrait of a young woman. Steven rose to examine the picture.

A pair of kind hazel eyes stared out at Steven from behind the glass, the girl's oval face framed by long locks of curly, auburn hair. Fine freckles decorated her cheeks and nose and her naturally full lips stretched wide in a jubilant smile.

"Audrey," Steven breathed.

"Yes. That one's a couple of years old now, but it's still how I think of her. So happy. She doesn't have much to smile about these days, but she still tries." Shuffling footsteps to his rear tightened the knot in Steven's stomach. He whirled around, ready to face whoever or whatever was coming, and for the second time in as many minutes, felt quite silly.

"Hey, Dad," the woman said. "How's our girl doing?"

"About as well as can be expected," Woody answered. "The nurse is almost done in there and, oh... Sorry, you've got company." He eyed Steven, a flash of recognition crossing his features. "Wait a minute." Woody crossed his arms, sending Amaryllis fluttering at Steven's chest. "You're the young man from the park."

"Yes, sir." He stood and extended a hand. "Steven Bauer."

"Steven's an old friend of Audrey's from Stanford," the woman said. "He's in town and dropped by to visit."

"Huh. I wish I would've known who you were." Flustered, Woody's face went red. "I would've invited you back with me and... Wait, that doesn't make any sense. When I told you about Audrey, you acted like you'd never heard of her before. What's going on here?"

"Now, don't get all paranoid, Dad," Audrey's mother said. "I'm sure Steven has a perfectly good explanation. He's been nothing but pleasant since he got here."

The old man bristled for a moment, but quickly calmed. "You're right, Deb. Sorry, Steven. It's been a long day, and I haven't had dinner yet. You know how it goes." Woody sat by his daughter. "I think the new nurse from hospice is going to work out. Audrey really perked up having someone more her own age to talk to." He let out a mischievous chuckle. "Plus, she's a lot easier on the eyes than the last one, that's for sure."

At Amaryllis' sharp pinch, a cold realization shot through Steven like a bolt of lightning. "The nurse. She's new?"

"Umm, yeah," Deb answered. "Today's her first day with us. She said Audrey's usual nurse had come down with pneumonia and that she'd be filling in."

"What does she look like?" Steven already knew the answer.

"Young, attractive, brunette. No more than a few years older than Audrey." Alarm blossomed on Deb's face. "Why are you asking?"

"No time to explain. Where is Audrey's room?"

"But—" the mother stammered, her eyes wide with fear.

"No time," Steven said. "Tell me where she is."

"Down the hall, last door on the left, but I don't understand—"

"Last on the left. Got it. Now get out of here and take your father with you. I don't have time to explain, but trust me. It's not safe in here."

"But what about—"

"I'll get Audrey. I promise." Steven summoned the shield. "Now, run."

Steven launched himself down the darkened hallway, the shield's radiance growing in magnitude with each hurried step. The dark scintillation coming from beneath the last door on the left confirmed his worst fears. He rushed the door, lowering his shoulder to knock it down, and was hurled back by the dark energy as if he'd grabbed a live wire. He got back to his feet and brought the pike from wherever it resided when not at his side, but the confined quarters left him little room to move.

"Lena!" Steven's call was answered with the rhythmic patter of sprinting sneakers. The girl was by his side in seconds. The head of the mace shone like a small sun in the dim hallway.

"Move." Lena swung full force at the door, the head of the mace disappearing in a burst of silver-white light. Despite the thunderous force of the blow, however, the door held fast. The shimmering sparks from the impact scattered along the obsidian glimmer of the door's surface like skipped stones across a pond. Lena's second swing produced similar results. Her frantic eyes met Steven's. "What now?"

"Aim here." Steven pointed to the wall adjacent to the door. "The darkness doesn't seem to extend past the doorframe."

Lena moved two steps to the right and brought the full force of the mace to bear against the adjoining section of hallway. The resultant thunderclap shattered the dry wall and timbers, leaving a gaping hole in their place.

His ears ringing from the impact, Steven had but a second before a jet of black fire shot from the jagged breach like flames from a dragon's dark maw. Before he could think, he shoved Lena out of the way and brought up his shield. Surrounded in a silver-white glow, the ebon flames rushed past his body like the roaring current of a diverging river. Engulfed but unharmed, Steven advanced on the jagged opening.

"All right, Lena. Back outside." Steven's voice grew quiet. "You know what to do."

"But—"

"No arguments." Steven pointed up the hall. "Go and make sure everyone else is out."

Lena sprinted back through the flames toward the front of the house and Steven turned back to the gaping hole in the wall.

*Looks like it's down to her and me.* Steven dove into the breach. *Again.*

As his feet found purchase on the other side, Steven crouched behind the oblong shield and took in his surroundings. The entire room ablaze, black flames licked across the ceiling, cascaded down the walls, and jetted across the room's hardwood floor. The flickering darkness cast a deep purple hue throughout the space and made the dimensions of the room inscrutable. At the center of this ebon inferno rested a scorched hospital bed and its lone occupant.

*Audrey.*

Barely visible through the conflagration, the young woman lay writhing under a single white sheet, her eyes clenched in terror. Black flames like writhing stalactites stretched down at her from the ceiling above and licked hungrily at the bedclothes from below. And there, perched by the head of the bed like a venomous serpent waiting to strike, stood the Black Queen.

"You know, Steven, we've really got to stop meeting like this." She shot him a wicked grin. "People are going to talk."

Steven took a step toward the bed, and the Queen touched the obsidian orb at the tip of her scepter to Audrey's temple.

"Now, now, little Pawn, you've proven to be quite formidable, but you're a fool if you believe you're fast enough to keep me from splattering her brains all over the wall."

The girl's sobs, just audible over the crackle of the flames, sent Steven's heart racing.

"All right," Steven said. "I get it. You're in charge here. You win." He peered out from behind his shield and the Queen stroked Audrey's cheek with the serpentine scepter. "What I don't get is why you've left the girl alive. What are you waiting for?"

"You watch too many movies, Steven. The whole reverse psychology ploy is a bit played, don't you think? Never fear. She will die, and soon."

An icy fist gripped Steven's heart at Audrey's terrified moan.

"As for why she's still breathing, it's very simple. The powers that be frown upon engagements between the White and Black prior to the start of play. You and your friend with the horse are therefore off limits, at least for the time being. However, if one or both of you met your end during the performance of my assigned task, it might simply be chalked up as one of those unavoidable consequences of playing our little Game."

The Queen raised her arms in a sweeping conductor's gesture and the dark flames engulfing the room rose around them. "Do you now understand, Steven Bauer?"

Another sweep of the scepter and a shimmering plane of black energy formed in the breach Lena left in the wall, blocking Steven's only avenue of escape. The heat around him doubled in intensity, rendering impotent whatever protection the shield afforded him. Worse, as tongues of flame danced close enough to scorch but not to burn, a simple fact became apparent.

The Queen was merely toying with him.

"Why so shocked, Steven? Did you think that scrap of metal there could protect you from me?" Cruel laughter echoed in the room. "I'm the Black Queen of this Game, you idiot. Your recent run of luck aside, you're still nothing but a Pawn."

She cast her malevolent stare on the girl's trembling form. "You know, I've changed my mind." The Queen ran her taloned fingers along Audrey's wasted cheek. "I think I'll let you watch her burn."

The edges of Audrey's bed, which had been smoldering since Steven entered the room, burst into flame. Fire nipped at her toes, bringing a hoarse scream from the girl's lips. Her knees curled up to her chest in a futile effort to escape the scorching heat. Steven's clothes and hair singed as the dark inferno rose around him.

*Come on, Emilio, where are you?*

An engine roared to life outside the room's bay window, its high whine just audible over the roar of the dark conflagration. Distracted but a moment by the sound, the Queen raised the bejeweled scepter above her head and a maelstrom of ink-black flame roared down from the ceiling and engulfed the bed.

"No!" His scream drowned out by the crackle of the flames, Steven slipped the shield from his arm, willed its form small and circular, and hurled it at the Queen. Like a giant discus, the shield's glowing platinum passed through the fiery funnel of dark energy, dissipating the flames for a moment. Before she could move, the shield smashed into the Queen's chest and sent her reeling into the far wall.

Not wasting a second, Steven rushed to Audrey's side and snatched her from the burning bed. As his fingers touched Audrey's charred skin, the searing heat at Steven's hip doubled in intensity. The pouch emitted a pulse of such volume, Steven's teeth shook in his head.

*No doubt about it. She's the one.*

The girl's emaciated body weighed less than ninety pounds. Her mottled scalp was hairless, most likely an effect of the cancer treatments, and the rest of her was little more than skin and bone. Each shallow breath appeared to hurt worse than the one before, the burns to her chest and flanks no doubt mirrored inside her lungs as well. As he studied the wasted features of Audrey's face, the girl's eyelids fluttered open, and though nothing else remained of the girl in the picture, her hazel eyes were unchanged.

*She's so far gone. How can she be the Queen?*

Her gaze distant, the confused gratitude in Audrey's eyes shifted back to terror. "Behind you," she croaked as loudly as her scorched vocal cords would allow.

Steven whirled and dove behind the charred remains of Audrey's armoire, narrowly avoiding a jet of black flame meant to immolate them where they stood.

The Black Queen laughed. "You're such a glutton for punishment." She leveled her scepter at Steven's chest. "To hell with Zed and his stupid rules. I'm going to enjoy this."

Audrey squeezed Steven's neck with all the force her wasted body could muster.

Trapped, Steven mouthed a desperate prayer to a deity he hadn't spoken to in years. "God, if you're listening, don't let it end like this." He met the Queen's gaze, refusing to let her see fear in his eyes. "Not like this."

At the Queen's silent command, the inferno engulfing the ceiling whirled like a dark cyclone, flowing down into her scepter in a vortex of ebon fire. Audrey buried her face in Steven's chest as her would-be rescuer cast about the room for anything resembling cover. He spied the glow of his shield no more than ten feet away. Resting at the Queen's feet, the metallic disc may as well have been on the moon.

"Now." The serpentine eyes of the Queen's scepter glowed deep violet and a column of jet-black flame erupted from its fanged mouth. Steven clenched his eyes shut and spun around in a last ditch effort to shield Audrey's body from the brunt of the firestorm.

A firestorm that never came.

Just audible above the crackling flames, the gentle purr of a motorcycle's engine filled the room, punctuated by the occasional staccato rev of the motor. Glancing across his shoulder, the scene before him exceeded his wildest imaginings.

Amid the blazing remnants of Audrey's room rested Rocinante in all its chrome-plated glory, its dazzling gleam at odds with the paradoxical darkness of the surrounding flames. Astride its shining pearl and silver body perched Emilio, his combination of street clothes and armor a peculiar sight. Though the lance was nowhere to be seen, in its stead rested an enormous double-edged axe Steven had difficulty believing Emilio could even lift, much less wield. The full-length shield on the boy's arm somehow repelled the Queen's fiery onslaught, though bitter experience had taught Steven she would only be balked for a moment.

"So," the Queen said, "you brought your Knight as well. We weren't sure if you would be so foolish as to throw one even less ready than yourself to the wolves. No matter. At least now we won't have to search him out ourselves."

"Don't listen to her crap, Steven," Emilio said. "I've got this. Get the girl out of here."

Steven rushed for the only viable exit from the room. The large bay window, obscured by smoke and flames, somehow remained intact despite Emilio's grand entrance. He raised his foot to kick out the glass but held back as the entire window lit up with a familiar silver-white glow.

"Close your eyes." Steven threw himself atop Audrey's emaciated form. No sooner had they hit the floor than the glass shattered inward with a thunderclap roar.

"Come on," Lena shouted from outside. "I'm not sure how long Emilio can hold her." A second swing from her mace finished the window and its frame, the resultant gouge large enough for two to climb through.

Steven cradled Audrey tight in his arms and leaped through the jagged opening and out into the twilight grey of early evening. As his feet hit the ground, he looked back, a cold question filling his mind.

*Did I just sacrifice my Knight to save my Queen?*

"They're out, *papi*," Lena screamed to Emilio over the pulsing of the pouch and the din of the inferno. "Get out of there." The girl's frantic tone sent chills up Steven's spine.

"Lena, we have to go." Steven made his way toward the front of the house with Audrey clinging weakly to his neck. "You can't imagine what she's capable of."

Audrey's bay window opened onto a gently sloping hill, terraced and planted with shrubs. No doubt a beautiful work of landscaping, the half-light of an Oregon forest at sunset transformed the woodland yard into an obstacle course. Even without Audrey's ninety pounds of dead weight, the going would have been difficult and slow. As he neared the front of the house, Steven turned his ankle on an exposed root and went to one knee, cursing as he fell.

"Steven?" Audrey whispered through a peal of hacking coughs. "That's your name?"

"That's it." Steven grunted as he regained his footing. "Are you making it?"

"What is all this?" Another fit of coughing. "Why is this happening to me?"

"No time to explain. Right now we've got to get you far away from here."

"But what about Mom? Grandpa? Are they okay?"

"We made sure they got out safe." Steven prayed he was telling the truth. "Right, Lena?"

Steven chanced a look back. There, outside the shattered bay window, Lena stood defenseless, mace by her side, her panicked face illuminated by alternating flashes of light and darkness from within.

"Lena," he shouted. "Come on."

"I can't." She stepped closer to the gaping hole. "Emilio needs me."

The hair on Steven's neck stood on end as a stray bolt of dark energy flew from the shattered window, missing Lena's head by inches. Unfazed, Lena wrapped her fingers around the splintered remains of an exposed wall stud and hauled herself up.

"Stay out of there," Steven yelled. "If you give her the chance, she'll kill you."

Fear flashed across Lena's features for less than a second, followed by the resolute stare Steven already knew all too well. "Go on without us," she shouted as she climbed through the open hole and into the dark inferno. "Get her out of here. We'll catch up when we can." And with that, Lena disappeared into the fray, leaving Steven and Audrey alone in the shadowy twilight of the Oregon evening.

"Dammit." Steven froze for a moment, unsure of what to do and cursing himself in the same breath for his indecision. "She's going to kill them."

Amaryllis fluttered at his neck.

"What now?" The frantic scraping above his collarbone brought a new sense of dread. Steven glanced down at the dragonfly on his chest. "What is it you're trying to tell me?"

"Steven?" Audrey whispered.

"What?"

Audrey winced at Steven's harsh tone. Though at the end of his patience, he hadn't meant to yell at the poor girl.

"Sorry," he said. "What is it?"

"Just a question." Her gaze shot past Steven. "Is *he* with us?"

# 20

# FLIGHT

*So, you brought your Knight as well.* The Queen's words echoed in Steven's mind.

At the center of the cobblestone drive, astride an armored stallion the color of midnight, waited a figure ripped from the pages of James Clavell. Outfitted head to toe in the traditional garb of the samurai, the Black Knight sat calmly with his hands in his lap, his swords still within their sheaths. His features hidden behind the grimacing mask of a kabuto helmet, he hailed Steven with a simple nod.

"Greetings, Steven Bauer, Pawn of the White. Greetings, Audrey Richards of Sisters, Oregon." Something in the way the Knight spoke fell strangely on Steven's ears. Though his meaning was clear, the sound, structure, and syntax were all wrong.

"I think he's speaking Japanese," Audrey said, confirming Steven's suspicions. "I heard him say our names, but that's all I could catch. Do you understand what he's saying?"

"I understand him all right." Though the language was foreign and harsh, he somehow understood every word. Steven put Audrey down and moved between her and their mounted foe. "I understand him fine."

"Surrender the girl, Bauer-Pawn." The dark samurai's impassive voice chilled Steven as much as the Queen's venom. "The time for Black and White to face each other has yet to come, but understand we will not be balked in this. Give her to me or face the consequences."

Steven glared up into the Knight's face, the dark menpó mask leering back beneath the tripartite crest of his helmet, a pair of hawks facing each other over a familiar horse icon. "You don't seriously believe I'm going to hand her over, do you?"

"Actually, no, but I was required to give you the option." The samurai shifted in his saddle and placed his hand on the hilt of his katana. "Shall we?"

Steven locked eyes with Audrey, his questioning gaze answered with a firm nod. "I don't know what you're seeing, but this is no ordinary man we're facing. He's—"

"I wear no cloak, Bauer-Pawn. She sees me as I am."

"The girl is already dying." Steven's eyes narrowed. "What more do you want?"

"A duel, then." The samurai evinced a slight bow. "Knight versus Pawn for the girl."

Steven pulled Audrey's ear to his lips. "I'll do everything I can to get you out of this."

"I know," she croaked. Somehow through her fear and pain Audrey managed a smile, and despite her withered features, the expression was beautiful. "Now, kick his ass."

Steven turned and faced his opponent. At his subvocal command, one became eight. Audrey gasped as seven armored warriors appeared in a flash of silver and again as Steven's clothing shifted to match the newcomers' anachronistic garb. The seven formed a tight circle around her and Steven's position while the samurai sat motionless atop his steed and studied the circle of Pawns, their helms, pikes and shields gleaming in the twilight.

"You four," Steven commanded, "go check on Lena and Emilio. The rest of you are with me." The quartet to Steven's rear moved out as the remaining triad stepped up to form a defensive line, the glimmering heads of their pikes all converging on their foe's dark mount.

"Your move," Steven said, all emotion stripped from his voice.

The Knight responded with a brisk salute, and disappeared from sight only to reappear to their rear. Before Steven could react, the samurai jerked Audrey from his arms and draped the girl's frail form unceremoniously across his steed's broad withers.

"A novice mistake, Bauer-Pawn." The samurai and his mount retreated into the forest. "In this Game, the battlefield is rarely linear. You must learn every aspect of both your Pieces and those of your opponent, or your cause is lost before you even begin."

Steven and the trio of Pawns spun around to charge their enemy, but before any or them could take a step, the Knight drew the shortest of his three blades and rested its edge under Audrey's chin.

"Your attack is ill-advised," the dark samurai continued in his bizarre monotone. "Regardless of the overzealous actions of my esteemed colleague, our only goal is to keep this young lady out of the Game. Rash action on your part, however, could force my hand." He drew the tanto's gleaming blade closer to Audrey's throat. The quartet of Pawns held their position.

"She won't be harmed," Steven said. "Your word."

The horse continued to back into the forest, the calm in its master's gaze in stark contrast to the wide-eye panic in Audrey's.

"I cannot speak for the King, but trust that unnecessary bloodshed is not on my agenda today." The Knight brought his horse about to depart. "Farewell, Bauer-Pawn. We will meet—"

The Knight's parting remark was cut off mid-sentence by the blunt poplar of a polearm thrust from the darkness. Nearly unseated from his perch, the winded samurai brought his horse around to confront his attacker, only to find the unaccounted for Pawn in mid-leap and coming fast, the spear-axe tip of a pike whistling toward his neck.

The Knight raised the tanto in defense and a moment later howled in pain as the gently curved dagger flew from his hand. Crimson blood spurted rhythmically from the stumps of his severed second and third digits. The horse reared, its flailing front hooves knocking the offending Pawn to the ground, but it was too little, too late.

Though the only head lost belonged to one of the hawks of the samurai's helmet crest, Steven's mad gambit had worked.

*Thank you, Lena Cervantes.*

Inspired by the girl's surprise attack on the Black Queen in Baltimore, Steven's thoughts went to her and Emilio. Kaleidoscope images of the other fight flashed across his mind's eye via the perception of the remaining three Pawns. Emilio was holding his own against the Black Queen, but only by the narrowest of margins. The flashing blade of his axe kept her physically out of range while the shield on his arm blocked the innumerable fiery tendrils that threatened from all sides.

Lena on the other hand was nowhere to be seen, a fact that left Steven with a ball of ice in his chest. As his remaining triad of emissaries joined the fight in his mind, he forced the images away so he could focus on the issue at hand.

*Hold on, Emilio. I'm coming.*

Steven charged the rearing horse, leaping at its wounded rider. His grasping fingers found purchase around the front of the saddle as the horse bolted away at a full gallop. The Knight pummeled away at Steven's grip with his bloody half-fist as his other hand, still intact, guided the panicked animal through the rushing forest. The merciless buffeting of his unguarded hands, along with the wrenching strain on his shoulder with each gallop soon proved more than he could bear. Steven prepared to let go his grip and face the racing forest floor when fate decided to throw a wild card.

Invisible in the wooded twilight, a low-hanging branch struck the samurai mid-chest, nearly unsaddling the dark rider for the second time that evening and giving Steven a desperately needed break. While the Knight recovered from the unexpected blow, Steven snaked first one hand and then the other across his opponent's armored legs and wrapped his bruised fingers around the hilts of the two blades tucked into the samurai's intricately woven belt.

*No way the Game will let me draw these blades, but as long as I'm holding on, he can't draw them either.*

Steven's improved grasp on the situation brought him face to face with Audrey. A clump of dark mane clutched in each of her white-knuckled fists, the emaciated girl held on with all the strength she could muster. Despite the terror and confusion, she maintained enough presence of mind to stay with the horse, regardless of the danger. Still, with each passing second, he imagined the moment when Audrey's weakened fingers would finally give out.

A pained grunt left Steven's lips as white-hot agony ran up his leg. So intent was he on Audrey's faltering grasp, he had failed to notice a cluster of jagged rocks jutting like teeth from the ground. The first caught at the toe of his shoe, nearly dragging him from the horse, while a second and third tore at his right shin like a rabid animal. The pain made his eyes swim.

"Concede, Bauer-Pawn." The Knight made a rapid course correction to the right. "Your cause is lost. Release my blades and live to fight another day. If you choose to continue with this fool's errand, it will not go well for you."

More and larger rocks blocked their path, the stony sentinels just visible in the dappled light of the rising crescent moon. Before Steven could pull himself up, a boulder struck him across the knees. His world red with pain, his throbbing fingers finally gave way, and a part of Steven welcomed the inevitable nothingness that was sure to follow.

Steven stood below a crimson sky and peered down into a vast chasm that smelled of death. Once the bed of a mighty river, only a brackish flow remained in the belly of the serpentine abyss. Thunder rolled like war drums in the distance and echoed through the gorge. A stone bridge of alternating squares of quartz and obsidian atop columns that stretched down into the dark oblivion spanned the cruel expanse, the bridge's checkered surface ending on a dark edifice that filled Steven with dread.

The black castle, its foundations rising precipitously from the far edge of the chasm, rested at the epicenter of a rising storm. The walls of the octagonal fortress, hewn from darkest granite, stood supported by eight flying buttresses, their massive span reminiscent of the legs of a colossal spider. Six towers rose from the center of this monstrosity, a cruel misshapen hand that appeared ready to wrench the very clouds from the sky. The howling winds seemed to call his name as the dark maelstrom continued to coalesce above the castle's highest spire.

*Steven... Steven...*

"Steven!"

First came searing pain coursing down both his legs. Then, a pounding headache like he'd gone one round too many in the ring. And finally, the rhythmic bounce of a rushing horse.

*Where am I?*

Steven's eyes fluttered open to find Audrey's panicked grimace set against a backdrop of rushing trees under a cobalt sky. One skeletal hand clutched the front of his shirt as the other clawed for his belt. Snared on the horse's tack, the strip of leather at his waist was all that kept Steven from falling.

Inching her trembling hand down his body, Audrey managed to get her fingers around his belt. Pulling with whatever strength she had left, tears of determination streamed down her face, the fear in her eyes melting into steely resolve.

"Let him fall." The Knight brought his mangled fist down on Audrey's flank, forcing the last bit of air out of the wasted girl's lungs. Still, she held on.

"Don't... let... go," she whispered between pained grunts.

His black steed charging onward, the Knight passed the reigns to his maimed hand and in one fluid motion drew his wakizashi. His first pass with the shorter blade a narrow miss, the dark samurai connected with his second thrust, leaving a gash in Steven's shoulder.

"Why will you not fall?" the Knight bellowed, his casual monotone at last showing signs of strain. "You must know you cannot win."

"I guess you're going to have to kill me then."

As his opponent brought the short-sword around for a third strike, Steven seized his armored wrist. Though his bruised fingers were still too numb to feel the cold steel of the samurai's gauntlet, Steven held on with a strength he didn't know he possessed. They wrestled for the weapon as the horse continued its mad charge through the forest.

Neither gave nor gained ground in their battle of wills. In the end though, neither Steven nor the Knight, nor even Audrey were the final arbiter of this struggle, but rather the splintered trunk of an ancient oak.

Knocked breathless to the forest floor, Steven watched helpless as horse, rider and girl faded into the darkening night. As they disappeared in the distance, Audrey screamed one last time, her voice cracking in terror. Even worse, the pouch was no longer at Steven's hip. Like the staccato beat of the horse's galloping hooves, the constant drone of the pouch soon faded into the gathering gloom.

"Dammit," Steven muttered as he struggled to sit up. "She's gone." The torn belt loop and twisted buckle at his waist, just visible in the failing light, told the whole story. Pulling himself half upright, he knelt by the gnarled stump and worked to keep himself from vomiting.

*They've got Audrey, God knows what's happened to Lena, and there's no way I'll get to Emilio in time. What else can—*

*Steven?* A terrified voice whispered into Steven's mind.

He leaped to his feet, his injuries for the moment forgotten.

*Audrey?* Steven asked silently. *Is that you?*

*Yes.* A pause. *I'm scared.*

*Are you all right? Where are you?* Steven held his breath, seconds ticking by like hours as he awaited an answer.

*Don't know,* the voice echoed after an interminable wait. *Trees rushing past. Dark. Please help me...*

As Audrey's voice faded into nothingness, Steven's brain went into overdrive. A quick shift of consciousness revealed the battle between Emilio, his seven Pawn doppelgangers, and the Black Queen had for the moment reached an impasse. Knowing Emilio was holding his own brought Steven some measure of relief, though one thing was clear.

No help was coming from that direction.

His icon, which had brought time to a screeching halt and enabled Steven to save Emilio from the dark archer's arrow, remained tied up in weapons resting a mile away inside a burning house. Even with the icon, Steven wasn't sure he could duplicate the life-saving jump.

*If only I still had—*

"The pouch."

Hope sprang anew in Steven's heart.

*Audrey? Can you hear me?*

Silence.

*Audrey?*

His mental cry unanswered, Steven returned to his perch on the overturned oak.

"Why me?" he shouted to the surrounding forest. "Why'd you pick me?" Steven drove his already bruised fist into the soft rotting wood. "If I can't even save one girl, how in the hell do you think I'm going to—"

*So cold... Dark... Mom...* Almost imperceptible, Audrey's scattered thoughts whispered across Steven's mind.

*Audrey.* Steven pictured himself shouting to the girl across a placid lake. *If you can hear me, let me know.*

*Steven? I thought I'd lost you. Are you all right?*

*I'm fine. Now, listen to me. Look down where I was hanging on the side of the horse. Do you see a white pouch with silver strings at the top?*

A pause. *Yes. It's hanging from one of the straps. Please, help me.*

The panic in her tone only steeled Steven's resolve.

*Listen, Audrey. You're going to be all right. I know you're scared, but you've got to keep it together if you want to make it through this. Okay?*

A pause. *Okay.*

*Good. Now listen and do exactly what I say. Got it?*

*Got it.*

*Can you reach the pouch?*

*I think so. It's barely hanging on though. If I go for it, it might fall.*

A shiver passed through Steven's body. *That cannot happen. Do you understand? The pouch may not look like much, but it's all you've got. Now, can you reach it or not?*

After another pause, Audrey answered, her tone a bit sullener than before. *I can reach it.*

Her feelings were bruised, but this wasn't the time for apologies.

*Okay. Grab the pouch, open it, and reach inside. Within the pouch rests something for you and you alone. I can't explain, but if you can get to it, everything will turn out fine. I promise.* For the second time, Steven prayed he wasn't lying to the girl. *Are you ready?*

A pause. *Ready.*

Her momentary hesitation spoke volumes, yet the sheer composure the dying girl displayed was already more than Steven could believe. He swallowed hard and then in the most confident tone he could summon, sent out one last thought. *All right. Do it.*

Steven spent the ensuing seconds cursing his ever-active imagination. *What if she can't reach it? What if it falls? What if she falls? What if—*

*I've got it Steven. I've got it.*

*Great, now open—*

*Oh Steven, I can hear it. It's singing to me. It's singing. So beautiful. So—*

Silence.

*Audrey?*

Answered only with a buzzing in his mind reminiscent of the static between radio stations, Steven sat and brooded alone in the pitch black forest. He briefly cast his mind back to the other fight, only to find Emilio and his seven Pawn brethren in retreat. His own eyes slid shut as his mind's eye skipped from one doppelganger to another, their fear the only constant.

The conflict had moved out of the burning house and into the adjoining woods, much to the Queen's advantage. Three of the seven Pawns were down, two of them weaponless and burned and the third unconscious with a cruel gash across his unprotected scalp. Emilio looked exhausted, his axe growing slower with each wide swing while the Queen appeared fresh and perhaps even a bit bored.

*I guess our luck couldn't hold out forever.* Steven focused his attention on the Pawn closest to Emilio, resolving to stay by his side at least by proxy until the end. He watched from every angle as the courageous young man on the gleaming motorcycle parried burst after burst of black flame, the Queen's attacks barely visible in the darkening twilight.

Just when it seemed Emilio couldn't hold out any longer, Steven's connection to the battle was interrupted by the sound of horse's hooves. A pale radiance filled the darkness beneath the forest's summer canopy, the quiet clip-clop continuing its slow crescendo as the forest grew brighter with each passing second.

Amaryllis remained still as Steven crouched behind the fallen oak. He scanned the ground for anything that might serve as a weapon, but a thick mist playing about his feet and ankles obscured his view. His groping hands seized upon a stone large enough to serve as a crude club. Holding it to his chest, he waited for the mounted stranger to grow close enough to strike.

"Don't worry, Steven." New to his ears, yet as familiar as his favorite song, the dulcet tones of the rider's voice filled Steven's heart with joy. "You won't be needing that."

Smiling despite the pain, Steven dropped the stone and rose to face the radiant young woman on the midnight steed. "Welcome back, Audrey."

# 21

## QUEEN

*S*he's beautiful...

Steven stared dumbfounded at the vision in white atop the samurai's dark stallion. Arrayed in a full ivory gown that shimmered silver and white in the darkness, Audrey's long legs draped gracefully sidesaddle along the horse's flank. She returned Steven's gaze, her broad smile at odds with the tears streaming down her face.

No evidence remained of the dying girl he had held in his arms minutes before. Gaunt, hollow cheeks were now full and flushed, vacant eyes now vibrant and aware, and her hairless scalp now boasted long auburn tresses that framed her faintly freckled face. The iridescent light of the Queen icon in her hand glistened off the silver and gold threads of the gown's samite bodice and danced between her eyes, those hazel eyes that held Steven transfixed as Audrey dismounted the anxious steed.

"You're... all right?" Steven asked.

"I think I'm a lot better than all right." Audrey swept her arms downward and bit her lip, cocking her head to one side. "I mean, look at me."

*No problem.* "So how did you—"

"No time for that now." Audrey wiped the tears from her flushed face. "We need to go help your friends."

In that moment, Steven knew. He wasn't sure what he knew, but he found himself filled with a sense of clarity and hope he hadn't experienced in months.

"So," Audrey asked. "This is uncharted territory for me. What do we do now?"

Steven closed his eyes, his face breaking into a subtle smile.

"Give me the pouch," he said. "If our luck holds out, we might still be able to pull this whole thing out of the fire."

Steven and Audrey's jaunt landed them just inside the front door of the Richards family home, the once noble manse a charred ruin. The ebon flames that had raged throughout the edifice now smoldered in the Black Queen's absence, ephemeral servants awaiting the return of their dark mistress. Thick, black smoke obscured every room, forcing Steven and Audrey to stay low as they felt their way down the inscrutable hallway leading to Audrey's bedroom.

As Steven had seen through the eyes of the other Pawns, the fight had indeed moved outside, leaving the bedroom a smoking ember. Taking positions on either side of the gaping hole left in the wall by Lena's mace, the pair stared out into the darkness at the veiled battle waged mere feet away. The scant light of the rising crescent moon, punctuated by the occasional glint of silver off the weapons of the White, illuminated this latest skirmish in a conflict that had lasted centuries.

Steven cast his consciousness among the other Pawns, his stomach cramping as the full gravity of their situation became clear.

The Black Queen stood triumphant over Emilio's battered form, her expression vacillating between enjoyment and annoyance as she fended off the advances of the three Pawns still able to raise arms. Emilio, his leg pinned beneath his overturned motorcycle, gritted his teeth in pain as he struggled to free his foot from the bike's dead weight. Though surrounded in flame, he remained untouched, the momentary distraction of the Pawns' renewed assault all that stood between him and fiery death.

"Even now, she's toying with them," Steven whispered. "What are we going to do when she finally cuts loose?"

"That'll be up to me, I guess." Audrey's tone was resolute, but Steven couldn't help but notice the underlying tremor in her voice. "Your friends aren't going to last much longer and that psycho bitch doesn't strike me as the type who takes prisoners. Any ideas?"

"I'm thinking. Whatever it is, we need to do it fast or... Oh God. Lena."

The spear-axe tips of a pair of the Pawns' pikes collided in midair above the Queen's head in a flash of silver. The resultant arc of energy lit up the forest like midday, the split-second flash revealing the answer to a question Steven had been too terrified to ask.

Thirty or so yards from the house, Lena's limp form lay sprawled like a discarded marionette against the base of a large pine, her neck turned at a queer angle. Steven balled up a fist and punched the smoking drywall.

"What is it?" Audrey peered out into the darkness, turning her eyes away as another flash illuminated Lena's crumpled form. "Oh my God. That girl. Is she—"

"No." Steven gathered up the shield and pike recovered from the smoke-filled hallway. "Listen, Audrey. I've got to go check on Lena. No matter what happens, stay here." The subtle glow of Steven's shield revealed the fear in both their eyes. "Not a sound, understand? Stay put, and if the Queen discovers you, run."

Audrey's brow furrowed in frustration, but her simple nod was all Steven needed to see. He brought the shield around to cover his flank and leaped through the remnants of the bay window, grunting as he landed hard on his turned ankle.

"Are you all right?" Audrey whispered from above.

"I'm fine. Now stay out of sight. I'll be right back." Keeping one eye on Lena and the other on the Queen, Steven felt his way across the uneven ground and limped to the girl's side.

"Lena?" Steven whispered into the girl's ear, gently shaking her shoulders. "Lena?" He placed two fingers beneath the corner of her jaw like he had seen on countless medical dramas and managed to find the girl's pulse. Far too fast and far too weak, but a pulse nonetheless.

He peered back at the jagged grimace the girl lying before him had left in the house's brick facade. Audrey had stayed hidden as asked. Steven attempted to broadcast the words *she's alive* over whatever mental frequency he and the new Queen shared minutes before. His mental whisper met with silence, he turned his attention back to the task at hand.

Memories from an old first aid class reminded Steven moving someone as badly injured as Lena could do more harm than good. Still, leaving her there wasn't an option. He knelt to scoop up the girl's twisted form and her chest rose and fell against his. That, along with the gentle warmth of her breath on his neck gave him no small measure of relief. He positioned the back of her head in the crook of his elbow and prayed his decision to move her wouldn't leave her paralyzed or worse.

Getting his legs beneath him, Steven edged his shoulder over to the gnarled tree and using its mass for support, came to his feet. With Lena cradled in his arms, he turned to head back toward the house when he noticed the battlefield had grown strangely quiet. The quiescent pain in his abdomen flared even as a flurry of metallic taps at his collarbone from Amaryllis let him know something had gone horribly wrong. Before he could take another breath, a familiar, mocking voice shattered the silence.

"Such a tender young thing. No business being out here among the big kids."

Steven whirled around to find the Black Queen floating in the air behind him, her feet resting on a dais of black energy in the shape of a diamond. She looked on Lena, her mercurial mien dancing between false pity and amusement.

"So, Steven," the Queen asked in singsong fashion, "where is the girl?" Steven kept his eyes fastened on the Queen's, afraid even a flicker of his gaze might reveal his entire hand.

"Don't play games with me, Your Highness. You know good and

well your Knight has her." Steven labored to keep any emotion from his face. "What are you going to do to her?"

The Queen peered down at Steven, the corners of her mouth turned down in a petulant frown. "I'm not the one playing games here, little Pawn. I lost contact with my Knight some time ago, though I'm guessing you know far more about that than you're letting on." She aimed the scepter's tip at Steven's head. "Enough with the distractions. Where is the girl?"

"I'm right here." A blinding white light emanated from the shattered bay window, illuminating the forest like a hunk of burning magnesium. An opaque white mist cascaded from every orifice of the burned-out building, spilling out onto the ground and covering the surrounding terrain in an impenetrable fog. Through clenched eyes, Steven could just make out the silhouette of a woman within the brilliant nimbus of silver incandescence.

Her hands, the focus of the blinding light, were clasped before her chest as if in prayer.

"Why do you waste your time with my Pawn and this wounded girl?" Audrey floated down from the gouge in the side of the house, her glistening gown billowing in the gentle breeze of the fledgling night. "If memory serves, you came here for me."

Her newly robust voice confident and mature, Audrey lit amid the gathering mist and brought the glowing icon to her brow. The four-inch piece of carved marble disappeared, replaced in an instant by a tiara of burnished silver and platinum.

The Black Queen seethed. "So, Steven, my Knight has failed and you have your Queen." Upon her dais of dark energy, the Black Queen's face drew down to a pensive moue. "Irrelevant. The girl is but a novice, your Knight lies trapped beneath a pile of twisted steel and chrome, and the remnants of your Pawn brethren lie strewn across the battlefield. Your cause is lost."

The corners of her mouth spread wide. The selfsame smile two nights before had filled Steven with a completely different emotion.

"You know, lady, you really need to learn when to shut up."

Steven and the Black Queen spun in the direction of the voice. His pearl and chrome steed roaring to life, Emilio leveled the lance's glowing tip at the Black Queen's midsection.

"How?" The Queen's eyes were wide in disbelief.

"Quick learner, I guess." Emilio gunned the engine and the rear wheel kicked up a spray of forest floor as Rocinante rocketed at the Queen. In retaliation, the Queen thrust her scepter at Emilio and a wall of dark flame spewed from its serpentine mouth.

Undeterred, Emilio punched the accelerator and headed straight for the heart of the dark conflagration. As the tip of the lance pierced the blazing barrier, however, the bike and its rider disappeared in a flash of silver only to reappear an instant later on their adversary's left flank and coming fast.

With no time to think and less to act, the Queen bolted from her platform of darkness, her usual poise a distant memory. She dove for the forest floor, the lance's platinum point grazing her side, eliciting a cry of pain that brought an almost guilty smile to Steven's face. The smile, much like the moment, lasted but a second.

Though winded by the impact, a tangle of brambles broke the Queen's fall, allowing her to regain her footing before Emilio could circle around for another pass. She took but a moment to check her wounded side before glaring up at Steven with eyes full of pain and rage and hate.

The White Knight's gambit done, it was the Black Queen's move.

In the blink of an eye, she was on top of Steven, her movements little more than a blur. She swept Lena from his arms and swung her coiled cudgel at his unprotected head. Steven scarcely registered what was happening before he found himself laid out on the soft pine straw and moss of the forest floor, his head pounding in time with his racing pulse.

Reaching up, his fingers found that the dripping fangs of the scepter's serpentine head had left their mark, an ugly pair of parallel gashes above his left temple. Hot blood pooling in his ear, Steven looked up into the eyes of his worst nightmare.

The Queen, injured and furious, stood above him, her scepter pointed at his head and Lena's limp form draped across her shoulder. "The archaic rules of this stupid Game may prevent me from finishing you and your junior Lancelot this night, but this *chiquita* is nothing but window dressing." The Queen looked down on Lena's unconscious face and grinned. "The Game won't miss her a bit."

Before Steven could respond, the high whine of Rocinante's engine approached from across Steven's shoulder.

"Get your hands off my girl." Emilio barreled at the Queen, the roar of the engine driving all thought from Steven's mind. "This is between you and me, bitch."

"Very well." The Queen waved her scepter at the oncoming machine like a magician's wand and the ground beneath the rear wheel erupted in an explosion of black fire, blowing the tire and hurling the rider from his seat. The chrome and ivory beast flipped end over end and came to rest at the Queen's feet.

Emilio's flight, on the other hand, came to an abrupt stop as his flailing body collided with the brick of the Richards home. The sickening crunch of impact and the sight of Emilio's limp form sliding to the ground chilled Steven to the core.

"Quick learner, indeed." The Queen turned to Steven and put on a face of mocking concern. "You know, I think he might be hurt." Her hand drifted down to her side, her fingers running along the bloody slash in her dress. "Steven, dear, if and when the boy wakes up, let him know he really should watch where he puts his pointy little stick. For him, it was but a matter of time, but the girl didn't have to die."

At the Queen's words, the dark shimmer surrounding her scepter grew in intensity. The strange white murk that coursed from the Richardson home played about her feet, a miniature sea of mist.

"Ah. Now your baby Queen wants to enter the fray." The Queen chuckled as Audrey glided across the clearing atop a lake of billowing white mist. "How predictably sad. You're all making this far too easy."

"Put the girl down." Possessed of a confidence beyond her years, Audrey's voice cut through the night. "You came here for me, not for her. Let's finish this."

"Do all of you have the same stupid death wish? No fairy godfather is coming to bail you out this time. No more hidden pieces to bring up from the back row to pull your asses out of the fire. Your Knight can't help you now, and this," she pointed a taloned finger at Steven, "this joke has already outlived any usefulness he might have once possessed. I hope you're ready, little girl, because it's down to you and me."

Audrey studied the ground at her feet for a moment and then raised her head to meet her opposite's gaze. "Are you done talking?"

The Queen gave no reply, her only response a subtle flick of the wrist that brought the scepter's serpentine eyes to life. In answer to her silent command, eight plumes of fire jetted from the ground around Audrey's feet, radiating outward like the petals of some dark flower. The eight sheets of flame rose about the White Queen, the fiery bloom blossoming in reverse, growing tighter and tighter until the girl's glowing form was enveloped in darkness.

"No," Steven cried. "Not her."

"Stop your blubbering." No more concerned than if she had swatted away an irritating gnat, the Queen returned her full attention to Steven. "Did you even dare to hope this evening would end a different way?" The Queen allowed Lena's lifeless form to slump to the unforgiving ground at her side. "Yet again, Steven, it's down to just the two of us. Now, are you going to lie there like a good boy, or are you going to force me to finish you as well?"

Steven rose to his feet. "I may go down fighting, but if you expect me to grovel, I—"

The ball of ebon fire surrounding Audrey was pierced from within by a cone of silver-white energy, the image for all the world like a shining baby bird emerging from a dark egg.

The Queen followed Steven's eyes, her smug air evaporating in an instant as the sphere of darkness shattered in a storm of silver brilliance. There at the heart of the blast, untouched by the black flames that still swept about her feet, stood Audrey defiant, her silver crown glowing like a fledgling star.

Undaunted by the sudden turn of events, the Queen's eyes fixed upon Audrey's form and a rushing torrent of dark flame followed her baleful glare. With a graceful wave of her hand, Audrey directed the mist at her feet to rise. The resultant pillar of silver fog engulfed the jet of obsidian fire like a ravenous wolf and for a moment, the Queen's face flashed with an emotion Steven never dreamed he would see there.

Fear.

"My move." Audrey held her hand before her and an orb of silver incandescence manifested above her open palm. She brought her fingers up around the bubble of force and the swirling haze at the Queen's feet answered.

Snaking tendrils of sentient mist played around her legs and feet, coiled about her midsection, and finally wound around her thin, pale neck. Bound head to toe by the whirling mists, the Black Queen tried to speak, but her best efforts produced no more than a muffled croak.

Audrey, swathed in a cocoon of silvery radiance, swept across the clearing, bringing herself nose-to-nose with her fettered adversary. "You're done here. Do you understand?"

The Black Queen stared back, the hate in her eyes palpable as a stifled moan escaped her lips. Audrey's knuckles went white, her fingers clenching around the ball of silver energy and forcing the last dregs of air from the Black Queen's lungs.

"The Arbiters have already spoken once today about your side playing out of turn. One of your Pieces has been removed from the Board. Pray they do not direct me to remove another." Audrey drew close to the Queen's ear. "Do we have an understanding?"

The Black Queen offered a subtle nod of acquiescence before passing into oblivion. Spent, Audrey released her hold on the Queen and the woman's unconscious form collapsed in a heap amid the spiraling fog that carpeted the forest floor.

"Audrey? How did you—"

"We've got to go," Audrey said. "I don't know how much time I've bought us, but I don't think the other side is going to take this lightly. Go get Emilio and bring him over here. I'll check on Lena."

The dimly lit forest spun like a carousel as Steven made his way to his feet and shuffled over to Emilio's side. In the limited light, Steven could still make out the shallow rise and fall of his young friend's chest, though the bruising about his face and the extra bend in his left arm left no doubt Emilio needed immediate medical attention.

"Emilio?" Steven shook his uninjured arm. "Emilio, can you hear me?"

A pain-filled moan escaped the boy's lips. "Lena?" he groaned.

"No, it's me, Steven."

"Where's Lena?" Blood bubbled from Emilio's mouth.

"Audrey's checking on her now," Steven said. "She's hurt pretty bad, but I think she'll be all right." He cursed himself a liar, but maintained a hopeful smile as he ensured Emilio could wiggle his fingers and toes and pulled him to a seated position.

"Did we—" A fit of blood-tinged coughing took Emilio's breath but Steven got the gist of what he was asking.

"Yeah. We stopped her. At least, Audrey did." Steven helped Emilio to his feet. "Right now, we've got to get you two to a hospital. You're both pretty banged up." He reached an aching hand up to inspect his own bleeding scalp. "Can you walk?"

"I'll try."

Steven helped Emilio to his feet, and the two of them hobbled over to Audrey and Lena.

"Lena's going to be all right, isn't she?" Emilio awaited an answer. "Isn't she?"

"I hope so, Emilio," Steven whispered. "I hope so."

# 22

# FAITH

The visitor area outside the surgical ICU overflowed with people: brothers and sisters, parents and children, husbands and wives. Steven sat on one of the plush purple couches that filled the room and watched the myriad of miniature dramas play out. To his right sat an elderly man sobbing alone with his head in his hands. To his left, a group of shell-shocked teenagers sat in a circle avoiding each other's eyes.

Across the room but within earshot, a doctor who reminded Steven of Peter Graves spoke to a family of twelve, informing them the bleed in their grandmother's head had left her with a serious neurological deficit. He didn't expect her to recover. Two broke into tears, others bowed their heads in prayer, and the rest merely stared into space as if they hadn't heard a thing.

The youngest, a six-year-old girl with curly brown hair, caught Steven's eye and waved, her ebullient grin a testament to the naiveté of youth. Steven returned her wave and managed a thin smile as Audrey returned from the snack bar with a biscuit and coffee for them both.

"Any news?" Audrey asked.

"I haven't seen the doctors yet, but I do know Emilio made it through surgery. They wheeled him back into the ICU a few minutes ago. He was still waking up from anesthesia, but he looked like he was doing all right."

"And Lena?"

"Not a clue. The doc in the ER said she didn't look good, but that they were going to do everything they could. That's the last I heard."

Though frustrated at being left in the dark, Steven couldn't fault the hospital staff. They were doing their jobs, and by every visible measure, doing them quite well. Truth be told, he was half-surprised things were going as smoothly as they were. Despite some gaping holes, the ER staff had bought their rapidly put together story about coming upon the pair at the scene of a motorcycle accident.

"It's not your fault, you know." Audrey put her hand on Steven's knee. "If it weren't for you, Emilio and I would both be dead, along with God knows how many others."

"Oh yeah, I'm a big hero." Steven rose from the couch and wandered over to the window. The large section of plate glass over-looked Roanoke and the eponymous river that wound its way through the heart of the city. Why the pouch had brought them all the way across the country to a hospital in his hometown, Steven hadn't the first clue and frankly, he didn't care.

Audrey gave Steven a few minutes of space before joining him. Together, they watched silently as the sky pinked with the rising sun.

"Better?" she asked eventually.

Steven had barely slept in over twenty-four hours, remaining vigilant through the night for even a twinge of the Black's presence. Audrey had dozed around two as Steven was in the midst of explaining the bizarre turn her life had taken. She managed a couple hours of fitful sleep before gasping awake from a nightmare filled with flames and darkness. Steven had a sneaking suspicion none of them would be sleeping well for the foreseeable future.

"It's not about me. It's about Lena. She's got to make it through this." Steven pounded gently on the window. "She's not even supposed to be here."

"From what you've told me, she insisted on staying by Emilio's side, and if Lena is anything like you described, I don't think you had much of a choice."

"There's always a choice." Steven yawned, rubbing his eyes. "On a different subject, I like the new duds. Scrubs are a good look for you." Her charred bedclothes neither functional nor appropriate, Audrey had changed into a set of blue scrubs with "Property of RMH" stenciled across the front pocket.

"One of the nurses let me borrow these. I told her my other clothes were ruined getting Emilio and Lena here."

"Smart, though with your cloak up, you could be dressed as Ronald McDonald and no one would give you a second look." Steven, like Audrey, had shifted back into what passed for normal clothes. Unfortunately, he found that while his cloak shielded his appearance from the eyes of casual onlookers, it did little to diminish the twin stenches of blood and sweat. He sniffed at his shirt and grinned. "Still, no two ways about it. We both need some new clothes."

Audrey returned his grin and took a sip of her coffee. A moment later, the ICU doors sprang open.

"Mr. Bauer?" A nurse in green scrubs stepped out of the ICU and scouted the room. "Steven Bauer?" Steven rubbed his eyes and raised a hand, waving her over to the window.

"I'm Steven Bauer."

"You two brought in the young Hispanic couple, right?"

"Yeah," Steven answered. "That's us. I saw you wheel the boy back a few minutes ago. How's he doing?"

"He's awake and his pain is well controlled, but he's got some significant facial fractures, a few broken ribs, and his left arm is in pretty bad shape. Still, he'll probably go up to the main floor tomorrow. He was asking for you."

"What about the girl?" Audrey asked.

"Miss Cervantes is still up in the OR with the neurosurgical team. Two of the vertebrae in her neck were fractured, but her spinal cord appears to be intact. With the kind of speed she must have been traveling when they went off the road, she's lucky to even be alive. Speaking of which, officially you two should have called 911 and let

EMS handle this. Between you and me, though, I think you saved that girl's life, bringing her in like you did."

Audrey returned Steven's knowing look but opted to maintain her silence.

"You said the boy was asking for me," Steven said. "Can we go back and see him?"

"Not quite yet. It's seven a.m. shift change, and his new nurse is getting report right now. She'll come and get you when Mr. Cruz is ready for visitors."

"How much longer until you know more about the girl?"

"I'm not sure, but I'll pass on to day shift you're still here. Someone should come let you know once she's out of surgery and stabilized."

"All right. Thanks."

The nurse hurried back to the ICU and Steven turned to face the window, his every breath leaving a moment of condensation on the cool glass. "So, I guess we keep waiting."

"Looks that way," Audrey said. "You know, I still think one of the doctors ought to check you out. I mean you got pretty banged up too—"

"I'm fine. Really. Never felt better." One look at Audrey's downcast expression and Steven wished the biting words back into his mouth. "Hey, I'm sorry. It's—"

"Look, Steven, I get it. Your friends are both in pretty bad shape, and it's basically all because of me. I know you didn't have any choice in the matter, but neither did I. I didn't ask to be part of this stupid Game, and I sure didn't ask to come out the other end of last night's main event untouched while everybody else got ripped to shreds."

"Audrey, I—"

"You think you're feeling horrible? This time yesterday, I was dying from end-stage leukemia. I've felt like total crap for a year and a half and was basically waiting to die. Then, some psychotic bitch comes along, does her level best to burn me alive in my bed, I get kidnapped by some freaky samurai, nearly get my throat slit, and come close to getting burned alive a second time.

"Now I'm stuck three time zones from home, my house and everything in it is a smoking ruin, and I have no idea where my family is or even if they're all right. To top it all off, I'm as whole and healthy as I've been in two years and I can't even feel good about it because some other girl is in a hospital bed instead of me." Audrey sobbed, her brave face cracking for the first time since their arrival in Virginia, and laid her head on Steven's shoulder.

His mind wrestling with a million emotions at once, Steven pulled her in tight and stroked her long auburn locks. "It's going to be okay," he murmured into her ear again and again. They clung to each other for a long moment until Audrey regained a measure of composure.

"Thanks." Audrey smiled up at Steven, her sheepish grin making his heart race anew. "So, who's Katherine?"

A fist of ice clutched Steven's heart. "Where did you hear that name?"

Audrey's eyes grew wide. "Late last night you dozed off. A few minutes, maybe. You kept moaning the name. I thought I'd ask."

"Katherine is... was my fiancé." For the thousandth time, Steven's heart froze as eighteen months of anger and self-doubt rushed to the surface. "She died a year and a half ago."

"Oh." Audrey's eyes welled up again.

"Hey. It's all right." Steven took Audrey's hand. "You didn't know."

"How did it happen?"

"It was a couple days before Christmas. We'd been out for a late dinner and were heading home around ten. I'd had a few drinks, so Katherine said she'd drive. We were almost home when a high school senior in a big black Suburban flew through a red light and hit us."

Audrey bit her lip. "Driver's side?"

Steven nodded. "She was killed instantly."

"God." Audrey squeezed his fingers. "I'm so sorry."

"Cops said the kid had a seizure. Epileptic since he was three, but hadn't had a seizure in ten years. Even took his meds that day." Steven ground his teeth. "Who the hell are you even supposed to be mad at in a situation like that?"

"Another accident." Audrey wiped her tears away with clenched fists. "You have to know, Steven. It wasn't my fault."

"What wasn't your fault?" Steven searched her eyes. "What are you talking about?"

"The samurai. Their Knight." Audrey swallowed. "He's dead."

"I kind of figured," Steven said. "Are you okay?"

Emotion choked Audrey's voice. "It was like a dream, Steven. Your voice in my head, the forest rushing by, the pouch singing to me like some kind of angelic chorus. I saw the silver cord start to slip from the stirrup and made a grab for it, but it was too far. No way I should have been able to reach it. Then, and I know this sounds crazy, I swear the pouch reached back."

"Honestly," Steven said, "after the last couple of days, that doesn't sound crazy at all."

"The Knight saw what I was doing and tried to stop me. Believe me, any issues he had about honor or keeping me alive were long gone by that point."

She passed a hand across her right side and shuddered. "He got in two mean jabs with that short sword of his. I thought I was dead for sure. I was up to my elbow in the pouch and nothing was happening. Then, as he raised the sword for a third strike, my fingers brushed something hard and smooth, like polished stone. I wrapped my fingers around it and drew the queen piece from the bag, the marble shining like a tiny sun. That's when everything changed."

"I can relate." Though scarcely two days had passed since Steven drew the pawn icon from the pouch, his life before the Game already seemed like ancient history.

"For a moment," Audrey continued, "time stood still and everything went away. An electricity ran up my arm, pulsing in time with my heart. It was like nothing I'd ever felt, yet as familiar as if I'd drawn the piece a thousand times." Audrey choked back a tear. "It was the first moment of peace I'd experienced in a really long time, but that's all it was, a moment."

"What happened?"

"The samurai panicked. He raised his sword to finish me, but as he brought the blade down, I stopped him."

"You... stopped him?"

"The mist stopped him." Audrey's eyes slipped out of focus and her voice grew distant. "One second the tip of his sword was heading for my neck, the next my body's surrounded in a cocoon of white haze and silver light. He kept hitting and hitting and hitting, but his blade couldn't get through. That's when it happened."

"Tell me."

"The same as with the Queen. The mists ran up his body, down his arms. Around his neck. I begged him to stop struggling." Audrey let out a quiet sob. "I begged him to stop."

Steven waited as she gathered herself. Together, they stared out the window, the Roanoke sky growing brighter with each passing minute. Audrey cradled her face in her hands and leaned her head against the glass.

"It was self-defense." Her head dropped. "I get that, but it doesn't change how I feel." She shot Steven a sidelong glance. "I've never killed anybody before."

"You cannot beat yourself up over this," Steven said. "You did what you had to do to survive. You know that, right?"

"I know. It's going to take some time, though." Audrey looked up at Steven, her face a bit brighter. "Hey, why don't you get some air? You've been up here all night. I can pull watch for a while if you want to take a break."

"You're sure?"

"Yeah, I've got this. Anything happens, I'll come get you. Just don't go too far."

Steven's heart skipped a beat at Audrey's winsome smile. "Sounds good. I'll go catch some morning air off the mountain." He shot her a weary two-fingered salute. "Look for me down on the ground floor if anything comes up."

Steven left the waiting area and wandered down the tiled hallway, stopping at the bank of elevators at the hospital's center. Though teetering on the edge of exhaustion, his sleep-deprived brain raced from thought to thought. Flashes from the night before competed with images of Audrey, so sad and yet so beautiful. After a brief wait, one of the elevators opened and a computerized voice stated coldly, "Ninth floor, going down." Steven boarded the empty elevator, his eyes sliding shut with the metal doors.

At first, he confused the sound with the normal hum of the elevator, but with each floor, the volume of the pouch's plaintive drone grew louder and louder. He rested his hand on the white leather and found it hot to the touch.

"Here?" Steven asked. "Now?"

The pouch pulsed, sending a charge through his body that nearly took him to his knees. The doors opened on the fourth floor and Steven stumbled out as a pair of nursing students boarded the elevator. A second pulse from the pouch confirmed another Piece was near.

The walls along the hallway bore a sickening shade of green that, coupled with the area's antiseptic stench, caused Steven's stomach to lurch. The placard above his head identified the floor as Mental Health. Down the hall to his right was another sign that read Inpatient Psychiatry. Steven made his way down the hall wondering what kind of person thought baby-puke-colored walls was the right call for the floor with all the crazy people.

Steven's reverie was cut short by another pulse from the pouch. A moment later, the heavy door that led to the inpatient ward opened, releasing a throng of figures in white coats.

Steven pulled the cloak tight about his body. None of the mob of doctors, residents, and students shuffling by seemed to take even the slightest notice of his presence. More importantly, the pouch maintained its low, monotonous drone as the entire entourage passed. Guessing the target of his search waited within, Steven rushed the doorway and slid his foot into the crack before the door could click closed.

After glancing around to ensure no one witnessed his mad dash, Steven let himself into the restricted area, marveling yet again at the power of the cloak about his shoulders. The door opened onto a common room filled with a disparate cast of characters.

In the center of the room, a fortyish appearing man with a handlebar mustache argued with one of the nurses, vehemently refusing his morning medication. A teenage girl with bandages covering both wrists sat in the corner and stared at nothing in particular. A manic-appearing woman paced the floor, giving Steven a quick puzzled look before continuing her earnest effort to wear a hole in the carpet. Fourteen in all filled the room, but not one of them elicited even the minutest reaction from the pouch.

A few feet down the opposite hallway, a young receptionist with platinum hair and a nose ring sat at the nurse station chatting on the phone while two medical students in short white coats sat behind her scribbling notes into overfilled charts. Steven drew close, but as in the common room, none of the three generated any response from his mystical Geiger counter.

"Sir? Can I help you?" The receptionist looked up at Steven from behind her red rectangular frames, one of her too-plucked eyebrows raised in a quizzical stare. Though perfectly reasonable, her question took him off guard.

"I'm, uh... looking for someone."

"Name?" she asked.

Steven was about to answer when down the hall he spotted a middle-aged man in a black shirt and priest's collar stepping out of a room. The pouch pulsed and the searing heat on Steven's hip caused him to wince.

"Ah, there he is. Thanks." Steven walked away before the receptionist could formulate a response and intercepted the priest as he headed for another room.

"Excuse me," Steven asked. "Are you the chaplain for this floor?"

"For today," the priest answered. "Chaplain Robertson is out sick, He asked me to fill in. I'm Father Hammond. How can I help you?"

Steven's ears grew hot as he put together what he needed to say.

"I'm sorry, Father. This might take a minute. I need to ask you something."

"Well, as it so happens, I'm between visits and have a few minutes right now. Would you care to go somewhere and talk?"

Steven followed the priest to a small conference room at the end of the hall and closed the door behind them. Father Hammond stayed by the door, his weathered face calm yet expectant, his expression that of a man who had taken his share of confessions. Broken only by the continued drone of the pouch, the two men stood in tense silence.

Steven searched for a way to begin. "You know, you may want to sit down for this."

"All right." Hammond pulled out a chair and motioned for Steven to join him. "So, young man, what's on your mind?"

The priest sat expectantly, awaiting an answer, an answer Steven wasn't ready to give. In his business, the cold call was his nemesis, at best a crapshoot, and at worst, a setup for failure. Convincing Emilio and Audrey of the truth about the Game had been relatively easy, considering the circumstances of each of their meetings. Pitching the Game to a Catholic priest while sitting on a hospital psych ward was a different story altogether.

Wrestling with how to begin, Steven locked gazes with the priest. "What would you say if I told you strange things are going on all around us that most people can't see or understand?"

Hammond's face shifted into a knowing smile.

Steven wished the words back into his mouth, realizing his statement was essentially the man's job description. "Sorry, Father. That didn't come out how I meant it."

"That's quite all right. It's hard to talk about the big concepts sometimes. Things happen every day that are beyond the ken of man. I certainly don't understand all the whys and wherefores of God's plan for His people, but I do believe He has a plan."

Steven sighed. "What if I told you I was caught up in something, a struggle so important it defies description and so old I believe it might even predate the church." His heart pounded in his chest. "Everything and everyone is depending on the outcome yet no one knows about it."

Hammond fixed him with an incredulous stare. "What's your name, young man?"

"Steven. Steven Bauer."

"Well, Steven, I would say you're definitely in the right place to work on those kind of issues. Which doctor is taking care of you?"

*Great. He thinks I'm a patient. Time for drastic measures.*

"Uncloak." In the blink of an eye, Steven stood revealed. His battered hands folded before him on the table, his torn clothes hung like rags from his bruised shoulders. He turned his burned, swollen face up into an ironic smile.

"Honestly, Father, I wish I was crazy. It would hurt a whole lot less."

"My God, what happened to you?" Hammond's eyes grew wide in disbelief. "And how did you do that?"

Steven spent the next while giving a chronicle of the events leading up to their arrival in Virginia. The priest's face vacillated between rapt attention and utter disbelief as Steven recounted the events of the preceding three days, his expression at times turning a bit sad as long held beliefs were inevitably called into question. At the end of his story, Steven unfastened the pouch from his belt and held it out to Father Hammond who took it from him as if it were a fragile newborn.

"The truth is, Father, I can tell you about the Game all day long, but to understand it, you have to experience it."

"What do you mean?" Hammond asked.

"I asked the pouch to take us to a place where Lena and Emilio could get help, but I think it brought us to this particular hospital for a reason."

Hammond's eyes filled with apprehension. "What reason?"

Steven closed his eyes and rubbed at the bridge of his nose. "I think we're here for you."

"Me?"

"When I first saw you in the hallway, the pouch made it pretty clear you're the next Piece to be claimed. Don't ask me to explain it more than that. If I'm right, everything will be clear very soon." Steven reached across the table, took the pouch back from the priest's trembling hand, and unwound the silver cord from the pouch's mouth.

"You reached inside and the piece was there, waiting for you?" Hammond's voice brimmed with excitement.

"That's how it happened for all of us so far." Steven handed the humming pouch back to Hammond. "I guess we'll have to see."

Hammond opened the pouch and stared into its open mouth like a child opening a gift on Christmas Day. Not wasting a moment, he reached inside for the prize awaiting him. A long couple of minutes passed as the priest ran his hand along every stitch of the bag inside and out, even turning it upside down and shaking it at one point.

After a brief pause, the priest laid the pouch on the table and looked up at Steven, his joyous expression replaced by one of defeat.

"It's... empty," Hammond said. "There's nothing there for me."

"But, that's impossible," Steven said. "I was there. I saw you. The pouch pulsed. Are you sure?"

Hammond rose and trudged toward the door. "Nothing there for me," he murmured again as he left the room. The door closed behind him with a crisp, metallic click, leaving Steven alone in the quiet conference room.

"Why did you bring us here, then?" Steven inquired of the still droning pouch. "What do you want?" Steven reattached the pouch to his frayed belt and headed back toward the nurse's desk, his mind a barrage of questions. Would Father Hammond wake tomorrow and think their encounter some strange dream? Or, would his near touch with destiny haunt him the rest of his days? Wrapped up in his own thoughts, Steven almost didn't hear the hushed voice coming from the door resting ajar to his right.

"Hey, you. Out in the hall." The harsh whisper set the hairs on the back of Steven's neck on end. "Get in here."

Steven walked to the door, knocked once, and entered to find a man at least forty years his senior lying in a hospital bed working on a half-eaten piece of French toast. His dark skin provided a stark contrast to his unkempt silver hair.

"Right floor, kid." The man coughed into his closed fist. "Wrong priest."

Amaryllis fluttered nervously at Steven's neck.

"Excuse me?" Steven asked.

The old man put down his fork and wiped his mouth.

"Hello, Steven Bauer. My name is Archibald Lacan, but you can call me Archie." The man flashed Steven a disquieting smile. "I believe you're looking for me."

## 23

## ARCHIE

Steven ventured farther into the old man's hospital room, his head buzzing with a thousand questions. An enigmatic grin upon his face, the man beckoned him to come closer, his hands and fingers gnarled with years of arthritis. The low drone of the pouch escalated with each careful step and soon attained its familiar high whine. As Steven came to the foot of the bed, the leather seared his hip. Without a doubt, he had found another of the Pieces, though Steven couldn't shake the feeling he was missing something. Something important.

"Mr. Lacan—"

"Father Lacan, but I prefer Archie. Less formal."

"All right, Archie," Steven said. "Do I know you from somewhere?"

"No, Steven Bauer, but I know you."

Steven's hand went to his pocket and gripped the Pawn icon, his eyes riveted on the old man's obscurant smile. "What do you want?"

"Now, now, you won't be needing any of the implements of your station here." The old man speared the last wedge of French toast. "Even if I meant you harm, I'm hardly a threat these days. Look for yourself. Not even a glimmer off your icon."

Steven studied the marble pawn in his hand and found only the fluorescence of the hospital lights reflecting off its polished surface. Still, a visceral sensation both like and unlike his various encounters with the Black, roiled through him.

"How could you possibly know the things you're saying? Who are you?"

"My apologies. I'm so thrilled to finally make your acquaintance, my enthusiasm has gotten the better of me. Not to mention, after the couple of days you've had, I'd be surprised if you weren't a bit skeptical. Sit for a moment and I'll try to explain."

Archie slapped an open hand on the arm of the blue recliner by the bed and though still dubious of the man's intentions, Steven accepted his offer and took a seat.

"So, you want to know how the crazy old man on the psych ward knows so much. Well, for starters, let me let you in on a little secret." Archie beckoned Steven to pull closer, feigning a quick look around the otherwise empty room for eavesdroppers. "I'm not crazy." His subsequent laughter ended in a hacking cough. "It's the visions, you see."

Archie grinned up at Steven, the crazed look in the man's eyes raising the hairs on his neck. "I see things no one else sees. Know things no one else knows. Can you imagine? For years, you dream about the end of the world, witness the great catastrophes of history, experience vicariously the various iterations of this insane Game that has taken over your life, Steven Bauer, and yet, you can't tell anyone. Who would believe you if you did?"

"Not even your fellow priests? Sounds like it'd be right up their alley."

"Truth be told," Archie said, "for a profession that deals in a lot of end of the world talk, most of my esteemed colleagues aren't all that keen on practical application." Archie laughed again. The resulting cough lasted over half a minute.

"I kept a journal," Archie continued, "studied the Scripture for anything that would bring meaning to what I had seen, but kept my tongue. Even managed to delude myself into believing the visions were nothing but dreams or, I suppose, nightmares."

"How'd you end up in here?" Steven asked.

"Over the last several weeks, the visions have been escalating. Before, they came only in the night, but as they encroached upon my daytime activities, I couldn't ignore their significance any longer. I feared I was losing my mind."

"What happened?"

"Before my recent... change in circumstance, I was the bishop of a small diocese north of New Orleans and had been invited to officiate Sunday morning mass at one of our local churches. I was finishing the homily that morning when I was hit by a vision of such intensity, it sent me staggering from the pulpit. I fell to the floor and from what I understand, laid there in front of a hundred parishioners, mumbling incoherently about kings and knights, good and evil, light and darkness, you get the picture."

"You scared the crap out of everybody." Steven smiled despite himself.

"To say the least. I understand the confessionals were packed for days."

Steven's initial apprehension waned. "So? What happened next?"

"I was admitted to Tulane for a few days. Got tested for every malady under the sun. The doctors seemed almost disappointed when they found nothing seriously wrong with me. They discharged me from the hospital, and after a few days, I tried to return to work. That's when the visions started coming daily. I couldn't function, but to be honest, I wouldn't have stayed even if I had been able to deal with the constant intrusion on my thoughts."

"Why not?"

"Around the same time, the visions shifted from rewind to fast forward. Instead of history, I started to receive glimpses of the future. Very precise, very accurate glimpses." Archie licked his lips and cast Steven a wistful grin. "Can you imagine knowing without a doubt what will happen an hour from now. Exactly what tomorrow will bring?"

"A skill like that must come in pretty handy."

"Not as much as you might think. As it became clear these weren't just dreams and I was actually predicting things to come, it occurred to me my problem might actually be a form of prophecy, perhaps a gift from God. So, as any priest worth his salt would, I brought my newfound talent to the attention of the archbishop down in New Orleans."

Steven ran his fingers through his hair. "I see where this is heading."

"He didn't know whether to call me senile or simply a heretic. Regardless, I was immediately suspended from my post. I've often wondered since then what the modern church would do if an actual prophet were to walk through their doors." Archie took a sip of coffee and cleared his throat.

"After a week, the archbishop again met with me. He'd gone so far as to discuss my case with representatives of the Vatican. They recommended I step down from my position and seek psychiatric help." Archie closed his eyes and lay back on his pillow. "Thirty-seven years, and I was out."

"I still don't understand." Steven asked, shifting the conversation in a hopefully less painful direction. "How'd you end up in Virginia?"

"My sister. Other than the job, I didn't really have anything holding me in Louisiana. The people from my local parish were very kind, but after that day, nothing was ever the same. I moved here a few weeks ago to stay with family while I figured out what to do next. Things were good for a while. The visions took a break. I wondered if maybe the Archbishop was right. Too much stress, or something like that." Archie sighed. "That's when it happened."

Archie took a breath to center himself. "My sister's grandkids decided to throw me a big party to celebrate my coming to stay with them. They called it Homecoming." Archie snorted back a laugh. "Still makes me laugh. I grew up in the bayou, Steven, and let me tell you, the mountains of Virginia are as different from southern Louisiana as anything you can imagine."

"Sounds like they were glad to have you. Nothing wrong with that."

"Oh, their hearts were in the right place, but it still stung a bit having to move after seven decades in one place."

"I can relate," Steven said. "I'm a bit of a transplant myself. I'm guessing something happened at the party?"

"The event was a huge picnic, must have been fifty or sixty people there. Family, friends, neighbors, kids running everywhere, lots of people I'd never met before. The kids were bringing out the cake when it hit me."

"Another vision?"

"The strongest one yet."

"What did you see?"

"You, Steven. I saw you." Archie's piercing gaze fixed Steven to the spot. "As plain as you sitting here next to me."

"What? How?"

"One minute I'm standing at the front table giving a speech and thanking everyone for coming. The next, I'm curled up on the floor, screaming over and over for someone named Steven to get the hell out of there." Archie laughed despite himself. "I guess Annie and Eli won't be throwing me another shindig any time soon."

"When was this?" Steven asked.

"Five nights ago. I've been a guest of this fine establishment ever since. The docs here ran all the same tests on me as the doctors at Tulane. They say I'm fit as a fiddle. Other than this stupid cough, I'm the healthiest seventy-three-year-old they've seen in a while."

"Your lungs bad?"

"No worse than anyone else who smoked their way through the fifties and sixties." Archie hawked the products of a wet cough into the cup by his bed. "Now I'm stuck down here on The Green Mile while the head docs try to figure out what to do with me next."

"The Green Mile, huh?"

"The movie was showing in the common room the night I was brought in. Name fits this place pretty well, don't you think? Especially considering my current predicament?"

"All that's missing are the bars and a trick mouse." Steven found himself warming to the old man, his initial misgivings fading into grudging fondness. "I take it you saw my first encounter with the Black Queen."

"She's cunning, that one. You're fortunate to still be alive and kicking." Archie rose from the bed and walked to the door, his shuffling gait slow but sure. After peering up and down the hallway, he turned and shut the door. "You think well on your feet, you know."

"Thanks." Steven raised an eyebrow. "So, you're saying you've followed everything that's happened to us over the last three days?"

"With a few exceptions, yes. You've had quite the eventful week."

"So, what's going to happen now? Do you know how all of this is going to turn out?"

"Unfortunately, no. While the clarity of my visions so far has been beyond reproach, I usually see things no more than a day or two in advance. Also, after today's events, everything gets muddier." Archie's face melted into an impish grin. "I did, however, experience a touch of déjà vu during our little talk."

Steven took a moment to process what the old man said, his face breaking into a similar grin as the implication became clear. "You've known everything I was going to say this whole time, haven't you?"

"More or less. I saw all of this a couple nights ago. Talking with you now is sort of like following along with a movie I've already seen. Believe it or not, I was half-afraid I might forget some of my lines."

"So you sat here for a day and a half and waited for me to walk by your door?"

"Well, you know, it's been pretty busy, what with all the group therapy and Jell-O breaks, but I was able to pencil you in."

Steven rose from the blue recliner and gazed out at the brightening Virginia sky. "Then I take it you know why we're here."

"I do. The girl, Lena, she was hurt pretty badly last night."

"She was still in surgery last I checked. Her boyfriend's here too, recuperating up in the ICU. I've got someone up there keeping an eye on him." Steven checked his watch. "Man, I've been down here forever. Audrey's probably hunting all over the hospital for me."

"Audrey. I assume that's the name of your lovely new Queen?"

Steven nodded. "Yeah. She's up there all by herself. I'd better go check on her." Steven half-opened the door. "Would you care to join me?"

"Certainly, but aren't you forgetting something?"

Steven stared blankly at Archie for a moment.

"Remember," Archie added, "I've been waiting for this a very long time."

"Oh, of course." Steven untied the silver cord from his waist and the pouch answered with a deafening pulse of sound. Though similar in many ways to his initial encounter with Emilio, the tone was subtly different this time, louder and more dissonant. Archie shed a tear as Steven opened the pouch, its glow filling the room with silver-white radiance.

The priest's hand trembled as it approached the shimmering light. "No turning back."

"From what I understand," Steven said, "that was never an option for any of us."

His fingers resting at the brink of discovery, Archie hesitated.

"Go ahead," Steven said. "It doesn't hurt, but be ready for whatever you might find."

Archie looked on for a moment longer and then dove his hand deep into the pouch's silver scintillation. His blind grope was fruitless for several long seconds, and frustration mounted on his face. As the moment unfolded, however, the priest's puzzled expression faded into a look of wonder, then rapture, as he brought forth his hand from the mouth of the pouch. His fingers, no longer twisted with years and arthritis, held an icon much like Steven's but larger and more ornate. The burnished marble surface of the bishop piece shone with fiery intensity, illuminating features of a man suddenly unmarked by time's relentless advance.

"Am I imagining this?" Archie asked, studying the fluid motion of his rejuvenated fingers. "Is this really happening?"

Steven looked on, barely believing what he was seeing. The man before him was still Archibald Lacan, but a younger, more virile Archie, as he must have looked in his prime. He stood tall and proud, the mild hunch in his back absent and his previously gaunt shoulders now broad and strong. Only the eyes were the same, filled with a look of wonder usually reserved for children on Christmas morning.

"Holy... It's like you dropped forty years." Steven put his hand on the man's shoulder. "How do you feel?"

Archie's newly young face broke into a wide grin. "It's indescribable. It's like I'm— oh…" With the advent of his awakening into the Game, Archie's perceptions were no longer obscured by Steven's cloak. "Your face."

"Don't worry," Steven said. "I'll heal." He ran his battered fingers along the cut above his brow. "It looks a lot worse than it feels."

"Right. I don't believe that for a second. Did you get one of the doctors to—"

"Archie?" A woman in her mid-forties, dressed in blue and green scrubs poked her head into the room. "Are you doing—oh, I'm sorry." The nurse checked to see if she was in the right room. "Excuse me. Where's Mr. Lacan?"

"He's taking a break." Archie thumbed at the bathroom door. "Prostate's not what it used to be." The nurse gave Archie's hospital-issued pajamas a quizzical once-over.

"We're down from the seventh floor," Steven said. "John here is a friend of the family. He wanted to come visit with Father Lacan for a minute."

"Tell Archie to buzz me when he gets out of the bathroom," the nurse said, her confused tone colored with mild annoyance. "It's time for his morning meds."

"Will do, Gladys," Archie said. "Will do."

The woman's face clouded over as she left the room, her mind making a connection Steven guessed she would deem impossible.

"Are you ready?" Steven asked as the door clicked shut.

"My clothes are all locked away down the hall." Archie ran his hands down his blue pajamas and gestured to his plaid slippers. "No belts on the psych floor, you know."

Steven reached into the pouch and produced a cloak fashioned of sheer white fabric. "Here, put this on. It'll make this a whole lot easier."

Archie fastened the cloak around his neck and brought up the hood. The silvery threads shimmered in the fluorescent light for a moment before the entire garment faded into obscurity.

"Fascinating," he said. "Can't wait to see what else I can do."

"We'll get you some real clothes once we're out of here, but your pajamas and cloak will have to do for now." Steven's gaze shot to the door. "I get the feeling Gladys didn't like our answers very much."

"All right," Archie agreed. "Let's go."

Steven headed for the door but Archie paused a second longer.

"Wait," he said. "One more thing." He rummaged in the drawer of his bedside table and drew out his rosary, crossing himself before stepping out into the hall.

"He's gotten me this far." A glimmer of excitement flashed in his eyes. "Shall we?"

Steven and Archie moved up the hall toward the door to the main hospital hallway. At the nursing station, Gladys sat at the desk working on a chart and sipping her morning coffee.

"Is the good Father done with his business?" Her mouth turned up in a half-smile.

"Almost," Archie said. "He said it might be a few more minutes."

"Anyway, we've got to go." Steven pointed to the door. "Can you let us out of here?"

"Sure, honey. I'll buzz you out." Gladys punched a code into the keypad on the wall, and the door leading off the unit clicked open. "Have a good day."

"Don't worry about that," Archie replied. "It's already a great one."

## 24

## MIRACLE

S teven and Archie stepped off the elevator onto the ninth floor and made their way toward the ICU waiting room. As Steven approached the double doors, he spotted Audrey huddled in the far corner of the room talking with a nurse he didn't recognize. Her hunched shoulders heaved with sobs and her eyes appeared even more puffed up and red than before. Rushing the last few steps, Steven caught the tail end of what the nurse was saying.

"...but for right now, at least she's stabilized." The nurse rose from her seat. "We'll do our best to keep you abreast of any developments in Miss Cervantes' condition."

"Wait," Steven said. "Before you go, how is Lena?"

"I'm sorry, sir, but I have to get back. Miss Cervantes is still in critical condition, and I've got one of the other nurses watching her while I'm out here. I just finished updating Miss Richards. She can fill you in. Also, the doctor should be making rounds sometime in the next hour and can probably answer your questions after he's seen her."

"Can you at least tell me if it looks like she's going to make it?"

"Steven," Audrey interjected, "Lena's in a coma. They're going to try to let her breathe without the machine tomorrow, but she's not waking up. The doctors think her brain may have taken too much damage to ever recover."

"We do appreciate your concern," the nurse added. "We've had other Good Samaritans bring in people from time to time, but few have taken such an active interest. Let me assure you we're doing everything we can. The doctors aren't optimistic her condition will improve much, but we're going to keep working with her and hope for the best. It's all we can do at this point."

"I understand," Steven said. "Thank you for your time."

The nurse nodded. "Any big developments, we'll let you know."

As Lena's nurse disappeared into the back, Audrey looked up at Steven, her eyes welling up anew. "I've been in and out of hospitals for longer than I care to remember," she said. "There were times when all I could think about was getting up and walking away, no matter what the cost. Well, if this is the cost, it's too high. A girl I've never even met is in there fighting for her life because she decided to help me." Audrey wiped the tears from her face. "I didn't think it was possible to feel any more helpless than I did when I was sick, but I was wrong. A part of me wishes the three of you hadn't come for me."

"Don't even go there." Steven rested a hand on Audrey's shoulder. "We all did what we had to do, and if it came down to it, we'd do it all again. Besides, if anybody put Lena and Emilio in danger, it was me."

"If I may intrude," came a third voice, "the truth is neither of you are at fault."

Audrey shot out of her seat and grasped her icon. She spun around to find Archie standing to one side, a bemused half-smile plastered across his face.

"Lena and Emilio are merely the latest casualties in our grand contest," Archie continued. "This Game we play is not for the weak of heart."

"Steven?" Audrey eyed the stranger warily. "Who is this?"

"Sorry," Steven answered. "This is Archie. He's with us."

"My Queen." The priest lowered his head in a show of deference. "Archibald Lacan, White Bishop, at your service."

"Where did he come from?" Audrey asked. "How is this possible?"

"It seems the pouch brought us to this particular hospital for a reason." Steven raised a shoulder in a subtle shrug and air escaped his nose in a quiet chuckle. "I didn't even make it to the ground floor before it went off like a car alarm."

"Well, then." Audrey extended Archie a hand. "Nice to meet you, Archie."

Archie took her hand and performed a graceful bow. "The pleasure is mine, my Queen."

"Seems you've picked up on all this pretty quickly. How did..." Audrey's eyes shot to Steven. "Wait, are *they* here?"

"If by 'they', you mean the Black," Archie answered, "then no. I believe for the moment you and yours have earned a well-deserved respite from their incessant assault."

Audrey shot Steven another quizzical look. "What is he talking about?"

"Apparently, Archie got the only copy of the instruction manual for this stupid Game. From what he's already told me, he understands more about all of this than anybody has a right to." Steven took a seat and motioned for the other two to join him. "He's right, though. I haven't felt even a glimmer of the Black since we hit Virginia. Let's hope our luck holds out."

"Some luck," Audrey said. "Emilio's not going to be up and about for at least a week, you heard what the nurse said about Lena, and as I understand it, the Game hasn't even started."

"We're going to make it through this," Steven said. "We don't have any other choice. Like it or not, ready or not, we're it. We may have to go on without our Knight, but as of last night, so do they."

Audrey buried her face in her hands. "Dammit, Steven, I didn't mean to do what I did." Her voice cracked as she broke into heaving sobs. "I didn't mean it."

"I'm sorry, Audrey," Steven said. "I wasn't trying to—"

"My dear," Archie interjected, "don't waste any emotion on their fallen Knight. Death, unfortunately, has become an intrinsic part of this Game, and for all his talk of noble intentions, his fate was no less than what his dark master meant for you. Had the Black awaited the Game's appointed time, their Knight may well have survived this time of upheaval. His fall is an unfortunate consequence of their King's hubris and greed."

"I don't want to play this godforsaken Game. I just want to go home." Audrey's teary eyes shot back and forth from Archie to Steven. "Or whatever's left of it."

"Make no mistake," Archie answered. "Though the Game proper has yet to begin, going back is not an option. Until this is over, we are all no more than Pieces on the great Board. Beyond what the Game provides, we can rely only on our strengths, our wits, and each other. The opposition may think they hold all the cards, but last night the four of you fought as one and achieved victory despite impossible odds." Archie took Audrey's hands in his. "When I saw what these three did for you last night and you for them—"

"What do you mean 'saw'? You weren't there." Audrey shot another puzzled look at Steven. "Was he?"

"Archie can see things." Steven met the priest's earnest gaze. "He's been having visions and dreams about the Game for years. Lately, they've been previews instead of recaps." He shook his head in disbelief. "He's known we were coming for days."

Audrey's eyes grew wide. "Then you must know what's going to happen to Lena. Is she going to be okay? Is she going to wake up?"

Archie's expression turned solemn. "Some visions are clearer than others," he said. "Sadly, my insights into the events that fall after my conscription are far vaguer than the others. A mechanism of the Game, no doubt."

"But you do have some idea, right?" She looked on with strained, yet hopeful eyes. "I mean, she's going to make it, isn't she?"

Archie cleared his throat and studied the floor for a moment before answering. "Her fate is unclear." Archie met Audrey's pained gaze. "The only thing I know with any clarity is that I have some role to play in the outcome."

Amaryllis fluttered at Steven's neck.

"What's that supposed to mean?" Steven asked.

"As I said, each of us brings certain abilities to the Game, some intrinsic to our nature and others associated with our position on the Board. I've gleaned from glimpses of the other iterations that the

Bishop's role is more than being simply another combatant, but also advisor to the King, and perhaps healer."

"You mean you can help her?" Audrey's eyes grew wide with hope.

"I'm not sure. From here on out, nothing's written in stone. Still, I can't escape the notion I'm supposed to minister to her in some way." Archie's voice grew quiet. "Actually, to all of you." The priest looked away, his already trademark zeal and confidence at a low ebb. "Not as easy to charge ahead full steam when you don't know what lies across the next hill."

"Welcome to our world." Steven slapped Archie on the back. "Lena's waiting. Ready to give it a shot?"

"No time like the present, I suppose." Archie rose from his seat, a concerned cast crossing his features. "What if I can't help her?"

"Then she's no worse off than she is right now," Steven said.

"The way I see it," Audrey added, "you're the best chance she's got."

"All right then," Archie said. "It's settled. Let's do it."

The trio moved to the entrance of the intensive care unit. Steven pressed the button, and the motorized double doorway opened revealing one of the physicians he'd seen earlier headed their way. His head buried in a chart, the slim man in the long white coat nearly knocked Archie over as he rushed past.

"Sorry about that," the doctor said. "Need to watch where I'm going, I suppose." When the trio wouldn't let him pass, his expression grew frustrated. "Can I help you?"

"Yes, Dr. Atkinson," Steven said, glancing at the man's badge. "We were hoping to go back and see Lena Cervantes."

"The girl from the motorcycle crash? She's in critical condition. Are you family?"

"No," Steven answered. "Audrey and I, we're the ones who brought her in. We wanted to go back and check on her before we left."

"I'm sorry, but the nurses are pretty busy with her right now. I can give you an update on her current status if you like."

"Thanks," Steven said, "but we just spoke to the nurse. Can we please just see her?"

"I'm sorry. It's against protocol and—"

"Sir," Archie interrupted, "my name is Father Archibald Lacan.

This fine couple has asked me to come and pray over the girl. I know it's unorthodox, but surely your staff can accommodate an old priest for a couple of minutes." Both Audrey and Atkinson adopted quizzical expressions at Archie's self-description, but the priest continued as if he didn't notice. "The girl is Catholic and if her situation is as dire as I've been told, she deserves last rites."

Atkinson paused for a moment and then slipped into a smile Steven suspected he reserved for only the most frustrating hospital visitors. "Of course. I'll go clear it with the charge nurse."

As Atkinson headed back into the ICU, Audrey caught Archie's eye. "Old priest?"

"Oh," Archie said, glancing down at his hands, "that's right." His lips turned up in an innocent smile. "I may not look it at the moment but I've been around the block once or twice."

"We'll explain later." Steven turned back to Archie. "So, what's next?"

"As I've watched the events of the last three days unfold," Archie said, "it's become apparent that play of the Game is in part instinctive. I could be wrong, Steven, but I suspect you'd never handled a halberd before two days ago."

"Yeah," Steven said, "always was more of a broadsword kind of guy. You think your healing whamma jamma might work the same way?"

"Won't know till I try. I hope—" Archie hushed himself as Dr. Atkinson reappeared and headed their way. "Why don't we hear what the good doctor has to say?"

"The nurses have just finished their assessment and the Cervantes girl is stable enough for a brief visit." Atkinson wore a stern, yet earnest expression. "You'll find her in Bay 2."

"Thanks," Steven said.

"Look." Atkinson crossed his arms. "So there are no surprises, I want you all to understand she's in pretty bad shape. We've cleaned her up as best we can, but her head and face are so swollen, I doubt you'll recognize her."

"The nurse told us it was bad." Audrey's face drew up into a pained grimace. "She said they had to drill a hole in her skull."

Steven's gaze shot to Audrey at this bit of information. "I didn't know that part."

"Her head CT revealed a pretty significant bleed," Atkinson said. "I think we were able to evacuate the clot in time, but we'll have to give it some time and see how she does."

"Thank you for allowing us in," Archie said. "We certainly appreciate all you and your staff have done to help."

"Yes." Audrey smiled. "Thank you, Dr. Atkinson."

Steven nodded his agreement and shook Atkinson's hand.

"We're all just doing our jobs." Atkinson paused as he turned to head for the elevators and caught Archie's eye with a grim stare. "Shape she's in, Father, that girl could use some divine intervention."

Steven led them through the intensive care unit's double doors and headed toward Lena's room. Set up in a half wheel configuration, the ICU wrapped around a central nursing area, each of the twelve rooms opening on large bay windows that looked out on the green mountains of the Roanoke Valley. Only a couple of bays sat empty, the rest occupied with a zoo-like menagerie of the sickest of the sick.

In one of the two rooms at the top of the key, Steven recognized the family who had received the bad news earlier. The girl with curly brown locks stood at the foot of the bed and watched solemnly as they passed, her previous carefree smile replaced by a look of profound desolation. Steven winked and raised a hand in a nonchalant salute as they passed, his warm gesture met with a cold stare.

As the threesome came to Bay 2, they found Emilio propped up at Lena's bedside in an old wheelchair of grey vinyl and chrome. Weeping over Lena's motionless form, the boy was a shadow of the impetuous youth Steven had met two days before. He held Lena's limp hand in his trembling grasp, the girl's fingers as white as the hospital linens she lay beneath.

"It's us," Steven said. "We would've come sooner, but we—"

Emilio cut Steven off with a raised hand. "Wouldn't have made a difference."

"How is she?" Audrey asked.

"She's dying." His cracked voice little more than a harsh whisper, Emilio shot Steven a bloodshot glare. "I guess my brother bleeding to death in an alley wasn't enough. Look at her. She's so pale..." Emilio turned his head away and ran his forearm across his tear-filled eyes.

Steven stepped into the room with Audrey in tow and did his best to stifle a gasp as the rest of Lena's body came into view. Even with Atkinson's warning fresh in their ears, the harsh reality was hard to stomach. Connected via a system of plastic tubes to a breathing machine that hissed intermittently as if alive, Lena's battered face was a study in blue and purple. Her head wrapped in several yards of white gauze, her features were so swollen she barely looked human. Coupled with the uneven rise and fall of her fractured chest with each forced mechanical breath, Steven began to lose hope in anything Archie had to offer.

"We're here to help." Steven did his best to keep the growing doubt out of his voice.

Emilio lips curled up in a snarl. "I think Lena's had about all the help she can take."

"Hang on, Emilio." Steven gestured to his rear. "I'd like you to meet Archie. He's... one of us. He thinks he can save Lena."

"One of us?" As Archie stepped into the room, Emilio shot out of his chair and went nose-to-nose with Steven. "So you found another sucker willing to listen to all of Grey's crap?"

"Young man," Archie said. "Everything in this life happens for a reason, and within the confines of the Game, infinitely more so. Last night, three of you were destined to be at a particular place at a particular time, and by your noble efforts, Miss Richards here is still among the living. Now, the four of you have been brought to me. I believe I can make this right, if you'll let me."

Emilio stared incredulous at Archie for a moment before fixing Steven with an angry glare. "Who the hell is this guy, and how is he spouting all this stuff?" His voice cracked in frustration as he turned his attention back on Archie. "What makes you think you can do anything to help Lena?"

"My name is Archibald Lacan, priest by vocation and the White Bishop of this iteration of the Game. For years I have been haunted by visions of this struggle and have witnessed the many cruel turns this so-called Game can take. I have seen death come from life, and life from death. I have seen things I cannot fathom, much less put into words. I know about your brother, Emilio Cruz, the tough decisions you've made, your strength, your honor, your love for this girl. In many ways, I know you and the others better than my own family." Archie sat on the bed next to Lena and took her bruised hand in his. "I'm not certain whether I can help Lena, but I do know I'm supposed to try."

"Then you don't know anything." Emilio turned and stared out the window.

"I'm sorry, Emilio. The Sight has shown me everything up to the moment of my transfiguration this morning, but little beyond." Archie grew pensive. "It's strange. For weeks now, I've been going through the motions of events I've already seen, but now that the future is again a blank slate, the newness of each moment is what feels odd.

"In that case," Emilio asked, "how are you so sure you're supposed to help her?"

"Faith," Archie said. "Belief without proof, conviction in the face of doubt, hope in the face of hopelessness. I have absolute faith this is what I'm supposed to do." Archie placed Lena's hand in Emilio's. "Can you have a little faith, Emilio Cruz?"

Emilio stared down at Lena's limp form a long moment and then leaned in and kissed her on the cheek. "Do it."

"How do we start?" Steven asked.

"First," Archie said, "we'll need to get rid of the tube in her throat. It's not natural. All the lines in her arms too. It all has to go."

Emilio turned to Archie, his expression incredulous. "Are you crazy? That tube is all that's keeping her alive."

"Answer me this," Archie said. "Last night, when you saw Steven and Audrey here about to burn at the Black Queen's hand, how did you know your steed would allow you to jump as it did? Was your intent to drive headlong into a brick wall, or did you trust your gut?"

"How could you know that?" Emilio's wide eyes filled with understanding. "Doesn't matter. What's your point?"

"My point is that in the last two days, you've relied on your instincts, and each time they've proven to be on target. What are those same instincts telling you now? Mine are telling me I can help Lena, but not as she is." Archie turned to Steven. "Close the door, if you will."

Steven stepped past Audrey and made a quick survey of the nursing station. Lena's nurse sat at one of the ubiquitous hospital computer terminals, her eyes riveted to the screen, her fingers dancing across the plastic keyboard. Of the remaining staff, only the cleaning lady paid Steven any mind, her grey eyebrow raised in a question mark as he slid closed the door to Lena's room and pulled the curtain.

"I don't think we have much time," Steven said. "What do you need us to do?"

"Help me disconnect her from all this machinery," Archie said. "Save the tube until the rest is done." Steven and Audrey descended on Lena's motionless form, pulling dripping IV's from both forearms and one from her wrist. Two different machines began to beep.

"Now for the last." Archie stepped forward to pull the tube from her throat.

"No." Emilio grasped Archie's wrist. "Let me do it."

"Are you sure?" Steven asked.

"I'm sure." Tears welled in Emilio's eyes as he undid the tape at the corner of Lena's mouth. His searching fingers found a small cannula that branched from the side of the tube. "Hand me a syringe," he said, pointing to the small table by the bed.

"How do you know what you're doing?" Audrey asked.

"I've watched the nurse adjust the tube," Emilio answered. "Not to mention, growing up, we used to watch a lot of medical shows. Carlos wanted me to be a doctor."

Emilio connected a syringe to the tube and pulled the plunger. A hissing sound accompanied the next breath from the machine. "All right, Archie, you ready?"

"As ready as I'm ever going to be." The priest mouthed a short prayer and laid his hands on Lena's brow and shoulder. "Pull it."

Emilio grasped the tube and withdrew it from Lena's mouth. Immediately, the ventilator alarm went off, filling the room with a high-pitched whine. Lena's chest fell and Steven's heart sank when it didn't rise again.

"Okay," Steven asked. "What now?"

Archie didn't answer.

"Archie." Steven shook the man by the shoulders. "What's next?"

"I'm... I'm not sure." A flash of panic crossed the priest's features.

"You're not sure?" Emilio grabbed the front of Archie's shirt. "What do you mean you're not sure?"

"Nothing's happening." Beads of sweat broke on the priest's forehead. "I don't know."

"Her lips are turning blue." Emilio said. "She's not breathing. Do something."

"What's going on in there?" a female voice shouted.

The door slid open a crack.

"Audrey," Steven shouted, "keep them out."

Audrey threw her full weight against the door, forcing it closed as Steven grabbed Archie by the shoulders.

"What's next, Archie?" Steven shook the man. "Think. You were talking about instincts before. Follow your own."

Archie's mouth worked in silent prayer, his fingers trembling as they caressed Lena's battered cheek, the dusky color of her skin growing more pronounced with each passing second. Steven found himself holding his own breath as Emilio's expression descended into sheer panic.

"It's not working." Emilio's voice filled with desperation. "She's dying. Let the doctors back in. At least before, she was still breathing. Please let them in."

The hubbub beyond the door grew louder by the second. "Listen to the kid," a male voice rumbled through the glass. "Let us in so we can help the girl."

As the door slid open an inch, a second, angry voice let them know security was on the way. A mop handle appeared in the crack, the improvised lever widening the gap with each passing second. Audrey dug in her heels and put her shoulder to the sliding door's handle.

"Whatever you're going to do, hurry," she shouted. "I can't hold them."

Despite the doubts eating at the edge of his consciousness, Steven's next words came out calmer than he would have dreamed possible. "Archie, we're out of time. Lena's out of time."

Archie looked up at Steven, the worry on his face more befitting the arthritis-ridden senior citizen from five floors down than the younger man who stood before him.

Steven rested his hand on the man's shoulder. "It has to be now."

The door slid open another inch. Several sets of hands appeared in the crack, knuckles white as they struggled against Audrey's waning efforts.

"They're coming in," Audrey shouted. "Steven, help me."

"Bring up the mist," Steven shouted. "Anything. You've got to hold them."

"No." The fear disappeared from Archie's voice. "Let them come." The priest's eyes fastened on Steven's, the despair in his gaze replaced with something like hope.

"What have you got?" Steven asked.

Emilio's desperate gaze shifted between the two of them as Archie ignored Steven's question and caught Audrey's eye.

"Audrey," he said, "come away from the door. To make this work, I'm going to need your full attention." Archie's eyes slid closed. "Everything you have to give."

Audrey shot Steven a questioning glance. "But—"

"Don't worry about them," Archie whispered, his voice calming with each word. "I need you over here. Lena needs you over here."

Audrey moved to join Archie at Lena's bedside as the priest continued.

"Steven, Emilio, you two as well. Gather round. If Lena's to make it through this day, it's going to take all of us." With that admonition, the four of them so recently strangers, converged on Lena's bed and interlocked hands, their faces resigned with a singular resolve that would not be denied.

No sooner had Audrey let go the handle than the heavy glass door to Lena's room slid open and a mob of nurses and doctors rushed in. In the lead was Lena's nurse, followed by half a dozen others in white coats and scrubs. Their shouts filled the room, but only for a moment, their protests fading into a silence of shared understanding. Though the corporate cloak of anonymity surrounding the bed ensured the specifics would be forgotten, the wonder of that day was forever emblazoned on Steven's mind and likely the mind of every person present.

The spectacle went on for several minutes and everyone in the ICU that could move under their own power, patient and visitor alike, left their rooms to gather in the central atrium and stare awestruck at the sheer power evidenced in the room marked Bay 2. Shafts of silver-white radiance filled the space and pulsed in time to a strange chanting that came from everywhere and nowhere at once. A careful mélange of English, Greek, and Latin mixed with segments of language barely recognizable as human speech, the singsong incantation echoed through the hallways of the hospital, and more, through the minds of all who heard it. In the years to follow, the event would come to be known as the Ninth Floor Miracle. Though anyone but the few present in the ICU that day dismissed the story as shared delusion or urban legend, the ones who were there knew they had witnessed something akin to the hand of God.

A perplexed Dr. Atkinson stepped through the door to the ICU. After surveying the odd scene of doctors and nurses, patients and guests all wandering the space aimlessly, he pushed his way through the listless crowd and headed for the opposite end of the atrium. He rounded the top of the key and poked his head into the room where the Armstrong family had kept a silent vigil over their dying matriarch for the majority of the morning. This time, however, he was met with teary smiles and gratitude.

"Dr. Atkinson, it's a miracle. Mama woke up. Only for a minute or so, but she woke up." Mrs. Armstrong's eldest daughter rose to meet Atkinson at the door. Glancing across her shoulder at the monitor, the doctor sighed. The poor woman had finally, mercifully, passed.

And yet...

"She woke up?" Atkinson asked.

"Yeah, Doc," added a man Atkinson didn't remember from earlier.

"From what you told us this morning, we didn't think we'd get the chance to say a proper goodbye." The man shook Atkinson's hand as Mrs. Armstrong's daughter wrapped her arm around his stethoscope-wrapped neck and gave him an impromptu hug.

"I think she was ready to go, but had a couple of things she wanted to say first. Even little Hannah got to say goodbye."

The doctor's eyes stole across the room and found the six-year-old scribbling away at a coloring book with a couple of broken crayons, her curly brown locks now pulled back in pigtails. Looking up from her coloring, she gave the doctor a quick wave.

"You're saying her grandmother spoke to her." Atkinson's brow furrowed. "And you could understand her?"

"Understand her?" the man asked, his tone as incredulous as Atkinson's. "She looked at Ginny there and told her she loved her, said her goodbyes to everyone, even told Hannah to keep the diamond ring Paps gave her for her wedding someday. 'Something to remember me by,' she said. Yeah, Doc. We understood her."

"Well," Atkinson said, "that is indeed a miracle. Consider yourselves blessed. A lot of families don't get such an opportunity."

"Thank you for all you did for Mama," Mrs. Armstrong's daughter said.

Atkinson raised a hand and gave them a confused smile. "I'm glad we were able to bring some peace to her final moments. I'll drop back by in a few minutes to help with arrangements, but another patient needs my attention first."

Atkinson left the room wondering if the family was suffering from some sort of group delusion. Mrs. Betty Jean Armstrong, age seventy-two, had suffered massive brain hemorrhage, a complication of impossible to control blood pressure and made worse by the blood thinner she was taking for her heart. He'd personally declared her brain dead hours before.

Their story seemed impossible.

*And yet, stranger things have happened,* he considered as he continued his trek toward Bay 2. *And speaking of people desperately in need of a miracle...*

The door to the Cervantes girl's room was closed with the curtain drawn. Taking a deep breath before entering, he slid the door open a few inches and poked his head inside. The absence of the ventilator's periodic hiss coupled with the high-pitched drone of the flatline marching across the cardiac monitor's screen set his hair on end. Neither, however, appeared to matter to the girl's nurse who stood dazed by the squealing machine, her hands moving with quiet efficiency as she silenced the alarm.

The girl's boyfriend was up from the ortho floor and standing at the bedside. His muscular back exposed by a hospital gown hanging askew, the boy obscured Atkinson's view of the girl's face. Though he couldn't see his features, it appeared he was crying. In sharp contrast, the three at the foot of the bed couldn't seem to stop smiling. The cute girl with the freckles and auburn hair from before stood arm in arm with the guy who brought the two kids in, sobbing like the credits were rolling on *It's a Wonderful Life*. Meanwhile, the priest who demanded to give the girl last rites sat in the corner panting, his brow dripping with sweat.

As Atkinson stepped into the room, the girl with the auburn hair smiled at him and winked, beckoning him closer. The boyfriend turned at the sound of his quiet footsteps, his surprising smile shining through the tears rolling down his cheeks. Nothing, however, compared to Atkinson's shock when he met the eyes of his patient.

Lena Cervantes looked up into the eyes of her doctor, her face whole and unblemished, her wounds healed and her expression buoyant. "Hello," she said, pausing as she read his nametag. "Dr. Atkinson. You're the one that's been taking care of me, right?"

Atkinson shifted from foot to foot, unsure of how to answer. "Yes, uh... I'm the surgeon who operated on you. I'm glad to see you're improving so quickly."

*Impossible.*

*Yet there she is.*

*A miracle.*

"Well, thanks for all you did. I've never felt better." The girl beamed up at him.

For a moment, Atkinson felt like a kid again. He wasn't a religious man, and didn't have much time for things that couldn't be explained by medical science, but this… "You're welcome." He smiled, the mood of the room infectious. "And you're sure you're all right? No headache? No pain?"

"Like I said, never better." Lena looked over at the man called Steven. "In fact, if you don't have any objections, I'm sure somebody else needs this bed more than me."

"Of course." The scientist in him wrestled with the childlike sense of wonder threatening to overtake him. "But—"

"No buts, Doc." Lena rose from the bed and shook Atkinson's hand. "You can check me out all you want, but I'm pretty sure I'm ready to go."

"Lena," the boy said. "Are you sure?"

Despite her boyfriend's scowl, the girl took his hand and repeated herself without an iota of doubt in her voice.

"I'm ready."

## 25

## SHIFT

For the better part of two hours, Steven, Audrey, and Archie stood by in the bustling family area waiting for Lena and Emilio to be discharged. Dr. Atkinson grudgingly agreed to let her go after the neurologist brought in to examine her hobbled away on his cane muttering that the girl was in better shape than he was.

During a lull in conversation, Steven excused himself, leaving Audrey and Archie alone to get better acquainted and returned to the large window that overlooked the southern tip of the city of Roanoke. He stared westward out at the verdant valley he once considered home and found himself reminiscing on better, simpler times.

The hospital sat at the western foot of Mill Mountain, the dominant terrain feature of the area. Atop this green mass of rock and trees rested the Mill Mountain Star, ninety feet in height and visible for miles to the north, especially at night when it's beacon cut the darkness like a pentacle forged of lightning and steel.

Steven grinned at memories from his high school years when most Friday nights found him with one girl or another basking in the star's gentle white glow and looking down on the city below. His mental trek led across the river and up the highway half a mile or so to the downtown area, a jewel nestled in the bosom of the Blue Ridge and Allegheny mountain ranges.

In his mind, Steven traced the highway as it snaked farther to the northeast, headed toward Lexington and Charlottesville.

*And him.*

His father's face loomed in his mind's eye.

*He's only fourteen miles and two right turns away.*

"Steven." Audrey rested her hand on Steven's shoulder, breaking his reverie.

"Yeah?"

"Come with me. You'll want to see this."

"What is it?"

"Live footage on CNN. It's happening now."

Steven followed Audrey to the opposite corner of the waiting area and sat between her and Archie. Within seconds, the television report made clear what had left Audrey at such a loss for words.

*"An earthquake fifty miles off the coast of California has resulted in the first significant tsunami to hit the west coast in over forty years.*

*"The largest earthquake previously recorded in the northern hemisphere, the Great Alaskan Earthquake of 1964, resulted in twenty-foot waves that struck various locations all along the west coast. California was hit the hardest, and one of the state's oldest communities, Crescent City, took the brunt of the disaster with damage in the millions and a total of eleven dead.*

*"Unfortunately, that number is miniscule when compared with the estimated death toll today in Long Beach. Reports are coming in now that push the projected number of fatalities into triple digits and..."*

"Jesus," Steven said.

"It's terrible." Audrey's voice trembled. "All those people."

"What's done is done," Archie said. "All we can do for them now is pray."

"You know," Audrey whispered, "you always think this kind of stuff happens to somebody else, far away from anything you know. Then one day the Twin Towers fall to the ground or a hurricane almost takes New Orleans off the map or a tidal wave puts Santa Monica underwater and all of a sudden it's—"

"All too real."

Not only was Steven not surprised by the familiar voice, he had been waiting for it. He peered across his shoulder and offered a quiet, "Hello, Grey."

"Good morning, Steven." Perched behind their couch in his usual out-of-season grey overcoat and hat, Steven's mentor watched the telecast, arms crossed and eyes disheartened. "As you can see," he said, "it has begun."

"This is Grey?" Audrey looked the new arrival up and down, her mouth turned down in a quizzical frown. Before anyone could answer her, she posed a second question. "What's begun?"

Archie cut in, his voice full of fire. "Don't you see? This is how it starts. The great upheaval, the latest in the eternal series of corrections."

Steven wasn't sure which he found more unnerving, Archie's odd comprehension of the events in play, or the glee with which he spoke of what was potentially the end of the world.

"Is he right, Grey? All those lives, is it our fault?"

"These events are not your fault, Steven, though the Bishop speaks true. The shift along the Pacific basin that led to the catastrophe you now witness is indeed evidence of the very forces the Game was designed to contain, control, and dissipate.

"For weeks, the signs have abounded. Colossal downpours in southern Texas. Drought and record temperatures across your southeastern states. Crop failure that has plagued your nation's breadbasket throughout this entire growing season.

"While the destruction along your west coast is the initial occurrence of any significant magnitude, make no mistake. The tsunami is not an isolated event, but the first of many such catastrophes. As time passes, these disasters will grow in force and scale, and unless the Game is played out at its appointed time, the devastation that ensues will make today's tragedy and the dozens of lives lost seem inconsequential."

"Inconsequential?" Audrey said. "This is crazy. People are dying. We need to warn them, the news, the government, somebody." Even as she spoke, a sad realization dawned upon her face and her impassioned rant ended in whispered certainty. "They'd never believe us."

"They never do." Grey doffed his hat and took a seat.

"There will be one difference this time though," Archie said.

"And what's that?" Audrey asked.

"In the past, the forces in question were responsible for countless unexplained phenomena. Great floods. The disappearance of continents from the face of the earth. The eradication of entire races, entire species even." Archie met Grey's gaze. "In the past, such events were often seen as the handiwork of the gods, and as a result have been relegated to the realm of myth, legend, folklore.

"Those people and places once existed, but if remembered at all, they are today dismissed as fiction, their toils faded by the obscurity of millennia." Archie gestured at the ongoing coverage of the California tsunami. "This time the world will watch disaster after disaster unfold from the relative comfort of their living rooms, all of it brought to them in high definition with exquisite detail and minute by minute updates, that is until the cataclysm comes for them.

"If you remember, in 1999, the world became a paranoid madhouse of doom seekers based on nothing but the irrational belief of a select few zealots and the off chance some unforeseen computer glitch might bring life as we know it to a screeching halt. What do you think the same people are going to do when confronted with irrefutable proof that this time, the end is actually coming?"

The room grew silent as grainy footage of a woman's body being dragged from a waterlogged car flashed across the screen.

Steven grunted. "I can't believe you people had the balls to call this a Game."

The doors to the ICU swung open. Lena strode out, her body in better condition than the tattered clothes draped about her. She smiled when she spotted Steven and the others. Emilio followed in her wake, though his reaction at seeing the party of four gathered around the television was far less enthusiastic.

"They finally finished all my discharge papers," Lena said, "though my doctor still isn't convinced it's the best idea for me to go. I don't think he knows what to make of all this. Almost kept me another night for observation."

"They cut me loose as well." Emilio shot a hard look at Grey. "So, mystery man, funny how you always show up *after* the shit hits the fan."

The unbridled anger in Emilio's voice surprised Steven, but only so much. The timing of Grey's frequent entrances and exits hadn't been lost on him either.

"Good to see you both on your feet," Steven interjected in an effort to change the subject. "None the worse for wear?"

"I'm fine," Lena said. "So, what's next?"

"What's next," Emilio said, "is we're taking you back to Baltimore."

Lena turned on him, her eyes afire. "We've already had this discussion."

"But—"

"No buts about it. No way I'm sitting home while you're God knows where, risking your life over this stupid Game. Like it or not, I'm a part of this, as much as you, and till it's over, I'm not letting you out of my sight."

Emilio slid his hands into his pockets and stared at the floor. "It was almost over last night." His face flushed in hopeless frustration. "Can one of you try to talk some sense into her? She won't listen to me."

"Lena—" Steven said.

"Save it, Steven." Lena crossed her arms. "If Emilio goes, I go. It's as simple as that."

Archie rose from his seat, his hands out in a conciliatory gesture. "Now, now, the young lady has made up her mind. No sense in arguing the point."

Placated for the moment, Lena moved into the circle and took a seat in the plush chair opposite the couch. Emilio, conversely, stood his ground, and remained sullen and quiet. Steven tried to catch his eye, understanding more than he cared to remember about the emotions boiling in the young man's gut, but found his sympathetic gaze met with something more akin to hate.

"Lena." Audrey broke the tense silence. "Something's been on my mind since we arrived here. I didn't ask before because you had just woken up, but..." She stopped for a moment, her face all screwed up with equal parts fear and hope. "Do you have any idea what happened to my mom and grandpa? Steven said you were the last one who might have seen them."

"Sorry." Lena sucked air in through her teeth. "I made sure they both got out of the house before I went back to help Steven and Emilio. Your mom was frantic, insisting on going back for you. It was all your grandfather and I could do to keep her from running back into the fire. Then the battle started. I told them to run and not look back. That's the last I saw of them."

"Did they say where they were going?" Audrey asked.

"Not that I... wait. Your mom said a name... Polly?"

"Polly? That's our neighbor up the street. They must have gone to her house to take cover." Audrey's face filled with hope. "Does anybody have a phone?"

Steven shook his head, his phone one of the many casualties in his initial encounter with the Black Queen. Emilio said his had gone missing in the previous night's battle while Lena pointed to the rags about her shoulders that twenty-four hours before had been a decent set of clothes. When Audrey turned to Archie, the priest chuckled.

"Sorry, child, but I'm the last person you ought to ask. Not that they would have let me keep it down on four, but I don't even own one."

"Well," Audrey said, "since we're apparently the only six people in the nation not sporting a mobile phone, I guess I'll run down to the lobby and see what I can find. Be back in a minute." Audrey turned to walk away when an unexpected voice cut in.

"Here." Grey produced a small silver flip phone from an inner pocket of his voluminous overcoat and held it out to Audrey. "Use mine."

Surprised, Audrey took the phone and made her way over to the window.

Steven let out an incredulous laugh. "*You* have a cell phone."

"Does not everyone these days?" Grey's face betrayed the slightest hint of a smile. "I keep it around for such occasions."

"You keep a cell phone handy in case the world decides to blow up?" Emilio asked.

"More or less." Grey's smile widened, and despite their collective despair, they laughed.

All of them.

Though the laughter lasted but a moment, it was a moment that each of them needed.

"So," Steven asked, "what do we do now?"

"The next Piece awaits," Grey said. "Zed has no doubt grown desperate watching his opening gambit fail at every turn. You must be wary."

"Something doesn't make sense," Steven said. "He didn't even try this time." Both his and Grey's gazes shot to Archie who was busy sharing a joke with Lena. "And when we were at our lowest. What do you make of that?"

"I don't know, Steven, but I fear that—" Grey stopped as Audrey rejoined the group, her face pale and eyes wide with panic. "Audrey. What is it, my dear?"

"They never made it." Her hands trembled as she returned Grey his phone. "I finally reached Polly. The whole town's been out at the house since the wee hours of the night putting out fires and sifting through ashes, but no one has seen Mom or Grandpa since the festival yesterday morning." Audrey choked back tears. "Polly was sure I'd been burned alive." Her frantic gaze shifted back and forth from Steven to Grey. "What's happened to them?"

Steven opened his mouth to say anything that might assuage Audrey's fears, and found himself at a loss for words. Every scenario he imagined was worse than the one before.

After moments of staring into Audrey's pleading eyes, Grey vocalized what all of them were thinking. "I fear your family has been taken by the Black." Cold. Matter of fact. Very different from the fatherly tone he evinced moments before. "Fortunately, and remember I have known our enemy for longer than you can imagine, I suspect your mother and grandfather still live. Dead, they would serve no purpose but to bring vengeance down upon his head. Even Zed respects the unbridled power of a Queen's wrath. Living, though—"

"They become pawns in a game they can't possibly understand." Anger rose in Steven's throat, swept away a moment later by a cold realization. "Lena, remember when we talked before and decided calling your family was a bad idea?"

"Yeah?"

"Scratch that. Get on Grey's phone and call home right now. Tell them to drop whatever they're doing and get out of town. You too, Emilio, anybody you can think of who might have a bullseye on their back. I have a feeling our friends in black may be changing their tactics a bit."

"The only person I've got left is standing right here," Emilio said. "You still plan on letting her tag along—"

Lena put her fingers over Emilio's lips as Steven turned to Archie.

"I'm not sure if they know about you yet, but I'm betting it won't take them long to figure out we've found our Bishop. You may want to get in touch with your family as well."

"I appreciate your concern, but everybody's out of town this week. They're down in Wilmington at my great niece's wedding. Doubt the bad guys will know to look there."

"You have a great niece?" Audrey raised an eyebrow.

"You know us black folk," Archie answered with a chuckle. "We age pretty well."

Lena broke into a hesitant laugh, unsure if Archie's comment was meant as a joke.

"Hey, Archie," Steven said, "maybe it's time to clear the air a bit."

Archie nodded, and all of them, Grey included, listened intently as the priest recounted the events that led to his hospitalization, the circumstances surrounding his induction into the Game, and the miraculous transformation that left him better than two generations younger than when he awoke that morning.

"You're really seventy-three?" Audrey asked when he was finished. "That's…"

"Impossible?" Archie said. "Yesterday, were you not eaten alive with cancer and waiting for the good Lord to call you home? Was not Lena here lying in a coma behind those very doors? If you ask me, miracles seem to be the order of the day."

"But why?" Lena asked.

"It is the Game's nature to desire to be played," Grey interjected.

233

"Regardless of circumstance or context, when the time of correction comes, the Game will use whatever means necessary to ensure its own eventuality. This instinct, if you will, was designed into the Game from the start, a failsafe to prevent another cataclysm." As if on cue, the cable news channel came off commercial and the ongoing coverage of the tsunami resumed in earnest. Grey grimaced as the image of several pale corpses being dragged from a swamped California storefront trailed across the screen, some no more than children. At his absent wave, the television flickered and went dark.

"I believe we've seen quite enough of that." Grey said. "Now, where was I? Oh yes." He steepled his fingers before his chin. "Understand that when the Game is played, it wishes to be played well." His gaze flitted around the room, lighting for a moment on Archie, Audrey, Lena, Emilio. "If any particular Piece is deemed too old, too infirm, or too injured to be a valid part of play, the Game moves to rectify the situation in as simple and direct a manner as possible."

"You talk like the Game is alive." Lena's statement captured everyone's attention. Even Emilio glanced up from his self-imposed silence as Grey answered her.

"No, Lena, the Game is not alive, though it does possess an inherent intelligence of sorts. As I explained to you before, the forces that empower its play exist whether the Game is played or not. The format, conventions, and rules, however, are intrinsic to the Game itself, all governed by the residual power and intellect of some of the greatest minds to ever walk the earth."

"When you defeated the Queen last night, you mentioned something about Arbiters," Steven said. "Do you remember that?"

"Like something out of a dream," Audrey said. "Or a nightmare."

"Arbiters?" Emilio asked.

Grey nodded. "The Great Arbiters have presided over every iteration of the Game since the beginning. They provide both the structure and the substance of the Game while containing the immense conceptual power of each correction and channeling those same forces into the various aspects of play. They reside in a place beyond perception and watch all that transpires, awaiting each iteration of the Game with a patience even I cannot begin to fathom."

"So, these people or ghosts or whatever sit around and wait hundreds of years for the universe to blow an alternator, all so they can watch a stupid chess game?"

"In a manner of speaking," Grey answered, "yes."

"And who are these Arbiters?" Audrey asked. "Where did they come from?"

"As Zed suggested he and I become the immortal champions for the Black and the White, so did I suggest some form of governing body be created to supervise and regulate play. Zed fought me on this, but I was able to convince the others of the wisdom of my words, wisdom that has certainly borne out over the past few days. The remaining seven, all of them approaching the end of their time on this plane, volunteered along with the two of us to become an immortal part of this construct we now call the Game."

"They were once your friends?" Audrey asked.

"Friends." Grey's eyes grew downcast. "Family."

"Your grandfather."

"Yes, Steven."

"But they're not like you, are they?" Steven asked. "I mean, you're still living and breathing after a thousand years, while they—"

"They are dead," Grey said, "at least from a conventional point of view. The seven who chose to become Arbiters of the Game volunteered to enter a twilight state between life and death, forfeiting their bodies and lives on this earth so their influence could last across the ages. While mine and Zed's link to the forces in question has contributed to our physical longevity, the remainder of our order now exist only in spirit, their disembodied essences a part of the very Game they helped design."

"Buddies or not, they're the ones letting Zed run all slipshod with the rules, right?"

Grey bowed his head at Emilio's pointed question. "I cannot fathom why our opponent's many deviations from even the most basic rules of play are not being met with appropriate consequences. Very few ways exist in today's world of empiricism to interact or communicate with the Arbiters, even for me. In the past, the various manifestations of their will upon the Game were anything but subtle. I would argue, however, that despite our opponent's blatant disregard for the many conventions of the Game, something has brought the lot of you safely through to this point."

"Safely?" Emilio's face went red. "Have you forgotten where we are? Why we're here?"

"Listen, boy." The fluorescent lights throughout the room dimmed as Grey turned on Emilio. "Do not presume to lecture me on matters of the Game. I have walked this sphere for longer than your limited mind can comprehend, buried friends from fifty different generations, watched lovers wither and die like cut flowers under the summer sun.

"I have lived through three iterations of this terrible Game I helped create, watched friends and enemies alike cut down in their prime, all to satisfy the capricious whim of an unfeeling universe. Though I understand those few deaths served to stave off the destruction that would otherwise have occurred, it does little to silence the voice inside me insisting there must have been another way."

Steven stepped in front of Emilio, the boy's wide-eyed face pale in the face of Grey's quiet fury. "What you're suggesting is maybe the Arbiters aren't as oblivious as we were led to believe. That's why we're all still breathing."

Grey, his anger already fading like a summer squall, nodded his assent. "In the last several days, have not each of you spoken with words not your own or become possessed of knowledge, however fleeting, outside of your specific frame of reference? It seems the Arbiters are not dealing with Zed directly, as this iteration has yet to commence. The fact that our young Queen was able to defeat her abductor mere moments after claiming her icon, however, makes their involvement undeniable fact."

Audrey's eyes brightened. "You mean they were there when I... when the—"

"Yes, Audrey," Grey answered. "Your encounter with the Black Knight was influenced by forces beyond your perception." He turned to face the rest of the group. "All of you should take some small measure of comfort knowing this iteration of the Game may not be quite the anarchy I had assumed. The enemy's absence at the recent conscription of our Bishop supports this theory. Zed may be playing his most aggressive Game yet, but he is no fool."

"So, what do we do now?" Lena asked.

"Claim the White Rook," Grey said. "The rest will play itself out as it will."

Somber silence filled the space for a moment as the gravity of Grey's words sunk in. Archie dropped his head in prayer, his silent lips working in earnest. For the moment, at least, Emilio put aside his sullen facade and comforted Lena, though his acerbic stare remained focused on Grey.

Audrey looked up at Steven, her eyes as full of sadness, fear, and longing as Lena's and he had to fight harder than he cared to admit not to follow Emilio's lead. He barely knew this woman, Audrey, yet she already held a place in his heart that had remained empty since he stood graveside at Katherine's funeral all those months before.

"Steven," Lena said. "I'm trying to get my aunt on Grey's phone but I keep getting the stupid machine. Do you think—"

"I don't know, Lena. We'll keep trying to get in touch with them, but for now, leave them a message. Say whatever it takes to get her and anyone else in your family out of town for at least a couple of days."

Steven turned to Grey. "I need you to do something for me."

Grey shook his head. "I cannot do what you ask. It violates the rules of—"

"Screw the rules. The way I see it, Zed is playing so hard and fast, it might as well be a different game." Steven's eyes narrowed. "You know what I need, don't you?"

"Yes, but—"

"Watch over them for a few hours," Steven said. "I'll be back before sundown."

"But the repercussions could be—"

"Look, for once, skip the cryptic crap. Are you going to do it or not?"

Grey sighed, his eyes the color of a thunderstorm on the horizon. "Very well. I will watch after them while you are gone." His gaze wandered the room, stopping briefly at each of the four in their now shared charge. "We shall await you at the town center."

As Steven turned for the exit, Audrey grabbed him by the arm. "Hey." More than a small measure of fear colored her words. "Where are you going?"

"There's someone I've got to see. Don't worry. I won't be long. Grey's going to keep an eye on you guys till I return."

"I want to come with you." Audrey bit her lip as her trembling gaze fell to the floor.

"I'm sorry, Audrey, but this is something I've got to do alone." Steven took her chin and brought her eyes back to his. "I'll be right back. I promise."

"All right," she whispered. "Hurry back."

Steven's gaze followed Audrey as she walked to a window. A summer shower pelted the thick glass like the angry tears of a thousand angels.

"Nothing can happen to them," Steven whispered to Grey. "Do you understand?"

"More than you know." Grey turned to join the others. "Sundown."

Steven took one last look at Audrey's auburn locks and headed for the elevators.

"Sundown."

## 26

## HOME

A family of white-billed American koots paddled by Steven's feet in the afternoon shadow of the old sycamore that had stood by the water's edge since he was a child. The river birches he and his dad planted by the lake when he was fourteen had thrived, their topmost branches swaying in the gentle breeze a good twenty feet above his head.

The roar of a Harley Davidson motorcycle sent the waterfowl flapping across the still water. Before Steven could stop himself, the pawn icon was in his hand.

"So, this is PTSD," he muttered, returning the icon to his pocket. The road crossing the dam was far busier than he remembered. Though he couldn't rule out the embellishment of time's passage, in the back of his mind Steven could recall hours of silent solitude spent by the lake when he was a boy. Life certainly seemed far simpler then.

A flopping fish broke the water's placid surface, jogging another memory that brought a smile to Steven's face even as it hurt his heart. In a flash, he was twelve again and on the lake in his family's old Coleman canoe. His mother sat in the front, reading one of those thrillers she loved by the fading light of early evening, while Steven and his father sat in the rear casting line after line in hopes of reeling in their dinner for the night.

Not long after, the raging hormones of adolescence had taken much of the joy out of such simple pleasures, but in that moment, the part of Steven's heart that still remembered his mother through the eyes of youthful innocence ached.

The familiar crunch of gravel under tires brought Steven back to the present. Up the hill sat the one-story ranch he used to call home. The red Chevy Blazer his father had been driving since the early nineties pulled to a stop by the small porch off their kitchen. As he headed up the hill to greet a man he hadn't spoken to in over two years, he struggled to come up with something—hell, anything—to say. The events of the preceding seventy-two hours were far beyond anything Don Bauer would listen to, much less believe.

An only child, Steven had always been close with his parents, his memories of growing up filled with images of his mother's unquenchable zeal for life and his father's quiet pride. In the summer of his junior year at Georgetown, however, everything had changed. He could still see the hastily scrawled note he found lying on the kitchen counter.

Steven,

Come to the hospital. 6th floor.

The only word Steven remembered hearing that day was cancer. He took a semester off from school to be with his mother as she fought with all she had against the malignancy that had grown unnoticed for months in her left breast. Despite the surgery and every therapy her team of doctors brought to bear, she succumbed less than three months after her diagnosis. "We were too late," the doctor said with a coldness Steven had never forgotten.

At age fifty-eight, his father lived alone, never having recovered from watching his childhood sweetheart wither away like some uprooted plant desperate for water. The last time Steven visited was weeks after Katherine's death on the fourth anniversary of his mother's passing. The visit hadn't gone well, the weekend culminating in a fight that pushed an already tenuous relationship with his father over the edge. He had picked up the phone a hundred times in the months since, but had never gotten up the nerve to make the call.

Steven reached the top of the hill and stepped onto the wooden deck that bore the spattered grease stains of a hundred summer cook-outs. Gazing through the blinding sunlight reflecting off the Chevy's dirty windshield, he spied the crest of his father's head as the man rummaged in the passenger side floorboard, his salt-and-pepper hair far more salt than Steven remembered.

"I can't believe it's been so long."

Donald Bauer rose back into his seat and spotted his son's hunched figure in the shadow of the house's eastern side. A flash of recognition bordering on pleasant surprise crossed his face, replaced in a blink by a mask of practiced indifference. He opened the door to his truck, stepped out onto the gravel, and looked Steven up and down for a moment before speaking.

"Hello, Steven." His father's voice came out muted, matter-of-fact.

"Dad." Somehow, this encounter wracked Steven's nerves even more than the insanity that had overtaken his life in the preceding days. "You're looking well."

"You should've called and let me know you were coming," Donald said. "I've been out all day running errands."

"It's all right. Pretty busy myself this morning. Besides, I've only been here a few minutes." Steven waited in vain for his father to respond. "So, when did you take out the pier?"

"Last year. The wood was getting pretty rickety." After another protracted pause, Steven's father finally caved. "So, what brings you out this way?"

*As if I lived around the corner.* "Believe it or not, I happened to be in the neighborhood. Had some business down in Roanoke. Thought I'd drop by."

"Well." Donald turned and headed for the house. "You still drink Dr. Pepper?"

A sad chuckle escaped Steven's lips. "Sure."

He followed his dad inside and took a seat at the round glass table where he used to eat Frosted Flakes every morning before school. The old parquet floor, still rippled from the edge of the kitchen counter all the way to the front door, had seen better days, its once glossy surface now dull and scratched from years of wear and tear.

The place looked clean for the most part. No one had ever accused Don Bauer of being a slob, but anything beyond the simple day-to-day upkeep of a home had clearly been ignored for a very long time.

Donald procured two bottles of Dr. Pepper from the old Kenmore refrigerator in the corner of the kitchen, popped the caps off of each using the edge of the counter, and set one down in front of Steven. He hadn't lost that bit of panache, it seemed. Steven wasn't sure how his dad was still able to score the old-school glass bottles of soda he routinely kept stocked in the fridge, but they had always agreed there was no comparison.

"So, Dad, how've you been?"

"Pretty good. Doc Hagy says my blood pressure's not too bad for an old man and other than my trick ankle, I'm still getting around pretty good. Truck's holding up fairly decent." Donald cleared his throat. "Can't complain, I guess."

"Guess not." Steven's eyes cut toward the front of the house. "Mrs. Chatsworth still stop by and check in on you?"

"Yeah, she comes by every couple of weeks. I'll fix some dinner, she brings apple pie, peach cobbler, or some such, and we watch the tube or sit and talk about better times."

"And how's Mr. Chatsworth these days?"

"Jim? From what Deb says his Parkinson's getting pretty bad. She's not sure how much longer he's going to be able to get around on his own."

"That's too bad," Steven said. "He was always a pretty decent guy."

"Steven."

"Yeah?"

"Shut up." Donald's eyes dropped for a moment, and when he again looked up, the face that had accompanied a thousand lectures during Steven's childhood looked back. "I don't believe for a minute you came all the way up here to ask about a bunch of long-in-the-tooth seniors you haven't laid eyes on since you were in high school. Hell, you haven't even darkened my doorstep in, what, going on two years now? What's going on?"

"The truth?"

"It'll set you free, isn't that what they say?" A half smile parted Donald's lips as he let Steven squirm. "Come on, son. Spill it. You have that look like when you skinned up the car back in tenth grade. You in trouble or something?"

"You could say that." Steven studied the ripple in the parquet floor.

"Is it money? Do you need some money?"

"No, it's nothing like that. It's, well… there are these people, Dad." Steven caught his father's skeptical eye. "God, this is going to sound paranoid." He took a breath. "The last few days, they've been after me. No matter where I go, they get there first. These people are serious trouble." His eyes slid closed. "I wanted to make sure they hadn't come after you."

"You're right, Steven." His dad drank the last swig of his Dr. Pepper and rested the empty bottle on the table between them. "That does sound paranoid."

Donald rose from the table and plopped down in the oversized recliner in the corner and flipped on the tube. There, he sat in silence as the television blared with one of those daytime court shows that made Steven want to bang his head against a wall. Compared to the man who once spent every possible second in the sun and air with a shovel, paddle, or walking stick in his hand, the Don Bauer before him was a shadow, a sad recluse who spent most of his hours in a darkened living room bathed in the cathode rays of the vintage Panasonic set.

"Turn that crap off." Steven followed him into the next room. "We're talking here."

His dad hit the power button on the remote and placed it back on the scarred end table. Not taking his eyes off the darkened screen, Donald sat in silence for a few moments before answering his son in a voice that was a bit too quiet.

"You want to talk, huh?" He shifted in his seat, his back cracking like a frozen lake on the first day of spring. "I'm not sure what you want me to say. Not a peep out of you for two years, and now you show up on my doorstep out of the blue talking out of your head about people who are out to get you. Way I see it, either you've gotten yourself into something way over your head, or that overactive imagination of yours has finally gotten the better of you."

"Look, I know I've been out of touch." The half laugh, half harrumph from his father sent a pang of guilt through Steven's gut. "All right, way out of touch, but that's beside the point. These people are real." Steven pounded the wall. "Dangerously real."

Baffled, Donald stared off into space, not saying a word.

"You know," Steven continued, "if this is how it's always going to be when I come home, then I'm glad I moved away. It's not like the last few years have been easy for me either. I miss Mom just as much as—"

"Stop. Don't you dare come here and tell me about how hard the last couple of years have been. And as far as missing your mother goes, I wrote the book, Steven. I wrote the damn book." Donald launched himself from his oversized recliner and walked out onto the front porch without another word.

Steven set his jaw and sighed as the front door slammed closed in his face. "Wow," he mumbled under his breath, "this is going well."

Out on the porch, his white-knuckled hands clutching the porch rail, Don Bauer stared westward, boldly defying the glaring sun of late afternoon. " You know, son. You've been running since you could stand. Fastest thing on two legs. It used to make your mom and me so proud." His father turned and looked at him, his sad eyes somewhere between regret and disappointment. "I guess I just never thought you'd run out on me."

"Don't you dare. That crap goes both ways and you know it." Heat rose in Steven's cheeks. "I barely heard from you my whole last year at Georgetown. Hell, you didn't even make Katherine's funeral. I know it's been rough since Mom died, but for God's sake, our wedding date was less than a month away. Were you going to skip that too?"

As his father's anger deflated, Steven fought the urge to hit him with one last dig.

He lost.

"Don't think for a minute I'm the only runner in this family."

Donald hung his head, and Steven wished the words back into his mouth. The sun continued its slow march across the sky as father and son stood in silence, neither ready to concede the point or admit the other was right.

Eventually, Steven made the first move, clasping his father's shoulder and pulling him back inside. "Come on, Dad. You've got to be starving. Let's go put together some dinner."

The smell of breaded pork chops soon filled the kitchen, and the growing pang in Steven's side reminded him a good ten hours had passed since he and Audrey choked down stale biscuits and coffee from the hospital snack bar. A drop of hot grease popped up from the frying pan and singed his wrist. He jerked his arm under the faucet and ran cool water over the burn.

His father took the pan of sizzling pork off the burner and speared a piece for his plate, tapping his foot as he waited for the rest of the meal to finish. After a few impatient seconds, he put his plate down on the counter and started to empty the dishwasher, a move Steven knew well.

"Veggies are almost done," Steven said. "A couple more minutes and we can eat."

His father chuckled. "You cook like your mom. She was a miracle worker. Always fixed it to where everything got done at the same time. Like magic." Donald glanced over at a picture of the three of them on the wall by the door. "Never got the hang of it myself."

Steven smiled. "I learned from the best."

"Remember how she finally got you to stop spitting out your lima beans?"

"I don't think adding bacon and ketchup to the mix is exactly playing fair. In fact, if I remember right, the vegetarians of the world lodged a formal complaint on that one."

"I miss her, Steven." The laughter left his voice, leaving only weariness. "Things have never been the same around here. Not even close."

"I know, Dad." Other than this brief island of conversation, the meal was an ocean of half-hearted questions and noncommittal answers. Beaming in the window that looked out onto the front yard, the sun was getting low in the sky.

"Do you think you could give me a ride back into town?" he asked.

"I'm meeting some associates for coffee. I could call another cab, but—"

"Shouldn't be a problem. I didn't have anywhere to be tonight. Hell, this week. Just do me a favor. Don't stay gone so long this time." Donald patted Steven's knee. "It was good seeing you again."

"Same here, Dad." Steven pulled in a breath. "Same here."

onald Bauer turned off the highway onto the busy two-and-a-half-mile stretch of road that led to his subdivision. *Coward of the County* blared from the truck's stereo speakers, the local country station in the middle of a mini-marathon of Kenny Rogers tunes. He laughed a bit as he sang along with *The Gambler*, but as Kenny's indictment of his life extended into *Through the Years*, his thoughts drifted into dangerous territory. He flipped the radio off.

The drive to Roanoke had been for the most part quiet. Steven had insisted he take a few days off and get out of town, and though Donald wasn't sure he bought Steven's convoluted story about money and mobsters, he agreed to pack up and visit his sister in Miami.

After that, Steven clammed up, gone to that place he retreated to when something was on his mind. The quiet didn't bother Donald. Long periods of silence had become the rule in his life, not the exception. The last thing he expected when he got out of bed that morning was a visit from his prodigal son. Still, despite all the conspiracy nonsense Steven had been spouting, Donald had enjoyed their brief time together more than he would ever admit, even to himself.

As Donald rounded the last curve before his street, his brain came off autopilot in an instant, his foot slamming the brakes well before his mind could completely register what he was seeing. Halfway off the road sat a black BMW Roadster with its hood in the air and its back bumper still sporting dealer tags. A silvery plume poured from under the open hood. Donald inched his truck around the stranded vehicle's left rear quarter panel and noted a female silhouette amidst the wafting steam.

"Excuse me," Donald asked through the passenger side window. "Can I help you?"

The woman extricated herself from the overheating engine and brushed a lock of dark hair from her face. Donald's first thought was the woman must be a model or a movie star.

*Not too many goddesses with fifty thousand dollar cars in this neck of the woods.*

"Thanks." She smiled, and for a moment Donald Bauer felt twenty-five again. "Sorry to bother you. I was driving to a friend's when all of a sudden steam started pouring out from under the hood." She pursed her lips into a playful pout. "So much for top of the line engineering."

"Probably the radiator." Donald slid the Blazer into park. "You sure you're all right?"

"Oh, I'm fine. Didn't get the car quite as far off the road as I would've liked before she stopped rolling, though. Can you give me a push?"

"Sure." Donald pulled his Blazer off the road and helped the woman guide the sleek black vehicle onto the shoulder.

"Thanks for your help." The woman stepped back out of her car. "Not to be even more of a bother, but do you happen to have a cell phone on you so I can call Triple A? I'm all paid up on my dues and want to get my money's worth."

"Sorry, don't own one. Against my religion and all that. I do live right around the corner, though. You're welcome to use my phone."

"Are you sure?" Her beaming smile was like something out of an old black-and-white movie. "I don't want to trouble you any more than I—"

"It's no trouble. No trouble at all." Donald opened the passenger door to his Blazer and made a polite bow. "You can lock up your car and hop in the truck with me. I'm literally right around the corner. Hopefully, we can get you taken care of before it gets too dark."

"Sounds great," she said. "Give me a minute to close up shop here and we can go."

Donald hopped back into his reliable old Chevy and patted the dash. "Two hundred and eleven thousand miles and you've never let me down. Wash and wax for you this weekend."

A moment later, the woman got in and closed the door. "Thanks for all your help. Good to know chivalry still exists in the world."

"Not a problem," Donald said as he pulled back onto the road. "So, I guess we didn't do too well with introductions. I'm Don."

"Hi, Don." Her face broke into another megawatt smile. "I'm Magdalene."

"Magdalene," Donald said. "That's pretty."

"Thanks."

"So, Miss Magdalene. Are you married? Kids?"

"Oh no, none of that. Still looking for the right guy, I guess." The woman shot Donald a playful wink. "Why do you ask?"

Donald's cheeks grew warm. "Oh, nothing like that. I'm well past my expiration date. Actually, I was thinking about my son. He dropped by today for a surprise visit. I just took him back into town for the night. He's about your age, I'm betting you'd be right up his alley."

Magdalene laughed. "Too bad I missed him. Would've been nice to meet the son of a true gentleman like yourself."

Donald pulled the truck onto his gravel driveway and dropped the gearshift into park. "His name's Steven and I believe he's in town for the next day or so. Who knows? Maybe you two will run into each other."

"Maybe we will, Don." Magdalene smiled. "Maybe we will."

# 27

## SQUARE

One by one, the streetlights along Roanoke's Market Square flickered to life as the dimming light of early evening continued its slow fade into night. For hours, the outdoor market had been slow but steady, peaking at lunch before entering its typical afternoon decrescendo. The aroma of thousands of flowers still hung in the air, a heady scent that mingled with the smell of coffee from the corner café.

Though all but the most tenacious of vendors had long since headed for home, a diverse crowd filled the open space at the heart of downtown, the best dressed among them trickling two by two into the double glass doors of the Mill Mountain Theatre for a production of *Godspell*.

Along the opposite corner, a smattering of teens congregated outside the open doors of The Daily Grind. Backlit by the light streaming from the coffee shop's front window, a wooden bench held two figures deep in conversation. Their long white cloaks draped along the uneven brick sidewalk, neither of them appeared to be uncomfortable in the sweltering evening heat.

Even stranger, of the multitude of people walking along the busy street, only one gave them more than a passing glance. A young girl with chocolate skin and her hair done up in tight braids waved to the man on the right and blew him a kiss. The man waved back, smiling up at the child's mother who returned nothing but a bland expression and a curt nod as she and her daughter hurried past and into the coffee shop's open doors.

"Huh," Emilio said, "she looked at you like you had two heads."

Archie laughed. "It's like we're not even here."

Emilio shook his head. "Steven told me he walked up to some woman on the street in Baltimore, did everything he could think of to get her to notice him, just to see what she'd do. Went so far as to hop down the sidewalk beside her for half a block."

Archie's lips curled into a smile. "And?"

"Nothing. Didn't bat an eye."

"To be ignored by everyone who passes you by, like your life doesn't matter." Any joviality in Archie's tone vanished like a candle's flame in a hurricane. He inclined his head toward a homeless man in flannel and corduroys panhandling outside the novelty shop two doors down. "How must he feel? The best among us may feel pity or even compassion toward such a troubled soul, but most feel only guilt, revulsion, apathy."

"Whoa, Archie." Emilio's scooted away from the suddenly morose priest. "You okay?"

"Sorry." The sparkle in Archie's eye reignited. "I let my mind get away from me."

Before Emilio could probe further, Lena and Audrey exited the café and headed in their direction. Their cloaks flowing in the gentle breeze, each carried a pair of iced coffees. Smiling, Lena handed one of hers to Emilio while Audrey offered her extra cup to Archie.

"Thank you, my dear." Archie took a sip of the icy beverage. "I've steered clear of anything with caffeine for years, but I think this young body will be able to handle it better than my previous trappings. Also, I suspect we're all going to be up for a while and anything that helps toward that end is welcome."

Lena glanced down at her watch and cast her gaze about the square. "Where is he? It's been hours and it's getting dark."

"Don't worry." Emilio took a gulp of his drink. "Steven can take care of himself."

"I would not be so quick to dismiss your concerns." Audrey and Lena started at the sound of Grey's voice, his form invisible among the deepening shadows of evening. "Steven assured me he would be along well before now."

"Do you think he's all right?" Lena asked.

"Have faith," Grey said. "If anything serious had happened to Steven, I would know. In fact, we all would."

"He'll be here," Audrey said. "That's what I know."

Lena nodded in agreement. "He's not let us down yet."

"Still, every moment wasted is a moment our opponent can turn against us. As it stands, two Pieces remain to be found. Though Steven and the four of you stand ready, your mettle proven, the Black stands fully assembled while we have yet to claim our Rook or King."

"The Rook is the Castle, right?" Lena asked.

"In a manner of speaking." Grey adjusted his hat. "You see, Lena—"

"I can see him, you know." Archie's mouth turned up into a strange grin.

"Who?" Audrey knelt before Archie. "Who can you see?"

"The White Rook." Archie's voice became strange and distant. "He is a strong one, though his life hangs by the most tenuous of threads. If someone isn't there to catch him..." A quiet giggle escaped the priest's lips a moment before his face resumed its previous solemnity. "Go on, Grey." His voice as well had returned to normal. "You were saying?"

Grey stared at him from beneath a furrowed brow, the wizard's incredulous expression mirrored on all their faces.

"Did I... say something?" Archie asked.

"Um... yeah," Emilio said. "You started talking out of your head again."

"You were talking about the White Rook," Lena said. "You said you could see him, that he was in some kind of danger."

Archie sat in baffled silence.

"Can you remember any of it?" Audrey asked. "Anything at all?"

Archie's eyes slid closed, and for a long while, he said nothing.

When he did speak, the words again left his mouth in a voice not quite his own. "I see two towers in the midst of a sprawling city. The King and the Queen. It is dark there, and he is alone." The priest shivered. "No. Not alone." His eyes sprung open, awash with fear. "He's anything but alone."

"It is as I feared." Grey stepped out of the circle and turned toward the center of town. "Wait here for Steven and no matter what, stay together. If the Black make an appearance, trust that I will not be far." And with that, he walked away without a single glance back.

As Lena and Emilio pumped Archie for further details of his vision, Grey meandered up the main thoroughfare away from the hubbub of Market Square. Reaching the far corner of the third block, he lingered for a moment by a small pawnshop that was closed for the evening.

He perused the wares on display behind its barred windows, his gaze stopping on a collection of old timepieces. A pocket watch fashioned of tarnished silver with gold trim rested at the center of the sixteen watches. The crystal's otherwise smooth surface marred by a single stellate crack at its center, the watch's hands were frozen in perpetuity at 10:57.

"Grey?"

It was the wizard's turn to be startled as the quiet voice shocked him out of his reverie.

"Audrey?"

"Sorry," she said. "I hope I'm not disturbing you."

"Of course not." Grey wiped the tear from his cheek before turning to face her. He noted Audrey had been crying as well. "What troubles you, my dear?"

"I need to ask you something." Audrey choked back a sob. "Something important."

Grey studied her for a long moment. "Very well."

"The others can't know I'm asking you this." Audrey shifted on her feet, her eyes welling with tears. "And no sugarcoating. I want it straight. The truth."

"I will do my best to keep your confidence, and if my suspicions about what you intend to ask are correct, I assure you my answer will be the truth, as well as I can say."

"Fair enough." Audrey took a breath. "I was thinking. Each of us: me, Steven, the others. The pouch picked us all for a reason, right?"

"That is correct."

"And if we're all in this thing because we're supposed to be, it means something about us sets us apart. Makes us different."

"True."

"Well, we've all been so focused on surviving and making it through to the Game that none of us have talked about what comes after. I mean, if we're all as special as you say, handpicked from millions to fill our various roles in the Game, who's to say we won't win?"

"A very astute observation."

"If we do win, what then? Do Lena and Emilio return to Baltimore and go back to high school like nothing ever happened? Does Archie go back to the hospital to live the rest of his days as a feeble old man after getting a second taste of youth?"

"Go on." Grey rested a fatherly hand on the girl's shoulder. "Ask the question you really want to ask."

Audrey stared at him, her shock melting into fury. "What's going to happen to me, Grey?" She blinked the tears from her eyes. "When this is all over and this Game of yours is through with me, what next? Am I cast aside like a broken toy? Do I survive all this shit just to let the leukemia finish me off? If that's the case, then all of this is nothing but a cruel joke."

Grey turned back toward the pawnshop window, his voice barely a whisper. "With each iteration, the Game takes the Pieces it needs and empowers them for the duration of play, briefly bringing together the opposing forces of that particular correction to fulfill its sole purpose. Once the Game is played out, however, the forces involved return to quiescence and the surviving Pieces return to their native state.

"In the past, some have chosen to remember their experiences, but most have opted to have the Arbiters return them to their places of origin and strip their memory of any recollection of the Game." Grey turned and faced Audrey's distraught stare. "These provisions were meant to be a kindness, a way to minimize the impact on the individuals' lives and—"

"You've got to be kidding." Audrey's body shook with righteous fury. "Want some advice on minimizing impact on people's lives? Don't kidnap us and force us to play a Game where the other side is doing its level best to kill us."

"It was never meant to be this way." Grey whispered. "No one was ever supposed to die. Zed's machinations over the centuries have warped the Game into something I never intended, but even so, it changes nothing. Regardless of the consequences, the Game must be played."

"That's a load of shit. You talk about consequences like *your* life is the one on the line. Well listen, Mister Immortal Wizard, it may be your Game that's being played, but we're the ones paying the price of admission."

Remembering Grey and Emilio's interaction from earlier in the afternoon, Audrey steeled herself for the brunt of Grey's ire and found herself unprepared for the words he spoke instead.

"I am truly sorry, Audrey Richards, for all of this—the danger, the false hope, all of it. Though the Game has become the very definition of a necessary evil, I have spent centuries searching for an alternate solution, a way to undo what we wrought all those many years ago.

"The power, and more importantly, the knowledge required to make such a change has long since vanished from this world. The only person alive who could conceivably aid me in such an endeavor clearly has other plans. It took a council of many to bring this terrible Game into being, and despite the accrued wisdom I have gleaned over nearly two millennia on this planet, I am still but one man."

"Answer me this, then." Audrey glared at Grey through bloodshot eyes. "Of all the billions of people on the planet, why pluck a girl off her deathbed to play this stupid Game if the end result, win or lose, is she ends up six feet in the ground?"

"The truth?"

Audrey's voice cracked. "Please…"

Grey drew close, his lips turned up in an enigmatic smile. "I cannot be sure, but perhaps the Game in its perverse wisdom chose you because of your illness, not despite it."

"And what's that supposed to mean?"

The wizard's eyes burned through her. "A person with nothing to gain is also a person with nothing to lose."

Before Audrey could respond, Grey's attention shifted back toward the square.

"What is it?" she asked.

"The others," Grey said. "Something is happening."

Audrey's heart froze as Grey took off at a dead sprint leaving her beneath the pawnshop's overhang. She retrieved the Queen icon from her pocket and noted its white marble surface gave off only the dimmest glimmer.

"Well, at least it's not them." Audrey raced down the sidewalk after Grey. Between the shadows and the thinning crowd, he was barely visible in his voluminous coat, but Audrey had learned how to pick out the wizard's form despite the murk and magic. She caught up to the grey-clad wizard by the theater entrance and scanned the square for Emilio and the others. Her heart sank with each stranger's face.

"Where are they?" she asked.

Where Archie and Emilio had been sitting, a young couple worked to quiet a screaming child, much to the dismay of the skateboard crowd gathered on the corner where Lena had stood minutes before.

"Grey?" Audrey's voice grew frantic. "Do you think—"

Before she could finish her question, her wandering gaze fixed on a face she had waited far longer than that night to see.

"Steven."

She sprinted across the crowded square, and blushed when Steven caught her gaze with a casual smile that was already far more than familiar. Flanked on either side by Emilio and Lena, Steven held up a hand to quiet Archie as Audrey negotiated a mob of children to join their circle.

"You're late, you big dummy." Audrey swatted his arm with half-playful ire, a jumble of mixed emotions tugging at her heart. "Is every-thing... okay?"

"Yeah. Everything's fine. Took a little longer than I... hey, have you been crying?"

Audrey rubbed at her eyes and forced a smile. "It's nothing. I'm just worried about Mom and Grandpa. Grey was doing his best to cheer me up, in his own morbid sort of way."

"And how's that, dare I ask?" Steven asked.

"As I said before," Grey said as he strode across the square toward them, "their deaths would serve no purpose other than to enrage our young Queen. Though such a tactic is far from beneath him, I fear Zed's plans for Audrey's mother and grandfather are far more insidious."

"See what I mean?" Audrey asked.

"Yeah," Steven agreed, "pretty morbid."

A large banner hanging between the buildings caught Steven's eye. "Center in the Square, huh?" He met Grey's gaze and smiled. "Nice."

"Where else would I bring the gathered White to wait? The center is after all the strongest position on the board." Grey returned Steven's grin, the expression odd on his wizened old face. "And your father? Is he well?"

"Still alive and kicking. As best I could tell, no one's come around to see him in the last week besides me. He agreed to get out of town, but God only knows if he'll follow through. Typical Don Bauer, stubborn to the end, not that I really blame him on this one. Even the most stripped-down version of the last four days would be pretty hard to swallow."

"At least you got to see your father," Audrey said. "I'd give anything if I could just know my mom was okay."

"He drove me back into town. Dropped me off a few minutes ago. Last thing he said before he pulled away was for me to get a haircut." Steven let out a sad chuckle. "What if that's the last thing he ever says to me?"

"All right. Enough with all the negative crap." Emilio held up his hands in exasperation. "We're going to make it through this, dammit."

"Not all of us," Archie said.

Steven spun and caught a glimpse of the strange glint in Archie's eye.

"What do you know?" Steven asked. "What have you seen?"

"Tell him about the Rook," Lena said.

"The Rook?" Steven asked.

Archie and the others worked together to recount the priest's brief insight into the White Rook's plight. Steven's expression grew more solemn with each detail of Archie's vision.

"No rest for the weary, it seems." Steven gazed around the circle at each face. "You ready, Emilio?"

"Enough talk." Emilio kept one eye on Archie as he stepped forward. "Let's go."

"I'll take that as a yes." Steven turned to Lena. "You still with us?"

"You know the answer to that one," Lena said. "Where Emilio goes, I go."

"All right. You two mount up and meet us back here." Steven locked gazes with the priest. "Archie, you good?"

"I am ready," he said, "though I fear we may be too late." His face lost all expression. "I see a white tower surrounded by a sea of black."

"That can't possibly be good." Steven cupped his hand at his mouth and shouted after Lena and Emilio to hurry. He turned to face Audrey and noticed her hands trembling at her side despite the stifling heat and the voluminous cloak draped about her shoulders.

"Are you all right?"

"I'm fine. Just a little case of the jitters. That's all. I'm good to go."

Steven pulled close to her. "Are you sure?"

Audrey's eyes narrowed, her voice taking on a new edge. "I'm fine."

"All right. I guess that leaves..." Steven scanned the area. "Grey?"

Their charcoal-clad mentor had again withdrawn, most likely watching from one of the many shadows in the square. No heartfelt goodbyes. No last words of advice. Merely the certainty that at some point, when the time was right, their paths would cross again.

The roar of Rocinante's motor returned Steven's attention to the here and now. Lena and Emilio pulled up astride the metallic beast's gleaming chrome body, its gentle purr punctuated by the occasional rev of the engine. Audrey and Archie joined them in the street, the bike parked diagonally across the middle of the intersection, and there the four of them waited. Steven had a flash of what Patton must have felt as he looked over his troops before they charged into battle.

"All right, everyone," Steven said. "Somewhere out there, the White Rook is in it deep, and chances are he doesn't even know it. I wish I could give you some idea of what to expect or what we're up against, but as usual, we're in the dark. It's just the five of us and you can be damn sure the Black will be there in force. Watch out for yourselves and each other."

Lena raised a timid hand as if she was addressing a teacher in school. Steven sighed. For all her bluster and bravery, she was still just a seventeen-year-old girl.

"Everything okay, Lena?"

The girl's trembling mouth turned up in a stubborn grin. "Just a thought. The coffee shop has a double door and it's the only one big enough for the bike." A young couple cut through the tight cloister of white cloaks. "No one will give us a second thought."

"Sounds like a plan." Pride swelled in Steven's chest. "All right everyone. Gather round and stay close."

Steven led the group toward the shop's open door, one hand clutching the pouch and the other gripped around the bike's left handlebar. Emilio guided the motorcycle toward the doorway while Lena held tight to Audrey and Archie's hands, the latter pair flanking the bike on either side. When they reached the door, Steven crossed its open frame, the pouch's low drone at once comforting and ominous.

Seconds later, a flash of blue-white lightning streaked across the cloudless sky, striking the copper roof of the twenty-story tower at the center of town. As every person in the square jerked their gaze skyward to witness the bizarre lightshow, Steven whispered, "Take us to the White Rook." The pouch pulsed in his hand, searing his fingers with its heat, and as one, the five stepped through the open doorway and vanished in a flash of silver.

## 28

## TOWER

T he sky above Atlanta was black, the stars obscured by foreboding thunderheads that stretched from horizon to horizon. The main arteries into and out of downtown sat sluggish and anemic as half a million people hunkered down in the face of the most violent storm to hit the southern metropolis in recent memory. Hail the size of small fists hammered down while gale force winds whipped through the steel and glass canyons of the city. Bolt after bolt of green lightning ripped the sky, the vehement punctuation of Mother Nature's latest missive to the far too complacent denizens of her little world.

Newscasters up and down the eastern seaboard spent the evening mocking the various meteorologists who had called for clear skies, though no sane person would have dreamed such a drastic shift in weather was possible. Common wisdom explained away the aberration as the exception that defines the rule. A small but vocal minority, however, believed the unprecedented storm a sign of the coming apocalypse. Regardless, all who faced the storm gained a better appreciation for the power of nature unfettered.

Off the beltway in the northwest corner of the city, the twin towers known to locals as the King and Queen dominated the darkened landscape. The regal latticework that crowned each of the two skyscrapers reflected the combined radiance of dozens of white spotlights, their angular spires piercing the night despite the blackened skies and pelting rain. At the base of the two towers, a brick courtyard sat empty save for the illuminated sculpture at its center, a dome divided into four quadrants sitting atop a fountain and circumscribed within an octagonal star. A banshee wind tore at the twin glass and steel edifices and whistled through the lattice walkway that connected the two buildings.

A streak of orange lightning struck between the two towers, not thirty feet from the stony dome at the courtyard's center. A deafening thunderclap reverberated in the space as five figures stepped out of nothingness into the driving rain. Cloaked in white, the quintet surrounded a wheeled machine of ivory and chrome. Their features inscrutable in the torrential downpour, the five drenched silhouettes scouted the area before converging at the base of one of the towers. A low, throbbing pulse sounded as the last of them joined the circle.

"Any luck?" Steven yelled over the pounding rain and the escalating drone resonating from his right hip, the pouch pulsing in time with his heartbeat.

"I don't think he's down here," Emilio said. "Who in their right mind would stay out in weather like this?"

"Then where is he?" The drone at Steven's side continued to rise and fall. "The pouch is going nuts."

"Maybe he's inside one of the buildings." Audrey held up an arm to block the rain from her face. "How are we possibly going to search two whole skyscrapers? It would take days."

"We won't have to." Archie's words cut through the roar of the downpour as he pointed skyward at the topmost reaches of the nearest tower. "He's up there."

Steven peered up through the raging storm. "Are you sure?"

Archie gave a curt nod. "Though the Sight is clouded by the storm, I can tell you with certainty that the person for whom we're searching waits atop the King tower and is alone." He retrieved the bishop icon from his pocket and held it before him, its glow growing brighter with each passing second. "But not for very much longer."

"What is he, crazy?" Audrey shouted over the whipping wind. "With all this lightning, he's going to get himself killed before the enemy even gets a chance."

"Maybe that's what he wants," Emilio muttered.

"What's that supposed to mean?" Steven asked. "You think he wants to die?"

"Look at us, Steven." Emilio's tone was flat, pragmatic. "All of us. Before you came along, Archie was stuck on a psych ward, Audrey was lying in her bed waiting to die, and Lena and I were about two seconds from becoming a statistic. Not exactly the dream team I would put together for this pickup game we've got going. Is it that big a stretch to think this guy might be on top of a skyscraper during a lightning storm for a reason?"

"You may be right." Steven studied the shimmering pawn icon in his hand. "But regardless of why he's up there, we all know what the opposition wants to do. Let's concentrate on getting our Rook safely away from here. We can sort out the rest later. Any ideas?"

"Maybe this is too obvious," Audrey asked, "but can the pouch get us up there?"

"I don't think so. From what Grey told me, the jaunts don't work like that. Even if I could get the pouch to make such a specific jump, the effort might leave us too drained to fight."

"What about the bike?" Lena asked Emilio as she stroked Rocinante's chrome handlebar. "Do you think a jump can cover that kind of distance?"

"I don't know, *mami*." Emilio's voice grew quiet. "I just don't know."

As the pair stared up at the glass and steel monstrosity, Steven clued in on what they were talking about. Twice in the battle with the Black Queen, Emilio astride Rocinante had somehow managed to leap from one place to another in an instant. These jumps had always been at most a few feet, though, and Steven more than understood Emilio's hesitation. Still, time was scarce.

"Give it a shot," Steven said. "It's the best idea we've got." He glanced skyward, afraid either might see the doubt in his eyes. "Take Lena with you and watch each other's backs."

Emilio climbed onto the ivory and silver motorcycle and revved the engine. "I'll try, but I'm not even sure how I did it before." He wiped the rain from his face. "I needed to be somewhere, and then I was there. Simple as that."

"Right now, we need you on top of that building," Steven said. "More importantly, the Rook needs you. Just have faith, and for God's sake, be careful."

"We're on it." Emilio's eyes narrowed. "You guys are coming too, right?"

Steven gestured at the tower's base. "As fast as the elevators will take us."

"We'll be right behind you," Audrey added. "Promise."

"Time's wasting, *papi*," Lena said. "Let's do this."

Leaping on the back of the bike, she wrapped her lithe arms around Emilio's chest. The faintest glimmer of a smile washed all fear from the boy's features. Emilio again revved the motor and he and Lena rocketed toward the base of the King tower.

The next few moments were a blur of motion, obscured by the driving rain that swept down between the twin skyscrapers. The roar of Rocinante's engine shook Steven's teeth as the bike sped headlong toward the columns that formed the building's foundation. Steven's every muscle tensed as he prayed their mad gambit didn't end in disaster.

With less than ten feet remaining between the motorcycle's head-light and the tower's unyielding stone, Rocinante vanished in a blinding flash, replaced by an ivory steed. Not slowing an iota, the stallion leaped to the side of the building, easily clearing three stories, and sprinted up the side of the tower as if gravity were merely a suggestion. In a second, the horse was out of sight, the sound of hooves on steel and glass drowned out by yet another surge of hail and rain.

"That was…" Archie looked on, eyes wide and mouth agape.

"Awesome." Audrey stared skyward in disbelief.

Steven headed for the door. "We can all be impressed with

ourselves later, but right now, Lena and Emilio are all alone up there with God knows what waiting for them. Come on."

Audrey and Archie followed Steven to the tower's nearest entrance, a large revolving door that opened onto a two-story, glass-enclosed atrium at the building's base. In stark contrast to the balmy humidity outside, the air filling the chamber was cool and dry, if not sterile in scent.

The large foyer opened onto four hallways, each of which led to a bank of elevators positioned at the building's center. The far left elevator stood open and empty. Steven stepped inside and reached for the button to the top floor when a subtle but familiar stab of ice pierced him to the core. He pulled the pawn icon from his pocket and found it glowing like a fallen star.

"They're here." Clutching his ribs as the stitch in his side flared, Steven found the same pain etched in his companions' features.

"What's happening to us?" The strain in Audrey's voice was unmistakable.

"That hot poker in your side?" Steven rested a hand just below his ribs. "That's the enemy." He took a breath. "Remember that feeling. It'll keep you alive." He held the icon before him, and with two muttered syllables, the shining marble figure disappeared from his hand only to be replaced an instant later by a long shield as his clothing shifted to the garb of the Pawn.

"Go ahead," Steven said, the pain in his side already fading. "Shift into your work clothes." He pressed the button for the twenty-fifth floor. "Once your icon knows you're ready for battle, the pain eases up pretty quickly."

Audrey was first. The marble icon held gingerly between her fingers vanished as her waterlogged street clothes shifted into the more regal raiment of the White Queen. Opaque mist billowed from beneath her gown as the jewels encrusted along her platinum and silver tiara shone with an inner fire. The silver-white radiance coalesced into a concentrated sphere of light that orbited her head like a small moon. The terrible juxtaposition of beauty and power manifest in the girl's graceful form left Steven speechless.

"Ready," Audrey said. She attempted to force a smile, but the result was at best a consigned grimace. "What do you think, Archie? Better in person?"

"You look radiant, my dear." Archie sighed, clutching the bishop icon tight to his chest, his fingers trembling around the shimmering hunk of marble. "My turn, I suppose."

The silver nimbus of light surrounding the bishop icon pulsed in time with the drone of the pouch. As the radiance crept up Archie's arm, a peculiar expression came across the priest's face, puzzled disorientation alternating with flashes of razor clarity. Steven reached out to touch Archie's shoulder and the priest's own hand shot out and grabbed Steven's wrist.

As if the Devil himself had come for his soul, a wide-eyed Archie launched into an unintelligible deluge of words, the verbiage not unlike the singsong chanting that had filled the ICU at the time of Lena's healing. Louder and faster with each breath, the priest's frenzied speech soon left the realm of forgotten language, however, and settled on a thick exaggeration of Archie's usually subtle Creole accent.

*"Faire attention à Le Fou. Faire attention à Le Fou. Faire..."*

Before he could repeat his bizarre warning a third time, Archie slumped to the floor, his knees buckling beneath him as if he were a puppet with cut strings. Steven leaped forward, catching Archie before his head hit the wall, and lowered the priest's body to the elevator floor. Audrey cradled Archie's head in her lap while Steven attempted to bring him around.

"Archie." Steven slapped him across the face. "Can you hear me?"

Another slap and Archie started out of his momentary delirium. His body shook as if he were waking from a nightmare. "Audrey?" he said weakly.

"Welcome back." Audrey smiled down at the suddenly frail face resting in her lap. "Are you all right?"

"That... remains to be seen." With Steven's help, Archie pulled himself to his feet and stood, still unsteady as the bishop icon in his fist pulsed faster and faster until its blinding silver radiance filled the elevator car with light.

"Thank you." Archie let go of Steven's arm. "But I must stand on my own two feet if I am to be worthy of my position on the Board."

Steven stepped back and gave Archie some space. Despite the priest's current youthful appearance, at his core was a man old enough to be his grandfather who deserved his respect.

The brilliance filling the car grew brighter with each passing floor, forcing Steven and Audrey to avert their eyes. As the light faded and their vision cleared, they found a very different Archibald Lacan.

The priest's soaked shirt and pants were replaced by a bishop's vestment, a gleaming white rochet over an ivory soutane, its sleeves adorned with silver thread. A miter rested upon his head, white and silver like his robes and covered with strange sigils Steven took to be some sort of ancient runes. In his hand, a staff of light poplar resided, its slender length terminating in a symbol resembling a Celtic cross ensconced within a crescent moon.

At that moment, the elevator doors opened onto the twenty-fifth floor.

"Shall we?" asked the White Bishop, his deep baritone reverberating through the space as he stepped into the floor's darkened hallway.

The trio made their way down the dim passage with Steven in the lead, Audrey close behind, and Archie watching their collective rear. They rushed up the stairs leading to the roof and found the steel door at the top ajar and the landing waterlogged. Steven put a finger to his lips and pushed open the door.

The three of them stepped out into the storm as one: Pawn, Bishop, and Queen.

A spike in the pouch's insistent drone confirmed the target of their search was nearby while the continued pang in Steven's side let him know they were far from alone. Blinded by the dozens of lights that illuminated the King tower's lattice crown, not to mention the escalating rain and gusts of wind, Steven perked his ears for any sign of life. Above the din of the storm, he could just make out the rumble of an engine to his forward right. Wrapping his cloak tightly about him, he headed in the direction of the sound with Audrey and Archie close behind.

Not far from the corner of the roof, its coarse motor howling like an injured beast, Rocinante rested precariously against one of the latticework uprights. The bike appeared intact, though Emilio and Lena were nowhere in sight. Peering through the rain, Steven cursed under his breath. A faint glow a few feet from the downed motorcycle emanated from Emilio's lance and Lena's mace, the pair of weapons lying crosswise next to two crumpled piles of white cloth.

Steven righted the chrome and ivory machine and stroked its warped handlebar. "Don't worry, boy," he muttered, his voice barely audible above the downpour. "We'll find them."

Archie's downcast gaze and Audrey's horror-stricken expression spoke volumes. "I know this looks bleak," Steven said, "but we have to assume Lena and Emilio are alive. From everything Grey's told me, they're off limits till the Game begins. For now, though, it's up to us." He peered into the rain-drenched darkness that surrounded them.

"The three of us could probably cover more ground if we spread out, but I think we'd better stick together. I have a nasty feeling we're being watched. These bastards would probably like nothing more than to pick us off one at a time." Steven assumed a low crouch and Audrey and Archie followed suit. "Eyes open, everyone."

The cloaked trio moved into a tight wedge and swept the roof's perimeter, though the deluge made it difficult to see more than a few feet in any direction. They'd barely covered half the roof's extent when Steven threw up his hands in frustration.

"This is pointless," he said in a harsh whisper. "I can't see anything."

"Patience, Steven." Archie's gaze dropped to the droning pouch at Steven's side. "The Rook is clearly still here somewhere."

"We've got to keep looking." Audrey pulled close. "What else can we do?"

Before Steven could answer, a form darted from behind a nearby air conditioning vent. The sprinting shape sent the pouch into an ear-piercing caterwaul.

"Stop!" Steven shouted.

"Leave me alone!" came a deep voice barely intelligible above the pounding storm.

Steven touched Audrey's shoulder, but she was already a step ahead of him. A tendril of white mist shot from beneath her feet, caught the runner about his midsection, and dragged him back. The image of a doomed fly snagged midair by a frog's facile tongue flashed across Steven's mind's eye as Audrey dropped her quarry in a heap at their feet. Dressed in a coat and tie and drenched to the skin, the man stared up at them, his gaze more fearful than angry.

"Who the hell are you?" The man's thick Polish accent cut through the sound of the rain as he struggled against the palpable haze that held him inert. "Let me go."

"Keep it down," Steven whispered. "We're not safe up here."

"No shit," the man said. "And what do you mean, 'we'?"

Steven let out a grim chuckle and signaled for Audrey to let him up.

At the White Queen's command, the mists dissipated. The stranger came to his feet and eyed his three captors with suspicion. An impressive cut of a man, the newcomer towered over all of them a good four inches and his broad shoulders spoke of someone who knew his way around the inside of a gym. Unsteady on his feet, he stumbled forward and nearly knocked Steven over. Even soaked to the bone, the reek of alcohol coming off the man turned Steven's stomach. Still, the pouch screamed its fervent endorsement from its master's scorched side.

Without a doubt, they had found their Rook.

"Listen." Steven shook the man's shoulders. "You don't know me, and you've got no reason to listen to anything I have to say, but here it is. My friends and I have been looking for you, and we're not the only ones. I have no idea what possessed you to head to the top of a skyscraper in the middle of a lightning storm, but it's probably the only reason you're still alive. The others looking for you, they want you dead, and unless I'm way off base, they're up here somewhere with us." He came nose-to-nose with the man. "Understand if they find you, they will end you without a thought."

The man's eyes cut to one side. "Like the two kids on the bike?"

The slurred words chilled Steven to the bone. "You saw them? Where are they? What happened to them?"

The flurry of metallic wings at Steven's chest answered his question all too well.

"I happened to them."

Steven hurled himself at Audrey and their newfound Rook before the taunt was complete, the sound of the Black Queen's icy voice spurring him like Pavlov's bell. The trio landed in a tangle of arms and legs, leaving Archie alone to face the full fury of the Queen's assault.

Scrambling back to his feet, Steven spun around in time to see the air around Archie erupt in dark flame. A kaleidoscope of images flashed through his mind—the immolated security guard in Chicago, the black arrow's near miss in Baltimore, Audrey's screams as she burned helpless in her bed, Lena's broken form after her first encounter with the Queen, the mangled motorcycle resting not thirty yards away.

*Dammit. Not Archie too.*

Steven summoned the pike and turned to face the woman who had in their three encounters become more than merely an adversary, but the very definition of nemesis. Surprisingly, Archie was holding his own, but there was no way he could last against the power of the Queen's flames. The silver ambience cast by his staff's headpiece shielded him from the brunt of her attack, but despite the rain, his robe already smoldered in the heat.

"I've got this," Archie shouted. "Get them out of here."

The Queen shot a wicked smile in Steven's direction as a river of fire swept out from beneath her feet, heading directly for Audrey and the Rook. Before Steven could move, Archie stepped into the path of the flame and brought his staff down upon the groundswell of fire, forcing the serpentine inferno away from them and toward the high wall that enclosed the diamond shaped rooftop.

"Go," Archie screamed as a twenty-foot section of concrete wall disintegrated into obsidian flame. "I'll hold her as long as I can."

Steven pulled Audrey to her feet, a different kind of pang hitting his side as he met her frightened gaze. "Look. I've got to get this guy out of here, but Archie isn't going to last long against the Queen." His voice dropped to a whisper. "Help him, but for God's sake, be careful."

Despite the rain, wind, and flames that surrounded them, Audrey managed a quick nod and a forced smile before turning her attention on the Queen.

The Rook, already on his feet, looked on in wide-eyed disbelief. "What the hell is all of this? Who are you people?"

"There's no time." Steven grabbed the man's arm. "We have to go."

"But—"

The whisper of shaft and fletching piercing the deluge ended in a sickening thunk of stone meeting flesh. The Rook cried out in agony, a black arrow protruding from his left shoulder, and lurched to one side.

Steven spotted a flash of movement along the latticework above their heads just before a second arrow buzzed down from above and embedded its head in the Rook's thigh. He brought up his shield to protect the defenseless man, though it was too little, too late.

"Your luck couldn't hold out forever, Steven Bauer." The Black Queen laughed as a third arrow flew in from a different angle and struck its target's muscular arm. "And if I've learned one thing from you, it's to never underestimate the effectiveness of a well-played Pawn." Her mocking voice cut the storm like a blade. "Wahnahtah, finish him."

At the Queen's command, a hail of arrows flew down from above, as if the storm had developed razor tips. Steven leaped in front of the wounded man with shield held high, but despite his best efforts, three more arrows found their mark. The threefold impact sent the man staggering, his stumbling course leading him dangerously near the interruption in the wall left by the Queen's previous attack.

Steven spun around, threw down his pike, and grabbed the Rook's thrashing hand, but the man's fingers, slick with rain and blood, slipped from his grasp, leaving him wavering at the edge of oblivion. He leaped forward to pull the man back from the brink and was driven to his knees by a searing impact between his shoulder blades.

Grey's voice echoed in his mind. *"As Pawn, your shield will protect you from any attack from the front, but you must ever watch your back."*

Struck breathless, Steven's chest throbbed as if he'd been impaled with a railroad spike as a high-pitched war cry from above pierced the storm's fury. Clambering to his feet as black shafts of death continued to rain down all around him, Steven threw down the shield and leaped forward, getting his fingers around the man's collar.

"Stay with me," he grunted through the pain. "We've got to—"

A second arrow hit Steven square in the back, forcing the remainder of air from his lungs. His vision suddenly filtered through a crimson haze, he jerked his head around and caught one last glimpse of Audrey's terrified gaze before his legs finally went out from beneath him. Her scream, the Black Queen's laughter, and the pounding rain all faded into nothingness as he and the Rook fell from the edge and out into the raging storm.

## 29

## ROOK

Steven plummeted headfirst toward the unforgiving concrete thirty stories below, the Rook's collar still held in his faltering grip. Gravity forced the blood to his brain and brought him back from the edge of unconsciousness. Hot blood trickled down his neck and a copper taste in his mouth threatened to make him retch.

Tangled within his cloak, Steven struggled to free his arms from the waterlogged shroud as he and the Rook hurtled toward the court-yard below.

*Only a few seconds till we hit.* Steven's numb fingers made it to the pouch, still droning at his waist. *Ground's coming up fast. If only...*

As if in answer to his unspoken request, the cloak unfurled from Steven's body like a giant pair of wings. A shimmering green glow lit up the space, and as their whirling fall brought them around again to face the building's mirrored glass windows, the source of the myste-rious light became clear. Shining like an emerald beacon in the night, Amaryllis had come to life, her metallic wings humming in concert with the droning of the pouch.

A glimmer of Ruth's smile flashed across Steven's memory, and only in that moment of desperation did he begin to fathom the depth of the old woman's generosity.

The jolt of rapid deceleration almost pulled the Rook from Steven's grasp, but somehow he found the strength to hold on with one hand and with the other undid the wet slipknot holding the pouch to his belt.

"Take this." Steven pushed the pouch into the man's clawing hands. "Something inside is calling to you." He closed the man's bloody fingers around the mouth of the leather bag. "Can you hear it?"

"I hear it," the Rook croaked, his voice barely audible over the rushing wind. "I—"

No sooner did Amaryllis pinch at Steven's collarbone than a tremendous force jerked him upward, forcing the air from his lungs anew and bringing an abrupt halt to his breakneck descent. The Rook, still subject to gravity's inexorable pull, wasn't as fortunate. Crying out more in fear than pain, his clawing fingers tore the white-hot pouch from Steven's hand as he disappeared into the obscuring gloom below.

Steven steeled himself for the pain-ending blow that was sure to follow this latest attack, but the ring of tangible mist encircling his midsection told a different tale. Amaryllis resumed her normal state, her piercing green glow fading quickly to black, leaving Steven again in darkness. There he hung like a worm on a hook, buffeted by the wind and rain. Head swimming from blood loss, his heartbeat pounded in his ears as the ephemeral tether of mist drew him upward. Adrenaline mixed with anger and defeat as he hung there impotent and the Rook's screams faded into nothingness.

"Steven," came Audrey's voice from above. "Thank God. Are you all right?"

"I had him, dammit." Despite the pain radiating between his shoulder blades, Steven turned his head and eyes skyward. There, silhouetted against menacing clouds lit by a fork of blue lightning, Audrey and Archie coasted down the side of the building atop a swirling cloudbank of silver and white, their impossible ride the size of a small bus.

"Steven?" Audrey asked again. "What's wrong?"

"I had him," Steven repeated, his voice full of anger. "Now he's gone."

"I'm sorry, Steven. I couldn't see him." She looked away, catching her breath. "Hell, if your cloak hadn't lit up all green—"

*THOOM.*

An explosion echoed up from below, the roar deafening as it reverberated through the steel and glass canyon.

"What in Heaven's name was that?" Archie asked.

"I don't have the first clue," Steven whispered as Audrey pulled him onto the floating dais of fog, "but I have a feeling we're about to find out."

"What next, then, fearless leader?" Audrey asked, refusing to meet Steven's gaze. "Ground floor? Explosions, bad guys, and certain death?"

"Look, Audrey." Steven tried to catch her eye. "I'm sorry—"

"Forget it, Steven." At Audrey's downward gesture, the flying carpet of cloud and mist began to descend. "No time now for hurt feelings."

"Leave her be for a moment." Archie moved behind Steven and went to work on his wounds. "God willing, there will be time for apologies later."

"Good advice," Steven hissed between clenched teeth. "So, how bad is it?"

"My apologies. This is going to smart a bit." Archie pulled the first arrow.

Biting back a cry of agony that welled up from his very soul, Steven let out a pained grunt and did his best not to hyperventilate. "The other one. Do it."

Archie wrapped his fingers around the remaining shaft. "Once I pull the second arrow, I can bring my powers to bear, but there are no guarantees I'll be able to get you back into fighting shape before we hit ground." Archie let out a quiet sigh. "To be honest, I'm still learning how all this works. Without the others, I'm not sure I'll be able to help much at all."

"Just do it." Steven sucked in what air he could and balled his hands into fists. "Right now, I'll take what I can get."

The searing pain as Archie worked the second arrow out of Steven's back was torture, almost as if the priest were burying the point deeper in his flesh. The grinding sensation of stone on bone triggered wave after wave of nausea. Steven teetered on the verge of unconsciousness when the barbed tip finally tore loose with a ripping sound he prayed he would someday forget. Still, he could finally again take something approaching a full breath.

"Hard part is over," Archie said. "Ready for the good stuff?"

Steven trembled, his body going into shock. "Hit me with your best shot."

Archie laid hands on the pair of wounds. Within seconds, a rush of warmth flowed along Steven's back. His body glowed within a subtle cocoon of silvery radiance. Soon, the throbbing in his upper back diminished while the trickle of blood along his back slowed for a moment and then stopped altogether.

"Better?" Archie asked.

"Better." Steven turned to face the priest, his ribcage aching like he'd just gone ten rounds. "Not great, but better."

Audrey stood silent at the edge of the misty bulwark, her back turned to the both of them and her arms crossed.

"Thanks for the save, Audrey." Steven trudged through the half-solid mist to join her. "But how did you guys manage to get away from the Queen and her nest of hornets?"

Either deep in concentration, or not in the mood to chat, Audrey didn't say a word.

"As soon as you and the Rook went over the edge," Archie offered, "the Black Queen and her archers disengaged from the fight. She and five of the Black Pawns gathered together and they all disappeared in a big black bubble of darkness. A second later, Audrey grabbed me and threw us both off the edge after you." Archie's half-lidded gaze shot to Audrey. "I'm glad our Queen knows how to produce an elevator out of thin air. It's an awful long way down."

"I wasn't even sure it would work," Audrey muttered under her breath, but loud and clear enough to be sure Steven heard every word.

They descended in silence, the familiar sound of rain on brick growing louder and louder until the courtyard between the towers finally came into view. Through the deluge, a pile of rubble was just visible at the heart of an eight-point star design in the stonework.

"Wasn't there a sculpture there before?" Audrey asked.

Steven nodded, motioning for Audrey to stay quiet and bring them to ground. He turned to check on Archie and found the priest's face turned up in that same strange look of absurd whimsy that always set his hair on end.

"The dome is shattered, and yet, there's no body." Archie's mischievous eyes looked up and to the left as if he were performing some incredibly complex computation. "I guess the priest was only half wrong..."

"What are you talking about, Archie?" Steven's harsh whisper brought the priest around.

"Hmm?" Archie's blank stare somehow frightened Steven more than the knowing smirk he had worn a second before.

"Steven." Audrey's voice was dead. "Look."

Through the rain, Steven could just make out what Audrey was referring to. At the periphery of the courtyard, surrounding them on all sides, stood a wall of black stone.

"Shit." Steven stepped off the bank of mist onto the wet concrete. "Stay alert, you two."

"Steven Bauer, I presume." The level timbre conveyed a politician's polish, though the derisive tone carried an undercurrent of danger. "And you have brought Miss Richards and Father Lacan as well. What a pleasure to finally make all of your acquaintances."

Within their prison of dark stone, the downpour tapered first to a drizzle and then to nothing, while the precipitation outside the circle continued in earnest.

"Thus far, Bauer," the taunting voice continued, "you and your little clutch have proven quite an interesting distraction, far more interesting than I could have dreamed, in fact. Grey has prepared you well for our Game."

Steven, Audrey, and Archie cast about the courtyard, attempting to isolate the voice. In his heart, however, Steven already knew all too well the identity of the speaker.

Audrey was the first to spot him. She nudged Steven and pointed a trembling finger at the lattice walkway that connected the two skyscrapers. Looking down on them from his perch atop one of the walkway's support pylons was a man who could be none other than the Black King. Dry despite the surrounding deluge, the King surveyed the three of them, his jet-black beard surrounding a contemptuous smirk Steven suspected was a permanent feature.

The King was of the same lineage as Grey—the same square chin, the slight hook to the nose, the not quite familiar accent. His dark eyes carried the same fire as the man Steven had come to consider mentor, if not friend, but there, the similarities ended. Even in his bluntest moments, Grey always carried about him a certain air of humility, a quality absent in the King's haughty demeanor.

Atop his head of lustrous black hair sat a crown of ornately engraved silver adorned with cut onyx. The stones cast a purplish glow much like the gems along the Black Queen's scepter. A regal robe draped across his shoulders, its entire length as black as ink and lined with the dark fur of some forgotten species. Though his outward dress appeared primarily ceremonial, the platinum breast-plate just visible beneath his robes and the dark steel broadsword resting lightly in his chain mail gauntlet indicated he had come prepared to fight.

Steven stepped forward. "What have you done with Lena and Emilio?"

"Do not concern yourself with them, Pawn of the White. Truth be told, I ordered your Knight and his little girlfriend removed from play primarily to prevent anything untoward from happening to them. Wouldn't want to violate any of Grey's precious rules, now would we?"

"I want to see them." Steven's eyes narrowed. "Now."

"Very well, though it changes nothing." The King looked back across his shoulder. "Pawn, bring out the children."

From behind a stone obelisk stepped five figures. With jagged stone daggers pressed against both their throats, Lena and Emilio led the march, the fear on the girl's face surpassed only by the anger on the boy's. The pair was led by two of the Black Pawns while a third brought up the rear, his nocked and drawn arrow trained on the back of Emilio's neck. The trio of Blackfoot warriors brought Lena and

Emilio to the center of the courtyard and threw them to the ground at Steven's feet.

"You all make this far too easy," taunted the one with the drawn bowstring. "Do not expect such mercy in the future."

The frightened pair scrambled to their feet and took their place with the others. "Eight on two, *pendejo*." Emilio spat at their captors' feet. "I'd like those odds too."

The Pawns of the Black retreated in silence to the section of lattice walkway that held their King and trained their bows on the huddle of White at the courtyard's center.

"What do you intend to do with us now?" Steven asked. "The Game proper has yet to begin. From what Grey told me, that makes us basically untouchable."

"Unkillable? Yes." The Black King smiled. "But untouchable? That's a matter of some interpretation."

Audrey stepped forward to address the King. "With all due respect, Your Highness, shouldn't we be fighting for our lives right now?" The streak of bravado couldn't hide the fear in Audrey's voice. "You killed that poor man on the roof without so much as a warning and now you're sitting here chatting with us like we're old friends."

"Agreed," came an icy voice from their rear. "Honestly, I'm all for killing the lot of you and dealing with whatever shitstorm it brings down upon our heads." The Black Queen strolled across the circle from the Queen tower's ground floor, her entourage of five Blackfoot archers taking positions along the periphery of the circular courtyard. "If it were up to me, I'd have had Wahnahtah use the two kids on the roof for target practice, but Zed figured your Knight and his girl-friend had already been through quite enough drama for one day, what with her brains leaking out her pretty little ear just last evening."

Emilio bristled at that last bit, but Lena's grip on his arm helped him keep his tongue.

The King brought a finger to his lips and everyone fell silent. "Now, now, my Queen. Do not antagonize the children." His face grew dark and sober. "And remember, Magdalene, what we discussed about names."

The Queen's smirk faded as she lowered her head in deference and took her place beneath the King's lofty vantage. "Yes, my King."

"King of the Black." Archie held his Bishop's staff before him. "I have little doubt that were it not for the rules of this cruel Game, we would indeed be fighting for our lives."

"An inconvenience, priest." The King studied Archie, a cunning smile across his face. "A quite temporary inconvenience."

Steven stepped in front of Archie. "What do you intend to do with us in the meantime?"

"That, Steven Bauer, is the question at hand." The King sheathed his sword and stroked his full beard. "I suppose the prudent thing would be to detain the five of you until this iteration of the Game is complete. It wouldn't serve anyone's purposes to let you run amok, regardless of the futility of your actions."

"What you do with us today is of little importance." The fire in Archie's voice grew with each word. "Regardless of your plans, the Game will still occur at its designated time and place and White will face Black and despite their apparent ambivalence of late, I doubt the Arbiters would allow such disaster to crown their centuries of vigilance."

"You misunderstand," the King said. "The Arbiters care nothing about your capacity to engage in play or the outcome of any particular iteration, only that a fair representation of the opposing forces are present at the moment of correction. In fact, once the two sides are brought face to face, the lot of you cease to matter whatsoever, less than a footnote in a history no one will ever read."

"You expect us to believe you're just going to pen us all up till this correction thing blows over?" Trembling with cold and rage and fear, Steven willed his hands to remain still at his sides. "We may be new to all of this, but we weren't born yesterday."

"No need to be so melodramatic, Bauer." The King laughed. "Your mentor always was fond of the pomp and circumstance surrounding these engagements but all that truly matters is the balance of power when the Game comes to a close. The rest is nothing but trivial pageantry."

The King descended from his perch atop a scintillating square of floating darkness that came to rest midway between the cluster of White and the dark wall at the courtyard's edge.

"Contrary to what you may have heard," he continued, "I care nothing for bloodshed. True, you live now because the Game requires it to be so. Once this iteration reaches its conclusion and victory is achieved, however, rest assured I will not waste precious time or energy on such petty concerns as your five insignificant lives." The King's dark brow furrowed. "Make no mistake, though. This iteration is mine, and I will brook no further opposition. Conduct yourselves appropriately and you may yet live. Cross me and you will follow in the footsteps of your Rook."

"What a load of bullshit." Emilio stumbled as the pile of rubble at the center of the courtyard shifted sending a miniature avalanche of stone and concrete into the back of his legs. "How do we know you won't kill us the moment the Game begins?"

"You don't, boy." Any pretense of cordiality in the King's voice evaporated. "Though trust me when I say your tone does little to bring out my benevolent side."

"So, that's it, then?" Steven asked. "After everything that's happened, you think we're going to roll over and play nice? Be good little captives? Not happening."

"That is your decision to make, Bauer, though the alternative involves significantly more pain for you and your friends. Look around you. You have nowhere to go, nowhere to hide, no magic bag to whisk you away, and my archers surround you on eight sides." The King took a step forward, his face a mask of mocking concern. "You and your line of Pawns have proven most formidable thus far, but you know as well as I that an black arrow or tongue of flame will eventually get through your defenses, and then your friends will suffer. I would spare you such pain." The King rested the tip of his sword on the concrete at his feet and leaned forward on the hilt. "Consider your next words wisely."

Steven held his tongue as the octet of Blackfoot archers converged on the huddled White. The King looked on, his impassive expression at odds with the utter glee evident in the Queen's wicked smile. Steven checked on Audrey, hoping to find some glimmer of inspiration in those amber eyes, but found her gaze along with the others' directed skyward. He followed their collective stare up, and there, galloping down the steel and glass facade of the King tower, Steven found a glimmer of hope.

A white blur in the pale light between the two towers, Rocinante sprinted down the side of the dark skyscraper in utter defiance of gravity or anything resembling the laws of nature. Seven of the eight archers shifted their aim skyward and launched volley after volley of razor arrows at the racing stallion, but not a single shaft found its mark as the pale charger continued his erratic sprint down the building's sheer face.

"My Queen," the King said, "I tire of all these interruptions. Bring that inbred nag to ground and for once, finish a task."

The Queen nodded and raised her scepter to the sky, its serpentine head erupting in a black inferno that flew at Rocinante like a blazing battering ram. Undaunted, the horse continued his mad descent, racing headlong toward his fiery rendezvous. A moment later, the racing stallion's form was lost amid a dark conflagration of burning steel and shattered glass.

"Rocinante," Lena screamed. "No!"

Audrey grasped Steven's hand and squeezed it tight. "What now?"

"Hold on," Steven whispered. "I wouldn't count our horse out of the race quite yet."

As the splintered fragments of five stories of the tower's face rained down, the King dropped back into a defensive posture, his arrogant mien mingled with watchful apprehension as he raised his shimmering broadsword to eye level. "My Queen and Pawn, keep your eyes open. This is far from over."

"But—" The Queen's rebuttal was cut short as Rocinante reappeared in a flash of silver and bore down on the King's position. The King leaped to one side, avoiding the hammering hooves of the horse's first pass, and brought his broadsword above his head.

"You are a brave beast indeed to face me without your rider," said the King as Rocinante circled for a second charge, "but bravery will take you only so far. Unlike my Queen, I have faced your like before."

"Rocinante," Lena screamed. "Don't."

The stallion raced at the King a second time, and again, the King dove to one side. This time, however, he expertly brought his broadsword around in a sweeping arc and dealt a glancing blow to Rocinante's flank.

"First blood," the King shouted. "Go now, beast, and stand with your master. You have well proven your mettle, but continue this and I will be forced to put you down here and now."

Without missing a stride, Rocinante lowered his head and circled around for a third run at his armored target. Laughing, the King raised his sword for another strike.

"That bastard's going to kill him," Lena cried. "Can't we do something?"

"I don't know what you want me to do, Lena," Steven said. "We even breathe funny, his Pawns will turn us into pin cushions. We almost lost you once today, Audrey and Emilio as well. I can't risk it." Steven winced as the King dealt Rocinante a second blow, the slash leaving a crimson gash across the horse's broad chest. "I'm sorry, but Rocinante's on his own."

"Perhaps I can help," came a gravelly voice that outstripped even the howling wind.

"Who?" Steven's eyes darted left and right.

"Sorry." The disembodied words reverberated from the rubble at the courtyard's center. "Still pulling myself together." The pile of shattered stone and concrete shifted one way, then the other, and then rose like clay on an enormous potter's wheel.

"What the—" Emilio stammered.

Resembling a serpent formed of jagged stone, the rubble encircled Steven and the others and continued to grow. Stone upon stone and row upon row, a shape began to take form.

A wall.

"Their Rook," shouted one of the Black Pawns. "He's alive."

The King's gaze shot to the center of the courtyard, his eyes cold as he caught sight of the mounting mass of rock and debris.

The momentary distraction cost him dearly.

Rocinante reared before the King, his front legs working like pistons. A spray of blood flew from the King's head as one of the horse's flailing hooves clouted him across the temple. The platinum crown flipped end over end into the waiting darkness, and the force of the blow flung the King to the ground. His sword clattering useless on the brick of the courtyard, he scrambled backward to evade Rocinante's trampling hooves.

"Stand down, beast, or face my fire." The Queen stepped between the King and the furious stallion, a maelstrom of black flame swirling in the air above her head. "I won't miss a second time."

The horse shot a hesitant look back at the circle of White with equal parts fear and fire in his equine eyes and let out a questioning neigh.

"Come on, boy," Emilio shouted. "Get away from her."

Rocinante spun and sprinted for his master with a triumphant whinny.

"Run, boy," Lena screamed. "Run."

As the horse neared the huddle of White, the Black Queen crouched by the fallen King, all the while barking orders at the octet of Black Pawns.

"The King is down," she screamed. "Fire, damn you, fire!"

As one, the archers drew their bows and launched a volley of black arrows into the cluster of cloaked forms at the courtyard's center.

"Phalanx." The word was out of Steven's mouth before his mind could fully grasp what was happening. The octet of shield bearers appeared a split second before the eightfold assault hit, the tight semi-circle of steel joining the now waist-high wall of concrete and brick rising around them. Though an impressive perimeter, both shields and stones still allowed a single arrow to pass.

"Oh, God…" Audrey whispered as she fell to her knees, the dark fletching of the shaft protruding from her abdomen hidden among the billowing folds of her cloak.

"Audrey!" The eight Pawns screamed in unison as the color drained from Audrey's cheeks and into the rapidly enlarging crimson circle on her gown's ivory bodice. An all too familiar panic gripped Steven's heart as their Queen fell limp to the pavement.

"Archie." Steven's voice cracked. "Help her. Please."

"I'm on it." The priest knelt by her side as the dark archers surrounding them launched a second barrage. "Just keep them off us." Archie closed his eyes to pray.

The curved wall of shattered concrete and brick continued to grow, extending to include the circumference of their small circle and leaving only a single door at its base. Within seconds, the structure was complete, a thirty-foot high embodiment of the tower seen on chessboards across the world.

Steven shifted seven of his phalanx of Pawns to cover the lone entrance. Two deep beneath the arched doorway, they raised their shields and prepared for the worst. The eighth Pawn remained inside with Audrey, who by the silver light of Archie's healing touch appeared to be getting paler by the minute.

A moment later, Rocinante passed ranks through the Pawn defense. Skirting Archie's hunched form as the priest ministered to Audrey's injuries, the horse joined Lena and Emilio along the wall's inner periphery and lowered his head before his young master and mistress.

"Good boy." Lena ran her fingers down the stallion's broad neck, but recoiled in fear as her hand came away hot and sticky.

"No." Lena leaped to the side as Rocinante's knees buckled and the horse fell. She gasped at the three feathered shafts jutting out of his neck, flank and hindquarter.

"Steven," she yelled. "Rocinante's hurt. He's hurt bad."

Emilio hunkered down by the wounded horse. "Archie," he asked, the emotion choking his voice, "will whatever it is you do work on a horse?"

"I believe so, but it's taking all I've got to keep Audrey's bleeding from getting worse." The priest wrung his hands, his eyes darting side to side. "We've got to get out of here."

In a rush of memory, Steven's subconscious took him back twenty years to the summer of his eighth birthday. His family vacationed in San Antonio that July. He remembered it well. The old church from a different time stuck in the heart of a modern city. The ancient tree that stretched from one end of the courtyard to the other. The detailed diorama of the battle resting under glass in the busy gift shop.

Surrounded by a seemingly infinite legion of troops dressed in blue and red, the situation depicted appeared unwinnable. Steven remembered asking his father what happened to all the brave men that fought from within the fort that day.

"They all died," his father whispered. "That's the lesson of the Alamo, Steven. Sometimes you fight even when you know in your heart it's over." The words left a lump in Steven's throat even as the mocking voice of the Queen dragged him back to the present.

"We can keep this up all night, Bauer." She hurled a flaming sphere of darkness at the phalanx of Pawns, the fireball exploding above the tower's arched doorway. "Even your run of luck won't last—"

"Silence, Magdalene." The King rose from the ground and retrieved his sword. "Did I not make myself clear? This battle is over." He looked to the eight Blackfoot archers around the periphery of the courtyard. "Pawns of the Black, hold your fire or face me."

Sullen, the Queen lowered her scepter. Her hate-filled eyes locked with Steven's eightfold gaze as the King shifted his attention back to the tower.

"Surrender, Bauer." The King's edict reverberated in the space. "I know full well your Queen is wounded. She might yet be saved, but not if we waste what precious time she has on yet another pointless skirmish."

"She's fading, Steven." The certainty in Archie's tone brought home the King's words. "I don't know how much longer she's going to last."

"Can't you do something?" The rattle in Audrey's breathing chilled Steven to the core. "Fix her like you did me?"

"Her wound is much deeper than either of yours. I'm afraid if I try to pull the arrow, she'll bleed out before I can do much of anything."

A trickle of crimson ran from the corner of Audrey's mouth and down her pale cheek.

"But, Lena was in worse shape—"

"Yes, Steven, and that took all of us, along with everything I had. We have neither the time nor the energy to commit to such an endeavor right now." Archie's voice grew quiet. "If we give in, at least for the moment, stop all of this, perhaps he would allow us to save her. Maybe the horse too. All of us could live to fight another day."

The glint in Archie's eye that unnerved Steven before had returned.

"No." Steven pounded the wall. "This is bigger than Audrey, bigger than us, even bigger than Zed and his Legion of Doom out there. The King said it himself. All that matters is the balance of power at the end. I say we tip that balance in our favor."

"What do you have in mind?" Archie asked.

Donald Bauer's words echoed in Steven's mind. *The best defense is a good offense.*

"If they want to start this Game with a few Pieces missing from the board, I say we oblige." Steven stepped around Rocinante's injured form and grasped Emilio's shoulder. "Are you with me?"

Emilio ran a trembling hand down the bleeding stallion's flank and stood. "Let's go get those bastards."

Lena lowered her head and turned her resigned gaze back to Rocinante's wounded side. Though she didn't say a word, her eyes spoke volumes.

"Take these." Steven handed Emilio his shield and pike. "They aren't yours, but they'll serve you well."

Emilio strapped on the shield and brandished the long pole arm.

"And you'll—"

"The seven Pawns at the door will fight with you, but I will stay with Lena." Steven rested a hand on the girl's shoulder. "No one will touch her. I swear."

Emilio cast one final look at the brave young girl at the horse's side and joined the remainder of the Pawns at the tower's opening.

"Rook?" Steven shouted up into the darkness of the tower structure. "Can you hear me?"

After a long pause, the gravelly voice spoke, as if waking from sleep.

"I can, though everything's strange. Your voice seems to be coming from somewhere... inside of me?"

"Where are you?" Steven's voice echoed in the space. "Somewhere in the tower?"

Several seconds passed before the stony voice answered, an undercurrent of growing panic evident in its wavering tone. "I think I am the tower."

Archie flinched at the Rook's confused response.

Steven rushed to his side. "What is it, Archie?"

"Oh, nothing," the priest answered a bit too quickly. "Audrey's stable for the moment, though I don't know how much longer I can keep this up."

Neither the rapid rise and fall of Audrey's chest nor the pool of blood forming between Rocinante's belly and Lena's bent knees filled Steven with confidence. "Stay with them. Do what you can. Either way, this will be over soon."

Steven turned his head upward to again address the Rook. "Are you still there?"

"You." The Rook's trembling voice echoed in the space. "You're called Steven?"

"Yes," he answered. "Steven Bauer."

"In that case, Steven Bauer," the gravelly voice demanded, "can you tell me what the hell is going on?" The trepidation in the Rook's crescendoing voice boiled over into anger. "In the last half hour, I've been shot off a skyscraper, had some idiot try to rescue me only to let me fall, and now, as best I can tell, I'm the latest construction project in downtown Atlanta."

*Was that a joke?*

"Listen. Try to stay calm." Steven brought his voice low. "What's your name?"

"Niklaus."

"Listen, Niklaus. This will all make a lot more sense later, but understand your world has just become a very dangerous game of chess, and you've been tagged as one of the Rooks."

"Rook," came the stony voice. "And that would make you what, exactly?"

"A Pawn in this stupid Game, not to mention the idiot that tried to save you before." Steven took a breath. "I didn't mean to let you fall." His gaze fell to Audrey's pale face. "It was out of my hands."

"Well, Steven the Pawn," said the gravelly voice that came from nowhere and everywhere at once, "I don't claim to understand a bit of this, but right now we've got a bigger problem. Those archers are coming around the base of the tower from both sides and they're nearing the door. What is it you need me to do?"

# 30

# CROWN

Т he divided band of Blackfoot warriors closed on the tower door from either side, bows slung and axes drawn. As the lead of each quartet caught sight of the other, all eight froze in place, and as one, turned to face their King. At his silent nod, they charged the arched doorway, but rather than two ranks of foot soldiers in white, the octet of Black Pawns found an enormous stone rolling into place from within the tower. After seconds of frustrated silence, the eight stowed their weapons and put their collective shoulder to the barrier, but despite their best efforts, the stone wouldn't budge.

The Queen let out an impatient sigh and joined her Pawns at the tower's base. "Is there a problem, Wahnahtah?"

"Their Rook's barrier," the lead Pawn said. "We cannot move it."

"Very well," she said. "Stand aside."

The Queen brought her serpentine scepter above her head and closed her eyes. Ebon fire swirled like a microcosmic cyclone about her weapon's fanged head as strange electricity flashed in the sky between the two towers of glass and steel. After a long moment, her eyes shot open, their usual green replaced by utter darkness.

"Pawns of the Black," she whispered, "prepare your assault."

A streak of lightning split the sky and struck the raised scepter, sending the Queen's body into spasm. The dark flames mixed with the indigo spark from above, spinning faster and faster until the pulsating globe of darkness achieved critical mass and flew from the Queen's outstretched arm. With a deafening boom, the fireball struck the colossal barrier and split the enormous stone in two. The resultant explosion shattered several stories of windows in both towers.

"Now, Wahnahtah. Through the breech."

Eager to penetrate the White's last line of defense, the first of the Black Pawns clambered through the narrow opening as the others fell into line. One after another, they charged the narrow aperture, but as the sixth made his way into the darkened tower, anxious shouting echoed from within. A moment later, the remaining two Pawns turned and addressed the Queen.

"Your Highness," they stammered in unison, "they're not inside."

"What?"

"The six within have scouted the entire structure." The lead Pawn's face grew blank as he looked through another set of eyes. "There's no one in the Tower. They're... gone."

"But that's impossible. Where could they..." Cold comprehension blossomed on the Queen's face. "Get them out, Wahnahtah. Get them out!"

As the last Pawn to enter the tower scrambled back toward the narrow opening, a voice like an avalanche echoed between the two skyscrapers, uttering a single, unmistakable word.

"Now."

The tower convulsed, the entire structure listing from side to side as if in the throes of a massive earthquake. The battlements shook themselves apart, and fell to the courtyard below.

The Queen screamed as she spun around on her floating dais of darkness and dove away from the tower, her desperate leap all that kept her from being trapped under the tons of rock and mortar that plummeted down as the castle disintegrated. Of the two remaining Pawns, only one reacted in time, his twin crushed beneath the tower's main parapet as it fell to the earth.

Scrambling to their feet, the Queen and the remaining Pawn

looked on as the thirty-foot tower imploded, the screams of the Pawns within drowned out by the horrendous cacophony of stone on falling stone. As the last remnants of the devastated structure settled into place, the Queen surveyed the debris and spat her adversary's name.

"*Bauer.*"

Glancing back across the courtyard for guidance from the King, she was surprised to find neither rage nor disappointment in his ancient, yet unlined face, but instead an expression of wry amusement.

"Your Majesty," she said. "The White have disappeared. I fear they have managed to escape." After a pained pause, she added a single whispered word. "Again."

"Don't worry, Magdalene." The King gestured at the cloud of dust that floated above the destroyed tower. "It would appear they haven't gone far."

The Queen jerked her head around to find Steven charging across the rubble at her. She yelped in pain as the blunt end of Steven's pole arm bore down on her unprotected wrist and sent her weapon flying.

"Phalanx." At Steven's command, his one became seven and surrounded the Queen, the gleaming razor tips of their pikes all leveled at her supple neck.

"For Rocinante!" Emilio leaped from the billowing dust cloud and charged the remaining Black Pawn. Still dazed from the loss of his seven brethren, the lone archer scarcely raised a hand before Emilio brought him to ground with a single blow to the jaw.

"How does it feel, *pendejo*?" Emilio lowered the pike's shining point at the Pawn's chest. "Little different when the blade's at your neck, wouldn't you say?"

The dark-skinned warrior squinted up at him through the trickle of blood coursing down his face, but offered no response, choosing instead to maintain proud silence.

"Enjoy your momentary advantage, Bauer." The Queen rubbed absently at her bruising wrist. "But don't forget the same rules apply to both sides of this Game. Quite the irony if it were White rather than Black that incurred the wrath of the high and mighty Arbiters."

"You're in no position to be making idle comments, Maggie." Each of Steven's seven doppelgangers advanced their pikes an inch. "As I understand it, those same Arbiters have been anything but attentive of late."

If the Queen felt the least bit of fear at Steven's words, she kept it from her face, her icy stare filled only with cool contempt, the only true emotion Steven guessed remained in the woman's black soul.

"So." The King watched from his vantage across the courtyard, "Grey's errand boy has teeth. Impressive."

Steven disengaged from the phalanx of Pawns, leaving the Queen under the watchful eyes of the remaining six. "You must be Zed."

"Indeed." The King scowled at Steven's use of his proper name. "I suppose you think that infinitesimal piece of knowledge gives you some sort of advantage?"

"Perhaps. No one knows the rules of this Game better than you, your Highness, and gauging from the fact we're standing here talking instead of fighting for our lives, I'm guessing Audrey was right. Like it or not, we're off limits till the main event." Steven's lips curled into a smirk. "Sucks doesn't it?"

"Ah, the baby bird stretches its wings." The King sheathed his sword. "Grey has truly found a worthy champion in you, Bauer— brave, resourceful, insightful." His eyes narrowed. "But still so very stupid. Do not presume, little man, to quote the rules of this Game to one of its very authors, regardless of whatever limited understanding you believe you've obtained from your esteemed mentor. Truth be told, his conception of the Game is at least as biased as mine."

"I've seen Stonehenge, you bastard. I know what you did."

The King laughed. "I have no doubt Grey has shown you exactly what he needed you to see to bring you to his side. He always did value blind loyalty. Regardless, the outcome today will remain the same. You put up a brave front, Bauer, but the fact that my Queen is still breathing is rather damning evidence that you are far too weak to be of any concern to me." He gestured in Emilio's direction. "Meanwhile, the boy there, for all his bluster, can barely keep his knees from knocking. Look at him. So sad, all that power wasted on one so young."

Steven glanced to his right and knew the King was right. Despite his bravado, Emilio's eyes were wide with as much terror as rage.

"The Arbiters require that you live." The King rested his hand on the jeweled hilt of his sword. "Anything beyond that is open to interpretation. I saw the wounds my Pawns dealt both your horse and Miss Richards. I suspect your Bishop, wherever you have hidden him, is far too busy keeping your lovely young Queen alive to be of much assistance."

Steven tensed at the King's calculated words, but held his tongue.

"Knight and Pawn alone to face a King." Zed's words dripped with false concern. "Your cause is lost."

"Then," interrupted a stony voice from the remains of the ruined tower, "I suppose they'll have to leave the heavy lifting to me."

The rubble folded and shifted, flowing and twisting until the shattered brick and concrete took the form of a gargantuan man of stone. Fifteen feet high and as broad as a dump truck, the rugged colossus stared down on them like an angry god. Then, as a butterfly shedding its chrysalis, the rough outer stone fell away and revealed the rippled white marble skin beneath. The Black Queen and Pawn each caught their breath, and even the King gazed at this latest addition to Steven's band with some measure of respect.

"So, Steven," came a voice that made James Earl Jones sound like a soprano, "is this the guy who ordered me shot off a skyscraper?"

"That's him." Steven mouth turned up in a half-smile.

"Would you rather I pound him into the ground or knock him into next week?"

"And so. Now the Rooks come out." The King raised his hand, his fingers curling into a fist. This simple gesture was answered with a massive boom. Then another. And another.

At the far side of the courtyard, a gap formed in the dark wall and a colossal female figure passed the jagged opening. Over a story high and formed of black stone and mortar, the monstrous form trudged in their direction. Her every step shattering windows as well as the pavement at her feet, the Black Rook came to rest behind her King.

"What is your will, my lord?" Her words reverberated through the space like the rumble of an earthquake.

"That depends." The King drew himself up straight and locked gazes with Steven. "It would appear, Bauer, that we have reached an impasse."

The King's taunting words were followed by another, softer voice, one far more familiar.

"Castling so early, old friend?"

His fedora and overcoat somehow dry despite the rain that still surrounded their small oasis from the storm, Grey strode across the devastated courtyard and stood before them.

"Good evening, Steven and Emilio." He shot a glance in the King's direction. "Zed."

"Grey." The King took his hand from his sword. "So, old friend, you've decided to take an active role in your own inevitable downfall. It's been so different this time, only matching wits with the hired help."

"The 'hired help', as you call them, just decimated your front row and nullified your Queen in short order." Grey crossed his arms. "Perhaps you should not be so quick to dismiss."

"You know as well as I do that Pawns are expendable." Zed turned his gaze on Steven. "Did you tell your protégé that, old friend? He was all wound up before regarding our altercation at Stonehenge, but does he know about Antarctica? How you managed to pull that victory from the jaws of defeat?" The King's mouth broke into a wicked smile even as Grey's face twisted into a frustrated scowl. "Hmmm... didn't come up, I suppose."

Grey let out a single sarcastic laugh. "If only I cared as much about the fate of my Pieces as you do yours." His eyes narrowed below the brim of his grey fedora. "At your hands, each of mine have already tasted of the sacrifices that come with playing this Game of ours, and yet, they still remain. Regardless of what you bring to bear against us, White will again persevere."

Zed inhaled to speak, but Grey cut him off, his tone harsh and insistent. "My side is now assembled, and yet you persist with this petty engagement. Are you really in such a rush to curry the Arbiters' displeasure?"

"Hmmph. I have seen no trace of their influence here this night."

Zed motioned to the phalanx of Pawns surrounding his Queen. "In fact, it appears the Arbiters care little about the indiscretions of either side anymore." The King's lips turned up in a smirk. "Plus, to my reckoning, a Piece still exists among the White that remains to be claimed. It is unfortunate the *Hvítr Kyll* lies lost among the rubble. Without it, you have no King."

Steven stepped forward. "And that, your Highness, is one assumption too many."

The Rook knelt down, so he could speak eye to eye with the King. "Do you think I left them inside that dark tower with nothing to light their way?"

"Steven?" Grey asked.

The Pawn closest to Grey produced a small white bundle from behind his shield. An audible hum filled the space.

"What?" The King stared, mouth agape. "How?"

"The cloak." Grey smiled. "Brilliant."

"It was the only way to keep it quiet." Steven peeled away each layer of the folded cloak, the drone of the pouch growing louder every second until the throbbing sound shook his teeth.

"Strange," he said, "it's louder than I've ever heard it..." He looked into Grey's eyes and knew the answer before he even knew the question.

"Yes, Steven," Grey said. "I am the last Piece." He shot a sidelong look at the Black King. "In every iteration since the Game's inception, I have served as the White King with Zed as my opposite."

"I knew," Steven said. "When I first saw the Black King, I knew."

"You aren't a part of the Game yet, old man," the Queen said. "Zed could still remove you from play with no repercussions."

"Foolish woman, you know not of what you speak," Grey said. "Do not think because you have tasted of the power inherent in the Game that you are its master. Not even your King, armed, armored, and an armsbreadth away would dare interfere at this point."

The Black King remained silent, though his cold eyes didn't leave Steven's hands as they worked at the *Hvítr Kyll's* silver cord.

"Open the pouch, Steven," Grey said. "Time to bring this phase of the Game to a close."

Steven presented the pouch to Grey and the Black King turned his back on the entire assemblage and strode off into the rain.

"Come," he said. "Let them have their little victory. The Game is nigh, and we will soon see how well the White fares without the Arbiters' much vaunted protection."

The ring of White Pawns bristled as the Black Queen scrambled to her feet, but at Grey's subtle nod, opened to let her pass.

The Black Rook held fast for a moment, staring strangely at the alabaster form of her opposite, and then turned to join the King. Her every step sent a tremor through the courtyard.

"Till next time, *'pendejo*,'" the Black Pawn said, offering Emilio a jaunty salute as he rose from the ground and collected his axe.

With a grunt, Emilio threw down Steven's pike and grabbed the nearest White Pawn by the shoulders.

"We're letting them walk? In case you forgot, these people spent the last three days trying to kill us." Emilio ground his teeth as he watched the Black Pawn swagger away.

"What about Lena?" Emilio drew Steven close, his breath hot on Steven's cheek. "And Audrey?"

The perceptions of the missing eighth Pawn, actively ignored to that point, flooded Steven's mind.

Lena crouched by the window in the King tower above, her head bowed in prayer.

Archie kneeling between his wounded Queen and Rocinante, a hand over each of their hearts as his lips worked the silent chant holding death at bay.

And Audrey.

*So pale.* An unbidden image of an open grave flashed through Steven's mind. Though his every instinct screamed to stay there by Audrey's side, Steven tore his mind's eye from the scene above and answered Emilio with words he only half believed himself.

"We have to let them go, Emilio. It's the only way."

A moment later, the King snapped his fingers and the four forms vanished in a bubble of inky darkness. The rain returned in earnest as if the storm bore them a personal grudge.

"Tell me we had no choice." Steven turned on Grey. "Tell me we didn't let those murderers go for no reason."

"We can discuss tonight's events later," Grey said. "For now, we have business to conduct and wounded friends that need our attention. The pouch, if you will."

For once, Steven didn't question, and instead held wide the mouth of the ancient artifact that had proven both blessing and curse in his life. Then, as if he had rehearsed the moment a thousand times, he knelt before Grey.

"My King."

"Rise, Steven," Grey said. "This is no time for ceremony."

Steven came to his feet and waited for what was to come. After a brief meditation, Grey reached his arm deep into the white leather's glowing aperture. Soon, the pouch shone brighter and droned louder than at any time in Steven's brief tenure as the White Pawn. The deafening roar shook the surrounding architecture with palpable force while the blinding radiance from the pouch's mouth lit the entire concourse as if it were midday. The light and sound buffeted him like a cyclone of silver radiance, and then, with one final burst of brilliance, the pouch went dark and silent.

The roar of the storm compounded the ringing in Steven's ears, while the blue haze burned into his retina along with the fractured kaleidoscopic perception of seven pairs of eyes left him helpless. Tortured seconds passed as the Pawns' vision readjusted to the darkness, their collective gaze eventually drifting to the circular object that rested in Grey's hand.

A simple crown of platinum, its burnished surface shone with an inner glow as if fresh from the forge. Though no stones adorned the grey metal, the glyphs inscribed along its surface shone in the night, the language they represented so old no record remained of its existence. Foreign yet hauntingly familiar, like so many things since he was brought into the Game, the ornate characters spoke to Steven, telling stories of a forgotten place and time.

Grey studied the circle of metal with brooding eyes, removed his battered fedora, and placed the crown to his brow. In a shimmering flash, Grey's attire shifted from its usual drab tones to blinding white, his dark overcoat iridescent for a moment before unfurling into robes more suited for royalty.

As the transformation continued, his already anachronistic clothing shifted into armor and trappings not dissimilar to that of the Black King. Still, while Zed's raiment had been ostentatious in its extravagance, Grey's somehow maintained that understated quality that permeated the man's every word and action. The sword at his side gleamed as if afire, and as the golden radiance washed across the wizard's ancient visage, the lines of centuries that marked his face were washed away.

"Thank you, Steven." Grey sheathed his sword. "The gathering is now complete. One task remains, and then we rest."

The seven Pawns gathered close and melded back into one.

"Are we too late?" Steven asked.

"I believe not," Grey answered, "though I sense our Bishop is nearly spent. He has poured more of himself into the others than is wise. He cannot go on this way."

"Let's not waste another second, then." Steven motioned for Emilio and Niklaus to rally around him. "Stay close, everyone."

He held aloft the pouch and with one final deafening pulse, the quartet disappeared, leaving only a spiral wisp of white smoke in their wake.

# 31

## PIECES

Steven stared out the window at the lake that had served as an aquatic playground throughout his childhood. Memories played across his mind's eye: exploring the far shore with his mother, feeding the Canada geese every spring, fishing with his dad by the tall sycamore in the corner.

No wind touched the lake's placid surface. No cloud blemished the azure sky. Not a single bird broke the welcome stillness with its morning call. Rocinante stood in silence, chewing at the tall grass at the water's edge.

A quarter mile out, Emilio and Lena sat unmoving in Steven's old rowboat, allowing the sun to brown their skin and the water's invisible current to take them wherever it would. Neither of the young couple had said much over the last thirty-six hours, and Steven didn't blame them. A part of him mourned their lost innocence, though he recognized the alternative was far worse.

A knock at the front door set Steven's heart racing. He checked his pocket before answering and breathed a sigh of relief when he found his icon's marble dark without even a glimmer of radiance. Steven turned the deadbolt and opened the door to find a diminutive older woman wearing a worn-out Mickey Mouse sweatshirt waiting on the porch.

"Steven." The woman peered across his shoulder into the house. "What a surprise."

"Hi, Mrs. Chatsworth."

She brought her gaze back to Steven. "Didn't know you were in from Chicago."

"Yeah." Steven did his best to evince a smile. "Hanging out at Dad's for a few days."

"It's good to see you. You and Don having fun catching up?"

"Yeah. Mostly catching up on some sleep today, though."

"Is he in?" She poked her head in the door and looked around.

Steven stepped into her field of vision. "He went into town." He hated lying to a woman who had babysat him for years when he was young, but he couldn't risk revealing anything close to the truth. "He should be back later on today."

"It's funny. He wasn't here yesterday either. He's usually such a homebody. I wonder what's gotten into him lately."

"Me too, Mrs. Chatsworth." *More than you could possibly know.*

"Oh, Steven, you're all grown up now." Her mouth spread wide in a friendly smile. "You can call me Marge if you want. I'm not all that old, I like to think."

"All right… Marge. Will do. Do you want me to leave a message?"

"Sure. Tell Don I dropped by to line up dinner next week. You're invited too, if you're still around. I'm itching to try out a new recipe. Don can handle food with some kick, right?"

"The hotter, the better, as I remember. I'll let him know."

"Thanks, Steven." Her face took on a mother's concern. "If you don't mind my asking, are you doing all right?"

"I'm fine." Steven donned a practiced smile. "I'm stuck in the middle of a big project for work. Just taking a break this morning."

"Oh," she said. "Well, good luck. Great seeing you back around these parts. I'm sure Don is glad to see you. Tell him to give me a call whenever he gets home."

"Will do."

Steven closed the door and returned to the window overlooking the lake. His stomach rumbled, reminding him he'd skipped breakfast.

A few minutes later, the sound of the door to the basement shook him from his reverie.

"Still no word?" Niklaus stretched as he came up the stairs. His tousled hair and rumpled sweats suggested he wasn't long out of bed.

"Nope. It's like he disappeared off the face of the earth." Steven peered out the window of the kitchen door at his father's red Blazer, gripping the keys he had retrieved from the porch the previous morning.

"I'm sure he's all right." Niklaus' thick Polish accent made the lie even more awkward.

"Yeah, Niklaus, my dad up and skipped town after our visit without keys, car, or even locking the stupid door. I'm sure that's it."

"Sorry. I only—" Niklaus' apology was cut short by an excited voice from the other end of the house.

"Steven! She's awake."

All other thought flew from Steven's mind as he raced down the hallway to the bedroom of his youth. Archie met Steven at the door, the priest's expression just short of giddy.

"She's still out of it, but praise the Lord. She's awake." Archie stepped back and allowed Steven into the brightly lit room.

There, resting against the headboard of his childhood bed and supported by every spare pillow they'd been able to gather, Audrey looked up at him through half-asleep eyes.

"Hi." Her voice came out as a harsh whisper.

"Welcome back." Despite a day and a half of pent-up questions, Steven could barely put two words together. "Are you okay?"

"I think so." Audrey's face broke into a wide grin. "You know, we've really got to stop meeting like this."

"I'm sorry about everything, Audrey." Steven took a step forward, his voice cracking as leaned across the bed. "I don't know what I would've done if—"

Audrey raised a feeble hand from the faded blue comforter and hushed him. "It's all right. Everything's kind of hazy, but I've got a sneaky suspicion you have something to do with the fact I'm still alive and breathing. We'll talk later, but for now, we're okay."

A weight left Steven's chest and he breathed freely for the first time since the battle in Atlanta.

"What happened, anyway?" Audrey searched Steven's eyes. "Last thing I remember, some kind of wall came out of the ground, and then…" She grew quiet as she absently rubbed at the area above her navel. "I don't remember much after that."

"That would be me." Niklaus stepped into the room. "The wall, that is."

"Wait." Audrey peered past Steven. "You're the guy from the roof. How did you—"

"Not end up splattered all over the courtyard? I owe it all to Steven here and that bag of tricks he carries. Another few seconds, though, and things would have turned out a lot different." Niklaus' eyes grew distant, his voice somber. "I guess you never really know if you're ready to die till death is staring you in the face."

"I can relate." She extended a weak hand. "I'm Audrey, by the way."

"Niklaus Zamek, the White Rook, apparently, and I am at your service." He took her hand and offered a slight bow. "And don't worry about introductions. I've heard all about you, Audrey. Can't get Steven here to shut up about—"

Steven cleared his throat. "Thank you, Niklaus."

The corner of Audrey's mouth turned up in a playful smile. "And what exactly did our fearless leader have to say?"

Prickly heat coursed across Steven's scalp. "You know, Niklaus, why don't you go check on Lena and Emilio while I fill Audrey in on the last couple of days?"

"Of course." Niklaus stepped out of the room.

"You too, Archie." Steven helped the priest to his feet. "You've been sitting here all night. You should take a break. Rest your eyes a bit."

"I could certainly use a walk to get the blood flowing." Archie shot Steven a wink. "I'm guessing you'll keep an eye on Audrey for me?"

"At least one." Steven took Archie's place on the corner of the bed. The priest in turn joined Niklaus in the hallway and closed the door behind them.

"It's good to have you back, Audrey," Steven said after far too long an awkward silence. "Lena's been your nurse for the last couple of days, and Archie has barely left your side."

"What about our new friend from Atlanta?" Audrey asked. "What's he like?"

"Niklaus? Don't worry. He grows on you pretty fast." Steven searched Audrey's eyes. "How do you feel?"

"I'm hurting in places I didn't even know I had, but considering the last thing I remember was an arrow sticking out of my chest, I think I'll take it."

"I've already replayed the whole night in my head about a thousand times." Steven's head dropped. "I'm so sorry. I never meant for you—"

"Stop. I'm fine." She took his hand in hers and squeezed it tight. "I promise."

They sat again in silence, neither sure exactly what to say.

"So," Audrey asked, "where are we this time?"

"Back in Virginia. My old house." Steven pointed to a collection of dusty high school trophies on top of a battered dresser. "This was my room growing up."

"Huh." Audrey scanned the room, the space filled with mementos of Steven's childhood. "So, what does your dad think about you bringing home a whole houseful of strangers?"

"I don't know." Steven bit his lip. "He's not here."

"When will he be back? I'd really like to meet him." Understanding blossomed on Audrey's face. "Oh. Is he—"

"Lena can't raise her aunt on the phone, your mom and grandfather are still MIA, and now Dad's fallen off the face of the earth." Steven's gaze wandered around the room. "It's not looking too good for the home team."

Audrey stared straight ahead, her face devoid of emotion. "I guess this is the part where we drive on and try to tell ourselves everything's going to be all right."

Steven nodded. "I try not to think about it too—" Steven jerked his head around as the bedroom door creaked open.

"Grey's back." Archie poked his head through the half-open doorway. "He wants to know if he's interrupting anything."

"No," Steven answered. "It's fine. Tell him to come on in."

Archie stood aside as Grey swept into the room dressed in a cobalt blue shirt, charcoal pants and his floor-length gabardine coat. He swept the battered fedora from his head and offered a slight bow. "Audrey, my dear. I am pleased to see you doing so well."

"Good to see you too, Grey," she said. "Though I'm not so sure about well."

"It was pretty touch and go for a while," Archie said, "but you're well on the road to recovery now. Grey made sure of that."

"What do you mean?" Audrey asked.

Archie grew quiet as Grey's slate gaze bore a hole through him.

"Steven," she asked. "What's Archie talking about?"

At Grey's subtle nod, Steven answered. "We almost lost you, Audrey. The Pawn's arrow hit some important stuff, and by the time we finished with Zed and the others, you were pretty far gone. Archie somehow managed to keep you alive but by the time we got to you he was way past his limit."

Archie nodded his head sadly. "It took everything we had to bring you back, and without the extra push from Grey, I'm not sure even that would have been enough."

"Oh." Audrey's face blanched. "Good to know, I guess."

"Now that all of us are within the Game," Grey said, "I am free to bring my abilities to bear for the good of the White. I did, in fact, provide a bit of aid at a moment when our Bishop's energies were at an ebb. The lion's share of thanks, however, remains with Archie and your friends. His abilities and their sacrifice were truly what saved both you and our Knight's fine steed."

Audrey peered around the room, pausing for a moment at each face that had played a part in saving her life. "I don't know what to say."

"It is our duty to come to the aid of our Queen," Grey said, "and our privilege. Truth be told, though, your role in the coming struggle has little to do with my gladness at seeing your bright eyes again." The wizard's smile was infectious and soon Audrey was laughing between sobs. Even the room seemed to breathe a sigh of relief. Seconds later, an excited voice from the hall galvanized the already festive mood.

"Audrey! You're awake." Lena ran through the open doorway and threw her arms around Audrey's neck.

"Ow!" Audrey said. "Not so hard." Her playful tone softened the edge to her words. "Wounded in action over here."

"Sorry," Lena said, "I'm just so glad to have you back." She slipped off the bed and slipped her arm around Emilio's waist as he stepped into the room. "It's been a two-day testosterone fest around here without you around."

"Good to see you, Audrey." Of them all, Emilio's response was by far the most reserved, which didn't surprise Steven in the least. The young man had avoided all of them except Lena since their return to Virginia, and Steven had chosen to give him his space.

"It's getting a bit crowded in here," Grey stepped out into the hallway. "Please allow me to get some air while the rest of you continue your reunion." He tapped Steven's shoulder. "A moment?"

Though Steven felt no desire whatsoever to leave Audrey's side, he rose to join Grey in the hall, squeezing Audrey's hand gently before he left. "I'll be back soon."

Audrey held his fingers a moment longer, the heat of her touch infusing Steven with a warmth that was both new and familiar. "Promise?"

Her playful grin set Steven's heart racing and in that brief instant, he gained serious insight into how a single face could launch a thousand ships.

"Promise."

Steven walked in silence with Grey by the still water of the lake that abutted his father's land and stopped amid the tall river birches he and his father planted a quarter century before. Grey picked up a single flat stone, stooped to one side, and flung the stone sidearm. The miniature discus skipped at least seven times before sinking to the muddy lake bottom.

Steven laughed. "If I remember right, my record's nine."

Grey stretched his hand out across the lake. "See the ripples? How they spread to encompass the lake's entire surface? The placid water is reality as you understand it. The stone represents the coming correction. Understand this. The earthquakes off your Pacific Coast and the storm we encountered in Atlanta are but the beginning."

"It gets worse from here?"

"The land I consider home is no more, claimed by the forces in question sixteen centuries ago. Like mighty Atlantis or fair Pompeii, the land of my people was destroyed by forces outside our understanding." Grey gazed across the lake, the loneliness of centuries played out in a moment. "This Game I helped create may keep such events from occurring, but those forces still exist, and the potential for disaster is no different than it was centuries ago."

"This correction has already hit both ends of the U.S." Steven squinted into the sun. "When we first discussed the Game, you said each of the three previous iterations had a certain geographic propensity. This big disaster you keep talking about. It's coming here, isn't it?"

"If this correction is consistent with previous iterations, the energies will indeed focus on a single land mass, in this case your North American continent. Each event stronger and more devastating than the one before, the destruction will crescendo toward an unprecedented release of energy onto this world. There and then, in the throes of this most recent correction's climax, the Game will be played."

"How will we know when it's time?"

"You will know, all of you, just as you know when the enemy is near or how to utilize the weapons of your various stations despite never having seen them before. The knowledge and skills necessary to play the Game are part and parcel of who you are."

"Got it." Steven shoved his hands in his pockets. "Different topic?"

"Certainly." Grey wore a knowing look.

"You've been gone since Atlanta, and I suspect you haven't been idle."

"No need for preamble, Steven. What is it you want to know?"

"Does Zed have my father? Audrey's family? Lena's aunt and uncle?"

Grey let out a plaintive sigh. "All evidence points toward that conclusion, I fear."

"Then here's what I want to know. Has the concept of taking hostages ever come up before?" The fire in Steven's eyes matched Grey's. "Is that now 'part and parcel' of who we are as well? It's bad enough all of our lives are at risk, but now he's got our families and we're still supposed to line up and play nice."

Grey lowered his gaze. "As my brethren and I brought this infernal Game into being, we planned for every eventuality of which we could conceive. Each individual Piece was meant to enter the field of battle as an anonymous cipher and complete the ritual, thus dissipating the energies in question. Survivors were then to return to their normal life as if nothing had happened. The involvement of families, friends, lovers was never even considered."

Steven and Grey were silent for a while. The trees swayed to and fro in the gentle breeze as a kingfisher flew in from the east and circled the lake. On its third circuit, the bird dropped from the sky, dove at the water at breakneck speed, and penetrated the water's still surface with a muted splash. Moments later, it rose from the water with a wriggling fish in its mouth and took to the sky, disappearing back across the trees. Steven shivered despite the summer heat.

"One last question." Steven's expression grew grim. "It's been on my mind ever since we returned to Roanoke." His gaze shot to the old house where his father's pine and walnut chessboard rested on a dusty shelf. "In every game of chess I've ever played, not once, win or lose, have I made it to the end without losing a piece or two."

Grey kept his silence.

"This isn't going to end well is it?" Steven asked. "Even if we win."

Grey sat by the still water. "This travesty you find yourself caught up in is what the great Game I conceived has devolved into. Though over the centuries, the ritual has saved the lives of thousands, nay millions, those like you have always borne the brunt of the cost. As it has been for the last sixteen centuries, those you have gathered may well be forced to pay the ultimate price for Zed's greed and the unfortunate naiveté of my youth."

"So what do we do now?"

"Wait. Heal. Prepare." Grey and Steven's eyes locked in a fiery dance. "Steel yourself, Steven. Zed's treachery is far from over. It is beyond certain he intends to use your loved ones as cruel leverage against you. You and the others must be prepared for this eventuality. Above all, however, you must maintain your focus on the one true goal—denying Zed his much-coveted victory. You and the others have already faced much in your brief time as part of the struggle, but what lies ahead will make the last week of your lives pale in comparison." Grey stroked his sparse beard. "The Game is nigh, and while your destiny awaits you, never forget that the Game waits for no one."

# AUTHOR'S NOTE

*This is not the end.*
*It is not even the beginning of the end.*
*But it is, perhaps, the end of the beginning.*
- Winston Churchill -

If you're reading this, you have either come to the end of the opening volume of my little chess story, or you're one of those compulsive people who, like me, jumps forward to the author's note just to see what makes a particular writer tick. To those of you who have already dropped some hard-earned cash and are the proud owner of this, the first novel I ever wrote, please accept my wholehearted thanks and know I hope you enjoyed reading it as much as I enjoyed writing it. Before we proceed, please note that I do discuss events from the story in the paragraphs that follow, so if you haven't finished the book yet, you may want to wait and read this part later.

This world that Steven Bauer and his friends inhabit has been kicking around in my head honestly for most of my life, but only in the last few years have I had the right combination of time, opportunity, and life experience to put it to paper. When I finished the first draft of Pawn's Gambit, lo these many years ago, I was two months from the end of my time as a United States Army family physician. In late 2002, however, a much younger "Captain Darin Kennedy" was gearing up to head to Kuwait in support of what would become Operation Iraqi Freedom. In February of 2003, I deployed with the 101st Airborne Division to Kuwait and early on the morning of March 20th, we crossed the berm into Iraq. My unit was a medical support company, responsible for the medical care of the hundreds of soldiers that made up the 1st Brigade Combat Team. Just behind the ever moving front line, we charged north through endless desert and raging sandstorms, and after two months of living like well-armored vagabonds, settled in an old Iraqi Air Force base about twenty minutes west of a small town called Quyarrah. It was there, living in an old MiG hangar amidst a decade of desiccated bird refuse and dust with no shower, no running water, and eating the same old "bagged lunch" (MRE) every day, that I borrowed our dentist's Panasonic Toughbook and began to chronicle the strange adventures of Steven Bauer. Both the story and the writer have come a long way since then, but if you get a hint of some underlying desolation while reading the first few chapters, I hope that explains it.

As those of you who have finished the book proper have probably already guessed, my father was the person who first introduced me to the game of chess. There are more than subtle parallels between Steven's childhood obsession with the game of kings and my own experiences growing up. Rather than the high end wood and marble set that young Steven and his father played on, however, ours was a well-used set of Anri Renaissance Chessmen as crafted by E.S. Lowe. The individual pieces of this particular set stood about three to four inches high and though made of plastic were fashioned to resemble marbled ivory and ebony. I can still visualize the pawns with their rounded helmets and triangular shields, the coned roofs and rocky foundations of the rooks, the rearing horses of the knights, the flowing robes and Prince Valiant haircuts of the bishops, the Queen's simple gown, and the King's stern expression as he stared at me from across the chessboard, tempting me and my little army of sixteen to cross the Rubicon and see if we could take him alive.

Growing up, I often wondered what it would be like if the

chessmen came to life and walked among us, and no, Mel Brooks' live action chess match from History of the World: Part I doesn't count. (Though I can't deny that it's still good to be the King.) To that end, the comic-book-crazed kid I once was created a character known as Chessmaster. This swashbuckling superhero carried around a bag of mystical chess pieces that he could animate and control at will. With an army of thirty-two at his beck and call, he was a force to be reckoned with. His little "bag of tricks" grew up to be the pouch that Steven carries on his hip and is probably the oldest piece of story that made it into the book you now hold in your hands.

Over the years and through almost countless incarnations and reimaginings, a story began to develop in my mind that looked a lot more like the events chronicled in these pages: the eternal Struggle, the collecting of the Pieces, the eventuality of a Game that would decide the fate of millions. As originally imagined, the order of indoctrination was totally different, and truth be told, I can't tell you how many different genders, races, orientations, backgrounds, relationships, etc. the various Pieces have been through. Emilio was originally a black kid from New York and—I'm a bit embarrassed to say—a member of a motorcycle gang known as the "Harlem Knights." Niklaus used to be much less European/cosmopolitan. In fact, my White Rook was originally a hulking construction worker with a name like Bob or John who worked for "Castle Construction" or some such. Lena was originally named Audrey, and though that name ended up belonging to another character, our spunky, mace-wielding maiden from the wrong side of Baltimore made it through otherwise pretty much intact. Audrey herself, on the other hand, wasn't even imagined until just a few pages before we first met the girl with auburn hair and hazel eyes. Each and every character in this book has come a long way, usually from very humble beginnings.

Don't even get me started on Steven.

I read in Stephen King's *On Writing* that he usually feels that his stories are "found" rather than created, that the character's stories are already in existence and he is merely the chronicler. I never truly understood or even fully believed him, that is until I sat down and started writing myself. I have honestly been surprised on more than one occasion at some of the turns this book has taken and some of the choices my characters have made and hope to continue to be astounded as work on the second volume continues in earnest.

So, many of you may be wondering what's next for Steven and his friends. Believe it or not, the entire story, beginning to end, was supposed to be contained in a single book, a tome I planned to call *The Pawn Stratagem*. As I got further and further into the writing process, however, it became evident that the book was heading for serious doorstopper length and, therefore, what was once a single book became three. The second volume, tentatively called *Four Corners*, is well underway. Once that one is done, I eagerly await the opportunity to bring this story full circle in the third and final volume, *Endgame*.

And now for a few acknowledgements.

To John, Jay, and Jaym at Falstaff Books, thanks for taking a chance on this book. I'm so excited that it finally has a home and can't wait to complete the series and share it with you and the world.

To Roy Mauritsen, I knew the first time I saw your awesome Chess Pieces artwork display at DragonCon all those years ago that you would be the only person I'd let do the artwork for this one. I certainly hope people judge this book by its cover.

To Sharon and Melissa, thanks to you both for awesome editing and proofreading. Readers can now walk the trail between these covers without tripping over random commas.

To Susan, big thanks for the awesome layout. You make this look good.

To the staff of the Barnes and Noble in Columbus, Georgia where much of the second half of this novel was written and all of it revised, thank you for your patience and for your ever present smiles, not to mention the endless supply of coffee.

To the fine people who made up Charlie Company, 426th Forward Support Battalion during our shared year in Iraq, thank you for your service, for all your hard work, for your daily sacrifices, for your friendship, and for making an untenable situation somehow bearable. I will never forget any of you.

To Lisa Postell, my first reader, thank you for the constant words of encouragement as I worked to get this book off the ground.

To Alis, Kevin, Kellie, Mary, Mark, Teresa, Dwight, Michi, Charlotte Writers, and the rest of my early readers, thank you for your excitement and enthusiasm over my little project and for helping me polish a good story into a great one.

To Mrs. Robbins, my ninth grade English teacher, thank you for all your encouragement and for giving me an A on my little Tolkien/Brooks rip-off/short story/novella when it probably deserved a C at best. I promise this one is better.

To Dad, thanks for being such an inspiration – there's a lot of you in these pages, and more to come.

Lastly, to Mom, thank you for four and a half decades of unwavering support and for never once thinking your son was crazy for wanting to write down all the insanity that bounces around in his head and actually trying to get other people to read it.

# ABOUT THE AUTHOR

Darin Kennedy, born and raised in Winston-Salem, North Carolina, is a graduate of Wake Forest University and Bowman Gray School of Medicine. After completing family medicine residency in the mountains of Virginia, he served eight years as a United States Army physician and wrote his first novel in the sands of northern Iraq, a novel you now hold in your hand. He is currently hard at work completing this trilogy for your reading enjoyment.

His Fugue and Fable trilogy, also available from Falstaff Books, was born from a fusion of two of his lifelong loves: classical music and world mythology. *The Mussorgsky Riddle*, *The Stravinsky Intrigue*, and *The Tchaikovsky Finale*, are the beginning, middle, and end of the closest he will likely ever come to writing his own symphony. His short stories can be found in numerous anthologies and magazines, and the best, particularly those about a certain Necromancer for Hire, are collected for your reading pleasure under Darin's imprint, 64Square Publishing.

Doctor by day and novelist by night, he writes and practices medicine in Charlotte, NC. When not engaged in either of the above activities, he has been known to strum the guitar, enjoy a bite of sushi, and, rumor has it, he even sleeps on occasion.

Find him online at darinkennedy.com.

# ALSO BY DARIN KENNEDY